THE
HAND

THE WHIP HAND

A HUNTER BUCHANON - BLACK HILLS WESTERN

WILLIAM W. JOHNSTONE

AND J.A. JOHNSTONE

PINNACLE BOOKS
Kensington Publishing Corp.
www.kensingtonbooks.com

PINNACLE BOOKS are published by

Kensington Publishing Corp.
900 Third Avenue
New York, NY 10022

All Kensington titles, imprints, and distributed lines are available at special quantity discounts for bulk purchases for sales promotion, premiums, fund-raising, and educational or institutional use.

Special book excerpts or customized printings can also be created to fit specific needs. For details, write or phone the office of the Kensington Sales Manager: Kensington Publishing Corp., 900 Third Avenue, New York, NY 10022. Attn. Sales Department. Phone: 1-800-221-2647.

PINNACLE BOOKS, the Pinnacle logo, and the WWJ steer head logo Reg. U.S. Pat. & TM Off.

First Printing: July 2024
ISBN-13: 978-0-7860-5048-2
ISBN-13: 978-0-7860-5049-9 (eBook)

10 9 8 7 6 5 4 3 2 1

Printed in the United States of America

CHAPTER 1

Hunter Buchanon whipped his hand to the big LeMat revolver jutting from the holster around which the shell belt was coiled on the ground beside him.

In a half second the big revolver was out of its holster and Hunter heard the hammer click back before he even knew what his thumb was doing. Lightning quick action honed by time and experience including four bloody years during which he fought for the Confederacy in the War of Northern Aggression.

He didn't know what had prompted his instinctive action until he sat half up from his saddle and peered across the red-glowing coals of the dying campfire to see Bobby Lee sitting nearby, peering down the slope into the southern darkness beyond, the coyote's tail curled tightly, ears pricked. Hunter's pet coyote gave another half moan, half growl like the one Hunter had heard in his sleep and shifted his weight from one foot to the other.

Hunter sat up slowly. "What is it, Bobby?"

A startled gasp sounded beside Hunter, and in the corner of his left eye he saw his wife, Annabelle, sit up quickly, grabbing her own hogleg from its holster and clicking the hammer back. Umber light from the fire danced in her thick, red hair. "What is it?" she whispered.

"Don't rightly know," Hunter said tightly, quietly. "But something's put a burr in Bobby's bonnet."

Down the slope behind Hunter, Annabelle, and Bobby Lee, their twelve horses whickered uneasily, drawing on their picket lines.

"Something's got the horses' blood up, too," Annabelle remarked, glancing over her shoulder at the fidgety mounts.

"Stay with the horses, honey," Hunter said, tossing his bedroll aside then rising, donning his Stetson, and stepping into his boots. As he grabbed his Henry repeating rifle, Annabelle said, "You be careful. We might have horse thieves on our hands, Hunter."

"Don't I know it." Hunter jacked a round into the Henry's action, then strode around the nearly dead fire, brushing fingers across the top of the coyote's head and starting down the hill to the south. "Come on, Bobby."

The coyote didn't need to be told twice. If there was one place for Bobby Lee, that was by the side of the big, blond man who'd adopted him when his mother had been killed by a rancher several years ago. Hunter moved slowly down the forested slope in the half darkness, one hand around the Henry's receiver so starlight didn't reflect off the brass and give him away.

Bobby Lee ran ahead, scouting for any human polecats after the ten horses Hunter and Annabelle were herding from their ranch near Tigerville deep in the Black Hills to a ranch outside of Denver. Hunter and Annabelle had caught the wild mustangs in the Hills near their ranch, and Annabelle had sat on the fence of the breaking corral, Bobby Lee near her feet, watching as Hunter had broken each wild-eyed bronc in turn.

Gentled them, rather. Hunter didn't believe in breaking a horse's spirit. He just wanted to turn them into "plug ponies," good ranch mounts that answered to the slightest tug on the reins or a squeeze of a rider's knees, and could turn on a dime, which was often necessary when working cattle, especially dangerous mavericks.

Hunter and Annabelle needed the money from the horse sale to help make up for the loss of several head of cattle to a rogue grizzly the previous summer. Times were hard on the ranch due to drought and low stock prices, and they were afraid they'd lose the Box Bar B without the money from the horses. They were getting two hundred dollars a head, because they were prime mounts—Hunter had a reputation as one of the best horse gentlers on the northern frontier—and that money would go far toward helping them keep the ranch.

Hunter wanted desperately to keep the Box Bar B not only for himself and Annabelle, but for Hunter's aged father, Angus, the boy they'd adopted, when Nathan's doxie mother had died after riding with would-be rustlers, including the boy's scoundrel father, whom Hunter had killed.

The boy was nothing like his father. He was good and hardworking, and he needed a good home.

Hunter moved off down the slope but stopped when Bobby Lee suddenly took off running and swinging left toward some rocks and a cedar thicket, growling. The coyote disappeared in the trees and brush and then started barking angrily. A man cursed and then there were three rocketing gun reports followed by Bobby's mewling howl.

"Damn coyote!" the man's voice called out.

"Bobby!" Hunter said and took off running in the direction in which Bobby Lee had disappeared.

"They know we're here now so be careful!" another man called out sharply.

Running footsteps sounded ahead of Hunter.

He stopped and dropped to a knee when a moving shadow appeared ahead of him and slightly down the slope. Starlight glinted off a rifle barrel and off the running man's cream Stetson.

"Hold it right there, you horse thief!" Hunter bellowed, pressing his cheek to the Henry's stock.

The man stopped suddenly and swung his rifle toward Hunter.

The Henry spoke once, twice, three times. The man grunted and flew backward, dropping his rifle and striking the ground with another grunt and a thud.

"Harvey!" the other man yelled from beyond the rocks and cedars.

Harvey yelled in a screeching voice filled with pain, "I'm a dead man, Buck! Buchanon got me, the rebel devil. He's over here. Get him for me!"

Hunter stepped behind a pine, peered out around it, and jacked another round into the Henry's action. He waited, pricking his ears, listening for the approach of Buck. Seconds passed. Then a minute. Then two minutes.

A figure appeared on the right side of the rocks and cedars, moving slowly, one step at a time. Buck held a carbine across his chest. Hunter lined up the Henry's sights on the man and was about to squeeze the trigger when something ran up behind the man and leaped onto his back. Buck screamed as he fell forward, Bobby Lee growling fiercely and tearing into the back of the man's neck.

Hunter smiled. Buck screamed as he tried in vain to fight off the fiercely protective Bobby Lee. Buck swung around suddenly and cursed loudly as he flung Bobby Lee off him. The coyote struck the ground with a yelp and rolled.

"You mangy cur!" Buck bellowed, drawing a pistol and aiming at Bobby.

Hunter's Henry spoke twice, flames lapping from the barrel.

Buck groaned and lay over on his back. "Ah, hell," he said, and died.

"Good work, Bobby," Hunter said, walking toward where

the coyote was climbing to his feet. Hunter dropped to a knee, placed his hand on Bobby Lee's back. "You all right?"

The coyote shook himself as if in an affirmative reply.

"All right," Hunter said, straightening. "Let's go check on—"

The shrill whinny of horses cut through the silence that had fallen over the night after Hunter had shot Buck.

"Annabelle!" Hunter yelled, swinging around to retrace his route back to the camp. "Come on, Bobby! There must be more of these scoundrels!"

The coyote mewled and took off running ahead of Hunter.

Only a minute after Hunter and Bobby had left the camp, the horses stirred more vigorously behind where Annabelle sat on a log near the cold fire, her Winchester carbine resting across her denim-clad thighs. She'd just risen from the log and started to walk toward the string of prize mounts when a man's voice called from the darkness down the hill behind the horses.

"Come here, purty li'l red-headed gal!" The voice was pitched with jeering, brash mockery.

Annabelle froze, stared into the darkness. Anger rose in her.

Again, the man's voice caromed quietly out of the darkness: "Come here, purty li'l red-headed gal!" The man chuckled.

Several of the horses lifted their heads and gave shrill whinnies.

The flame of anger burned more brightly in Annabelle, her heart quickening, her gloved hands tightening around the carbine she held high across her chest. She knew she shouldn't do it, but she couldn't stop herself. She moved slowly forward. Ahead and to her left, thirty feet away, the horses were whickering and shifting, pulling at the ropes securing them to the picket line.

Annabelle jacked a round into the carbine's action and moved toward the horses. She patted the blaze on the snout of a handsome black and said, "Easy, fellas. Easy. I got this."

She stepped around the horses and down the slope and stopped behind a broad-boled pine.

Again, the man's infuriating voice came from down the slope beyond her. "Come here, purty li'l red-haired gal. Come find me!"

Annabelle swallowed tightly and said quietly, mostly to herself: "All right—if you're sure about this, bucko . . ."

She continued forward, taking one step at a time. She had no spurs on her boots. Hunter's horses were so well-trained they didn't require them. She made virtually no sound as she continued down the slope, weaving among the columnar pines and firs silhouetted against the night's darkness relieved only by starlight.

"Come on, purty li'l red-headed gal," came the jeering voice again. "Wanna show ya somethin'."

"Oh, you do, do you?" Annabelle muttered beneath her breath. "Wonder what that could be."

She headed in the direction from which the voice had come, practically directly ahead of her now, maybe thirty, forty feet down the slope. On the one hand, that she was being lured into a trap, there could be no question. Hunter had always told her that her red-headed anger would get the best of her one day. Maybe he'd been right.

On the other hand, the open mockery in the voice of the man trying to lure her into the trap could not be denied. She imagined shooting him, and the thought stretched her rich, red lips back from her perfect, white teeth in a savage smile.

She took one step, then another . . . another . . . pausing briefly behind trees, edging cautious looks around them, knowing that she could see the lap of flames from a gun barrel at any second.

"That's it," came the man's voice again. "Just a bit closer, honey. That's it. Keep comin', purty li'l red-headed gal."

"All right," Annabelle said, tightly, loudly enough for the man to hear her now. "But you're gonna regret it, you son of a b—"

She'd smelled the rancid odor of unwashed man and raw whiskey two seconds before she heard the pine needle crunch of a stealthy tread behind her. She froze as a man's body pressed against her from behind. Just as the man started to wrap his arm around her, intending to close his hand over her mouth, Annabelle ducked and swung around, swinging the carbine, as well—and rammed the butt into her would-be assailant's solar plexus.

The man gave a great exhalation of whiskey-soaked breath, and folded.

Annabelle turned farther and rammed her right knee into the man's face. She felt the wetness of blood on her knee from the man's exploding nose. He gave a wheezy, *"Mercy!"* as he fell straight back against the ground and lay moaning and writhing.

Knowing she was about to have lead sent her way, Annabelle threw herself to her left and rolled. Sure enough, the rifle of the man on the slope below thundered once, twice, three times, the bullets caroming through the air where Annabelle had been a second before. The man whom she'd taken to the proverbial woodshed howled, apparently having taken one of the bullets meant for her.

Annabelle rolled onto her belly and aimed the carbine straight out before her. She'd seen the flash of the second man's rifle, and she aimed toward him now, sending three quick shots his way. The second shooter howled. Annabelle heard the heavy thud as he struck the ground.

"Gallblastit!" he cried. "You like to shot my dang ear off, you wicked, red-haired hussy!"

"What happened to 'purty li'l red-haired gal'?" Annabelle spat out as she shoved to her feet and righted her Stetson.

She heard the second shooter thrashing around down the slope, jostling the branches of an evergreen shrub. He gave another cry, and then Annabelle could hear him running in a shambling fashion downhill.

"Oh, you're running away from the 'purty li'l red-haired gal,' now, tough guy?"

Anna strode after him, following the sounds of his shambling retreat.

She pushed through the shrubs and saw his shadow moving downhill, holding a hand to his right ear, groaning. He'd left his rifle up where Anna had shot him. "Turn around or take it in the back, tough guy," she said, following him, taking long, purposeful strides.

"You're crazy!" the man cried, casting a fearful glance behind him. "What'd you do to H.J.?"

"What I started, you finished."

"He's my cousin!"

"Was your cousin."

He gave another sobbing cry as he continued running so awkwardly that Anna, walking, steadily gained on him as she held the carbine down low against her right leg.

"You're just evil is what you are!"

"You were after our horses, I take it?"

The man only sobbed again.

"How'd you get on our trail?"

"Seen you passin' wide around Lusk," the man said, breathless, grunting. "We was huntin' antelope on the ridge."

"Market hunters?"

"Fer a woodcuttin' crew."

"Ah. You figured you'd make more money selling my

and my husband's horses. At least you have a good eye for horse flesh."

The man gained the bottom of the ridge. He stopped and turned to see Anna moving within twenty feet of him, gaining on him steadily—a tall, slender, well-put-together young lady outfitted in men's trail gear, though, judging by all her curves in all the right places, she was all woman. He gave another wail, moonlight glinting in his wide, terrified eyes, then swung around and ran into the creek, the water splashing like quicksilver up around his knees.

He'd likely never been stalked by a woman before. Especially no "purty li'l red-headed gal."

Anna followed the coward into the creek. "What's your name?"

"Oh, go to hell!"

"What's your name?"

He shot another silver-eyed gaze back over his shoulder. "Wally. Leave me be. I'm in major pain here!"

Now that Anna was closing on him, she could see the man was tall and slender, mid- to late-twenties, with long, stringy hair brushing his shoulders while the top of his head was bald. He had small, mean eyes and now as he turned to face her, he lowered his bloody right hand to the pistol bristling on his right hip.

"You stop there, now," he warned, stretching his lips back from his teeth in pain. "You stop there. I'm done. Finished. You go on back to your camp!"

Anna stopped ten feet away from him. She rested the Winchester on her shoulder. "You know what happens to rustlers in these parts—don't you, Wally?"

He thrust his left arm and index finger out at her. "N-now, you ain't gonna hang me. You done blowed my ear off!" Wally slid the old Smith & Wesson from its holster and held it straight down against his right leg. "Besides, you're a woman. Women don't behave like that!"

He clicked the Smithy's hammer back.

"You're right—we don't behave like that. Not even we 'purty li'l red-headed gals'!" Anna racked a fresh round into the carbine's action, raised the rifle to her shoulder, and grinned coldly. "Why waste the hemp on vermin like you, Wally?"

Wally's little eyes grew wide in terror as he jerked his pistol up. "Don't you—!"

"We just shoot 'em!" Anna said.

And shot him.

Wally flew back into the creek with a splash. He went under and bobbed to the surface, arms and legs spread wide. Slowly, the current carried him downstream.

Anna heard running footsteps and a man's raking breaths behind her. She swung around, bringing the carbine up again, ready to shoot, but held fire when she saw the big, broad-shouldered man in the gray Stetson, buckskin tunic, and denims running toward her, the coyote running just ahead.

"Anna!" Hunter yelled. "Are you all right, honey?"

He and Bobby stopped at the edge of the stream. Both their gazes caught on the man bobbing downstream, and Hunter shuttled his incredulous gaze back to his wife. Raking deep breaths, he hooked a thumb over his shoulder. "Saw the other man up the hill. Dead as a post." Hunter Buchanon planted his fists on his hips and scowled his reproof at his young wife. "I told you to stay at the camp!"

Anna strode back out of the stream. She stopped before her husband, who was a whole head taller than she. "We purty li'l red-headed gals just need us a little bloodletting once in a while. Sort of like bleeding the sap off a tree."

She grinned, rose up on her toes to kiss Hunter's lips, then ticked the brim of his hat with her right index finger and started walking back toward the camp and the horses. "Come on, Bobby Lee," she said. "I'll race ya!"

CHAPTER 2

The next day, late in the afternoon, Hunter had a strange sense of foreboding as he rode into the Arapaho Creek headquarters.

He stopped his horse just inside the wooden portal in the overhead crossbar of which the Arapaho Creek brand—A/C—had been burned. He curvetted his fine grullo stallion, Nasty Pete, and took a quick study of the place.

The house sat off to the right and just ahead of him—a large, two-and-a-half story stone-and-log affair. A large, fieldstone hearth ran up the lodge's near wall shaded by a large, dusty cottonwood, its leaves flashing silver in the breeze blowing in from the bastion of the Rocky Mountain Front Range rising in the west. A couple of log barns and a stable as well as a windmill and blacksmith shop sat ahead on Hunter's left, beyond a large corral.

The wooden blades of the windmill creaked in the wind, and that hot, dry, vagrant breeze kicked up finely churned dirt and horse apples in the yard just ahead of him; they made a mini, short-lived tornado out of them. The breeze brought to Hunter's nostrils the pungent tang of sage and horse manure.

Likely impressive at one time, the place had a time-worn look. Brush grew up around the house and most of the outbuildings. Rusted tin washtubs hung from nails in the front wall of the bunkhouse. Also, there were few men working around the headquarters. Hunter spotted only four. Only one was actually working. A big, burly man in a leather apron, likely the blacksmith, was greasing the axle of a dilapidated supply wagon, the A/C brand painted on both sides badly faded.

One man sat on the corral fence to Hunter's left, rolling a sharpened matchstick from one corner of his mouth to the other with a desultory air. Two others sat outside the bunkhouse between the stable and the windmill, straddling a bench and playing two-handed poker.

Of course, most of the hands could be out on the range, tending the herds, but Hunter had spied few cattle after he, Annabelle, and the ten horses they would sell here, had ridden onto Navajo Creek graze roughly twenty miles north of Denver, near a little town called Javelina. The graze itself was sparse. It was a motley looking country under a broad, blue bowl of sky from which the sun hammered down relentlessly.

It was all bunch grass and sage, a few cedars here and there peppering low, chalky buttes and meandering, dry arroyos. It was, indeed, a big, broad, open country with damn few trees, the First Front of the Rocky Mountains cropping up in the west, some of the highest peaks showing the ermine of the previous winter's snow. This dry, dun brown country lay in grim contrast to those high, formidable ridges that bespoke deep, lush pine forests and roaring creeks and rivers.

What also appeared odd was that three of the four men Hunter could see appeared old. Late fifties to mid-sixties. Only the man sitting with his boot heels hooked over a corral slat to Hunter's left appeared under forty. He regarded Hunter blandly from beneath the weathered, funneled brim of his once-cream Stetson that was now, after enduring much sun, wind, rain, and hail of this harsh country—a washed-out yellow.

The man slid his gaze from Hunter to the main house and said, tonelessly, "Looks like the hosses are here, boss."

Hunter followed the man's gaze toward where an old man with thin gray, curly hair and a long, gray tangle of beard stood on the house's front porch. He had to be somewhere in his late-sixties—hard-earned years, judging by the man's slump and general air of fragility.

He appeared to be carrying a great weight and was damned weary of it. He wore wash-worn, broadcloth trousers, a thin cream longhandle top, and suspenders. He squinted at Hunter, his bony features long and drawn. He looked as though he might have just woken from a nap.

"Hunter Buchanon?" the man called raspily.

"Rufus Scanlon?" Hunter countered.

The man dipped his chin, his long beard brushing his flat, bony chest.

"We have the horses up on the ridge," Hunter said, hooking a thumb to indicate the low, pine-peppered ridge behind him. "I rode down to see if you were ready for 'em."

He glanced into the corral where only three horses stood still as stone save switching their tails at flies, hang-headed, regarding the newcomer dubiously.

The man beckoned broadly with a thin arm; his lips spread an eager smile, giving sudden life to the otherwise lifeless tangle of beard. "Bring 'em on down!"

Hunter glanced around the yard once more. He was selling his prized horses for two hundred apiece. He had a hard time reconciling such a price with such a humble looking headquarters. He hoped he and Anna hadn't ridden all this way for nothing.

"All right, then," he said.

He neck-reined Nasty Pete around and galloped back out through the portal. He followed the trail across Navajo Creek and up to the crest of the ridge where Anna was holding the horses in scattered pines. They stood spread out, calmly grazing, Anna sitting her calico mare, Ruthie, among them.

When they'd stopped here on the ridge, Bobby Lee had disappeared. Likely sensing they'd come to the end of the trail, the coyote had lit out on a rabbit or gopher hunt. Seeing Hunter, Anna booted the mare over to him, frowning incredulously beneath the brim of her dark green Stetson, its horsehair thong drawn up securely beneath her chin. The Rocky Mountain sun glinted fetchingly in her deep red hair.

"What is it?" she asked, the mare nuzzling Nasty Pete with teasing affection.

"What's what?"

"I know that look. What's wrong?"

Hunter shrugged and leaned forward against his saddle horn. "Not sure. Humble place, the Arapaho Creek. Doesn't look like the kind of outfit that can afford these hosses. I told Scanlon in my letter that this was a cash deal only. That's two thousand dollars. Just a might skeptical that old man down there has two thousand dollars laying around, lonely an' in need of a home." The big ex-Confederate gave his wife a pointed look. "I'll guaran-damn-tee you, though, I'm not goin' home without the cash he agreed to pay or without the horses he agreed to buy if he can't buy 'em!"

"You should've had him put cash down."

"Yeah, well, I've never had to do that before."

"That's because you've always known the men you were selling to."

Hunter sighed and raked a thumb through a two-day growth of blond beard stubble. "I gotta admit I ain't the shrewdest businessman."

"No, you're not. You're a simple, honest ex-rebel from

Georgia." Anna sidled Ruthie up next to Nasty Pete, thumbed Hunter's hat up on his forehead, and kissed him. "And that's why this Yankee girl loves you. Not sure I could've fallen in love with a shrewd businessman. My father was one of those."

Hunter smiled.

Annabelle frowned with sudden concern. "You don't think he might try to take them from us, do you? The horses."

Hunter shook his head. "Doesn't seem the type. Besides, not enough men around, and those who are, all but one, don't look like they could raise a hogleg. Nah, he's probably one of those tight Yankees who let his place go to pot because he was too cheap to hire the men to keep it up. He probably has a mattress stuffed with money somewhere in that old house. He's likely ready to spend some of that cash on horses, maybe try to build up his own remuda. Hope so, anyways." Hunter glanced around, again seeing no sign of a herd. "Looks like he might be out of the cattle business."

Anna straightened in her saddle. "Let's go see. With any luck, we'll be in Javelina by sundown, flush as railroad magnates and sitting down to a big surrounding of steak and beans!"

"Mrs. Buchanon, you are indeed a lady after my own heart."

"Oh, I think you've known for a while now that you have that, dear heart." Anna narrowed an eye at him and hooked her mouth in a crooked smile, jade eyes shimmering in the late afternoon light. "Lock, stock, and barrel!" She started to rein her calico around, saying, "Let's go drive these broomtails down to—"

Hunter touched her arm. "Hold on."

She turned back to him, frowning. "What is it?"

"Whatever happens down there." He gave her a commanding look and jerked his chin to indicate the humble headquarters at the base of the ridge. "Don't go off half-cocked like you did last night."

"Oh, I went off fully cocked last night, dear heart."

"Anna!"

But she'd already reined away from him and was working Ruthie around to the far side of the herd.

Hunter stared after her, shaking his head in frustration. But wasn't it his own damn fault—letting himself tumble for a fiery Yankee girl, a redhead spawned and reared by the equally stubborn and warrior-like Yankee Black Hills Rancher, Graham Ludlow, who'd become Hunter's blood enemy when the man had tried to keep his prized daughter from marrying into the Confederate Buchanon family?

In fact, the two families had nearly destroyed each other in the feud that had followed.

But after the smoke and dust had cleared, Hunter had found himself with the prize he'd lost two brothers, and nearly his father, old Angus, in winning. Annabelle's father had been ruined, his ranch, nearly reduced to ashes, now defunct. Hunter had to admit, as he watched Anna now, expertly working the mustangs, that she'd been worth it.

If anything had, she had . . .

He chuckled wryly. "You romantic fool, Buchanon."

He rode out and joined his young wife in gathering the herd and hazing them on down the trail, across the creek, and into the Arapaho Creek headquarters, where the man who'd been sitting on the corral fence stood holding the gate wide. When Hunter and Anna had all the horses inside the corral, obscured by a heavy cloud of roiling, sunlit dust, Rufus Scanlon strode over from the main lodge, grinning again inside the tangle of beard.

He wore a corduroy jacket over his underwear top—a concession to having guests, especially one of the female variety, Hunter silently opined—and rested his bony arms on the top corral slat, inspecting his new remuda.

"Nice, nice," he said, blinking against the dust. "Say that brown and white pinto looks to have some Spanish blood. Look at the fire in his eyes!"

Hunter and Anna sat their horses behind him.

"Most of these do," Hunter said, surveying the fine-looking remuda, all ten stallions stomping around, skirmishing, nosing the air, getting the lay of the new land. A lineback dun tried to mount a steeldust with a long, black snout and black tail and nearly got into a fight for his trouble. Others gazed off into the distance, wild-eyed, wanting to be free once more. "Some very old bloodlines in this string. Old Spanish an' Injun blood. You'll have some good breeders here, Mister Scanlon. Get you a coupla fine mares, an' you'll have one hell of a remuda."

"Were they hard to break?"

"Oh, they're not broke," Hunter said with a dry chuckle. "Do they look broke to you? Nah, their spirits are intact. But you try to throw a saddle on any of the ten, an' they'll give you no trouble. Now, when you try to mount . . ."

"That's when you'll have trouble," Anna cut in. "They'll test any one of your riders"—she grinned beautifully, gazing at the herd fondly and with a sadness at the thought of parting with them—"just to make sure they're man enough."

"Or woman enough?"

Hunter turned to see a young woman striding over from the main house—a well setup brunette in a white blouse and long, black wool skirt and riding boots. She took long, lunging strides, chin in the air, a glowing smile on her classically beautifully face.

Her hair hung messily down about her shoulders, blowing back in the wind, strands catching at the corners of her mouth. She was olive skinned, likely betraying some Spanish blood of her own, and there was a wild clarity and untethered delight in her eyes as brown as a mountain stream late in the day—as late as the day was getting now, in fact.

"Or, yeah," Anna said uncertainly, cutting a territorial glance at Hunter whom she'd no doubt spied eyeing the newcomer with keen male interest, "woman enough. Even gentled, they'll throw you for sure if they sense you're afraid of them." She glanced at Scanlon who stood packing a pipe he'd produced from the breast pocket of his worn corduroy jacket. "Who's this, Mr. Scanlon? The lady of the house?"

Scanlon merely chuckled as though at a private joke, eyes slitted, as he fired a match to life on his thumbnail and touched the flame to the pipe bowl.

"Lucinda Scanlon," said the young lady, somewhere in her early twenties, Hunter judged while trying not to scrutinize her too closely, knowing he was under his wife's watchful eye. She extended a hand to Anna. "The lady of the house and the whole damn range!" Chuckling, she added, "Pleased to meet you . . . Mrs. Buchanon, I assume?"

"Annabelle," Anna said, returning the young lady's shake and regarding her dubiously, as though a wildcat— tame or untamed, was yet to be determined—had so unexpectedly entered the conversation.

"Annabelle, of course," said Lucinda Scanlon, casting Anna a broad, warm smile before turning to Hunter whom she also offered a firm handshake and welcoming smile. Her eyes were not only as brown as a mountain creek but as deep as any lake up high in the Rockies, Hunter found himself noting. "And you're Mr. Buchanon."

"Hunter." He felt a sudden restriction in his throat at this sudden newcomer's obvious charms and forthright, refined, open, and friendly manner. Appearing so suddenly out of nowhere here at this humble, going-to-seed headquarters, she was definitely a diamond in the rough. A bluebird in a flock of crows.

"Indeed, Hunter. I enjoyed your letters describing the remuda."

"Well, uh," Hunter said, hiking a shoulder in chagrin.

"Anna helped me with it. I can ride all day, but I ain't . . . *haven't* . . . exactly perfected my sentences." He chuckled self-consciously. "Letters, but not always my sentences."

Annabelle cut him a sharp look as though silently throwing a loop over his head and reining him in. He realized he'd removed his hat and quickly donned it.

Scanlon saw the interplay and laughed.

CHAPTER 3

"It's an impressive string of horses, Mr. Buchanon," intoned Lucinda Scanlon, standing next to her father at the corral fence, inspecting the stallions jostling like schoolboys inside the corral while at times testing the fence, clawing at it with their front hooves, to see if the enclosure would hold them.

They might have been gentled and ready to saddle and bridle and to ride out on a fall gather, but they still had enough "pitch" in them, as the saying went, to keep any would-be rider on his or her toes. No rider worth his salt wanted a horse without at least a little "pitch" in him. A horse without pitch and spleen—and heart—wouldn't be worth its salt in rope-to-horn combat with a colicky steer.

Just as a ranch hand without the same thing wouldn't be worth his salt in the same situation or in a fight against rustlers or competing ranchers. Hunter had trained his horses with some of the roughest steers on the Box Bar B. Just as he wouldn't hire a hand without a little fight in him, he wouldn't train the heart and fight out of any horse meant for a working ranch. He didn't train horses for any other employ. He wouldn't know how to.

"Please, Miss Scanlon," Hunter said, smiling down at the lovely gal. "It's Hunter."

Sitting her calico beside him, Annabelle cleared her throat and gave him the stink eye.

Hunter wiped the smile off his face.

"Absolutely magnificent, Hunter," the young lady said, shaking her head in awe at the splendid spectacle of male horse flesh before her, the dust rising and turning copper yellow as the sun continued its descent in the west. "Absolutely mag-ni-fi-cent . . . Oh, look there—that zebra dun is staring at me."

"Watch out for that one," Anna warned. "He'll give you one heckuva nip. He'll sneak up behind you and give you a nice tear in your shirt . . . won't he, Hunter?"

"Oh, he's not that bad," Hunter said, chuckling.

"Look, look," said Lucinda Scanlon, her voice hushed with awe. "He's coming over here."

"Sure enough he is," said her father, puffing his pipe while he, too, inspected the herd.

"Easy, Rob Roy," Annabelle said. "That's what I call him. Rob Roy."

"Ah, yes," Miss Scanlon said as though equal to the challenge. "After Sir Walter Scott's character . . . in one of the Waverly novels."

Anna scowled down at the pretty and obviously well-read young woman. Hunter could fairly feel his young wife's pique rising off her like the heat from a high temperature. Inwardly, knowing how hot-tempered Anna could be, he cringed. He'd faced down many a gnarly rustler and a whole army of Yankee soldiers before that. It was his wife he feared the most, he begrudgingly admitted to himself.

"Well, hello, there, Rob Roy," Lucinda said as, sure enough, the big dun walked slowly toward her. He stopped seven feet away from her, slowly lowered his head, and slid his snout toward her. He laid his ears partway back as the young woman ran the backs of her fingers slowly, gently down the long, fine snout between the dark copper eyes that regarded her with—what?

Affection?

You could have knocked Hunter out of his saddle with a feather duster.

He'd never seen that expression in the horse's eyes before.

"Ahh," the young woman cooed. "Aren't we just so sweet? And beautiful. Oh, what a beautiful, boy." She turned to the old man puffing his pipe beside her. "Father, I think I'm going to claim this horse for my very own!"

Scanlon chuckled, aromatic pipe smoke wreathing the air around his weathered gray head. "Don't doubt it a bit, my dear. Don't doubt it a bit."

"Well, I reckon *Mister Buchanon* and I better be striking out for Javelina," Annabelle said, curtly. "Gonna be dark soon. So, if we could settle up, Mr. Scanlon . . ."

Lucinda whipped around, shocked, dark brown eyes imploring. "Oh, no—you must stay! Why, we were expecting you to stay. Four Bulls has corn on the cob, oyster stew, and an elk haunch on the spit in the backyard. And he's prepared a guest room. I admit, the room isn't much. The house fell into disrepair when Father was doing his government work in Denver and I was in school in England with Mother, but Four Bulls has fixed it up rather comfortably. I'm sure he has water for baths heated. Oh, you must stay. We were expecting you to stay!"

Hunter and Annabelle shared a conferring glance. Hunter arched a brow.

Then Annabelle turned to Lucinda Scanlon and said, "Did you say bath?"

Miss Scanlon shaped another warm, broad smile. "I did, indeed."

Hunter chuckled, then turned to see the man who'd been sitting on the fence earlier, and who'd opened the gate for the horses, sitting on the fence again. He was giving Hunter the proverbial woolly eyeball, but now he promptly turned away and rolled that sharpened matchstick from one corner of his mouth to the other again.

Later, as Hunter and Annabelle each soaked in their own separate, copper tubs, side by side in an upstairs guest room at the rear of the house, staring out of a pair of open French doors onto a wooden balcony that ran along the house's backside, Hunter chuckled and said, "Didn't take much to convince you to stay the night."

Her thick red hair pinned atop her head, Annabelle slumped back against the tub, arms resting on its sides, eyes half closed. She flared a nostril and splashed water at him as she said, "Yeah, well, it didn't take much to convince you, either."

Hunter sniffed the air like a dog. Apparently, the spit upon which their supper was cooking was just below the balcony, in a paved courtyard of sorts. "Yeah, well, that elk haunch sure smells good!"

"I wasn't talking about the elk haunch, and you know it."

"Oh, you mean Miss Lucinda? Pshaw. She's ain't got nothin' on you, darlin'."

"If it were she up here, you'd clean up your English. Or at least *try*!"

Slumped back in his own tub, Hunter laughed. "Why, you're jealous."

"As soon as she joined the little party there by the corral, you were blushing like a lovestruck schoolboy!"

"Ah, heck. Now, that's not true at all. She's just a right fetchin' gal, is all. And, hey, she can't be too bad—she likes our hosses."

"If it were she up here, you'd say 'horses.'"

Hunter gave a throaty chuckle.

Anna turned to him, frowning. "Did you and Scanlon talk money yet?"

Hunter shook his head. "No, not yet." They'd been given a quick tour of the sprawling, timeworn house appointed with mostly out-of-date furnishings before being led to their room where, indeed, the Indian servant, Four Bulls, had provided them with the steaming baths.

"I ain't so worried about it now, though. Sounds like Scanlon worked in Denver for a time, for the government, an' you heard Miss Lucinda said she'd been to England. They must have the cash layin' around somewhere. Sounds like this might not be their only home."

"Just the same, I'll feel a lot better when that money's in our saddlebags, Hunter."

"Oh, I will, too, honey. I will, too. I'll bring it up just as soon as I get the chance." Hunter scowled pensively through the open French doors toward a broad, panoramic view of open, dun brown prairie stretching away from the ranch yard to the distant, hazy southern horizon. "Hmm," he said, tapping his thumbs on the edge of the tub.

"What is it?"

"That fella sittin' on the corral fence? You seen him, didn't you?"

"I *saw* him."

"He looked dang familiar."

"Really? You think you've seen him before?"

Hunter nodded. "Yeah. I think I might know where, too."

"Where?"

"Tigerville. Leastways, for a while. Pretty sure he was a deputy sheriff out of Deadwood for a while. Jack Tatum, I think is his name. If that's Tatum, he was caught with a group of rustlers and hanged by a rancher up that away— Noble Price. Only, somehow Tatum cut himself down and skedaddled. The story was told by Price's men who went out to bury the bodies after they'd hung there a good long time as a lesson to others. Tatum's noose was still there but Tatum was gone."

"Why would such a scoundrel be working for Scanlon?"

"Got no idea. I sure caught him givin' me the woolly eyeball, though."

"He knows you?"

"Yeah, we had a run-in in Deadwood, a few years back."

"Over what?"

Hunter felt his ears warm. "Uh . . ."

"What?"

"Uh . . . well . . . remember, this was long before we met, honey . . ."

Again, she splashed water at him. "You cad!"

A woman's scream rose from the courtyard below, making both Hunter and Annabelle jerk with such starts that water overflowed both tubs. "Oh, my gosh. There's a coyote out here! He's eyeing the haunch!"

"Oh, no," Hunter said, bounding up out of the tub.

"Um . . . Hunter . . ." Annabelle said as her big husband ran out onto the balcony.

He peered over the rusty iron rail to see Bobby Lee sitting on a hillock about twenty feet from the edge of the paving stones, tail curled behind him. Sure enough, General Robert E. Lee's namesake was out there, eyeing the haunch on the large, bowl-shaped, cast-iron spit below Hunter and to his right.

"Bobby!" Hunter yelled, waving an angry arm. "Get away from there! Get away, you idiot. You wanna get yourself shot? Most people wouldn't understand . . . you know . . . our relationship!"

Bobby's gaze found his lord and master on the balcony. He rose and wagged his tail delightedly.

"Bobby!" Hunter said, again waving his arm. "Get away. We'll be back on the trail again tomorrow!"

"Um, Hunter . . ." came Annabelle's voice behind Hunter again.

The coyote lifted his long, pointed snout and gave a single, mournful wail. Then he turned and, casting dejected glances behind him, trotted off into the stage-stippled prairie.

Behind Hunter, Anna cleared her throat. "Um, Hunter . . ."

"That's *your* coyote?" asked Lucinda Scanlon.

She was standing by the smoking spit, beside a short, broad-shouldered, large-gutted Indian wearing a stained white apron, long, salt-and-pepper hair hanging in a braid down his broad back. Four Bulls, no doubt. Hunter hadn't met the Scanlon servant and housekeeper yet. Both he and Lucinda, who also wore an apron, her hair piled prettily atop her head, held large wooden bowls and long-handled brushes of what Hunter assumed was basting sauce for the haunch.

"Yeah, well," Hunter said, opening and closing his hands on the balcony rail, "I reckon you could say me an' Bobby Lee . . . I mean, Bobby Lee and *I* . . . sorta belong to each other. He and me . . . er, *I* . . . are pretty much joined at the hip. Don't worry about him. He'll stay away now until . . ."

He let his voice trail off when he looked down and just then realized he was standing out here on the balcony as naked as the proverbial jaybird. Both Lucinda and the stout Indian were gazing up at him shiny eyed and with lips stretched amusedly, as though at a great joke only they were in on.

Which, in a sense, they had been.

"Oh, Lordy!" Hunter exclaimed, crouching to cover himself with both hands as he whipped around and ran back into the room.

"I tried to tell you, you big galoot," Annabelle said.

CHAPTER 4

Hunter sat through most of the meal, served by the gastronomically gifted Lakota, Four Bulls, with his ears still afire with embarrassment. Lucinda and Four Bulls must have told Scanlon about the . . . um, *incident* . . . earlier, for the rancher kept regarding Hunter with a bemused smirk. Not helping any, Anna occasionally gave her hulking husband a jeering poke in the ribs.

A welcome distraction was the meal itself, which was nothing less than delicious. Especially after nearly a week on the trail herding horses down from the Hills. The haunch, corn on the cob, oyster stew, and mashed potatoes served with a rich, dark gravy spiced with mint and wild onions were all cooked to perfection.

The meal was served with coffee and milk, which Scanlon informed his guests had come from a neighboring ranch stocked with several Holsteins. More coffee was served when Four Bulls hauled out a big silver tray loaded with large wedges of dried apple pie topped with generous dollops of freshly whipped cream.

During table conversation, Hunter learned that Scanlon had several years ago served in the Colorado Territorial Senate before opening a gold and silver mine in the mountains near Leadville. His family had owned the Arapaho

Creek Ranch for two generations, his father and two brothers having fought the land away from the Arapaho and Utes. Scanlon and two uncles had run the ranch for several years after Scanlon's father died. Scanlon left the ranch and moved to Denver when he'd been elected to the territorial senate.

When both his unmarried uncles died from typhoid, the house was closed, the herd sold off. Only a year ago, Scanlon and his daughter, who'd been educated in England where the man's estranged wife still lived, had returned to Arapaho Creek to reopen the ranch and restock the range as well as its remuda. They both very much wanted to build back up the Scanlon family holdings to its former glory and to call it home again, far from the madding crowd of both England and Leadville.

Their start were the horses the man and his daughter had bought from Hunter and Annabelle. They were having several blooded mares hauled up from Texas with which to sow the seed of a larger remuda.

Hunter kept wanting to ask Scanlon why he had a man of Jack Tatum's lowly ilk on his roll, but supper didn't seem the right time or place.

Neither did after supper cigars and brandy in the parlor, for the women were invited to join them. Scanlon coerced his daughter, decked out in a creamy, low-cut gown and earrings of pearl and a pearl necklace, her hair coifed fetchingly, to entertain them at the piano. Now, Hunter Buchanon was not a good judge of musical talent, you would not be surprised to learn, but some of the piano "concertos"—at least, that's what he thought Scanlon had called the music the young woman was playing—tied knots in his throat. Not only the music itself but the way she tilted her head this way and that and the way her hands floated over the keys, seeming to barely touch the ivory yet evoking such affecting sounds.

Hunter could see that Annabelle, despite her pique at the lovely, young, cultured woman and Hunter's male fascination with her, was as moved as Hunter was. The notes fairly floated like little birds around the room, and at one point, Hunter glanced at his beloved sitting beside him and saw tears rolling down her cheeks. Annabelle caught his glance, frowned self-consciously, and quickly brushed them away.

Beneath the piano's soft chiming, a lone coyote howled mournfully somewhere on the prairie beyond the ranch house. Hunter smiled. Bobby Lee, too, had found an appreciation for fine music.

During one particularly affecting rendition at the baby grand piano, Miss Scanlon's hands suddenly lifted from the keys. She sat frozen. Hunter couldn't see the expression on her face, because her back was to him, but then she lowered her head slightly, and she sobbed. She rose suddenly and stepped out away from the piano.

"I do apologize," she said through another strangled sob and, hurrying out of the room, said, "That was mother's favorite!"

Then she was gone.

Scanlon sat in an overstuffed leather chair across from Hunter and Anna, smiling bittersweetly. He removed the ubiquitous pipe from his mouth and said, "She lost her mother only last year, you understand."

"I'm sorry to hear that," Annabelle said.

She leaned forward to set her empty brandy snifter on the small table before her, and said, "If you'll excuse me, gentleman. I'm very tired. I think I'll turn in." She rose and faced the rancher. "Thank you for your hospitality, Mr. Scanlon. Hunter and I will likely be back on the trail at first light."

"Without breakfast?" the rancher asked, rising from his chair.

Anna smiled. "Yes, but not without regret. But we, too, have a ranch to run. Maybe see you again sometime."

She shook the man's hand, kissed her husband's cheek, then left the room, leaving Hunter and Scanlon standing in a heavy, awkward silence following Miss Scanlon's poignant, lingering music.

Hunter and the rancher slacked back into their seats. Hunter cleared his throat but before he could say a word, Scanlon said, "I bet you'd like to get paid."

"That's sort of what I was getting around to."

"Yes, yes, of course." He turned his head toward the parlor's open door. "Four Bulls?"

Silence.

Heavy footsteps sounded. They grew louder, the old wooden floor creaking, until Four Bulls entered the room, wearing as he had earlier a broadcloth jacket over a white shirt decked out with a necklace of Indian-colored beads. He wore broadcloth trousers and beaded moccasins. In his right hand he held a fat manilla envelope.

"Mhmm," he said, and gave the envelope to Scanlon, and then turned and left the room, leaving the smoky smell of the buckskin moccasins and the spit on which he'd roasted the elk in the room behind him.

Scanlon hefted the envelope in his hands, smiling. "A goodly amount." He set the envelope on the table between him and Hunter. "And worth every penny. Thank you for bringing them to me."

Hunter stood and stuffed the envelope in his back pocket. "My pleasure, sir. Been nice doing business with you. And like my lovely wife said, much obliged for your hospitality."

Scanlon rose creakily from his chair and shook Hunter's hand.

"Good night, young man," he said, regarding Hunter almost sadly.

That took Hunter aback a bit, but he just smiled, said goodnight, and left the room, hoping he could remember how to find his way back to his and Anna's.

Later that night, in the night's deep bowels, in fact, Anna found herself lying awake, arms crossed behind her head.

It was hot so she and Hunter had left the French doors open, hoping for a breeze. There was a slight one now, somewhat relieving the heat. Still, she found herself sleepless, for some reason.

Why?

She frowned as she stared at the ceiling.

She'd felt a strange unease all evening, but she hadn't been able to put a finger on its cause. She couldn't now, either. Likely, it was just that she was far from home and now that their job of delivering the horses to the Arapaho Creek Ranch was complete, she just wanted to be back on the trail home with her husband. Though she'd let on otherwise, she was not jealous of Lucinda Scanlon. She knew Hunter's love for her was complete. What man with red blood in his veins wouldn't be taken with the lovely and cultivated young woman?

No, Miss Scanlon was not the reason for her unease.

Whatever the cause, she couldn't sleep while Hunter lay snoring softly beside her. She'd swear the man could sleep through a cyclone. Not she.

Restless, she slid the covers back and rose from the bed.

Hunter stirred, grumbling.

"Just gonna take a walk," she whispered. "Go back to sleep."

Hunter smacked his lips and made the bed quake as he rolled onto his side and resumed snoring.

Anna gave a dry chuckle.

Clad in only her longhandles, she pulled on her plaid wool shirt and stepped into her boots. She grabbed her hat off a wall peg, set it on her head, and walked softly out the two open French doors and onto the balcony, the old boards creaking beneath her feet. She stood gazing out over the star-capped prairie, enjoying the fresh breeze sliding against her face, rife with the wine of cottonwoods, cedars, and sage.

She turned sideways to the balcony rail and crossed her arms on her chest, over the shirt she'd buttoned only partway. She closed her eyes, drew a deep breath. The only sounds were the breeze and the pulsating hum of crickets.

A twig snapped.

Anna opened her eyes and looked around. Beneath her were only the paving stones and old, rotting benches of the courtyard. Beyond a fringe of cedars, shrubs, and a few small cottonwoods at the edge of the courtyard, below and to her left, was only vast, open prairie mantled with twinkling stars. The twig had snapped somewhere in the shrubs. It hadn't snapped itself. Someone or something had snapped it.

Anna had a sense she was being watched.

"Who's down there?" she wanted to yell but did not. She didn't want to wake the house. She considered waking Hunter, but she might be alarmed about nothing. It could just be a cat or a dog down there. Possibly Bobby Lee.

She'd find out for herself.

She walked back into the room where Hunter still lay snoring on his side, and grabbed her carbine from where she'd leaned it against the wall. She walked back out onto the balcony, swung left ,and, staring into the black mass of moving shrubs and small trees, she walked to the end of the balcony and then followed the steps down to the courtyard, where the heat from the now-covered spit still radiated.

She walked out along the courtyard to its backside and stared into the thicket, the branches being nudged this way and that by the fickle night breeze.

"Hello?" she said very quietly.

She'd feel foolish if someone saw or heard her out here, frightened as a child who couldn't sleep, possibly only pestered by specters from her own imagination.

She glanced back at the house hulking up darkly behind her, making sure she wasn't being watched, then followed a thin path into the thicket, holding the carbine up high across her chest. She walked six feet, ten, stepping around the breeze-brushed shrubs, squinting into the darkness around her. The rustling of the breeze was louder out here.

Again, a twig snapped. Anna gasped and turned to her left.

"Who's there?" she said, louder this time, hearing the tremor of fear in her voice. Still more loudly: "Who's there? I know you're out here. Who are you? What do you want?"

Ahead now the trees and shrubs made a heavier, blacker line. That was the area from which the last sound had come.

Anger building in her, tempering her fear—someone was toying with her—she strode forward quickly, squeezing the carbine in her hands.

A growling sounded from that dark mass ahead of her.

A man cursed.

More growling and snarling and then a man said, "Git, damn you!"

An angry bark and then there rose the thudding of a galloping horse.

The thuds dwindled quickly to silence, to only the rustling of the breeze in the branches around her. A figure moved ahead of her, growing larger until the gray-brown coyote took shape ten feet in front of her.

"Bobby!" Anna cried in relief.

The coyote came up to her, mewling and panting, obviously troubled.

Anna dropped to a knee and wrapped an arm around the frightened beast's neck.

"What happened, boy? Who was out there?"

Bobby mewled, gave a brief, low howl, then licked Anna's cheek.

"Whoever it was, you scared him off, didn't you? Thank you." Anna hugged the coyote more tightly. Bobby Lee had likely been out here all night, watching over her and Hunter.

A tear came to Anna's eye.

A wild beast, eh?

"You run along now, Bobby," she said, straightening. "I'm going to go back to bed, see if I can get some sleep. We'll be leaving first thing in the morning."

She knew she didn't have to tell Bobby Lee that. He'd be watching and waiting. As soon as Anna and Hunter were back on the trail, he'd show himself and run along beside them. She gave the coyote one more pat, then swung around and started to retrace her route through the trees and shrubs. She'd taken only a few steps when a young woman's cry of *"Oh, God!"* sailed from the direction of the house.

Anna froze, frowning toward the house, which she could not see from this vantage.

"Now what?"

She broke into a run.

CHAPTER 5

A few minutes earlier, Hunter thought he'd heard Anna's voice in his sleep.

He opened his eyes and turned to see that her side of the bed was empty. Then through the fog of sleep and dreams, he remembered she'd awakened and said she was going to take a walk. He didn't much care for that idea, he realized now but had been too tired to realize earlier.

He rose from the bed. Having learned from his experience earlier, he pulled on his denims and buckskin tunic and stepped into his boots. He even donned his hat just because, like most westerners, he didn't feel complete without it. He didn't feel complete without his knife and gun, either, but he decided to leave them. He was just going to go out and have a look around for Anna.

To that end, he strode through the open French doors onto the balcony and, leaning forward, rested his arms on the balcony rail. Peering down into the courtyard, he couldn't see much. There being no moon, the darkness was relieved only by starlight.

Deciding to go down and have a closer look, he turned to his left and gave a sharp grunt as someone walked straight into him, her warm body pressing against his. At first, he thought she was Anna but then Lucinda Scanlon lifted her face to his and she was smiling, lips stretched back from all those perfect, white teeth, starlight glinting in her eyes.

"My gosh, you're a big man! You know, I didn't realize just how big till now! Why I feel like a child in your arms!"

"Miss Scanlon—what in the holy hob are you doin' out here this time o' the night?" And dressed in only a thin nightgown? he did not add, but wondered. Obviously, she wore nothing under it. Her hair was down again and blowing in the breeze. He could smell her perfume that had fairly filled both the dining room and parlor earlier and as well as brandy and . . . what?

He'd frolicked in Deadwood enough times before he'd married Anna to recognize the distinctive, cloying aroma of the midnight oil.

Why, this little scamp of an English-educated debutante had an opium pipe in her room!

"I'm so sorry," she said. "I couldn't sleep, and I guess I was just wandering around and . . . found myself up here." She peered into the guest room. "Is your wife asleep?"

"No, she's out here, too." Hunter looked over the balcony rail again. "Somewhere."

"Getting some air, eh?"

"I reckon."

"Did you have an argument . . . big man?" she said, jeer-ingly, obviously drunk and addled from the Chinese to-bacco. She wrapped her arms around Hunter's neck and stepped up close to him. "It's okay if you did . . . if you're alone. I'm always alone. I'm always alone and . . . well, sad, if you must know. My brothers are dead. Mother is dead. And . . . well, if you must know—*shhh!*" She placed a finger to her bee-stung lips, then wrapped her arms around his neck again. "Father is dying."

Hunter gently lowered her arms from his neck, frowning

down at her with genuine concern. "I'm sorry to hear that, Miss Scanlon."

"Lucinda."

"Lucinda, I mean." Hunter's head was suddenly aswirl with questions and conflicting feelings.

If the man was dying, why on earth had he bought the horses?

Standing before him, entwining her fingers down low before her, Lucinda Scanlon looked up at him and shook her hair from her eyes. "I think that buying the horses was his way of trying to stave off death. Of denying it, somehow. Of telling it to go to hell—it's not going to get him. Not Rufus Scanlon!"

Suddenly, her eyes filled with tears. She leaned forward and placed her cheek against Hunter's chest. "I'm so sad," she sobbed.

Hunter felt about as awkward as he'd ever felt. Having all this female flesh in his arms and yet not wanting her here. Yet she was obviously feeling very dark and depressed, and she was crying against his chest, dampening his shirt. He couldn't very well just push her away—now, could he?

But what if Annabelle returned?

He steeled himself with a deep breath, filling up his chest. He placed his hands on the sobbing young woman's shoulders. "I'm very sorry to hear that about your pa, Miss . . . er, I mean, Lucinda. But I need to go out lookin' for my wife. I'm afraid she might've taken a walk and got turned around. I'd best see to—"

She reached up and placed a finger on his lips. "Wait." She tilted her head back, looking up at him, a devilish little light in her eyes and curling her lips. "Kiss me first. You'll make it better that way." She started to rise up onto her toes, sliding her mouth toward his. "Please. She has enough man . . . she can share . . ."

Hunter pushed her back away from him again. "I'm sorry, Lucinda. Truly, I am, but—"

"Oh, God!" she cried and, hardening her jaws, slapped him hard across the jaw.

It was a stinging, burning blow.

"You go to hell, then," she seethed.

She swung around and stumbled away on her bare feet. Her pale nightgown was quickly absorbed by the darkness.

Hunter stared after her in shock.

"Hunter?"

Annabelle's voice nudged him out of the fog.

He turned to peer down into the courtyard. Anna stood there, gazing up at him. It was then he realized that during his enervating encounter with Lucinda Scanlon he'd heard a commotion out in the darkness beyond the yard. "Anna?" he said, turning and squeezing the balcony rail in his hands. "Where on earth have you been?"

"Bobby Lee and I have been chasing away a shadow."

Hunter scowled. "A what?"

Anna walked to the stairs and then stood before her husband, looking up at him, incredulous. "How has your night been?"

Hunter chuckled and took his young wife in his arms, drew her close against him.

"Your shirt's wet," she said.

"Yeah, well, it's been rainin' Lucinda Scanlon."

Anna looked up at him. "Pretty rain."

He turned Anna toward the open French doors. "I'll tell you tomorrow. Let's go back to bed. We might get a couple of hours in before dawn . . . if we're lucky."

"If we're very lucky," Anna said.

* * *

On the trail early the next day, headed back in the direction of their ranch near Tigerville, in the Black Hills, Hunter said, "Whoa!"

He reined Nasty Pete to a halt.

Riding on his left, Annabelle stopped Ruthie and glanced at Hunter. "What is it?"

The ex-Confederate glanced up at the high rocks lining the trail. "Seen a shadow of some—"

He stopped as that shadow dropped straight down onto the trail from the rocks above it. *Plop!* Bobby Lee turned to face them both, giving a devilish smile with those long eyes of his, and shook himself.

"Bobby Lee," Hunter said, removing his hand from the grips of the LeMat holstered on his right thigh, "you about took another seven years off my life!"

The coyote swung around and trotted up the trail, riding point.

Annabelle laughed as she and Hunter booted their mounts on up the trail. "I was sure glad he was out there last night, looking out for me."

"That's the strangest dang thing," Hunter said. "What in holy blazes would someone be doin' out there in the middle of the night?"

"I think he or whoever it was, was keeping an eye on us. For some reason. I don't know why."

"You know who I think it was?" Hunter said.

"Who?"

"Jack Tatum."

"You think Tatum still holds a grudge over the *dove du pave* you two were fighting over in Deadwood?"

"Well, she wasn't just any *dove du pave*," Hunter said.

"Oh, really?" Annabelle said, arching both brows in that schoolmarmish way of hers. "Do tell!"

"Well, she was really purty an' I think he wanted to marry her. You know—make an honest woman out of her. But then I came along—an' I have to make a confession here. I ain't braggin' or nothin' like that. But I think I mighta stole her heart a little."

"Oh, you did. And you left her high and dry?"

Hunter laughed. "Heck, no. She's one of the biggest, notorious madams in Deadwood even to this day."

Annabelle stared at him, aghast. "This dove didn't happen to be Maud 'Frenchie' Devereaux?"

Hunter grinned. "Gentlemen keep their secrets."

Annabelle beat him with her hat, saying, "You big rebel galoot—I had no idea I was married to such a man about Deadwood!"

"Annabelle—stop!" Hunter said, raising an arm to defend himself. More seriously, he said, "Wait—hold on. Stop!"

He was staring up trail, his eyes wide and serious.

Annabelle stopped and followed his gaze to where Bobby Lee sat on a flat rock fifty feet ahead and on the trail's left side.

He checked Nasty Pete down to a stop. Annabelle did the same with Ruthie. At nearly the same time, something buzzed through the air between them to smash into a boulder just behind them. The loud *thud!* was followed by a rifle's distant bark.

"*Bushwhack!*" Hunter yelled just as Nasty Pete gave a shrill whinny and rose sharply up off his front hooves.

He'd been so concerned about Annabelle that the horse's sudden start caught him off guard. He reached for the horn, but his fingers merely brushed it before he was rolling down the horse's left hip. The ground came up fast, rocks and pebbles growing in his vision, until he slammed onto the trail with an ear-ringing crash. He struck on his left shoulder and hip; his hat flew off his head. Bobby came mewling around him, raking him with his nose, worried about his master.

Another bullet tore up dirt inches to his right, throwing

grit in his eyes. Bobby screeched and ran off into the brush. He was a brave, protective coyote, but when it came to bullets coming too close for comfort, jackrabbits became more important.

"Hunter!"

In his blurred vision, he saw Annabelle leap out of her saddle and Ruthie go tearing up the trail after Nasty Pete, dust roiling behind the frightened mounts.

"No!" Hunter said, shaking his head to clear his vision. "Grab Pete—the money!"

Annabelle dropped to a knee beside him. "Are you all right?"

Another bullet buzzed through the air over both their heads before slamming into the same rock the first one had. It was followed by the distant, echoing bark of the rifle that had fired it.

Hunter leaped to his feet, grabbed Annabelle's arm, and pulled her off the side of the trail and behind the large boulder the bullets had slammed into. He edged a look around the edge of the boulder, staring up trail in the direction in which the horses had fled. "The hosses!" Hunter bellowed. "The money's in the saddlebags—my saddlebags!"

As another rocketing report echoed from a pine-stippled ridge off the trail's right side, following the bullet it had fired an eye wink earlier, Annabelle said, "At the moment, I think we have more important things to worry about!"

"Nothin' more important than that money!" Hunter barked, edging another look to the north as both horses disappeared around a bend in the trail. "Pete has my rifle, too."

Annabelle said with no little mockery, "I thought to grab mine!" She held out the carbine she'd shucked from her saddle boot just before Ruthie went thundering after Nasty Pete.

Hunter looked at it. His ears warmed with chagrin. "Well, ain't you so handy."

"For a horseman, you know little about leaving a saddle!"

"Oh, hell, this ain't no time to add insult to injury, my sweet Yankee darlin'!" He turned to where Annabelle stood pressing her back against the boulder behind him. "Cover me. I'm gonna work my way up that ridge!"

"Hunter, hold on!"

He turned to her. "What is it?"

"Our lives are more important than that money."

"So—what? You don't want me to try and save it?"

"No." Annabelle shook her head and gave a grim smile. "I just wanted you to hear it."

"Oh, hell—I know that." Hunter grabbed her by the back of the neck, drawing her to him brusquely and kissing her lips. "But if we don't get that money back, we'll be movin' to town soon an' you'll likely have to go back to saloon work. Not that the men of Tigerville wouldn't love to see you in a pair of fishnet stockings again, but—"

Taking advantage of a lull in the shooting, Hunter turned away from Annabelle and ran across the trail and into the prickly brush beyond.

CHAPTER 6

Behind Hunter, Annabelle dropped to a knee and fired a couple of rounds up toward the rocky ridge atop which Hunter assumed their assailants were cowering.

He had no idea who they were, but he assumed they were your average trail devils after his and Anna's horses and possibly Anna herself—but he aimed to find out and to show them the error of their ways. The problem, he realized now, hunkering behind a rock and gazing up the long slope, was that there was little cover between him and them.

The top of the ridge was roughly a hundred yards away. That was a long, open run. He'd never make it. Another problem he had was that he was armed with only his LeMat, a gift from a Confederate general whose life he'd saved during the War of Northern Aggression. Great for close range work, but darn near useless in this situation.

Scrutinizing the country from this vantage, however, he saw a ravine running up the ridge, just ahead and to his right. It was broad and shallow, but if he kept his head down, he should be able to make it to the top of the ridge and over to a nest of rocks on top of it, where he assumed his assailants were firing from, without getting himself perforated.

It was his only chance.

He glanced behind. Anna knelt behind the boulder, holding her Winchester, ready.

"All right!"

He bounded up and out from behind his covering rock. He'd taken only one long, running stride before a bullet plumed dirt just in front of him. The shooters had anticipated his ploy. Nothing he could do but keep running, which he did—hard, scissoring his arms and legs. Behind him, Anna's carbine spoke. It stopped speaking, likely having fired its last round, just as he dove forward the last few yards, flying over the lip of the ravine and landing on the floor of the cut below, cursing as nails of pain bit his joints already sore from his earlier unceremonious unseating.

Two rounds landed just beyond him, the rifles echoing a second later.

Hunter heaved himself to his feet, grunting, again shaking the cobwebs from his vision. His LeMat in hand, keeping his head just beneath the lip of the arroyo, he ran up the ravine that cut down the long slope of the ridge. After ten or so strides, he stopped, pressed a shoulder against the ravine wall on his left, and edged a look over the top, toward the ridge crest.

They knew he was in the ravine, so he had to assume they'd come to meet him at some point.

Not yet.

He continued running.

After another forty feet, he stopped again. Breathing hard, he gazed up toward the ridge crest again. Still nothing. They'd stopped shooting because they didn't have a target.

They were waiting for him.

He looked at the LeMat in his gloved right hand, shook his head. He sure wished he had his Henry.

He pulled his head back down beneath the ravine's lip and continued running, breathing hard against the climb. When he'd been running guerilla missions behind Union lines during the war, he'd gone barefoot just as he had when he'd been a kid, running wild through the north Georgia hills, sometimes armed with only a slingshot. He could run like the wind in those days. The boots he wore now were not made for running, but he was afraid to take them off. His feet were far more tender than they were back in those gay olden times . . .

The ridge crest was now a hundred feet beyond.

He stopped and dropped to a knee. The ravine played out at the crest, opening like the main part of a bottle, the ravine banks dropping to ground level.

"See him?"

Hunter dropped still lower and thrust his shoulder against the ravine wall on his left. The man's query had not come from far away.

"No," said another man's voice, a little farther away than the first. "He's in there, though. I seen him."

Hunter waited.

Footsteps sounded—the crunch of boot soles on grass.

When he could hear both men breathing nervously, he lifted his head as well as the LcMat, clicking the hammer back.

"Right here, fellas!"

They swung their heads toward him and froze—both clad in motley trail gear, pistols wedged behind their belts. Petty road agents, most likely. The stockier of the two was nearest Hunter. He had a hound dog look beneath the round brim of his Stetson. The taller of the two was also the youngest, with longish blond hair hanging down from a ragged bowler hat to the collar of his sack shirt. He stood about ten yards upslope of the stocky gent.

Hunter slid the LeMat from left to right, keeping them both in his sights.

"What're you after?"

"Uh . . . uh . . ." said the stocky gent. He held an old

Springfield rifle held together with baling wire in his right hand. He held up his left hand, palm out. "Now, uh . . . now, uh . . ."

"What're you after?" Hunter asked again, more sharply.

The younger man smiled seedily and said, "You know what we're after." His look told Hunter he and the other man knew he and Annabelle had sold the horses. They'd likely followed them from a distance, waiting for them to return without the horses but with a packet full of money. They were likely just bright enough to know such fine horse flesh would bring in a sizeable cache.

The skinny blond swung his Spencer repeater toward Hunter, spreading his feet and crouching.

Hunter's LeMat bucked and roared. The bullet took the kid through the dead center of his chest and knocked him straight backward, throwing the Spencer out away from him.

The stocky gent brought his Springfield to bear and fired, the bullet flying wide as Hunter's own bullet drilled a puckered purple hole in his forehead, just above his right eye. The second man hadn't stopped groaning, dying hard, when Hunter sprang up out of the ravine, holstered his LeMat, grabbed the kid's Spencer, and ran toward the rocks scattered atop the ridge crest.

He ran crouching, holding the cocked LeMat straight out before him. From the trail below, he thought he'd spied three or four shooters in the rocks, which meant there was at least one more. The rocks were twenty feet away from him now.

Ten . . .

He ran around them, swinging the big pistol around and tightening his finger on the trigger.

Nothing but spent cartridges and a single cigarette butt still smoldering in a patch of sand.

Hoof thuds sounded. Annabelle was riding her calico up

the shoulder of the ridge, straight ahead of Hunter. "Found
Ruthie," she said, holding her carbine across her saddle-
bows. "You all right?"

"Yeah, I'm all right. No sign of Nasty Pe—?"

Hunter stopped. He'd spied movement in the corner of
his right eye.

"What is it?" Annabelle asked.

"Think I just found him."

He squinted at two riders leading one saddled horse up
a low, distant ridge. Bobby Lee was hot on their trail but
when one of the riders twisted around in his saddle to send
three rounds pluming dirt around Bobby's scissoring legs,
the coyote gave a yip and swerved off into the brush.

"I just found him," Hunter said as the riders crested the
ridge and then disappeared down its opposite side.

Hunter thrust his right hand up at his wife. "Hop down,
Anna. We're gonna have to ride double."

Anna leaped down, then Hunter toed a stirrup and swung
up into the leather. He extended a hand to Anna again and
pulled her up behind him. He swung the calico around
and booted her on down the backside of the ridge.

"Go easy, now, Hunter," Anna admonished behind him,
wrapping her arms around his waist. "Remember, she's
carrying double, and you are no little man."

"I know, I know—damn the luck!"

It wasn't easy, but Hunter didn't push the calico.

Anna was right. Ruthie was carrying more than double
her usual weight. Killing the mare wouldn't get them to
the men who'd stolen Nasty Pete as well as Hunter's rifle—
which had belonged to his now-deceased brother, Shep—
and the money in his saddlebags. The money he and Anna
needed to continue running the ranch in the wake of last
year's costly bear killings.

Speed wasn't all that necessary, anyway. The two riders had left plenty of sign and only after a mile or so of tracking them, Hunter thought he knew where they were headed. As they were moving northeast, they were likely headed for the Buffalo Gulch Roadhouse. Save a few raggedy-heeled shotgun ranches, that was about all that lay between here and North Platte, Nebraska.

Bobby Lee caught up to them but held back, wary of more lead being hurled his way. That was all right. Bobby was good in a fight but he was no match for lead.

They rested Ruthie every half hour, giving her water from Anna's canteen. Hunter and Anna themselves drank sparingly, saving the water for the horse. It was late in the day, almost evening, when they heard the off-key patter of a distant piano issuing from maybe half a mile ahead on the nearly featureless prairie. They dipped down into a ravine and when they bounded up through willows on the other side, the roadhouse lay ahead—a sprawling, ramshackle, adobe brick affair with a rusted tin roof.

The trail split the yard down the middle. A log barn with connecting corral and a windmill lay to the right. The roadhouse with a large, brush-roofed ramada lay to the left. Several horses milled in the corral. Five or six more stood at the hitchrack beneath the ramada. An old, beat-up wagon sat there, too, a mule standing hang-headed in the traces.

A large, shaggy dog was skirmishing with a small, brown, short-haired dog in the yard. They were fighting over a stick, the little dog following the large dog and barking angrily. The shaggy dog trotted around proudly, as though he'd found the bone of all bones, and wouldn't the little dog just love to get its teeth on it?

The yard had turned a deep copper, as the sun was hovering just above the western horizon, behind Hunter and Anna as they rode into the yard astride the calico. Seeing them, the big dog dropped the stick and came running, wagging his tail as though the roadhouse hadn't seen a visitor in weeks. The little dog yipped and grabbed the stick. The dogs kept Bobby Lee at the edge of the yard. The coyote had no time for dogs. Hunter swung his right leg over the saddle horn, dropped to the ground, gave the shaggy dog a pat, and glanced at one of the horses tied to the hitchrack beneath the ramada.

Anna had seen Nasty Pete, too. She gave Hunter a dark look, then leaped straight back over the calico's tail to the ground.

She slid her carbine from the boot, cocked it, and said, "How do you want to play it?"

Hunter walked over to Nasty Pete, who had already craned his neck to regard his rider, delightedly switching his tail.

"Hey, boy," Hunter said, patting the horse's rump. "Hey, there, old fella. Hope they treated you right."

The grullo whickered.

The tinny piano clatter still issued from inside the tumbledown place.

Hunter reached into the saddlebag pouch, felt around. The envelope containing the money from the broncs was gone.

He looked at Anna. She read his expression, pursed her lips, and nodded.

He looked at his scabbard. Empty.

"They really cleaned me out," he said. "Not for long."

"I doubt they had time to spend much money."

"Never know," Hunter said. "They're about to find out how expensive that money came. Be ready to back me if I need it."

"You're not going to just walk right in there?"

"I doubt they got a good look at either of us."

"How will you know who they are?"

"I'll know."

Anna placed her hand on his arm. "Be careful. Like I said . . ."

"I know." Hunter grinned. "But I don't want you in fishnet stockings again, neither. At least, not in no saloon." He winked, turned, and mounted the steps of the small porch fronting the place.

He peered over the batwings. Twenty or so men were patronizing the humble hole, five standing at the bar running along the right wall, the rest sitting at tables before Hunter and to his left. A staircase ran up the room's rear wall, on the opposite side of the room from the batwings.

There were two girls—a thin blond in bloomers and not much else except a few feathers in her hair playing the piano at the far end of the bar as though she knew what she was doing. Hunter was surprised she hadn't run all the drinkers out of the place or gotten herself shot. He noticed there were three bullet holes in the side of the piano and one in the bench she was sitting on. He'd have thought she'd have learned her lesson. She was working the peddles barefoot.

The other girl appeared a half-breed. She sat on the knee of a cow puncher—one of five playing poker at a table in the middle of the room. One of the punchers appeared a midget. He sat on cushions piled high on his chair, and he was smoking a fat stogie and laughing as he cajoled the others, who appeared none too pleased with the haranguing. The girl was dressed in a simple nightgown; her near-black hair hung long, and she had a knife scar on her cheek. She appeared bored with the proceedings.

Another quick survey of the room, and Hunter found his men.

They were standing at the bar side by side, to the left of a man in a long, canvas coat and canvas hat—likely a prospector who belonged to the wagon parked outside. The two men to his left, standing maybe six feet away from him, leaned forward, elbows on the bar. In the back bar mirror, Hunter could see they were drinking from a labeled bottle. Neither appeared the type to drink from a bottle with a label on it. Both wore a combination of sack clothes and time-worn broadcloth. Hunter's Henry rested atop the bar to the right of the man standing to the right of the other man.

Outside, the little dog was yipping again, angrily. Apparently, his skirmish with the shaggy dog had resumed. Hunter could just barely hear above the thunder of that consarned piano.

If the two gents at the bar hadn't stolen a sizeable, badly needed stake from him, he would have turned around and walked away, believing his ears deserved better.

Instead, he strode to his right and bellied up to the bar to the right of the man who had his Henry resting on the bar beside him.

The barman, a tall thin man with dead eyes and a pencil-line mustache, walked over and said, "What's your pleasure?"

"Not that piano. That's for sure."

He and the two men standing to Hunter's left laughed. Then the two to his left continued drinking and staring dully at the bar before them. In the backbar mirror Hunter could see they were much like the two he'd dispatched—dull-witted, pennyante road agents and, most likely, stock thieves. They'd spied Hunter and Annabelle and their two fine horses from a distance and, knowing they'd sold the ten horses, decided they could line their pockets for the rest of the year and, if they played it right, a good part of the winter.

"You're welcome," Hunter said.

Both men looked at him. The man nearest him frowned and said, "What?"

"For the drinks," Hunter said. "I bought 'em."

Understanding grew slowly in their gazes.

Hunter reached under the coat of the man standing nearest him and pulled the manilla envelope out of his back pocket. He slapped the envelope down on the bar. Both men jerked with starts and reached for the hoglegs tied low on their thighs. Hunter grabbed the Henry off the bar and smashed the butt plate into the face of the man nearest him then cocked the rifle and shot the other man, who was just then bringing up an old-model Schofield.

The other man was staggering backward, screaming, blood oozing from his smashed lips. As he did, he raised his own .44 and got a shot off, flames lapping from the barrel, the bullet plunking into the bar to Hunter's left, a half second before Hunter recocked the Henry and fired a round into the man's chest.

As both men piled up on the floor at the base of the bar, the infernal piano fell silent. The girl who'd been playing it turned toward Hunter and the two dead men with a gasp, covering her mouth with her hand.

One of the other customers raked out a shocked curse, and then silence fell over the room.

"Good Lord, man," said the bartender.

"Sorry about the disturbance," Hunter said, stuffing the envelope into his shirt pocket, then scooping the Henry up off the bar and resting it on his shoulder. He smiled and pinched his hat brim to the apron. "I'll be gettin' outta your hair straightaway."

The barman glanced at the labeled bottle on the bar. "They haven't paid for that yet."

"And they never will."

Hunter swung around and began walking toward the batwings. He stopped when one of the customers rose from a table ahead and to his right, and said, "Hunter Buchanon . . . rebel vermin from Tigerville!"

Hunter stopped and turned to the man—a big, broad-shouldered man with black eyes and a thick, curly black beard. "You ran me outta Tigerville a few years ago, when you was playin' town marshal."

Hunter grinned. "Oh, I wasn't just playin'. I landed the job, all right. Didn't like it much . . . less'n I was runnin' filth like you outta town, Boyd Simms." Hunter hardened his gaze. "Still slappin' up soiled doves just for fun, Boyd?"

"Why you . . . !"

Simms drew the revolver hanging low on his right thigh but not before the LeMat was in Hunter's hand, blasting. Simms fired his own gun into the floor and flew back into the table he'd been sitting at. That caused the five men he'd been playing poker with to make a similar play, leaping to their feet and slapping leather. Hunter shot one, and Annabelle went to work with her Winchester and in seconds all five men were down, obscured by a cloud of pale gun smoke.

The rest of the room tensed. Hands went to pistols or rifles lying across tables, but the guns remained where they were. For both Hunter and Annabelle were covering the room with their own smoking weapons.

"Why, thank you, darlin'," Hunter said.

"Don't mention it, darling," Annabelle returned.

To the room, Hunter said, "Everybody just stay put now, hear? Been enough killin' here tonight, I think you will agree."

As he spoke, he backed slowly to the door. Annabelle joined him. Once outside, they mounted their horses, turned them away from the hitchrack, and put the steel to them, riding out of the road ranch yard at hard gallops, casting cautious glances behind them. They rode into a narrow canyon and checked their blowing mounts down. They made a hasty, rudimentary camp and brewed a pot of coffee, leaning back against their saddles to sip it.

Bobby Lee slunk into the camp and curled up between Hunter's spread legs, instantly asleep.

"Close one," Hunter said and took another sip.

"You can say that again. We almost lost that stake, Hunt."

Hunter removed his hat and ran a big hand through his shaggy, blond hair. "Don't I know it. Lots of bad folks out here."

Annabelle gazed darkly into the night. "Yeah . . . and I fear there's more where those came from."

CHAPTER 7

Meanwhile, back at Hunter and Annabelle's Box Bar B Ranch in the Black Hills west of Tigerville, Dakota Territory, Hunter's father, old Angus, set a case of his homemade, coffee-colored ale into the box of his supply wagon.

Not an easy task with only one arm, but Angus was a stalwart Southern soul, and he always got by. He had no complaint in him. He especially wouldn't complain in front of his foster grandson, Nathan Jones, whom he saw was smiling admiringly up at the old man as he set his own crate of bottles into the back of the wagon.

"Why the smile, boy?" Angus asked.

"Hunter's right about you. You got the bark on." Nathan, a sandy-haired, freckle-faced boy of thirteen, clad in denim overalls, work shirt, and stockmen's boots, smiled up again at Angus.

Angus grinned then, too. "In this world, you got to, son."

"Sure you don't want me to ride into town with you, help you unload the beer?"

"Nah, you stay here and look after the place with Casey." Angus ruffled the young man's hair.

After the Buchanons had lost most of their men in the attack of the rogue grizzly of the previous year, they'd hired only one man—Casey McQuade, who lived alone in the bunkhouse. They were too short of scratch, as Angus would call the money needed to pay such men. So Hunter, Annabelle, Nathan, and Angus had to do the work of ten, which meant long days. Angus fortified their income by selling his ale in town to saloons.

"You know where my extra shotgun is," Angus said. "Inside by the front door." He glanced at the sprawling log ranch house standing amidst pines and painted by the early morning sun. "Any owlhoots show up stirrin' up trouble, you know what to do and so does Casey."

"We do."

"All right, then." Angus clambered into the wagon, grunting with the effort. The graybeard pinched his battered brown Stetson at the boy, released the brake, and swung the wagon out away from his brewing shed, the area around it rife with the smell of wort and hops. He whipped up the roan in the traces and rolled on out of the yard and into a deep valley hemmed in by high, pine-carpeted ridges.

It was a beautiful morning with birds piping and squirrels chittering in the pine boughs. The sky was a clear, faultless blue, and the sun glistened off the pine needles. The air was spiced with the heady, gin-like aroma of the pine resin. Angus was stove up with arthritis, but he was still alive, gallblastit, and he was going to enjoy the day, maybe even have a beer with Bill Wheatly in the Sundown Saloon. As the wagon rolled along, he found himself humming and sometimes even singing songs his Mam and Pappy had taught him when he'd been just a younker down in Georgia, in the peaceful years before the war during which he'd lost his arm.

He'd ridden a few miles when three riders appeared ahead of him, rounding a bend in the trail. Angus was instantly suspicious, for owlhoots roamed these hills, on the run from the law or looking to long loop a few cattle and sell them to outlaw ranchers. He shoved his foot back under the wagon seat where his double-barrel resided, making sure it was there. These men were gun-hung, he saw as they approached, so he wouldn't have much time to bring up the twelve-gauge if they made trouble, but he'd do his best, by God.

"Hello, old-timer," said one of the men as they rode on by him. "Lovely morning, eh?"

"That it is, that it is," Angus said rotely, and was happy to continue unharassed toward town.

These three had rough faces, mustached or bearded, but they were otherwise well set up in suits and string or foulard ties—tall men, all three. They sat their horses well.

"Hmm," Angus said as they continued up the trail. He wondered where they were going. There wasn't much out here except the Box Bar B and a few mine diggings. There was one large mine, the Lady Dancer, so maybe they were ore guards. Yeah, that was probably it.

Ore guards.

He rode on into Tigerville and negotiated his way through the horse and wagon traffic and pulled the wagon up to the Sundown Saloon. He bid good day to several folks he knew as he climbed down from the wagon. As he did, two rough-looking young men in trail garb who'd been standing out front of the saloon, leaning against awning support posts and chinning, stepped off the boardwalk and came over.

"Hey, Buchanon, you old rebel," the taller of the two said. He was seedy featured and bucktoothed, with a six-shooter thonged low on his thigh and clad in baggy, faded denim trousers. "Why don't you give us a couple of your beers? We're plum out of jingle, Roy an' me, and the day is still young."

Judging by the glitter in their eyes, they'd likely been drinking all night. And doing a few other things, to boot.

Angus recognized the young man who'd spoken as a bottom-feeding near-do-well, Eddie Price. His friend was Roy Shannon—shorter and bearded. They were card cheats, known rustlers, and hay thieves. Shannon had been in jail for beating a doxie.

"Get away from here," Angus said. "I don't have the time of day for you two."

As he reached into the wagon bed to remove one of the beer crates, Eddie Price shouldered him aside. "Here, let me help you with that, you old devil." He and Shannon both chuckled.

Angus cursed and pulled his shotgun out from under the wagon seat, aiming and cocking rather adeptly for a one-armed man. "You set that crate back in the box, Price, or you'll have so much buck in you you'll rattle when you walk!"

"I was only tryin' to help," Price said, indignant.

"Set it back in the box. I know what you're tryin' to do. You're tryin' to steal my beer!"

Shannon stepped forward. "Put that shotgun down, you old rebel dog!"

"I'll put it down when your ugly friend here returns my beer to the wagon!"

Price and Shannon shared a look. Then Price cursed and returned the crate to the wagon.

"Now get the hell out of here," Angus ordered. "Bottom feeders!"

Both men held up their hands, palm out, and backed up slowly. "Man, you got a temper on you—don't you, Buchanon?"

"When it come to my family and my beer, yes I do. Not necessarily in that order."

Angus uncocked the shotgun and had just started to return it to the wagon when he saw a shadow slide up beside him. Price grabbed him by the back of his collar. Angus pulled the barn blaster back out, swung around, and drove the barrel deep in the firebrand's solar plexus.

Price screamed and folded, dropping to his knees.

Shannon drew his six-shooter and Angus planted the twelve-gauge on him, grinning. "You want some o' this, Shannon? Open wide, you son of a dog!"

Shannon looked at the big maws aimed at his belly and his dark-brown eyes grew darker. He raised his gloved left-hand palm out. "Now, now . . ." He returned his shooter to its holster. He glared at Angus, then reached down to help his partner to his feet. "Come on, Eddie. Let's head back to camp. There's no dealin' with this grayback scalawag."

"You got that right," Angus said.

Price glared at Angus and yelled, "You liked to have killed me!"

"You got that right, too," Angus said.

He watched the two climb into their saddles. For Eddie Price, it was a tender maneuver. They rode off through the dust and the midmorning street traffic, casting angry looks behind them.

Angus returned his gut shredder to the wagon, then reached for a crate of beer, muttering epithets. He'd no sooner got the crate raised once more when a voice said behind him, "Are you Angus Buchanon?"

Angus sighed and turned around, cradling the case against him with his one arm. He was surprised to see the three well setup men he'd seen on the trail to town. The man who appeared the leader was tall and broad-shouldered. He had blue eyes and a thick, black mustache. He was dressed almost entirely in black. The one to his right was short and fair-skinned, sandy hair curling down from his cream hat to the collar of his vest. The other man was thick, stocky, with a big fleshy face and a red beard. Wearing a fancy paisley vest and red string tie under his black frock coat, he leaned forward against his saddle horn, regarding Angus with a vague amusement in his amber eyes.

Angus said, "Who the hell wants to know?"

"I'm Bryce Jackson," the lead rider said, then introduced the man with the longish sandy hair and the beefy gent as Leech Davis and Dutch McCrae, respectively. "We're Pinkerton agents on the trail of a pair of cutthroats and a girl who robbed a train a few days back, down near Denver. They were seen in this area, and we think they're headed to a cabin they've been known to hole up in till their trail cools. The cabin's up near Ghost Mountain. Now, we know where the mountain is on the map, but we don't know how to get to it. We're looking for a guide. In Deadwood, we were told you know as much about these hills as anyone and you've guided before. You and your sons."

"I only have one son left and he's down near Denver selling horses."

"Well, damn the luck." Jackson pulled his mouth corners down in disappointment, then exchanged glances with the other two Pinkertons before turning back to Angus. "We'd still like you to do it."

Angus laughed as he started hauling the beer crate up on the boardwalk fronting the saloon. "You three are crazier'n a tree full of owls. I'm a stove-up old scudder with just one arm!"

He laughed again, then pushed through the batwings.

When he came out a couple minutes later, they were still there.

Jackson leaned forward against his saddle horn. He gave Angus a direct look. "We want you to do it, Buchanon. Rest assured, you'll be well paid for your time and trouble."

* * *

That night in the Buchanon lodge at the Bar Box B, Angus couldn't sleep.

He went downstairs, brewed a pot of coffee, poured himself a cup, and sat at the long, oilcloth-covered table in the kitchen, sipping the coffee to which he added a liberal jigger of skull pop, and smoked a cigarette. Annabelle would read to him from the book when she and Hunter returned and smelled the smoke; she strictly forbade smoking in the house.

Angus smiled at the young woman's spirit. But he felt like smoking tonight, by God, so he would; it helped him think. Besides, he was the founder of the Box Bar B in the years after the war, his own self and his three sons. He'd endure Annabelle's wrath later.

He was in a quandary.

He kept thinking about the steep, mysterious, forested slopes up around Ghost Mountain. He and Hunter and his other two sons—Shep and Tyrell—used to hunt that wild country for elk, staying out for sometimes a week at a time. Those were the days! When he was younger and could sit a horse for more than a few hours without growing cankers.

Could he now?

No. He was old.

But he hadn't yet made his decision.

Dammit, he was confounded. He hadn't been able to tell the Pinkertons no or yes. He'd told them he'd think about it overnight and they could ride out and get his answer. He'd made no promises, but he was leaning against it now. At his age, the ride would likely kill him.

But ah, the hunt!

He sipped his coffee and set the cup down, frowning.

He'd heard something.

He rose from the table, moved to the door, and stepped out on the broad front porch.

He stood there, frowning out into the darkness.

Then it came again—the long, mournful bugle of an elk on one of the ridges between the Box Bar B and Ghost Mountain, recalling the memories of those storied hunts once more, when they were all together again.

Abruptly, he turned and went back inside and yelled up the stairs: "Nathan, get yourself up an' dressed an' help me pack. We're takin' to the trail tomorrow bright and early!"

CHAPTER 8

Hunter and Annabelle arrived in Lusk along the Deadwood to Cheyenne Stage Trail, just north of Hat Creek Station in the arid eastern Wyoming plains, two days after they'd recovered the money for their horses.

"Best make yourself scarce, Bobby," Hunter told the coyote riding point. "Lusk ain't no place for rebel coyotes."

He did not have to tell the coyote twice. Instantly, Bobby found a big jack to chase.

Lusk was a rollicking town founded by ranchers and frequented by outlaws such as Bill Mccoy, Jack Slade, Kid Curry, and the Sundance Kid. Hunter knew it was probably foolhardy to spend the night with Annabelle in such a wide-open town, and with a pocketful of money, but they were both exhausted from their ordeal and were craving big steaks and a platter of steaming beans. They'd secure a room in the Yellow Hotel then a meal at the H.G. Herbert Dining Room, then return to the hotel and turn in early.

Besides, no one here in town would know he'd sold horses because he'd skirted the town by way of the Rawhide Hills on the way down to Arapaho Creek. Of course, the ones he'd recently turned toe down had seen them, but then they must have followed them from a distance. He doubted others had, or he'd have known about it by now. Life was not without risk, and Annabelle needed a good meal and a bed.

They were at a window seat in the H.G. Herbert Dining Room, enjoying their meal, when Annabelle glanced out the window and said "Uh-oh."

Hunter followed her gaze to six riders galloping into town from the south.

They were as dangerous looking a lot as Hunter had seen. Young, old, thin, tall, broad-shouldered, stocky. One—a man on a cream horse and wearing a stovepipe hat—had a nasty scar trailing down from a patch over his eye. The one with the patch Hunter recognized as Saguaro Machado, a killer for hire out of Dakota Territory. He'd run into the man a few times in Deadwood and Tigerville, and they'd fought until they'd both been dumped like trash in the street and left to sober up in the mud.

"They are trouble and only trouble," Annabelle told Hunter.

"Trouble and only trouble." Hunter was glad when the gang had passed the restaurant and disappeared around a bend in the street. "We'll head on back to the hotel and stay there. I don't want them seeing you."

Annabelle clutched herself and shivered. "I don't want them seeing me, either."

They finished their steaks and beans and left. They walked back toward the hotel, in the opposite direction in which Machado's gang had gone, weaving through the foot traffic on the boardwalks fronting the businesses. Hunter saw a few lusty looks cast Annabelle's way, but he was a big, imposing man himself and most of the men quickly diverted their attention.

He was relieved when he and his bride gained their destination.

They picked up their key, then walked through the Yellow Hotel's long, narrow lobby to the high, dark, narrow stairs. They strode hand in hand down the hall. Just before they came to their room, a door opened on their right and a big, beefy man with a beard and an eye patch—Saguaro Machado himself—stepped into the hall. The man grinned and before Hunter could react, the man's gloved right fist slammed into his jaw.

It was an ear-ringing blow, and Hunter staggered backward. Before he could fall, he was aware of more doors opening around him, on both sides of the hall. Annabelle screamed and then Machado's gang was all over Hunter, beating him mercilessly—bone crunching punches to his face, belly, ribs. Behind the cacophony of the beating, Hunter could hear Annabelle screaming and crying. He glimpsed a man holding her down toward the end of the hall, laughing and nuzzling her neck while she kicked at him and scratched at his face.

Seemingly out of nowhere, Bobby Lee ran in to offer a hand, grabbing one of the men's arms and chomping down hard.

"Damn coyote!" one of the men bellowed.

A gun blasted three times. Bobby yipped and ran back down the stairs.

Hunter heard Annabelle scream once more before he rolled onto his belly, and someone slammed something hard against the back of his head. Likely a gun butt.

Darkness followed and he lay in pounding torment remembering the smell of whiskey and hearing Machado's voice say from only inches away, "Gonna leave you alive, grayback, so you can imagine what's happening to her. Gonna be a doozy, believe me!"

Then there was the thudding of boots on wood, gradually fading, and the world went silent.

"Mister?" The young man's voice came from far away. Someone nudged Hunter's shoulder.

"Are you alive, mister?"

"I think he's dead," said a young woman's voice also from far away.

Hunter groaned against the pain in every inch of him. He forced his eyes open to see two faces staring at him with concern in their gazes. He was on the bed in the room he and Annabelle had rented, but he had no memory of how he got there.

Annabelle . . .

"They took my wife," Hunter said through a groan, trying to push himself into a sitting position.

"Wait, wait, wait," the young man said, both he and the girl—a pretty brunette maybe twenty years old—pushing Hunter back down against the bed. "You're busted up pretty good."

"Think you have some busted ribs," the girl said.

"How long . . . ?"

"Have you been here?" the girl said. "Overnight. It's morning."

"Ah, hell." Hunter remembered Annabelle's screams.

He pressed his fists against his temples, trying to funnel some strength back into his aching body. It did not work.

"Some nasty fightin' up here, Mister," the young man said. "The town marshal came, but when he heard who was at the center of it, he left."

Hunter reached into his back pocket. The money meant nothing to him now, but of course it was gone. "So no one went after them?"

"Doubt it," said the girl. "Nobody around here is going after Saguaro Machado."

"Well, I am." Hunter howled as he pushed himself to a sitting position with success this time, though every nerve and muscle in his body shivered against the agony. He shook his head in a futile attempt to fight away the pain, then turned to the young man and the girl gazing at him incredulously. "Who are you two?"

"I'm Billy Lancaster," said the young man. "Folks call me 'Powwow' for short." He gave a sheepish smile. "I have a little Comanch blood. Cow puncher but I'm between jobs at the moment. This is Sylvie Todd." He gave another wry grin. "We were in the room next to yours when . . . the trouble started. Thought there was an earthquake. Even heard a dog growlin'. After that the place went quiet as a church at midnight." He shook his head. "No one wants to mess with ol' Saguaro's bunch." Again, he shook his head, and guilt shone in his eyes. "Not even me."

"They would have killed you," Hunter said. "Does either of you have any whiskey?" He wasn't much for imbibing these days, but if ever there was a situation . . ."

"I do."

The girl ran out of the room and came back a minute later with a brown bottle.

"Thanks." Hunter took several healthy pulls, then gave the bottle back to Sylvie. "Now, do me another favor. Both of you. Take the sheet out from under me." He heaved himself to his feet with another howl of unadulterated misery and leaned against the wall, panting like a winded dog. "Cut it into large strips and tie them around my waist to hold these ribs in place."

"You need time to heal, mister," said the girl, slowly shaking her head.

"Don't have time to heal. Cut that sheet up for me!" Hunter unbuttoned his shirt, shrugged out of it, and dropped it to the floor.

Powwow and Sylvie both rose and regarding Hunter as though they'd just discovered a rabid dog in the room, pulled the sheet off the bed. The young man produced a folding knife from his pocket, slashed the sheet, then he and the girl tore it in half. They tore it again, and Hunter said,

"Now fold both up, wrap them around may waist, and tie them tight."

They did as instructed, wrapping the wide strips around Hunter's waist, drawing them taut.

"Tighter," Hunter cried.

They both grunted as together they tightened the sheet.

Hunter fell back against the wall, trying desperately to remain conscious. It was not an easy fight. His vision blurred, then darkened, and the room pitched around him. When his senses returned, he panted out, "Obliged."

He turned to the young man. "Could I ask you for another favor?"

Powwow hiked a shoulder.

"Carry that rifle and those saddlebags over to the livery barn for me. Don't think I can manage it quite yet."

"Sure, sure."

"Don't want to get you hurt."

"I ain't worried. I shoulda helped last night"—Powwow glanced at the girl, again guiltily—"and I didn't."

"Like I said, kid, they'd have killed you deader'n a boot."

"You're Hunter Buchanon, aren't you?"

Hunter frowned at him questioningly.

"It's an honor to help you, Mister Buchanon. Heard a lot about your exploits during the Misunderstandin' and then the land war up north."

"Oh, that was no land war." Hunter chuckled dryly. Tears came to his eyes. "That was a battle for the girl that old sinner Machado just took from me." He choked down a sob, then cleared his throat in embarrassment. "Let's go."

"Here's your hat," the girl said. She'd retrieved it from the hall.

"Obliged, Miss Sylvie."

"Good luck, Mister Buchanon."

"Hunter." Hunter staggered out into the hall, Powwow Billy on his heels with his Henry and saddlebags.

Hunter stumbled more than walked out of the room and down the stairs. He went outside and bought a bottle at the first saloon he came to. He wasn't going to make it without some painkiller. Powwow in tow, he stumbled more than walked down the street to the livery barn. The liveryman eyed him warily, incredulously, as the man saddled his horse for him.

Hunter swung into the saddle with another howl.

"You sure about this, Mister Buchanon?" the lad asked, a perpetual wince on his young face.

"No, I'm not sure, but I have no choice." As Powwow Billy draped his saddlebags over Nasty Pete's back, Hunter said, "Did you get a chance to see where Machado's gang was headed?"

"East as far as I could tell."

"Likely Dakota," Hunter said. "His gang usually holes up between jobs along the Missouri River. I'll likely cut their sign on the old stage trail just outside of town."

He was about to boot Nasty Pete along the main street to the east but stopped when Powwow grabbed his saddle horn and said, "What're you gonna do once you catch up to 'em?"

"Kick 'em all out with a cold shovel and get my woman back!" Hunter howled in pain as he booted Pete into a hard gallop, feeling as though every sharp-edged broken rib in his body was ripping right through him.

He couldn't manage the gallop for long. Just outside of town, on the trail that led east across the old Deadwood to Cheyenne Trail, he slowed him to a walk. Not only because he thought the pain was about to kill him but because he needed to scour the ground for the hoof prints of six riders. It didn't take him long. Machado was headed east, all right. Cross-country to the northeast. It made sense he'd avoid the main trails. That was all right. It would make it easier for

Hunter to track him, his trail being unadulterated by other horsebackers or ranch wagons.

What had his gut in knots was knowing that Machado was known for kidnapping women and girls and selling them to slave traders out in the eastern part of the territory, mostly to remote wood cutters working for the river boats.

He followed the trail out across the vast, gently rolling, sage- and buckbrush-stippled desert country of eastern Wyoming. A Godless country, he'd always considered it and considered it even more so now. Impatient, he gigged Pete into a faster pace, but cursed himself for not being able to hold it.

At one point he looked back to see Bobby Lee shadowing him from about twenty feet back. He gave a feeble smile. Bobby wanted to help him make it, but Hunter could tell by the way the coyote carried himself, favoring a back leg, he'd taken a graze the night before in the Yellow Hotel.

Across the prairie he rode, slumped low in the saddle, an arm over his ribs, keeping an eye on the tracks he was following. The short grass prairie did not hold a track well, so he often had to stop and look around before picking up Machado's trail again. It didn't help that he also felt himself passing out in the saddle and had to shake himself back to consciousness.

At midday he stopped at a shallow creek to let Pete draw water and to fill his canteen. It was hellish, climbing in and out of the saddle but once back in the leather, he took a deep pull from the hooch in his saddlebags. It helped; he rode on. An hour later he and Pete descended a deep dry wash. Pete lunged up the opposite side. It was like having railroad spikes driven through Hunter's chest.

The world went dark. He tumbled from the saddle and struck the ground with a thud.

He howled and passed out.

Bobby ran up to him and nuzzled him, mewling, and curled up beside him.

Hunter had no idea how much time had passed when, distantly, he heard the clomp of hooves growing louder as a rider approached.

CHAPTER 9

The Box Bar B's hired man, Casey McQuade, lean and gray-bearded in late middle-age, handed Angus the reins of a zebra dun, glanced at the three Pinkertons sitting their horses expectantly in the middle of the Box Bar B Ranch yard, and said, "You sure you wanna do this, boss?"

Angus accepted the reins. "No, I ain't sure I wanna do it, Casey. But for some consarned reason I sorta feel the need. Know what I mean?"

They were standing between the open stable doors.

It was dawn. The sun hadn't even poked the top of its head above the eastern ridges.

Casey looked deeply consternated. "But . . . but . . ."

"I know, I know," Angus said, adjusting the saddlebags on the dun's back, as well as the war sack he'd filled with grub. "I'm old an' stove up an' I got only one arm. But you know what, Casey?" He grinned at his hired man, nearly as old as Angus was but still capable with a plug pony and a lariat. "I'm lookin' forward to it."

"You know what Hunter would say about this."

"Oh, I know, I know." Angus chuckled as he walked over to where young Nathan stood holding the reins of a steel-dust, short and stocky as an Indian pony. "Climb up, boy."

He held the reins while Nathan clambered up into the

saddle. Nathan had been riding and roping ever since he came to the Box Bar B over a year ago.

"Saddle snug?"

"Feels snug, Angus."

"Stirrups the right length?"

"Yep." Nathan grinned down at the old man pridefully. He loved the notion of riding along with Angus and the three officious looking Pinkertons. "I'm ready."

"Why you takin' the boy?" Casey asked Angus.

"'Cause his eyes are better than mine," Angus said, walking around to the left side of his dun. "And he needs the experience. Might never get the chance again. I raised all my boys on the huntin' trail, and they grew up tough an' mean? He winked at Casey, then grabbed the horn with his one hand, toed a stirrup, and swung up into the leather.

"Hey, Buchanon," called the lead Pinkerton, Bryce Jackson. "We're sorta burnin' daylight here, if you know what I mean. What do you say you stop palaverin' with that old man, and let's get a move on?"

Casey scowled up at Angus. "Kinda peevish, ain't they?"

Angus chuckled. "Yeah, well, they're law and they're goin' after the lawless, so I reckon they got the bark on. Just gotta live with it. Look after the place, Casey. We'll likely see you in a few days."

Angus reined the dun around and booted it out into the yard, calling for Nathan to follow.

"I hope so," Angus heard Casey say fatefully behind him. "I do hope so. Go with God, boss."

Angus threw up an acknowledging arm, then called to the three Pinkertons, "Come along, Pinks. Come along. We're burnin' daylight!"

He glanced at Nathan, winked, and said, "Come on, boy!" And he gigged the dun into a trot, crossing the yard toward the old woodcutting trail that would lead them up into the fur-carpeted ridges showing a dark, furry, purple green in the dawn light, toward the northwest and the distant bulge of Ghost Mountain.

Angus was no sooner out of the yard when he felt as though he'd shed twenty years or more. He had an important job. He was leading lawmen after the lawless. He was riding up into his old haunts, where a man felt as though he could spread his wings. Not only that, but he had his foster grandson with him. He'd teach the boy the ways of the mountains just as he'd taught Shep, Tyrell, and Hunter oh so many years ago now.

He and Nathan led the Pinkertons across a flat stretch of valley, then into a canyon that rose gradually between high, fur-carpeted ridges. At times the climb was steep, so he kept a slow, gradual pace though he knew the slow speed was graveling the Pinkertons, whom he could hear muttering peevishly behind him. When they came to a creek crossing the trail—Old Man Cranston Creek, it was called, after the old man who'd gone mad in his later years but who'd had a cabin just upstream, he reined in and swung down from the saddle. The Pinkertons were climbing the slope behind him and Nathan, grim sets to their naturally grim features.

"What're we stopping for?" asked the tall, dark, broad-shouldered Jackson.

"What're we stoppin' for?" Angus asked, incredulous, as Nathan swung down from his steeldust's back. "We been climbin' hard for over an hour. These hosses need a rest." He glanced at Nathan. "Come on, boy."

He and Nathan led their horses over to the stream to let them draw water.

The Pinkertons conferred in nettled tones though Angus couldn't hear what they said above the stream's rush over rocks. He glanced back at them and said, "Lead 'em on over here. They're all three hot and need water, an' you oughta fill your canteens. Be awhile till we get to another creek."

Impatiently, the Pinkertons dismounted, led their horses

over to the stream, and let them drink. Casting Angus the woolly eyeball, they knelt to fill their canteens. Angus was starting to get riled himself.

"You boys haven't had much experience with mountain travel, have you?"

"No," said the beefy Dutch McCrae as he sunk his canteen in the stream to fill it. "That's why we hired you. But we need to go a little faster than what we've been traveling or those three are going to get away with the loot *we're being paid* to retrieve."

"You're not gonna do that by killin' your horses," Nathan put in, standing and capping his canteen.

Angus glanced at the boy in surprise. Nathan was normally meek and reserved, downright shy. But he, too, had felt the impatience of the Pinkertons and, a horse lover himself, was miffed about how they were treating their mounts. Inwardly, Angus smiled at the boy's pluck but said quietly, "Easy, boy. I'll take care of it."

"Didn't realize the kid had a mouth on him," said the lean Pinkerton with long, sandy hair tumbling down from his low-crowned cream Stetson. He had flat, colorless, washed-out eyes and a long, aquiline nose. He grinned at the other two men, and they chuckled dryly, subtly mockingly.

Nathan flushed and cast Angus an indignant glance.

Angus smiled and pressed two fingers to his lips.

"All right," said the beefy, red-bearded McCrae, capping his canteen and hooking the lanyard over his saddle horn. "Let's get a move on before those three pull their picket pins and head down out of the mountains."

"This is the only way up or down from Ghost Mountain," Angus said, stepping into the leather. "We ain't in any hurry, fellas."

"That's what you say," Jackson said, stepping into his own saddle and sponging water from his thick, dragoon-style mustache.

"What I say goes, fellas," Angus said, chuckling as he put the dun into the stream. "I'm the trail boss. What I say goes."

He doubted he'd be able to convince these officious Pinkertons of that, but he'd give it a try, anyway. He'd put up with more difficult cases. His own, young, wild, and impatient sons, for instance. He gave another chuckle, still enjoying himself as he put the dun up the opposite bank and back onto the rocky trail, Nathan riding close behind him.

A half hour later, as they were climbing another in a series of steep ridges, Angus checked the dun down abruptly, saying, "Whoa, boy. Whoah!"

Nathan almost rode up into Angus but quickly checked his own mount down, as well.

"Now what we stopping for?" asked Jackson, riding up into Nathan before jerking back on his own reins, his mount lifting its head and fighting the bit.

"Bear," Nathan said quietly.

Angus had heard the thrashing in the brush off the trail's right side, maybe fifty yards away. He watched as the big, lumbering beast climbed the ridge to disappear into pines and furs, snorting. He didn't see much but its big hind end, but it was a bear, all right.

"So, it's a bear," McCrae said. "It's headed *away* from us. Not comin' *toward* us."

"If we stop for every bear we'll likely see in these hills," said Jackson, "we won't make it to Ghost Mountain until fall."

"Like Dutch said," said Leech Davis. "It's headed away from us."

"Yeah," Angus said, putting his dun ahead once more. "For now."

They climbed the ridge and descended into a shallow valley. The sun was sinking low in the west, and the pines carpeting a stream running through the heart of the valley were casting long shadows. The air was misty with an early mountain nightfall. Angus led his charges off the trail's right side and toward a stone escarpment rising along the stream's near side.

"Where we goin'?" McCrae wanted to know.

"We're stoppin' for the night," Angus said. "It'll be dark in another half hour."

"Well, then I say we stop in a half hour," Jackson said.

"No, no," Angus said. "That ain't how you do it, boys. You stop while there's still enough light to make camp."

Jackson angrily booted his horse up ahead of Angus, stopped, and curveted it, facing Angus with a belligerent scowl. Angus reined up and so did Nathan.

"I say we ride for another half hour. There'll still be enough light to make camp."

"You go ahead," Angus said defiantly. "The boy and I are stoppin' here because that's the smart thing to do. These hills are honeycombed with outlaw hideouts, outlaws on the dodge from the law in Denver and Colorado Springs. Even some from New Mexico and Utah. You ride up on one of those camps in the dark and there'll be hell to pave an' no hot pitch!"

"Not to mention wild animals," Nathan put in. "Remember the bear?"

Jackson jutted an angry finger at the boy. "You know, I'm gettin' tired of that boy's sass."

"Then ride on." Anger rose in Angus. "I back the boy!"

Jackson glanced at the other two Pinkertons sitting their mounts behind Nathan. Finally, he drew a deep, disgusted breath and let it out slowly, loudly. "All right, all right. *Trail boss*!"

He yielded the trail and Angus led them to the base of the escarpment, and they tied the horses to a picket line and set up camp between the escarpment and the stream.

The scarp would offer cover from behind, the stream from in front. They'd still have to keep an eye on the pines, darkening now, lined out to either side along the water. It was the best place Angus had spied over the past hour. It would have to do.

Nathan gathered wood and Angus built a fire and cooked a pot of beans that he had soaked in his coffeepot on their way into the mountains. They hung the pot filled with water for coffee over the fire and only forty-five minutes or so after they'd stopped for the night, they were all eating the beans to which Angus had added a goodly amount of bacon, and drinking piping black coffee.

The night closed down, black as a glove save the high, arching firmament sprinkled with twinkling stars.

When the Pinkertons had finished their meals, they set their plates aside and leaned back against their saddles, ready to settle in for the night.

"Don't get too cozy just yet," Angus said, swirling the last of his coffee in his cup where he leaned back against his saddle abutting the scarp, Nathan on one side, Jackson on the other, the two other Pinkertons, Davis and McCrae, sitting with their backs to the stream. "One of you three has to do the dishes."

"What?" said the beefy McCrae. "Have the boy do it."

Angus shook his head. "He and I built the fire and cooked the meal. One of you has to do the dishes. Take 'em down to the stream and scrub 'em out with sand and water."

To a man, they cast him withering glares.

Only, it didn't wither Angus. He'd raised sons.

He only chuckled.

CHAPTER 10

Hunter poked his hat brim up off his forehead and stared across the fire at Powwow Billy, the kid's round, brown-eyed face bronzed by the dancing flames over which a coffeepot hung from an iron tripod.

They were in the ravine Hunter had tried to cross. At least, he thought so. It was so dark now that everything looked different than it had earlier. Somehow the kid had managed to drag him into the draw where there was more shelter than on the bank above. He remembered the pain of being dragged; he'd regained only semiconsciousness briefly.

Now he saw that Bobby Lee lay curled beside him, looking up at him dubiously.

"What in holy blazes, junior?" he said now as the kid used a leather swatch to remove the pot from over the flames and fill a tin cup to which he added a good splash of whiskey from Hunter's bottle.

Powwow Billy carried the smoking cup around the fire and set it down beside Hunter. "There. Have you some of that. Make you feel better. Say, that coyote seems to really like you."

"So much for Bobby's taste."

"Bobby?"

"Bobby Lee."

"Well, I'll be hanged. Never seen the like!"

"I get that a lot. What're you doing here?"

Powwow hiked a shoulder. "Had a feelin' you wouldn't make it. Didn't set right with me, I reckon. Lettin' you ride out alone after that whole, nasty bunch. Thought I'd throw in. I ain't worth much in a lead swap, but I can put in my two cents."

"You best go back to Lusk." Hunter picked up the cup in both hands, blew on it, sipped. "Dang. That is good."

"I'm a pretty good trail cook, an' you're gonna need one. I don't think you can do much for yourself, and I doubt Bobby Lee can cook. I know one thing for a fact." Powwow gave Hunter a direct, dark look. "I know you can't take down Saguaro Machado your ownself. Not in your condition."

Hunter took another sip of the nicely spiced mud and pondered on what the kid had said. Of course, he was right. But Hunter had had no choice. He'd had to ride out after Annabelle. Obviously, the cowardly law in Lusk wasn't going to do it.

Still, if he caught up to Machado, he'd likely die a hard death. That wouldn't do Annabelle any good. If she was still alive, that was. The possibility that she might already be dead tied his throat in a tight knot and drove a stake through his heart. He didn't know what he'd do without her. They were planning on someday raising a family together, complete with sons and daughters and a whole passel of grandchildren running wild on the Box Bar B. Maybe even some of Bobby's pups if the contrary coyote could ever find him a mate.

Not a man known for crying, Hunter sucked back a sob and regarded Powwow. The kid had returned to the other side of the fire and was leaning against his saddle, sipping his own coffee and regarding Hunter with expectancy from beneath the brim of his battered hat.

How much help would he be?

Not much. But he was all Hunter had, and Hunter had no

choice but to continue in his quest for the savage Machado and Annabelle. Somehow, he had to find a way to run Machado down and get his wife back. He didn't care about the money. Only Annabelle.

"I'll likely get you killed, Kit, but . . . I don't know"—he offered a grim smile—"I reckon I could use a cookie."

Powwow smiled over the smoking brim of his cup.

Bobby Lee flopped his tail.

The next morning, after a hurried breakfast of coffee and beans, Hunter and Powwow mounted their horses and they and Bobby Lee continued their long journey, following Machado's sometimes hard-to-follow trail. The kid proved to be a pretty good tracker, which helped when Hunter was in too much pain to be much good himself. When the kid couldn't find the trail, Bobby Lee could.

The next two days were long and painful for Hunter as they steadily followed the outlaws' trail, camping in dry washes both nights and starting out early again the next morning. The next night they again settled into a wash. Hunter leaned back against his saddle for a post-supper cup of coffee spiced with the last of his whiskey. He hoped they came to a road ranch soon, as he needed to resupply the painkiller. It was about the only thing keeping him in the saddle. That and his need to find Annabelle, of course.

The next day they rode through open ranch country. Cattle broadly peppered the sides of low hills and cedar-stippled buttes. They appeared to be Herefords bred with longhorns. Around one o'clock that afternoon, Powwow said, "Uh-oh."

Hunter had been resting in his saddle with his eyes closed. Now he opened them with a start and said, "What is it?"

"Riders."

Then Hunter saw them riding down out of cedars topping a high mesa off the trail's right side. Three men coming fast and riding Indian file on an interception course with Hunter, Powwow, and Bobby Lee. They wore Stetsons and billowy neckerchiefs. Batwing chaps flapped around their thighs. Rifles resided in saddle scabbards.

"Ah, hell," Hunter said.

The men came down onto the trail Hunter and Powwow were following and then they booted their mounts into trots toward the two trail pards.

"How you want to play it, Hunter?"

"How the hell should I know? Take out your repeater, lever a round into the action, and set it across your saddle-bow. If it comes to a lead swap, let me make the first move . . . if I can."

Bobby Lee sat off the side of the trail, showed the riders his teeth, and growled.

Hunter knew he himself was fast. At least, he was fast when he was healthy. Now he had no idea. All he did know as these grim-faced riders drew near was that they were trouble. Their faces were drawn in hard lines, jaws hard, two sporting brushy mustaches on their copper, sun-seasoned faces while the third and smallest of the bunch was clean-shaven.

He wore a low-crowned cream hat and a green silk neckerchief. Each rode a clean-lined ranch pony, and the thuds of the horses' hooves grew louder until the obvious cow punchers reined up ten feet in front of Hunter and Powwow and curveted their mounts, making them less easy targets than if they faced the pair head on. They shuttled their incredulous gazes from Hunter to Powwow to Bobby Lee showing them his teeth.

"How do," Hunter said, benignly. "Just passin' through, fellas. No need to get your necks in a hump."

The lead rider was in his mid-forties. He had a broad face that might have been crudely chipped out of stone by a half-drunk sculptor. He wore a black hat and a black vest, and two walnut gripped Colt Lightnings bristled on his hips. "That . . . coyote . . . yours . . . ?"

"Nah. I'm his."

The lead rider regarded Bobby with a deeply befuddled expression, then turned to Hunter. "There's no passin' through Ironwood Creek Range. You'll have to turn back and take another route to wherever you're goin'." He had a deep voice that was oddly resonate and pitched with barely restrained fury.

"Unless they're here to throw long loops on Ironwood cattle," said the clean-shaven young man, smartly, one hand on the grips of his Colt.

"Shut up, junior," Hunter snapped at the kid. He was not in the mood for these three at all.

The kid stiffened his back and tightened his grip on the .44.

"Keep it holstered, Giff," the lead rider said, smiling shrewdly at Hunter. To Hunter, he said, "You got a smart mouth for a trespasser."

"We ain't trespassin' an' you know it. This is open range. You might call it yours, but it's mine and my partner's an' my coyote's just as much as it yours. Now, I'm in no mood, so yield the trail!"

The kid, whose face had swollen up and turned crimson, said, "Why's he's nothin' but a smart-mouthed grayback!"

He started to unpouch his six-shooter. Hunter was as surprised as the kid was when he found that he'd managed to pull the LeMat before the barrel of the kid's Bisley had cleared leather. Hunter clicked the hammer back. The other two men, including the one who Hunter assumed was the Ironwood Creek foreman, eyed him as though they'd just realized they had a wildcat in their midst.

Bobby Lee rose and gave an angry bark at the three range riders.

"Why, he's got him a whip hand!" exclaimed the third

rider, eyes riveted on the big, wicked-looking LeMat covering all three of them.

"Stop!" came a woman's voice amidst the distant rataplan of galloping hooves. "Stop right there. That's enough!"

Hunter looked off the trail's right side to see a young woman galloping a fine Palomino down the ridge toward him and his and Powwow's sudden enemies.

"Stop!" she yelled again, long tawny hair blowing out behind her in the wind. She wore a white blouse, the sleeves rolled up to her elbows, a spruce green riding skirt, and black patent riding boots.

Bobby barked at her.

"Easy, Bobby Lee. Female."

At first, Hunter thought his pain and all the whiskey he'd drunk to quell it was making him hallucinate. Especially the nearer she came and he saw her cameo perfect features, tanned to the texture of a half-breed Indian's. And a beautiful one, at that. She wore no hat; the tails of her neck-knotted bandanna, the same color as her skirt, blew out behind her with her hair, which Hunter guessed likely hung down to the small of her back. She galloped up to within twenty feet of Hunter, Powwow, and the others, and drew sudden rein, the Palomino skidding to a halt, turning slightly sideways and giving a spirited whinny.

Again, Bobby Lee barked at her.

She regarded the coyote dubiously, then turned to her foreman. "What's going on here? Kendall, what is the meaning of this?"

"Think we just caught us some long loopers. Miss McGovern. And a coyote."

Slowly, Hunter let the LeMat sag in his hand as she turned to him and appraised him thoroughly with intelligent gray eyes, and said, "This man is injured. Can't you see that? I could tell as much, the way he sits his saddle, through my spyglass from up on the ridge." She snapped another angry look at Kendall and said, "And he still got the drop on you!"

There was no little jeering in her voice.

She turned back to Hunter. "Who are you, sir?"

"The name's Hunter Buchanon, ma'am."

She frowned, puzzled at first. Then recognition shone in those soulful gray orbs. "Ahh. The rebel freedom fighter." Hunter just then realized she, too, spoke with a deep Southern accent. "My father used to talk about you. He was a Confederate general back during the War of Northern Aggression."

Hunter almost smiled. She pronounced "war" as "whah" and "Northern" as "Noh-thenn."

He hadn't heard an accent that thick in years.

"How bad are you hurt?"

"Just some ribs. I'll make it."

"I trained with a doctor in Denver for two years. Ride back to the Ironwood Creek headquarters with me, and I can make you feel much better than I can tell you're feeling now. You need salve on the ribs and a much tighter brace. Otherwise, I doubt you'll make it another two miles . . . wherever you're headed."

She glanced curiously at Hunter's trail partner.

"That's Powwow," Hunter said.

Quicky, Powwow fumbled his hat off his head and held it deferentially over his chest. "How do, ma'am."

"Powwow?" she asked.

Powwow held up his right hand, thumb and index finger about a half-inch apart. "I have about that much Comanch in my veins, ma'am."

She looked at Bobby Lee and wrinkled the skin above the bridge of her nose.

"That's General Robert E. Lee, ma'am," Hunter said. "You can call him Bobby. Everybody does."

She gave a skeptical nod, then turned to her men. "Kendall, you and your men get back to work."

Kendall sighed and, looking chagrined, said, "Yes, Miss McCloud."

He and the other two cast Hunter one more glare, then galloped back in the direction from which they'd come.

Cynthia McCloud turned to Hunter. "Please . . . ride with me to the headquarters. I'll have you feeling better in no time. Then you can return to the trail. Where are you headed, anyway?"

"My wife was kidnapped by cutthroats. I'm on their trail."

She nodded again, more deeply. "Then all the more reason to help me fix those ribs for you. You'll be delayed one way or the other, Mister Buchanon."

"How far away?" Hunter asked.

She hiked a shoulder. "Only about a mile. I'll fix those ribs and make you a good meal. Hospitality from one Southerner to another. And for you, of course, as well, Powwow. I'm told I have a little Cherokee to go with my own Scottish ancestry."

"Oh, is that a fact, Miss McGovern?"

"Please, it's Cynthia. My mother is Mrs. McGovern."

Hunter thought it over quickly. She was right. He likely wouldn't make it another mile. It made sense to get help.

He pinched his hat brim to her. "All right, then, ma'am . . . er, I mean Cynthia. We'll follow your lead. And thank you in advance for your hospitality."

He felt keenly guilty for accepting hospitality when Annabelle was in the hands of Saguaro Machado, but it made sense to get himself feeling well enough to continue on the trail to rescue her and to turn Saguaro Machado and his cohorts toes down.

CHAPTER 11

"It's a rather humble place, I'm afraid," said Cynthia McGovern as they reined up on a cedar-stippled rise and stared down at a small ranch headquarters sprawled at the bottom of the hill. "When my father died, I returned here to try to keep the Ironwood up and running. My mother moved to Denver some years ago. She refused to return. She didn't want me to either, but . . . Those men you met are my only hands. Just me here . . . and them. They're good men, all in all."

The cabin was all chinked log, tin-roofed, one story and rambling, smoke unfurling from the stone hearth abutting the far side. There was a small log bunkhouse, a log stable attached to a small barn, and a corral. The place had likely been built before the Little Misunderstanding and not much had been done to it since. Still, it appeared neat and well-tended. A few fine-looking horses milled in the corral, some eating from a hay crib.

"My father built the place but had trouble keeping it due to falling stock prices and rustlers, not to mention the occasional Indian attack. I was raised here, but my parents sent me away to read for the law back east. They wanted better for me. Instead, I studied with a surgeon I met in a Christmas ball. That seemed to be my calling." Cynthia clucked her Palomino on down the ridge. "Come on, gentlemen. Let's get those ribs tended!"

Hunter grunted as he booted Nasty Pete down the ridge after the young woman, whose beauty and sophistication he was having trouble marrying to the humility of the shotgun ranch she'd grown up on. No wonder her parents had wanted better for her. He knew from his own experience that even a shotgun ranch was not a bad place for a kid to grow up. But then, when he and his father and brothers had come north after the war and built the Box Bar B, Hunter had been a veteran Confederate guerilla fighter albeit one not yet twenty years old. He'd been a rustic young man running off his leash, just like his brothers. Not a beautiful, precocious girl who'd likely yearned for broader horizons.

There was only one man about the place—a willowy young Indian named Vincent, who'd come out of the barn to tend Cynthia's and the newcomers' horses. Then Hunter and Powwow followed Cynthia to the sprawling, humble, rustically yet comfortably appointed cabin, and she promptly ordered Hunter to take off his shirt and sit down at her long eating table in the kitchen part of the dwelling that was fairly filled with comfortably slumbering cats—some on cushions, some in wicker baskets, some on shelves, two on a badly faded and tattered fainting couch in the living room part of the cabin.

"We have very few mice here at Ironwood Creek," Cynthia quipped when she saw Hunter regarding the sleeping felines.

She poured him and Powwow, who also took a seat at the table, each a cup of coffee and then got to work mixing up some sort of stinky poultice at the kitchen's rear counter. A stew pot bubbling over the fire in the hearth took some of the edge off the stench, but just some.

She laid what almost appeared to be a lady's corset on the table and then dolloped a goodly portion of the poultice onto the corset. Then she gently removed the strips of sheet holding Hunter's ribs in place. Hunter groaned at the release in pressure. She tossed the sheet strips aside and then examined Hunter's ribs closely, gently probing with her fingers, leaning so close over Hunter, that he could feel her long hair brushing his chest.

Some places she probed hurt more than others. Hunter set his jaws against the pain.

"Hmm," she said finally, straightening. "You took a good beating, all right. I would say no dangerous breaks but a few cracks. Mostly bad bruising. I think you must have strong bones, Hunter."

"Well, they've been through the mill, Miss Cynthia. I reckon they had no choice."

She chuckled throatily, fetchingly. She wrapped the corset poultice around Hunter's chest and belly and tied it tightly behind his back, grunting as she drew it tighter and tighter until he could barely breath.

Powwow chuckled.

"Shut up, kid."

"That'll be uncomfortable for a while," Cynthia said, a little breathless with her efforts. "It will loosen some, but it should make those ribs feel a whole lot better."

"They already do, thank you."

"This will make you feel even better."

She pulled a bottle down from a shelf and set three goblets on the table. She uncorked the bottle and, filling one of the glasses, said, "My father's own homemade chokecherry wine. He was a master fermenter. This pretty much cures anything that ails you. I know. I've indulged a few times myself. Found a whole cache of the stuff in the root cellar."

She filled the other two glasses, set the bottle on the table, and raised her glass. "To success in getting your wife back, Hunter."

"To success," Powwow said.

"To success," Hunter said.

They clinked glasses together.

Hunter slept fitfully after a goodly portion of the strong wine and a large bowl of beef stew. He and Powwow occupied the room in which Cynthia's parents had slept together albeit in separate beds. Powwow snored loudly, peacefully, in the bed on the opposite side of the room from where Hunter lay, restless and thinking of Annabelle.

Annabelle . . .

His ribs felt better now. Cynthia had taken at least half the pain away. He and Powwow would ride at first light, which couldn't come soon enough for Hunter.

Too restless for sleep, he rose, pulled on his pants, stepped into his boots, and donned his hat. Quietly, he left the room, stole quietly across the dark cabin, and stepped out onto the cabin's front stoop. He stood staring into the night, toward the northeast where Saguaro Machado was headed with Annabelle, wondering what was happening to her now, wondering if she was alive or . . .

No.

He couldn't even think it.

Worry mixed with the rage inside him as well as a keen frustration at his not having been able to catch up to Machado by now because of the beating he'd taken at his hands.

He jerked with a start when the cabin door opened behind him.

He glanced over his shoulder to see Cynthia McGovern step out of the cabin and quietly draw the door closed behind her. She was clad in a ratty, oversized, plaid robe that Hunter assumed had belonged to her father. It looked lovely on her, her prettily disheveled hair curling onto her shoulders.

"Hope I didn't wake you," Hunter said.

She shook her head as, arms crossed on her chest, she walked up to stand beside him. "I couldn't sleep, either."

"Why's that?"

She smiled sheepishly, shook her head. "You don't want to know."

"Sure, I do."

She gave a husky chuckle as she gazed up at him, standing a whole head taller than she, admiringly. "No. You don't."

"Ah."

"Yeah."

"Been awhile?"

"Yes. Anyway . . . I know what's going through your head. Your wife . . . what is happening to her."

Hunter gazed to the northwest once more, beyond the dark bunkhouse and the corral in which a half-dozen horses either lay or stood sleeping, still as statues. "Yeah, I just don't know. Whether she's alive or . . . if I'll find her somewhere along the trail." He shook his head. "Just never expected this. We've been through so much, Annabelle an' me. After surviving all that . . . a bloody feud between our families when we made plans to marry . . . being trapped in a mine shaft together . . . having a stake of gold dust I built up for us stolen . . . having survived all that, I guess I was just fool enough to believe we wouldn't be tested anymore."

"She's very lucky to have you. To have a man who loves her so much."

"I'm lucky, too."

"You are."

Hunter sighed.

"You don't mind my feeling jealous, do you?"

Hunter gave her a tender smile, gently slid a few strands of her hair from her cheek. "Nah. You must be very lonely out here."

"I was lonely back east, too. I reckon it's just my fate."

"I'm sorry."

She shook her head. "It's nothing compared to what you have on your mind. Still, I'm jealous of your history . . . of your love for Annabelle."

"That's all right."

She looked up at him, her eyes dark beneath the porch's awning. "I hope you make it, Hunter. Honestly, I do. You and Powwow."

"I do, too."

"Do you think you have a chance?"

"I reckon we'll find out."

"Do you know where this Machado fellow is headed with her?"

"He holes up along the Missouri River. I have a feeling he might be intending to sell her to slavers who work along the river . . . selling women to woodcutting parties who work in that remote country most of the year to fuel riverboats. I've heard marshals have worked for years to break up that ring, but they've had little luck. It's remote country. Remote, savage country filled with savage, downright uncivilized men the slavers sell kidnapped girls and women to. Soldiers among them."

Cynthia squeezed herself and shuddered.

"Yeah." Hunter turned to the northwest again. "I'll find her. Sooner or later, I'll find her." He gritted his teeth. "And I'll find Machado, too."

Cynthia slid her arm around his waist and canted her head against his chest. "I'll prepare trail food for you and Powwow. I know you'll want to leave early."

"You've done enough, Cynthia."

"No, I have not."

She returned to the cabin and closed the door quietly behind her.

Hunter stood staring toward the northwest.

* * *

He sat on the porch until dawn.

He could smell coffee and fried bacon emanating from inside the cabin, could hear the clatter of pans and dishes. When he went inside, Powwow was already at the table, hunkered over a plate of eggs, bacon, and fried potatoes. Hunter wasn't hungry. He hadn't really felt hungry since his last meal with Annabelle. But since Cynthia had gone to the work to feed him and Powwow, he sat down and ate a full meal and drank two cups of coffee.

When they were finished, he and Powwow went outside to see that their horses were saddled and tied to the hitchrack fronting the cabin. Young Vincent was walking back toward the stable. Julia came out behind him and Powwow. She handed Hunter a burlap sack bulging with foodstuffs.

"Thank you, Julia," Hunter said, accepting the bag. "Truly. For everything."

She smiled. "Anytime. Good luck."

Hunter pinched his hat brim to her.

Powwow said, "Thank you, ma'am," and then he and Hunter mounted up and rode out of the yard, toward the northwest.

They'd ridden only a hundred yards or so when Hunter stopped Nasty Pete and told Powwow to ride ahead. "I'll catch up to you."

He rode back into the Ironwood Creek headquarters.

She stood in her plaid robe at the foot of the porch steps, waiting for him, a beguiling smile quirking her mouth corners.

Hunter checked Pete down, stepped down from the saddle, took her in his arms, and hugged her very tightly, very closely to him. She groaned against him, returning his hug. He held her for nearly a minute, rocking her gently, then kissed her cheek, gave her one last parting smile, mounted up, and headed back out on the range toward Powwow and, hopefully, Saguaro Machado and Annabelle.

CHAPTER 12

Annabelle was so tired she was having trouble staying awake in the saddle.

Her head kept bobbing, and sometimes she would slide forward and down over one of her horse's withers. She didn't fall completely out of the saddle because one of Machado's men had tied her wrists to her saddle horn. He was the one leading her horse—a thickset block of a man with long, greasy hair hanging over his shoulders. She could smell the sickly sweet stench of the man. They all smelled like sweat, wool, leather, and whiskey. They passed a bottle around as they rode.

She pulled herself up out of another doze and looked around. It was late in the day. Almost dusk. She wished they'd stop soon. Almost as severe as the terror of being these savages' prisoner was her exhaustion.

She just wanted to sleep.

She didn't want to eat. Just sleep.

The thought had no sooner passed through her mind than she saw a crooked wooden sign poking up from the brush on the trail's right side.

RIVER BEND STATION

She leaned out from her saddle to look ahead through the six men riding in front of her, including the lead-riding, big, top-hatted Machado, who wore his long, gray-brown hair down his back in a braid threaded with rawhide. Annabelle ground her teeth in fury. He was big, ugly, and savage. But her heart lightened a little when she saw a large, two-story log cabin sitting on the bank of a muddy, slow-moving river beyond a screen of shrubs, the green, late-summer stench of which she could now smell.

She could smell the aromas of cooking food, as well.

Maybe they'd feed her tonight. They hadn't fed her last night because Machado hadn't liked the way she'd looked at him, which of course was laughable. What did he expect? Not only was he an uncouth savage, but he'd kidnapped her and left Hunter in God knows what condition in the hall of the hotel in Lusk.

As they approached the cabin, there came a low roar of conversation and the clinking of coins and glasses. The succulent aromas of cooking food grew stronger. A woman's loud laugh suddenly cut through the din. Machado stopped his big paint horse in front of the cabin and the seven others checked their mounts down, as well.

"Hey, you big ugly German!" Machado shouted toward a stable on the opposite side of the trail from the cabin. "Get out here an' stable these hosses! They been rode a long way, so treat 'em right or I'll whip your big Kraut behind!"

Machado's men laughed.

Machado turned to the man trailing Annabelle's horse and said, "Cut her down!"

The man leading Annabelle's horse—Tobin, she thought he was called—swung down from his own horse, came back, and used his bowie knife to cut Annabelle's wrists free of her saddle horn. He sheathed the knife and stepped back and ordered brusquely, gutturally, "Down!" None of these men spoke like humans but only like animals, wild ones, at that. They never really spoke but aways yelled.

Annabelle's head swirled. She'd just started to dismount but apparently not fast enough for Tobin. "Why, you . . . !" he said, and stepped forward and smashed the back of his hand against her mouth.

She was too exhausted to even scream. She just flew down the opposite side of her mount to strike the ground with ear-ringing, vision-clouding violence. She lay on her back, feeling like a turtle, impossible to right herself.

She heard loud footsteps moving toward her, saw Machado's red boots with white stitching pass by her. She heard the savage crack of a fist on flesh and then Machado bellowing, "What did I tell you about messing her up? Corazon don't pay for damaged merchandise, you damn fool!"

Another resounding punch and a loud grunt and the resolute thud of a heavy body striking the ground. Then Machado came around, picked Annabelle up by her shoulders, and shoved her toward the cabin's now open door. A heavy-set woman in a long, flowered dress stood there and suddenly sprang into hearty laughter.

"Hah! You got you a redhead, Machado. Why, she's purty! Where'd you find her? Oh, Corazon's gonna *love* her. He'll get top dollar for her!"

"Let's just say she's the woman of a friend of mine," Machado said and laughed his deep, animal-like laugh. The laugh of a wolf if a wolf could laugh. "Take her in and clean her up. Usual price."

"You got it, you got it." The woman took Annabelle's hand and pulled her into the cabin, Annabelle stumbling because she was still reeling from the blow. "Come on, honey. Let Ann-Marie make you presentable."

When Annabelle entered the cabin, a hush fell over the smoky place.

"Henrietta, come over here and take this young lady upstairs, give her a good, long bath and then fetch her a plate of food. Why, I bet she's so hungry her tummy's gotten way too familiar with her backbone!"

Lusty male chuckles from around the room.

And then a girl took Annabelle's hand and led her upstairs. Annabelle was so exhausted and still so stunned from Tobin's blow that she wasn't fully conscious of what was happening until she found herself in a steaming hot copper tub and the girl, Henrietta, was slowly scrubbing her back with a sponge.

Anna jerked with a start with the sudden realization.

But the water felt good. Henrietta cooed in her ear to soothe her.

"Easy, now. Easy, now, Miss Annabelle. Machado said that's your name, Annabelle. Real pretty name. Everything will be all right, Miss Annabelle. The journey's almost over now. That's the hardest part. After that, if you just give into it, you'll feel much better."

Annabelle turned to her, dumbfounded. "Did Machado bring you, too?"

"Yep. It was hard. But when you know you don't got no other choice, I reckon it's just best to give into it. I hear you'll be movin' on, though."

"Where . . . where am I going?"

"Probably the river. The Missouri. He gets the best prices for the best girls there. A man named Corazon will pay top dollar for a redhead."

"Oh, God," Annabelle said, dully.

"You should be thankful. Machado's men will leave you alone because you're special. Corazon won't pay for damaged goods. Your lip will probably heal by the time you get to the river. Before you leave, I'll touch it up for you."

Annabelle placed her hand on the girl's forearm. "Isn't

there a way out of this place? A back way? Henrietta, surely you've tried to escape!"

"Oh, no, no." Deep lines cut across Henrietta's pale forehead. "There's no point in even trying. There's nowhere to go. Why, the nearest town is upstream a good twenty miles. Besides, if Machado catches you . . . well, then, it ain't gonna matter how pretty you are." She gave Annabelle's rich, red hair a flip with her hand.

Henrietta gave the sponge to Annabelle. "Here, you finish up yourself. I'll go down and fetch you a plate of food. Courtney—that's the old cook—knows how to cook a mean venison steak!"

The girl rose, opened the door, and stepped into the hall. When she closed the door, Annabelle heard the scrape of a key in the lock.

"Damn," Annabelle said.

She felt a sudden urgency to somehow flee her captors. After all, they were likely all downstairs getting stone drunk, and she was up here, a good distance from them, no longer under their close scrutiny. As tired as she was—the effect of Tobin's abuse was fading—she fairly leaped up out of the tub, grabbed a towel, and dried herself, toweling her lower legs and feet as she stepped out of the tub onto the crude puncheons of the floor.

She tossed the towel over the scrolled wooden room divider with painted glass panels running across the top, then grabbed the fresh underwear Henrietta had laid out for her— pink pantalettes, wool socks, and a fresh chemise. Then she pulled on the denims and wool shirt she'd worn on the trail. She drew her hair up and used one of Henrietta's silver clips to secure it, then stepped into her boots.

Her heart was beating quickly, urgently. If she was going to escape these savages, now was the time to do it.

Again, she turned to the door.

Locked from the outside.

She walked over to the door and crouched down to peer through the lock. Yep, there was a key securely inside it. Footsteps sounded and suddenly someone stood on the other side of the door, a small, pink hand moving to the key in the lock. Two knocks, and Henrietta's voice said, "Knock-knock—I'm back and I've come bearing gifts!"

Annabelle stepped quickly back as the door opened and Henrietta came in carrying a tray with a plate of meat, potatoes, and gravy on it. Henrietta turned back to the door to poke the key in the lock and turn it, locking the door. Annabelle watched her, almost trembling with anticipation. The door was locked from the inside. All she had to do now was unlock it.

But there was Henrietta, whose obvious duty it was to not only tend to Machado's prisoner but also to make sure she stayed in the room.

Henrietta set the tray on a small table outfitted with two brocade-upholstered armchairs, and said, "Here, now . . . you sit down an' eat. Smells so good, doesn't it? One of the benefits of being here is Mister Courtney's cookin'. He doesn't say much on account of the Cheyenne cut out his tongue when he was soldierin', but he cooks one hell of a plate of food. You should taste his stew—cooked from turtles he catches in the Cheyenne just behind the roadhouse!"

Annabelle gave a mirthless chuckle and shuddered.

She looked at the food on the table. She looked at Henrietta standing between her and the door. Henrietta was a slender girl dressed in cream underwear, two blue sleeping feathers in her hair. Anna was taller and probably had a good ten pounds on the girl. She could easily overtake her.

But there was just something so sweet and innocent about the girl. And there was that damnable plate of food filling the entire room with the smell of fried venison, potatoes, and rich brown gravy obviously spiced with wild onion. Her stomach groaned. Her hunger made her weak. If she was going to try to make her escape tonight, she could not do it on an empty stomach.

With a sigh, she sat down at the table, unwrapped the cloth napkin from around her silverware, and dug into her food. Henrietta sat down across from her to watch her, smiling in delight at Annabelle's obvious delight at the food, which, she had to admit, was some of the best venison she'd tasted. Henrietta made her feel a little self-conscious, for she knew she was eating with the abandon of a drunken gandy dancer at midnight; still, she enjoyed the food right down to the last ragged bit of biscuit with which she swabbed the last of the gravy from her plate, then popped it into her mouth.

She chewed, swallowed, washed it down with the last of her coffee.

"Oh, God—that was good!" Annabelle said.

Henrietta gave her small hands a single scalp. "See—I told you you'd like it!"

Annabelle scrubbed her mouth with her napkin, looked across the table at Henrietta. She felt like a snake eyeing a kitten. She had to subdue Henrietta so she could leave the room and find a way out of this place. She'd already inspected the room's two windows. They would open, but the drop was too steep from each—straight down to the ground. She'd at least get a broken ankle out of the deal.

Hanging from a hook above the table were a pair of silk stockings. She could use them as a gag and then secure poor Henrietta to the bed using sheets. Her heart quickened. Henrietta was still smiling at her from across the table, chin resting on the heels of her hands.

Annabelle smiled back at the girl.

"Want to play some pinochle?" Henrietta asked her. "That's my favorite."

"Pinochle . . . hmmm." Annabelle's hand started to rise toward the stockings. There was a sudden knock on the door.

Annabelle jerked with a start, gasping, and lowered her hand to her lap.

"Who is it?" Henrietta said as she rose from her chair and walked to the door.

A raspy male voice said, "Honey, it's me—Horace. Let me in, will ya? Come fer a visit."

Oh, no, Annabelle thought. Oh, no. Why now of all times does Henrietta have to get business? Right when Annabelle was about to make her escape.

"I'm sorry—I'm not takin' visitors tonight, Horace," Henrietta said, canting her head toward the door.

"Oh, come on, honey—I come all this way to see you!"

"Oh, Horace, please, no . . ."

There you go, honey, Annabelle thought. Stand your ground.

Or . . .

A sudden idea dawned on Annabelle. Maybe they should entertain ol' Horace, after all . . .

"Henrietta," she said. "Invite him in. We could play three-handed pinochle. Make the time go by a little faster."

Henrietta regarded her incredulously.

Inwardly, Annabelle smiled.

CHAPTER 13

Henrietta shrugged a pale, bare shoulder.
"All right—if you say so, Annabelle."

Henrietta turned the key in the lock and opened the door. "Horace, hello!" she exclaimed as though delighted to see a close friend she hadn't seen in years. "Come in, come in. Where have you been? Henrietta has missed you so!"

A man who stank like a barn stepped into the room, grinning, his hat in his hand. He was a little taller than Annabelle, but not by much. Maybe in his mid-thirties with a ratlike face and a generally seedy look. Obviously, a cow puncher, he came in grinning like the cat that ate the canary, and Henrietta closed the door. Annabelle had picked up a coal shovel from the little brazier in the corner by the table.

Now she squeezed it and when Horace turned to her, still grinning, she beaned him over the head with it. He fell with a groan. Henrietta gasped and leaped back in shock, staring wide-eyed at Annabelle, speechless.

Annabelle grabbed the stockings from the hook and rushed over to the girl before she could scream. Just as Henrietta opened her mouth to scream, Annabelle thrust the stockings into her mouth. She drove her to the floor saying, "I'm so sorry, Henrietta—but I can't stay here. I'm so sorry . . ." Quickly she knotted the sock behind the girl's head.

Minutes later, she had Henrietta gagged and tied to all four bed posters with sheets. Henrietta stared at her in wide-eyed shock and dismay.

Horace lay on the floor, unmoving.

A walnut-gripped six-shooter bristled on his right hip.

Quickly, Annabelle grabbed the gun and shoved it down behind her belt. She stepped over Horace, removed the key from the lock, opened the door, went out, and locked the door behind her. Enough sound emanated from downstairs and enough sounds of love, if you could call it that, issued from behind the doors around Annabelle, that the man, once he returned to consciousness, would have to call pretty loudly before anyone could hear him. If Annabelle hadn't killed him, that was. She hadn't cared enough to check. At least he was out for now and hopefully a while longer.

There was a window at the end of the hall to her left.

She hurried to it. It was cracked about three inches for ventilation. It was hot and cloying with body sweat here on the second floor. The window was designed to rise up and down, and there appeared a shake-shingled roof several feet below it—probably a small rear porch. She shoved the window up, but the frame was swollen likely from summer humidity and from the river that ran behind the place. On her first try, Anna could get the window up only about ten inches.

Behind her came the sounds of someone moving up the stairs. A man was talking, and a girl was laughing.

Oh, God, no!

Anna grunted as she took the window in both hands and slid it up farther—but only a few more inches. There wasn't enough room for her to climb through.

Behind her, the footsteps and the man's voice and the girl's laughter grew louder.

Annabelle drew a deep breath, flexed her hands, grabbed

the window, and gave another grunt as she funneled every bit of strength she had into the window. Now there might be just enough room for her to squirm through. There better be. The man and the girl were almost to the second story. She caught a first glimpse of them. She hoped like hell they didn't glimpse her . . .

In desperation, she thrust her head through the window and shoved off with her feet. She dove through the opening, flew straight down, and landed on the roof below headfirst, the rest of her body close behind.

She grunted with the impact, wood slivers from the shakes digging into her chin, hands, and wrists. Again, she was dazed but not as badly as when Tobin had smacked her off her horse. She shook her head to clear the cobwebs, then heaved herself to her feet. She made sure Horace's six-shooter was still behind her belt. It was. She took mincing steps to the edge of the porch roof and peered over the side.

There was about a ten-foot drop to the ground.

She looked around but saw no easy way down, so she looked around again to make sure there was no one in the road ranch's backyard. Seeing no one, she said, "Here goes nothin' . . ." and dropped to her hands and knees.

She dropped her legs over the lip of the roof.

She twisted around until she was belly down. She crabbed closer and closer to the edge, her legs dropping lower and lower. Finally, she hooked her fingers over the edge of the roof, hung there for a second, then, sucking a deep breath, let go.

She dropped straight down to the ground, bending her knees to distribute the force of the blow.

Again, she grunted. She fell back on her butt. She still had Horace's gun.

She looked around. The road ranch's windows were

brightly lit on each side, but back here in the rear yard, it was nearly as dark as pitch.

Good.

She rose, looked around.

Anxious hope made her heart beat fast, but she wasn't out of the woods yet. Now she needed to get her hands on a horse.

Or . . .

When she'd scouted the area from above, she'd seen something along the shore of the river that glistened silver in the starlight.

Hmmm.

She shoved Horace's pistol down snugger behind her belt, then started walking toward the snake of the river glistening behind shrubs lining the shore. There was the squawk and scrape of a door opening on her right. She dove forward and rolled up behind a sage shrub. She peered through the shrub toward the privy on her right. A man was just emerging from the rickety structure, sighing and breathing as though he'd run a great distance.

He stopped in front of the open door, set his hat on his head, and stared toward Annabelle.

"Someone out here?"

Annabelle gritted her teeth in dread.

"No jokes, now, ya hear? I ain't in no mood." He started moving toward the far side of the cabin. "A little off my feed's all . . ."

Then he was gone.

Annabelle heaved a heavy sigh.

She jerked with a start when she heard a commotion inside the building behind her.

A man's voice—Machado's voice—bellowed: "SHE'S GONE! THE REDHEAD'S GONE! FIND HERRRR!"

The commotion inside the place grew louder.

Heart racing, Annabelle ran through the shrubs to the river. What she'd seen from the room but hadn't been able to make out clearly was a rowboat. Likely the boat the tongue-less cook took out to catch the turtles for his stew.

As a door of the cabin opened and men began to run out into the yard, yelling angrily, Annabelle crouched to shove the boat into the dark, glistening water. She leaped over the stern and took up the paddle. She dipped the paddle into the water, rammed it into the river's muddy bottom, and, using both hands at the end of the paddle, gave a great shove, pushing herself and the boat out farther into the river.

Almost instantly, the river's current grabbed her and—*oh, thank God, thank God, thank God!*—slid her downriver away from the road ranch and the men running around in the yard, howling and cursing like a rabid pack of half-human wolves.

Annabelle sat down facing the boat's stern and began paddling, keeping the boat aimed straight downstream. With every inch, every foot, every five feet . . . ten feet . . . the merciful river took her farther away from the roadhouse, she muttered a genuine thank-you to the fates.

She'd been on the river maybe seven or eight minutes when a man's deep yell cut through the night, rising above the din around the roadhouse—"THE ROWBOAT'S GONE!"

Annabelle's heart leaped into her throat.

Immediately, she paddled harder, faster, picking up speed.

In the starlit darkness alive with crickets and the screech of an occasional nightbird, the boat traced a long curve in the river. She could no longer hear the angry shouts and bellows of Machado's men. She paddled until she was so exhausted, and her hands were so badly blistered, that she could paddle no longer.

The boat slid along with the river.

Around one bend, around another one.

She nearly got caught in a snag of trees that had fallen over the river from the right shoreline and had to use the paddle to shove the boat away from it, around it. It was a frustrating maneuver that cost her precious minutes, and she couldn't afford to be delayed even a single second.

Machado's men would be coming after her.

Only a few minutes after that nettling thought had snagged at her brain, distant hoof thuds sounded. The thudding grew louder and then a man shouted, "She's in here somewhere! Keep your eyes open, boys!"

The thrashing of shrubs and bushes accompanied the thudding of the hooves.

They were close and they were getting closer.

To Annabelle's left as she faced upstream, the bank was roughly ten feet above the river. She could see shrubs rustling up there, just upstream from her. Through the branches, she glimpsed the glistening hide of a horse. Desperately, she paddled to bring the boat close to shore where tree roots poked out of the bank. When she was close enough, she set down the paddle and grabbed the roots with both hands, holding her and the boat still, though the current kept pushing and pulling.

She clung desperately to the roots and kept her feet pressed hard against the bottom of the boat.

Above her, the bank bulged outward slightly, offering her a modicum of cover from above.

Above her, the hoof thuds grew louder.

She steeled herself, tried to quiet her racing heart to no avail.

Closer and closer the riders came until she could hear the squawk of tack and the faint rattle of bit chains. Brush snapped under hooves. Horses snorted.

Suddenly, straight above Annabelle, the sound stopped.

An eerie silence save for the sucking sound of the river

and the breathing of horses fell over the night around Annabelle.

So suddenly that Anna jerked with a start, Machado's voice said, "When I find that damn tramp, I'm gonna shoot her!"

Again, hooves thudded and snapped twigs and brush as the riders moved off downstream along the top of the bank.

Annabelle removed her hand from the roots and let the river continue to shepherd her downstream. She was glad to see boulders and cedars growing along the crest of the bank. They would make it harder for her stalkers to see her in the river. She followed another long bend in the stream to the left. Trees grew tall on both embankments, making it seem as though she were floating through a deep tunnel. More darkness meant better protection.

Her heart grew lighter when fifteen minutes passed, then twenty . . . then thirty and she neither heard nor saw anything of Machado's men.

Vaguely she heard a whispering sound from straight ahead along the river.

She frowned, gazing curiously upstream.

That whispering became a rushing sound and then her heart sank.

She was heading straight for a rapid, and there was no place to take refuge along either steep bank.

"No," she said, turning the boat around and trying to paddle backward. "No, no, no!"

But there was nothing she could do.

The river had her.

The rushing grew louder and louder and then she could see the white of the water dropping before her in the starry darkness . . . just before the rapids sucked her and the boat straight down that ladder of white, rippling water. The front of the boat dipped violently, and she went flying forward over the prow . . . and straight down . . . down . . . into the angry tangle of rushing water.

She couldn't help but scream just before she went head-first into the stream.

CHAPTER 14

The three Pinkertons stared at Angus in pugnacious silence.

"You heard me," Angus said. "The boy and I cooked. One of you fellas does the dishes. That's how it works in hunt camp. Since you're havin' such a gallbasted time decidin' on your own, why don't you draw straws? Want me to cut one for you?"

He gave a dry chuckle.

The three exchanged dark, frustrated glances.

"Oh, hell," said Leech Davis, running a hand through his long, sandy hair. He set his hat on his head, rose, and began gathering up the dishes until he had an armful. Then he stomped over to the stream and dropped the whole mess into the water before coming back and, huffing and puffing his exasperation, gathered up another armful.

Jackson sipped his coffee, then turned a knowing grin on Angus. "You're loving this, aren't you, Buchanon?"

"What's that?"

"Bein' out here . . . deep in the hills . . . bein' *trail boss*. This is your element."

Angus sipped his own brew, holding the warm tin cup in his gnarled hand. He chuckled. "Yes, yes, I reckon I do. Reminds me of the old days."

"What old days?"

"When my boys an' me moved up here from the South. After the War of Northern Aggression. We all four had a lotta forgettin' to do. The war. The boys' mother dyin' while Hunter and I were off fightin' the bloody fight." Angus shook his head. "Bad days down there. We came up here to start over. That includin' regular hunts up in these mountains. Elk, griz, deer, wild turkeys, pheasants, partridge. Yessir, after the work was done at home, we'd take a week or so off in the spring or fall and come up here and live free and shoot an' bring our kill home an' fill the larder an' the keeper shed."

Jackson glanced at Nathan poking at the fire with a stick. "That why you brought him?"

"That an' because his eyes are better'n mine. He's been up here before. Not this high or very often—there's been little time—but he knows his way around a Winchester. But, yeah, I wanted him to have more experience and a chance to fall in love with these hills just like my other boys did."

"Where'd he come from?"

Nathan looked at Angus.

"Hell," Angus said. "Ain't that right, boy? He was raised by outlaws."

Nathan pulled his mouth corners down, nodded, and continued poking a stick at the fire. "I like it at the Box Bar B a whole lot better."

Jackson looked at Angus sidelong. "You do realize we're hunting men—right, Buchanon? Two nasty hardtails and a crazy woman."

Angus returned the look. "They're up to *you*. Gettin' you fellas up to Ghost Mountain is *our* job, and when we get you there, *our* job is over."

Jackson nodded.

Angus said, "Keep in mind, we're your trail *guides*. Not your *hosts*. We'll pull our weight—Nate an' me. You fellas pull yours, an' we'll get along just fine."

With that, Angus tossed the dregs of his coffee into the fire. He set his cup aside, picked up his canteen, then rose with a grunt, and pushed through some pine boughs as he walked over to the river, around a bend from where Davis was busily, disgustedly cleaning the dishes with sand and water. He dropped to an arthritic knee, uncapped his flask, and submerged it in the stream.

Footsteps sounded behind him, and he turned to see Nate pushing through the shrubs, carrying his own canteen. The boy looked tired, drawn, sun- and windburned.

Nate dropped to a knee beside Angus and submerged his own canteen in the river.

"How you holdin' up, son?"

"I'm all right. How you holdin' up, Angus?"

"When you get to be my age, and you're still on this side of the sod, you're holdin' up all right." Angus chuckled as he pulled his canteen out of the river and capped it.

"Those men back there," Nate said, tossing his head to indicate the fire's glow in the camp beyond the shrubs, "I don't like them much. Do you?"

"Nah, nah, I don't like them all that much. Then again, there's not a whole lotta men I do like, so . . ."

"They're the law, you say?"

"Yeah, I reckon they're Pinkertons. That's law, so . . ."

"I don't know. They just seem kinda strange."

"They may be law, but they're pilgrims. They're not used to the life up here, an' I reckon they have a lot on their minds. When we catch up to them owlhoots, they'll have to take them down while we just fall back and keep our heads down."

"I reckon."

"They're kinda rough—I'll admit. But you get to meet all kinds in this life, boy. It's a good experience—you an' me leading such men into the mountains. They don't have much experience in the high an' rocky. We best watch out for 'em, no matter how sharp-tongued they can be. How impatient they can be." Angus gave another dry chuckle. "They're pilgrims, all right. We'll just keep to our own pace, an' they'll have to hold it, or they can ride on alone. And believe you me, they do not want to do that. But you an' me, we know how to make a trek like this."

Nate smiled up at the older man. "You really like this."

"I reckon I do. I reckon I do. Without them"—Angus tossed his head to indicate the glowing camp in the dark pines—"I reckon I'd be stuck back at the ranch. Never woulda made a trek like this alone. Even with Hunter. Never woulda occurred to me I could still make a ride like this. I just hope . . . well, I just hope . . ." He cast his gaze to the northwest where Ghost Mountain humped up unseen in the darkness.

"Hope what?"

Angus smiled a little sheepishly at the boy. "Well, that I can make it without embarrassin' myself, that's all."

"You're not gonna embarrass yourself, Angus. Like Hunter says, you got the bark on." Nate grinned.

"The bark on. Yeah, I reckon I used to think so. Now, you know, I think I'm comin' around again." Angus pushed to his feet. "But we still have two hard days left. The hardest days. The apron slopes around Ghost Mountain is rough country. Outlaws up thataway. So we both gotta keep our eyes skinned. The terrain is tough enough. But then when you throw in desperadoes from bank and train robberies around Denver an' Manitou an' Colorado Springs—well, then you gotta really ride careful. I sorta wish I hadn't brought you now, thinkin' more clearly on it."

"I'll be all right."

"You an' Hunter been practice shooting with that Winchester?"

"Yes. I'm a good shot. Of course, I've only been shooting rabbits an' gophers . . ."

Angus squeezed the boy's shoulder. "Let's hope that's all you have to shoot. Come on, boy. Let's head back to camp an' get some shut-eye. Mornin' will be here before we know it."

"I'm already hungry for pancakes."

"Of course, you are!" Angus laughed.

Flies buzzed around the dead man's lips, the mouth twisted into a grimace, probably the last, agonized grimace before his demise.

Birds had been pecking at him.

He twisted slightly on the rope wrapped around his neck, thrown up over a branch above him and then tied off near the bottom of the tree. He'd kicked out of one of his boots. It lay on the ground beneath him. The toe of his sock flopped like a dirty cream tongue in the midmorning breeze.

He'd been shot before he'd been hanged. Blood crusted the moon-and-star badge pinned to the lapel of his frock coat.

"U.S. Marshal," Jackson observed.

"This is a hard place for lawmen," Angus said.

"Wow," murmured Nate, who'd been strangely quiet ever since they'd first spied the dead man hanging from a branch of the aspen in this narrow valley along a slender stream between high, craggy ridges.

"Look away if you need to, son," Angus said. "No shame in lookin' away. Death is nothin' nobody needs to look at."

"Who do you suppose killed him?" Nate asked.

"Maybe those he was after. Can't believe he was out here alone. There's likely at least one more lawdog out here. Likely dead, too."

Angus said, "We should probably bury him."

"No time," Davis said. "His misfortune an' none of our own."

"I agree," said Dutch McCrae, packing chewing tobacco

between his cheek and gum. "Time to ride on. We got a timetable to keep."

Jackson said, "If we stop to bury every dead man we'll likely find out here, we won't make it to Ghost Mountain—"

"I know, I know," Angus said. "We won't make it to Ghost Mountain till fall."

He gigged his dun forward and they set out again, heading west up the valley, the valley floor rising gradually until they rode up and over another pass. At the bottom of the pass was another stream. On the far side of the stream, off the left side of the trail, and up a slight rise, lay a small, weathered gray log cabin.

"Whoa, whoa," Angus said, checking down the dun.

Jackson rode up beside him. "Now, what the hell is . . ."

He let his voice trail off when his gaze had followed Angus's gaze to the cabin and the two bearded men milling out in front of it. One sat in a chair in front of the cabin, leaning forward, elbows on his knees, twirling a revolver on his finger. The other was carving up a puma hanging upside down from the bough of a pine tree fronting the cabin. Both were bearded, badly disheveled, clad in denims or buckskins. At least, partly clad. The man doing the carving was bare chested, his skin as dark as an Indian's. Both wore long, tangled beards.

The man twirling the gun on his finger had looked up to see Angus and his trail partners sitting just down from the top of the pass. He said something to the other man, who stopped carving to turn his own attention on the newcomers. Angus could see smoke rising from behind the cabin. He sniffed the air.

Mmhmm.

Angus glanced behind him. "Let's ride in slow, gents. No sudden moves."

"Hell," McCrae said. "Just look like a couple old mountain men to me."

"Mebbe so, mebbe so."

Angus booted the dun on down the ridge. As he did, he turned to Nate riding just off the dun's right hip. "Stay close to me, boy."

Nate nodded.

Angus bottomed out in the valley, crossed the creek, and reined up near the cabin, giving an affable smile and saying, "How-do, gents."

The man in the chair rose, reached into the cabin, and pulled out an old Sharps .56, which must have been leaning against the wall beside the door. He sat down in the chair again and rested the Sharps across his denim-clad thighs. He was barefoot and wore a ratty underwear top under a smoke-stained buckskin vest. His tangled, gray-brown beard hung halfway down his bony chest. Both men were scrawny, deeply tanned, and they both had feral, paranoid looks in their eyes.

Behind all that grime and those beards, Angus saw a family resemblance.

"No need for that, now!" Jackson told the man with the Sharps. "We're just passin' through."

"Easy," Angus said out the side of his mouth.

The man who'd been carving the wildcat stood with his bloody knife hanging straight down at his side. Blood stained his chest and the front of his buckskin trousers. It stained his beard, as well. Angus wrinkled his nose at the smell of the dead cat. It might have been hanging there in the sun a little too long. But then, there was nothing as foul as the smell of dead, butchered wildcat, no matter how long they'd been dead. It was, however, somewhat of a delicacy to the old mountain men and fur trappers, who called them "painters." He had no idea why it was so special to them, but it was. Dead and butchered, they smelled like skunks. At least, to Angus's nose.

"Who're you?" said the man with the knife, giving Angus and his trail partners the woolly eyeball.

Paranoia hung over this place, as thick as mountain fog in the morning.

"No one special," Angus said. "We're just passin'—"

Jackson put his horse two steps forward and in his best official voice said, "Pinkerton agents out of Denver. I'm Jackson. That's Davis, the big fella's McCrae. We're looking for two men riding with a woman. They robbed a train. You happen to see 'em? Might've passed through here a week or so ago."

Angus winced, giving the head Pinkerton a stink eye of his own.

The man with the knife turned his head to share an inscrutable look with his brother or cousin with the Sharps. The man with the Sharps only blinked. No expression at all. Not on either face as the man with the knife turned back to regard the obviously unwanted strangers.

"Is that a yes or a no?" Jackson persisted.

Behind him, McCrae gave a wry snort.

Peeved, Jackson raised his voice. "Look, like I said, we're Pinkertons out of—"

"That'll be enough," Angus said with fake congeniality. "Sorry to bother you fellas. We'll be on our way. Sorry to bother you. Enjoy the painter."

He was about to gig the dun forward when the man with the Sharps suddenly rose from his chair and started walking forward. As he did, the man with the knife dropped the knife and reached for an old double-barrel shotgun leaning against the tree from which the wildcat hung.

Angus had anticipated the moves.

He pulled his old Colt, poking up from behind his belt, over his belly, and clicked the hammer back.

"No, no, no," he said, startling the Pinkertons as well as Nate, all of whom had also turned away from the mountain salts and gigged their horses forward. "There ain't no need for that. We're not here for you. Yeah, I know you got a still behind the cabin. Can smell it from here. You'd best clean out your copper cables, 'cause you got a skunky batch brewin' back there. We seen the dead marshal. The way I see it, he had him a run of bad luck, as do most lawmen in these mountains. They know that ridin' in. But neither he nor you are any of our business. So don't make it so!"

Both men had frozen in place.

They both regarded Angus with dull incredulity.

They exchanged a look and then the man with the Sharps returned to his chair and sat down, resting the rifle across his thighs once more. The other man left his shotgun leaning against the tree, picked up his knife, and resumed carving the wildcat.

Angus cast a disgusted look back at Jackson, then depressed his Colt's hammer and returned the old popper to its place behind his belt, angled slightly over his belly.

Jackson and the others shared sheepish looks.

Angus spat in disgust, then booted the dun on ahead along the trail toward Ghost Mountain.

CHAPTER 15

Hunter, Powwow, and Bobby Lee pushed hard for the next two days.

The riding was miserable but not nearly as miserable as it had been before Cynthia McGovern had tended his ribs. He didn't like having to rely on the whiskey because he wanted to be sharp and ready for anything, but the pain was just too intense if he didn't. So, essentially, he stayed mildly drunk and relied on Powwow and Bobby Lee to help him stay on Machado's trail, which they still lost from time to time but managed to pick up again soon after.

This was Indian country, and several times they came upon small bands of hunting Indians, most of whom ignored them. They were still after buffalo, which were getting sparser and sparser, the hide hunters having killed most of them for only their hides and left the rest of the meat on the prairie to spoil. They crossed several streams with water in them but mainly it was one dry wash after another and monotonous, open expanses of sun-cured grass. The only creatures they saw were scattered antelope, jackrabbits, and coyotes. Occasionally, they spied a buffalo or two, but mostly those poor creatures were gone and seeing one or two alive was like coming upon ghosts of the prairie's ancient past.

Late in the day of their third day on the trail out from Cynthia McGovern's place, they found themselves following Machado's trail along an old, abandoned stage trace. Off the trail's right side, they came to a worn, tilting wooden sign announcing RIVER BEND STATION.

Hope rose in Hunter.

Machado had likely stopped here. Judging by the age of the tracks he and Powwow were following, Machado's bunch had likely stopped here two or three nights ago, but Hunter should be able to pick up some information here, anyway. At least, how long ago the gang had stopped, if there'd been a pretty redhead with them, and which way they'd headed after they'd left the road ranch.

Hope rose higher.

By God, he and Powwow were closing the gap. He could feel it in his bones.

Now, he just had to figure out, once he'd caught up to them, how to take them down in the condition he was in. He had Powwow to back his play, but he could rely on the sometime cow puncher only so far. Bobby Lee was no good in a lead swap.

They rode into the yard and almost instantly a big, long-haired, round-faced man surfaced from the stable to which a corral was attached. Without a word, after Hunter and Powwow had dismounted, he snatched up the reins of both horses and led them both off to the corral around which sat three big lumber drays. A dozen or so mules milled with a dozen or so horses in the paddock. A dozen or so saddles adorned the corral's top pole. Nasty Pete glanced warily over his shoulder at Hunter, and Hunter gave a dry chuckle and said, "Go with God, boy. Go with God."

He and Powwow shared an incredulous look.

"You best head out now, Bobby," Hunter told the coyote sitting nearby, an expectant cast to his long-eyed gaze, ears pricked. "Stay close, though. We'll head out first thing in the mornin'"

The coyote gave a low, clipped howl, then headed off into the brush. Hunter knew he'd likely stand vigil over the roadhouse. He might not have understood the exact details of Hunter's situation, but he understood instinctively that things were dire . . . and dangerous.

No sooner had Hunter and Powwow gained the front porch than the roadhouse door opened and a woman of considerable girth that a large, loose, flowered dress could not conceal, said, "Come on in an' name your poison, gents. The more the merrier! You like whiskey, I got whiskey. You like girls, I got girls!"

She clapped her hands, tipped her head back, and roared.

Hunter and Powwow shared another incredulous glance.

Hunter pinched his hat brim to the woman and said, "Much obliged ma'am."

"Ma'am nothing. It's Ann-Marie or nothing at all!"

Hunter sidled past the woman as did Powwow, who also pinched his hat brim to the hardy gal. Hunter stepped to one side out of instinct in such matters—not wanting to be outlined by the open doors. Powwow followed his lead. Hunter scanned the large, smoky, low-ceilinged room, picking out the mule skinners who likely belonged to those big drays, cow punchers, and owlhoots. He wasn't sure how he could tell them all apart, but he could. Especially the owlhoots. They had a guarded, paranoid look, and those obvious owlhoots here now had lowered their hands to their six-shooters as soon as Hunter and Powwow had entered, always on the scout for the law that could ruin their whole day—or their night, as the case was here.

He was impatient to gather the information he was after but decided to wait a few hours, when the liquor had been running and possibly loosened a few tongues and the other diners and drinkers had gotten accustomed to his and

Powwow's presence. He and his partner would have a few drinks, some food—he could smell something cooking in the kitchen that appeared to open through a doorway flanking the bar on the room's left wall—and then he'd broach the topic.

When he was relatively sure he wasn't about to be back-shot, he and Powwow moseyed up to the bar. Only three other men stood at it—two bearded muleskinners with trail dirt crusting the deep lines in their weathered faces and speaking in hushed Scandinavian brogues. There was also a dandy, likely a gambler, in a three-piece suit complete with black and gold brocade vest and gold watch chain. In the back bar mirror, Hunter could see he had one of those mustaches that appeared to be nothing so much as a dead raccoon, albeit a well-groomed one, mantling his upper lip. A pearl-handled, silver-capped knife jutted up from inside his right, black boot into which his red-checked twill trousers were tucked.

The bartender appeared Mexican, short and big gutted with a black mustache and one wandering eye, but judging by his accent he was Scandinavian. He set Hunter and Powwow up with beers and whiskey shots and when they'd finished the first round, Hunter inquired about the food whose aromas he could smell issuing from the kitchen. He'd seen several of the drinkers enjoying wooden bowls of some kind of chunky, clear-broth stew but he hadn't been able to tell what it was.

"Mr. Courtney's got a big kettle of turtle stew back there. Locally famous. He's a little long in the face, however, because someone ran off with the boat he goes out to trap his turtles in." The Swede shook his head. "Practical jokers, tsk, tsk, tsk."

"Ah, too bad," Hunter said. "What the hell? I'm brave. Set us each up with a bowl of the stew."

Not ten minutes later, he dropped his spoon into his empty bowl and said, "I'll be hanged if that wasn't half bad."

Powwow agreed with a mouthful of the last of his stew in his mouth. He swallowed the stew quickly and with a start when a pretty, little blond doxie clad in so little that Hunter thought he could stuff the whole outfit in his mouth and still have room to chew, sidled up to him, giving his shoulder a playful nudge with his own.

"Hello there, you," she said. "You got a friendly face."

Powwow choked a little, cleared his throat. Hunter saw his ears turn red.

"I . . . do . . . ?"

"Yes, you do. Don't you know that? I can tell a friendly face as soon one walks through the door 'cause there's so many that ain't friendly. Why, I got bruises where the sun don't shine, if you must know. Still, you can't beat Mr. Courtney's stew, can you?"

"It sure was good stew. Not that I'm an expert, but . . ."

"What's your name? I'm Henrietta."

Powwow fumbled his hat off his head and held it over his chest. "I'm, uh . . . Billy Lancaster. Folks call me Powwow since I got about that much Injun blood in my veins." He held his right hand up, thumb and index finger about a half inch apart. He gave a laugh like a mule braying.

"Powwow, I like that."

"I like Henrietta, too. That's purty."

"You got any money, Powwow?"

"Uh . . . uh . . ." He glanced self-consciously at Hunter and said, "Well . . . I got me a little jingle. Likely gonna need it on the trail, though."

"No time for a dalliance, Powwow?"

Hunter gave the younger man a playful nudge with his elbow. Powwow ignored him as he gave a regretful wince. "Uh . . . well . . . uh . . . prob'ly not. If I had any extry, though, I would spend it on you, Miss Henrietta. You sure are purty . . . to go along with your purty name."

"Why, thank you, Powwow. You're so nice I'm tempted to give you a free one." Henrietta pressed two fingers to her lips, dramatically. "Shhh! Mustn't tell Ann-Marie!" She cupped her hand to her mouth and gave a devilish giggle. "Are you spending the night? Ann-Marie rents rooms upstairs even if you're not . . . you know . . . partaking."

"Uh . . ."

Powwow glanced at Hunter, who nodded. They might as well sleep in beds here, get a fresh start in the morning. Besides, if he was going to learn anything about where Machado was headed, he'd likely find it here as anywhere. Machado had to have stopped here at least for food and drinks. Hunter had a feeling every traveler to this remote end of the territory stopped here for drinks, food, and women . . . not necessarily in that order.

That meant Annabelle must have stopped here, too.

"I reckon we are, Miss Henrietta," Powwow said.

"All right, then." Henrietta gave a smile no less alluring for appearing so girlish. "Maybe see you later . . . upstairs. Shhh!"

She giggled and flounced away.

Hunter chuckled. "'You sure are purty . . . to go along with your purty name' . . . ?"

Powwow's ears turned red again. "I thought that was purty good. Leastways, it was all I could come up with spur-o'-the-moment . . . an' with you standin' here."

Again, Hunter chuckled. "Go for it, kid. Life is short." He threw back the last of his beer, set the mug on the bar, and said, "Meanwhile, I got some business to tend to."

He picked up his spoon as well as his beer mug and turned to the room.

"Attention, please," he said, loudly. "Attention, everyone. Attention, please!" He rapped the spoon against the glass until he had the attention of everyone in the smoky watering hole. Faces turned to him, incredulous, some with quirleys or cigars dangling from between their lips, drinks being set back down on tables, two poker games halting, the poker players freezing in mid-call and casting the big, Viking-handsome blond man in denims and buckskins the woolly eyeball.

"I happen to be missing a very precious possession of mine. My wife. She was taken by a big ugly half-Mex lout named Saguaro Machado and the rest of his gang. If anyone can tell me he's been here and where you think he might be heading—which direction he did head when he left—I have one hundred crisp dollar bills for you!"

The room was as quiet as a Lutheran church on Saturday night.

All eyes regarded him skeptically.

Some with downright shock.

One man's mouth opened involuntarily, and the cigarette that had been dangling from between his lips dropped to the table before him and sparked.

The rotund Ann-Marie in her flowered tent dress had been hovering over a poker game at the rear of the room. Now she regarded Hunter with wide-eyed exasperation, pushing off the table she'd been leaning against, and hurried over to him, making swishing sounds as she strode, her cloying perfume growing heavier and heavier as she approached.

She smiled broadly and turned to the room saying, "Carry on, everyone. Carry on. The big reb has just had a little too much to drink is all. You know how they are. Carry on!"

She turned back to Hunter and her suety face became a rogue grizzly's mask of bald disdain and exasperation. "Are you out of your mind?" she hissed, getting right up close to Hunter and keeping her voice low. "No one mentions Machado's name here or anywhere else. He has spies everywhere! You're liable to get yourself shot and my place *shot up*!"

The low hum of conversation had returned to the room but more stiffly, tensely than before, men fatefully conferring.

"So he has been here," Hunter said. "Did he have my wife with him? A pretty redhead?"

"That is not a question you ask me or anyone else. You ask it again, I'll have to *tell* you to leave!"

"All right, all right—don't get your bloomers in a twist, lady. You got a room for me an' Casanova here?"

Hunter was enduring a fitful sleep, slumbering beside Powwow in a too-small bed, listening to the sometimes-drover's raucous snores grind up from the very bottom of his lungs to rumble out of him like a freight train trundling out of a deep tunnel into the open.

He was about to get up and go out and sleep in the stable with the horses when he heard a floorboard creak outside his room. Three soft taps on his door.

Instantly, the big LeMat was in his hand, his thumb ratcheting the hammer back.

He tossed back the covers, rose, and padded barefoot to the door, pressing his shoulder against the wall to the left of it. He didn't want to stand in front of it in case someone decided to pump lead through it. This wasn't his first rodeo.

Again came three soft taps.

"Who is it?" Hunter said, his voice sounding inordinately loud between Powwow's snores.

"Henrietta," came the girl's soft voice on the other side of the door.

Holding the LeMat in his right hand, Hunter twisted the knob and opened the door one foot with his left, scowling curiously at the delicate, shadowy little figure standing on the other side of it.

"Let me in!" she whispered and rammed the door wide with her shoulder.

Hunter quickly closed the door, turned to the girl who was mostly in shadow, and said, "Romeo's asleep."

She shook her head. "I'm not hear about him. I'm hear about Machado . . . an' Annabelle."

CHAPTER 16

Anna dropped down, down, down along the slanting falls. She fell until she didn't think there was any way she could make it to the surface of the river from here.

She dropped until her fingers touched seaweed and mud. It was a dark, soundless world devoid of light. She was in a black prism. Fear was no longer a part of her. She'd tumbled beyond fear into a mindset focused entirely on survival, the blackness of watery death pressing against every inch of her.

She'd thought that over the past couple of days she'd lost her will to survive. Tobin's lip-smacking blow had finalized the notion for her. When Henrietta had led her up the stairs at River Bend Station, she hadn't cared if she were being led to the smoking gates of hell. She'd just wanted the ordeal over.

Now her instincts took over and she swung her feet down beneath her, kicked off the muddy bottom, and swam hard for the surface, swinging her arms broadly and kicking her legs while her lungs felt as though they would burst. When her head finally broke the river's moving surface, she sucked a deep draught of the night air and fought to keep her head above water. At the bottom of the falls, the river had picked up speed and it shuttled her quickly downstream through darkness that made her feel as though she were drifting through space. Only by the stream's current could she tell which way was upstream and which way downstream. She had no visual reference points; otherwise, the entire world around her was as dark as the bottom of a deep well.

Fighting to keep her head above the surface quickly exhausted her. Several times the current pulled her under, and weakness almost made her give in to the stream's demands. Each time, however, she belted out, "No!" through gritted teeth and shoved her head up into open air again.

The current twisted and turned her, took her from one side of the river to the other. Until the river's will began to relent. Gradually at first but then there was hardly any current at all.

The banks had dropped away on both sides of the river, she could see now in the first wash of pearlescent dawn light emanating from the far eastern prairie. She swam toward the shore on her left and was surprised and delighted in a vague, exhausted way to feel sand under her feet. She got her feet beneath her and stumbled toward the shore, so exhausted that her temples throbbed, and her heart felt as though it were being squeezed by some sadist's iron fist.

Shore lay just ahead, beyond a short cutbank. A sunbleached log lay on it, beside a fire ring in which a small pile of long-cold ashes and some burned airtight tins resided. She was five feet from the cutbank, walking in water only an inch or so deep, when her knees buckled and she dropped, out like a blown lamp even before she hit the ground.

She slept the sleep of the half dead. Dreamless. Soundless. Touchless. Emotionless.

No desires or anxieties. No cares, no worries.

Complete as the still blackness at the heart of the universe.

Something hard and cold and round pressed against her forehead, hard.

Even before she opened her eyes, she knew what it was.

She gazed up the long barrel of Saguaro Machado's ivory gripped .45. His hideous mask of a scarred, one-eyed face beneath the narrow brim of his ridiculous, black stovepipe hat gazed down the barrel at her, his one dung-brown eye blazing. His jaws were set in hard lines, ensconced in tangled, dark-brown beard.

The sun was full up, and the birds were singing. The sky above Machado was a faultless lake blue.

Annabelle smiled up at him. "My, you have a big gun, Senor Machado. You know what they say about men with big guns. Compensation for small . . . brains."

She reached up and placed both hands around the barrel. "Go ahead. Shoot me. I want you to." She hardened her voice, rage and exasperation creeping back into her repertoire of emotions. "Go ahead, tough man. You said you were going to do it. So do it, you useless, cowardly miscreant!"

Machado's mouth screwed up into a grimace and he pressed the barrel of his .45 harder against Anna's forehead. Anna gritted her teeth against the pain but kept her smile in place, albeit stiffly, as she kept her hands wrapped around the .45's seven-and-a-half-inch barrel. "Do it!" she screamed.

Somewhere behind the outlaw leader, a horse whinnied.

Abruptly, Machado pulled the gun away. He holstered the pistol, then bent down and pulled Anna up by her left hand. It was then that Anna saw the five other members of the man's gang sitting their horses in a semicircle behind their fearless leader. Machado pulled Anna up and over his left shoulder. He carried her over to the mount they'd appropriated for her by shooting an innocent cow puncher off his horse. The look of shock and horror she'd seen in the drover's eyes—he'd been alone, stopped at a creek to let his horse draw water—when he'd seen Machado calmly pull his big gun and ratchet back the hammer.

Machado had killed the man as easily as he would have shot any game animal he might had come upon, helpless.

Now he brusquely slung Annabelle up onto the saddle. He held out his hand, and a length of rope was promptly placed in it by one of the other riders. Silently, morosely, without saying anything to anyone and not looking at Anna, he tied Anna's wrists to her saddle horn. When he had them secure, he took the reins himself, mounted his own horse, and pulled out, glancing at his men behind him and merely saying, "Let's go!"

Then they were off at hard gallops, continuing east and north upon the nearly featureless land. It was as though the outlaw leader was following some trail in his head alone. Rarely since they'd left Lusk had the gang followed a bone fide trail. Here and there they would pick up a corner of a freight or stagecoach trail and follow it for a mile or two but inevitably Machado would swing off said trail and head cross-country once more.

It was as though he'd ridden this way often, and he probably had. He likely knew the shortest route and the one that would be hardest for others to follow.

Everything about the man. . . about the men he rode with . . . was diabolical.

Anna didn't even want to think about how many women and girls had endured the same indignity she was enduring. She'd gotten off relatively easily so far. She hadn't been ravaged. Tobin was the first who'd directly assaulted her. She'd just been tortured with fear and by riding tied too long, being underfed and watered, and made to do most of the chores when it came time to camp. At the point of several pistols aimed at her from blanket folds.

She couldn't help wondering why he hadn't shot her when she'd been unconscious by the Cheyenne. He'd wanted to do it. Anna had seen it in his lone, cold, snake-flat eye. Yet he hadn't. Surely, even a redhead couldn't be worth that much money. She wondered vaguely if her being married to the notorious rebel freedom fighter, Hunter Buchanon, had upped her value.

Most folks in the territory had either heard of Hunter's exploits during the war or they'd heard of the now-legendary feud that had broken out when Hunter had first asked for Anna's hand in marriage and her father, Graham Ludlow, had refused. Most newspapers had reported on that infamous war, and even a few pulp writers had ridden out to the Box Bar B for additional information. Of course, Annabelle and Hunter had driven them off the place, but they'd still penned their stories. They'd just made up most of the details.

Also, Anna might be seen as a trophy. An invitingly dangerous one, at that, to a sporting man. After all, she was married to a man who, if still alive, would hunt for her. That danger aspect might up her value.

Which meant one thing and one thing only: Many men were sick puppies, indeed.

They stopped for the night in the early dusk, setting up camp and tending the horses in a cottonwood copse along another, narrow, muddy stream. The red-brown patch of up-turned earth that was the vast Dakota badlands lay ahead to the north and east. Annabelle had never seen that wild country before, but she'd read about it in books and magazines— mostly archaeological reports of excavations of dinosaur and ancient Indian burial sites and old settlements situated in the heart of that colorful, picturesque, and unforgiving land.

She didn't have time to scrutinize that storied patch of wind- and water-eroded castle-like earth, for the sun was fast going down and she was prodded to build a fire and to cook these savages another supper of fatback and beans. Anna merely walked over to a tree near the stone ring one of the men had arranged, and sat down. She drew her knees up to her chest and wrapped her arms around them.

She was miserable, still a little damp from her swim in the river. Wrung out. Wind- and sunburned. Where her clothes had dried, they were stiff.

She herself was as hollow as an old tree stump.

She would work for these men no more.

"What're you doin'?" Machado asked her.

"Go to hell."

"What?"

"You heard me."

He stopped for her, set his feet a little more than shoulder width apart, and thrust an arm and angry finger at her, narrowing his lone, shallow, stupid eye. "You will cook as I tell you to do it!"

Annabelle smiled at him in delighted defiance. "Go to hell, you half-breed whore."

The other men stopped what they were doing—tending the horses and hauling tack into the camp—to stare in shock from Machado to the pretty redhead who'd defied him again. Not only defied him but desecrated his honor.

He grunted furiously and strode up to Anna. He whipped his right hand back behind his left shoulder and started to swing it forward and down, toward her face, but stopped himself. Anger burned in that lone eye. He stared down at Anna in silent rage for nearly a minute before he whipped around and barked at one of his men: "Tie her!"

That was the end of the discussion.

She would not work for them tonight. All Machado would do about it was tie her to the tree. She was shocked. Even a little frightened. Sometimes the withholding of punishment was more menacing than the punishment itself. Likely, a powerful rage was burning in Machado. Annabelle knew he didn't one bit care for how she'd spoken to him in front of his men.

Her only punishment seemed to be the withholding of food. When the men had eaten, they drew straws and then the two losers gathered up all the pans, dishes, and silverware, hauled them down to the stream, and began cleaning, conversing in hushed tones, which Anna could hear, though not make out the words themselves, beneath the cool night breeze.

Two men were sent out on guard duty. The others passed a bottle for a while, conversing in desultory tones, then, around eleven or maybe closer to midnight, they rolled up in their soogans and went to sleep. Anna slept then, as well, wrists tied before her, chin dipping toward her chest. She was sound asleep despite the uncomfortable position when a dirty hand closed over her mouth, jerking her head up harshly.

Here it comes, was in the back of her mind. *Here it comes at long last.*

A face slid up close to hers from behind the tree. It was not Machado. It was one of his men—a man the others called Big Nick. He wasn't tall but he was wide, and he wore only buckskins and had a big, sheathed Bowie knife on each hip.

He had a long, narrow, craggy face, close-set eyes, and long, grizzled silver hair that never laid flat but that just sort of fanned out around his head beneath his cream, leather-banded hat adorned with a feather from a red-tail hawk. He'd been eyeing Anna covertly for days. She'd often spied him staring at her, maybe from one side or the other, and when she returned his gaze, he held hers and his thin lips quirked a dubious smile that betrayed the workings of his devious mind.

Now he held up one of his big knives in front of her face, threateningly.

He pressed two fingers to his lips and then, as if to show her what would happen if she didn't stay quiet, he made a slashing motion with his knife across her throat, the razor-edged, upturned tip grazing it slightly.

Then, keeping his hand over her mouth, he began to cut the ropes securing her to the tree.

CHAPTER 17

Walking his dun up a gentle rise through pines and aspens that were beginning to turn with the early mountain fall, following an old woodcutters' trail, the grass and sage growing lush and green around him, Angus sniffed the breeze like a dog, snorting in large drafts of the cool, clean-scoured air.

"Smell that? That's mule."

"What is?" asked Jackson, again riding behind Nate, all three Pinkertons surly again because of what they saw as an overly conservative pace.

"That smell. For some reason, I've aways been able to sniff mule from a long way off. We're not too far off now, though. I got me a feelin' there's a muleskinners' camp a little farther up the rise."

As if to validate the old ex-rebel's estimation, a mule's distant bray sounded beneath the breeze rattling the aspen leaves.

Angus laughed and slapped his thigh.

"That old buzzard's got a beak on him," Leech Davis groused to Jackson.

The two Pinkertons rode side by side. McCrae, who'd gotten up on the wrong side of his bedroll that morning, brought up the rear. He hadn't said two words to anyone for most of the morning nor even after they'd stopped for a quick noon lunch of bacon sandwiches and coffee. Another delay Angus had insisted on to rest themselves as well as their horses. "In the mountains, you need food an' coffee, plenty of water, an' fresh hosses."

That was Angus's motto that all three Pinkertons were getting tired of hearing.

Which was just fine with the agreeably defiant Angus. Because the old scudder knew he was right.

They followed the two-track trail through pines and when they came out into the clearing beyond, Angus saw two large lumber drays parked off to the far left, along a creek that tumbled straight down the slope from probably a spring above. He could see a good dozen or so mules tied to a long picket line on the other side of the stream. Another of the mules brayed and stomped. They all looked a might jumpy.

He stopped the dun, cupped his hand to his mouth, and yelled, "Halloo the camp!"

No response.

Angus could see no smoke rising from the large cook fire he could see between the parked wagons, each bearing the burden of a good load of long, unpeeled pine logs.

"Halloo-oo the camp!" Angus yelled again.

"Let 'em sleep," grouched Ten Jackson.

"I don't think they're sleepin'."

"What makes you say so?" asked Jackson.

"Them soogans under both wagons look empty. Besides, it's after noon. No good muleskinner would sleep till afternoon."

"Maybe they stop for naps."

"They don't stop for naps. They work."

He could see the blanket rolls under each wagon. At least two under each. Muleskinners just naturally slept under their wagons in case it rained, which it nearly aways did up in this high country every late afternoon.

"I'm gonna check it out." Angus glanced at Nate. "You stay here, boy."

"All right, Angus."

As he booted the dun into a trot toward the parked wagons, each one facing him with their tongues drooping into the sage, Leech Davis called behind him, "What business are they to you, old man?"

"Maybe none," Angus said and checked the dun down between the wagons and near the fire ring piled with dead ashes but over which an iron tripod stood with a scorched, black, white-specked coffeepot hanging from its hook.

"Hmm," he said, scratching under his chin with his gloved hand. "Damn peculiar."

He rode back and forth between the wagons a couple of times before coming upon the tracks of what appeared four shod horses leading away from the camp. "Oh, I see," Angus said to himself, leaning out a little from his saddle and following the tracks toward the saddle ahead. "Maybe they rode off huntin' game."

They probably trailed horses behind the wagons for that very purpose.

He turned the dun off the trail of the two shod horses and rode back over to where the Pinkertons waited impatiently with Nate, whose stocky pony was nibbling the green grass growing thickly along the rocky, two-track wagon trail carved by many drays pulled by mules on woodcutting expeditions. Usually, the woodcutters would haul the long chunks of wood—the stems of pines, firs, and aspens—and sell them in surrounding villages like Lead, Tigerville, Hot Springs, and Deadwood.

They'd sell the uncut logs for one price, then ask a little more if the buyer wanted the sawyers to stay and cut the logs up into stove-sized chunks. They'd ask a little more if, say, the buyer wanted the wood all split and neatly stacked. Of course, they'd finagle a meal or two thrown in for free . . .

maybe even a place to throw down for the night in a barn or stable.

That's how it worked. Great American capitalism at work. Albeit Yankee capitalism . . .

"They must've left to hunt," Angus said, retaking his place at the head of the pack. "They're headed back to town so they likely figure they can sell some game, too. They're business jacks, these fellas!"

He chuckled, then booted the dun ahead along the two-track trail rising gently toward the saddle maybe a hundred yards beyond.

"You're too damn curious, Buchanon," Leech Davis castigated behind Angus and Nate. "We got a job to do. How many times do I have to tell you that?"

"What's the hurry?" Angus said, hipping around in his saddle to scowl incredulously at the long-haired Pinkerton, whose face had turned a deep red from the sun and wind. He had a haggard look, likely from sleeping on the ground and riding too long in the saddle despite his desire for haste. There was even a sort of inexplicable desperation in the Pinkerton's eyes. "Like I done told you, this is the only way to or from Ghost Mountain. If them three decide to come back down from their hideout, they'll run smack into us!"

"Just the same!" Davis said in disgust.

"You never know what Avery's gonna pull." That was the first complete sentence Angus had heard Dutch McCrae utter all day. He'd almost said it too quietly for Angus to hear, but he'd heard it, all right.

Damn puzzling, these three . . .

"Whoah, whoah, whoah . . ." Angus said when they'd crossed the saddle and were riding through a grassy valley with scattered pines and aspens.

The trail forked ahead, the main one climbing up the distant ridge straight ahead, the left tine taking the ridge at a westward angle, off the main trail's left side, through heavy pine forest.

"Christ almighty, Buchanon!" intoned Jackson behind him.

"Horse," Nate said, pointing at the saddled mount Angus had spied standing at the edge of the forest sixty yards away on his left. The horse stood peering toward Angus and his trail mates, reins hanging. His saddle hung down his left side. It appeared to be nearly falling off the stocky sorrel.

"Wait here, Nate!" Angus said and booted the dun into a gallop.

As he and the dun approached the sorrel, the sorrel shied, trying to pull away, but Angus saw that its reins were not on the ground but twisted around a small pine. Wrapped tightly. Not by a man but by happenstance, most likely. The horse had been galloping past the tree when the reins had become entangled with the sapling, wrapped tightly around the main stem.

"Easy, boy. Easy fella," Angus said, stepping slowly down from the dun's back. "No one's gonna hurt . . ."

He let his voice trail off when he saw the bloody gashes raked into the horse's hide over its left hip. The gelding was sweat lathered and blowing hard, eyes wide and white ringed. "Shhh, shhh, shhh," Angus said, holding the sorrel's reins tightly in his fist and stepping back to inspect the horse's hind end. The gashes were long and deep, the blood glistening redly against the sorrel's dark hide. They could have been made by four razor-edged Bowie knives raked simultaneously across the horse's hip.

But no Bowie knives had made those cuts.

The only thing that could have made those cuts was the long, razor-edged claws of a grizzly. Possibly a wildcat but most likely a grizzly. A year ago, Angus had gotten way too familiar with the havoc a grizzly could make not only on stock flesh but on man flesh, as well.

He gave an involuntary shudder at the savage, atavistic terror connoted by those wounds.

"Oh, boy," he said under his breath, those grisly wounds holding his gaze. "Oh . . . boy . . ."

He released the horse's reins, reached under the mount's belly, and freed the latigo with one jerk of his lone hand, which had become more powerful than the rest of his old self with the need to compensate for the one lost to a Yankee's minié ball. The saddle dropped to the ground. There was no bedroll or saddlebags. The hunters had intended to head back to the wagons for the night. With one sweep of his lone hand, Angus slid the bridle off the sorrel's snout. Suddenly free, the horse whinnied shrilly, swung around, and galloped off into the forest beyond Angus, quickly absorbed by the forest's deep, early afternoon shadows.

Angus scrutinized the ground around the sapling closely. He easily picked up the sorrel's backtrail in the thick, soft, mustily fragrant forest duff. Climbing back onto the dun's back, he backtracked the trail along the edge of the woods and then where it angled into the forest and up to the top of the pass and down the other side. The smell of wood smoke touched his nostrils, growing in intensity as he bottomed out in the valley at the bottom of the pass.

In more woods beyond, fifty yards away, he saw a tendril of gray smoke rising through pine boughs.

He stopped, again sniffed the air.

He frowned.

Another aroma now mixed with the smell of the woodsmoke.

He didn't like this smell at all. It was a sweet, wild smell laced with the metallic stench of—what?

He booted the dun ahead. He had to give it several kicks to get it moving. It shied, snorted, not liking the smell issuing from ahead any more than Angus did.

Haltingly, the dun lurched into a trot.

Horse and rider angled across the brushy meadow into the woods. Almost immediately, Angus checked the gelding down to a stop. The dun stood breathing heavily, its ribs expanding and contracting beneath Angus, who stared into the woods at the fire ring roughly twenty feet away from which the tendril of gray smoke rose from a pile of pale ashes. A small coffeepot lay in the fire, near a flat rock from which it must have been knocked.

Angus now realized what that third smell was.

Blood. Fresh blood. The badly scuffed forest floor beyond the fire ring was splashed with the stuff. Blood-soaked clothing and pieces of men were strewn beyond it, as well.

Hoof thuds sounded behind Angus. He was slow to register them, for his attention was riveted on the carnage before him.

He'd seen such carnage once before. The previous summer on Box Bar B Range, when the rogue grizzly had decided to prey on Box Bar B cattle and then on the men who'd gone out to kill it, nearly killing Hunter, as well. A cold sweat broke out over Angus now, basting his shirt against his back. Several beads of it, like ice water, ran down from his temples to moisten his thick, gray beard.

"No," he muttered. "No, no, no . . . not again."

"What's going on, Buchanon?" came Bryce Jackson's voice behind him as the two sets of hoof thuds grew louder.

"Best stop where you are," Angus said, staring straight ahead. "Unless you wanna see somethin' a might unholy. Might interrupt your sleep tonight. I know it's gonna mine."

Jackson stopped off the dun's left hip. "What is—?"

Leech Davis reined up just off Angus's right stirrup. "What in holy . . . *blazes*?"

"Griz." Angus brushed his fist across his nose. He looked around warily. "And he ain't far away, neither."

"Good God," Jackson said. "How many . . . how many . . . ?"

"Four men. Hard to tell the way they'd all been torn apart, half-eaten. But there were four sets of tracks. He . . . the griz . . . got all four, all right. They must've been hunting and stopped for coffee. That's when he hit 'em." He motioned to what appeared a horse . . . or part of a horse . . . lying a good way beyond the fire ring. "He got one of the horses, too. At least one. No tellin' where the others are."

"Let's get the hell out of here," Jackson said.

Angus turned to him pointedly. "Where's the boy? Where's Nathan?"

"Back on the trail with Dutch."

A rifle barked from back in the direction from which Angus had come.

"Christ!" Angus reined the dun around sharply and booted him into an instant, lunging run.

CHAPTER 18

A few minutes earlier, Dutch McCrae said, "What the hell was that?"

Nathan had heard it, too—a thrashing in the mixed aspens, junipers, and cedars near the top of the pass and along the right side of the main trail. Along with the thrashing came guttural snorting sounds.

"Judgin' by the sounds," Nathan said, "I'd say it's a bear." He heard the tremor in his own voice as he stared into that moving foliage near the top of the ridge. "Prob'ly the same one we seen the other day."

"Well, I'll be jiggered," McCrae said. "Maybe it's time to put an end to this foolishness."

"Oh, it ain't no foolishness. We had bear trouble at the Box Bar B last summer. I seen an' heard it my ownself, an'. . . believe me, it ain't nothing to trifle abou—"

He stopped himself when Dutch put the spurs to his mount and sent him rocketing up the trail, sliding his Winchester repeater from his saddle boot.

"No, no, no," Nathan said, booting his own mount haltingly ahead. "You don't wanna do that!"

Near the top of the pass, Dutch swung his horse off the trail's right side and into the brush, aiming his Winchester straight out from his right shoulder and firing. "Hy-yahhh, you four-legged vermin. Get the hell outta here. I got me a rifle—what you got to say about that?"

He laughed as he continued firing.

He disappeared into the brush and then the shooting stopped.

Silence issued from the foliage.

Then Nate saw Dutch ride up out of the brush, heading toward the top of the pass, plucking cartridges from his shell belt and thumbing them through his Winchester's loading gate.

"Hold on!" Nate called.

Dutch glanced over his shoulder at Nathan and yelled, "Stay there, boy. This is a man's work!"

He rode up and over the pass and disappeared from Nate's sight.

"Oh, hell!"

Nate put the spurs to his steeldust, and the gelding lunged into a hard run up the trail. Halfway to the pass, Nate slid his Winchester carbine from its saddle scabbard and racked a round into the action one-handed, the way he'd seen Hunter do more than a few times. He almost lost the rifle in the process and had to grab it with both hands, but he'd amazed himself there for a minute.

Beneath his bravado was the fear that was making his heart race.

"Hold on, Dutch!" he shouted at the tops of his lungs, angling off the trail and over to where Dutch had climbed to the top of the pass. "You don't know bears. They're nothin' to trifle with less'n you got one hell of big-caliber—"

On the other side of the pass, a rifle spoke once, twice, three times.

Dutch whooped.

His horse gave a shrill whinny. Judging by the sound, they were quite a way down the pass, at least sixty, seventy yards beyond.

Nate halted the steeldust atop the pass. His heart was really banging away against his breastbone now. Fear and revulsion made him want to stay where he was, but a dark curiosity made him boot the stocky gelding slowly down the backside of the ridge, weaving through white-stemmed aspens.

"D-Dutch," he said, probably only loudly enough for himself to hear.

Straight down the slope from him, a horse whinnied shrilly.

Nate jerked and gasped with a start, his blood turning cold. He stared straight down the pass, holding his breath.

Again, the horse whinnied—a bone-splintering, screaming whinny that seemed to express all the horror in the universe.

Dutch wailed.

A violent thrashing came from the forest maybe a sixty yards down the pass. Then suddenly Dutch yelled, "HELP!" and the man appeared, running up through the trees, weaving around them, limping on a bad ankle. His face above his bushy red beard was a red mask of bloated horror.

Something moved beyond the man.

Fast.

It was big, too.

It was the consarned bear. It was running up the slope, weaving through the pines and aspens, hot on Dutch's heels, groaning with each lunging run, fur rippling across its rippling muscles.

"Oh, GOD!" exploded Nate, whose steeldust pitched, tossing him from the saddle and galloping back in the direction from which they'd come.

The forest floor made for a relatively soft landing. At least, Nate didn't notice much pain. His mind was focused on the raging bruin galloping up the slope faster than any horse, closing quickly on Dutch who was only about two hundred feet from Nathan now.

Nathan picked up his rifle, dusted it off quickly, and levered a round into the action. He dropped to a knee. He was shaking so bad he was sure he'd never be able to plant a bead on the bruin that was so close now that Nate could feel the reverberations of the raging beast's heavy, running paws in the ground beneath him. Nate shouldered the rifle. He aimed at the beast racing toward him and Dutch, who just now threw himself back behind Nate now, and rolled, wailing his horror at his imminent demise.

Nate aimed at the bear. Or tried to. His hands were shaking. He tried to draw his right index finger back against the trigger, but it was as though that finger had turned to stone. He couldn't move it.

Which meant he was dead.

He closed his eyes, let the rifle droop in his hands.

A gun blasted so close to Nate that he wondered for a second if he hadn't snapped a shot off with the Winchester, after all. Maybe he was just in too much shock to realize it.

He opened his eyes and saw Angus on one knee beside him, aiming his big Sharps with his lone right hand. Firing, then working the heavy trigger guard cocking mechanism, aiming quickly, and firing again.

Nate saw the heavy bullets slam into the big bruin's shoulders, parting the hair and making dust billow. It gave an enormous roar of unbridled fury, then stopped and rose up on its hind feet. It was so close it looked like a mountain to Nathan. Its peppery sweet stench made Nate's eyes water.

Angus cursed as he pumped two more heavy rounds into the beast's thick hide. It waved its heavy paws in even more fury, razor-like claws extended. Then it dropped back down to all fours, gave its head a quick wag, flicking its ears, then turned around and lumbered back in the direction from

which it had come, breaking into a run when Angus drilled
another round into its ass.

"N-never seen nothin' so damn big in my life!"

Dutch tipped back the flat, brown bottle he'd produced
from his saddlebags. He must have had more than one bottle
in there, for he'd had several liberal tipples every night
they'd been on the trail, before he'd rolled up in his soogan.
"I mean, that was not no ordinary bear. I mean, when it
poked its head out of those shrubs, I swear that head was the
size of a *rain barrel*! And eyes as dark as . . . *Christ!*. . . eyes
as dark as a damn eight ball and just as *big*!"

He took another deep pull from the bottle.

Angus was refilling his coffee cup. As he did, he looked
over at where Dutch sat against his saddle. Sweat beads
glinting in the firelight rolled down into his beard, soaking
it. He had a wild, crazed look in his eyes.

"Better have some coffee to go with that whiskey,"
Angus suggested.

"I'll never forget that look in its eyes when it came after
me. After it took down my horse. I don't know how I got
away. Have no memory of anything except that look in its
eyes when it saw me scramble to my feet and start running
up that hill. It waited. I swear, it waited . . . like it wanted to
give me a chance. Then it roared and came after me, and I
could feel the ground shake beneath my boots as it closed
on me."

Angus fished a second coffee cup out of his saddlebags.
He used a leather swatch to remove the steaming pot from
the tripod over the fire, filled the cup three-quarters. While
Dutch continued reliving the bear attack in his mind, Angus
walked over to where Nathan sat against his own saddle,
blankets drawn up to his chin. He'd said little since the
attack. Now he sat staring into the dancing flames.

"Here, boy," Angus said, setting the cup down beside the boy. "Have you a cup of that. Make you feel better. Lift your spirits."

Nathan only gave a slight nod and continued staring into the fire.

"Nice," Ten Jackson interjected into Dutch's monologue. "Now we're out a horse and until we can find another one, I reckon you'll be riding double with me or Leech."

Angus got himself settled back against his own saddle, beside Nathan. He cast an incredulous look across the fire at the bright-eyed, sweating Dutch, who just then took another pull from the bottle. "What on earth made you think you could tangle with a *bear*?"

He was more than a little piss-burned at the Pinkerton. He'd damn near got Nathan killed. There was no way Nate would have pulled a stunt like that alone—riding after a grizzly. He'd gone after the bear because he'd had it in his head that he might be able to help Dutch. That was just the way the boy was. Angus would have a talk with him about that. Some men were just too stupid to save from themselves, and Dutch was one of those—Pinkerton or not.

"Hell, I don't know." Dutch brushed sweat from his brow with a sleeve of his coat. "Just had me a wild hair, I reckon. Never seen one before. Sure as hell never tangled with one before!" He chuckled, took another pull from the bottle.

"That's enough, Dutch," Jackson said. "You won't be fit to ride tomorrow."

"Hell, I'd like to stay right here." Again, Dutch laughed his nervous, almost lunatic laugh. "I'd like to stay right here, throw in with you fellas on your way back out of the mountains. After you've run down Baxter an' Thayer and little Miss Frannie from San Francisco an' the strongbox!"

Another pull from the bottle. Only, it was empty, so with an angry grunt he tossed it into the dark woods beyond the fire. That startled the horses where they were tied to a picket line thirty feet from the fire. They whickered and pulled at their halter ropes.

"Dutch!" Leech Davis scolded. "Get control of yourself, you damn fool. The bruin didn't get you. You aren't dead. But if you keep on . . . !" He leaned forward angrily and closed his hand around the six-shooter holstered on his hip.

"Easy, Leech, easy," Jackson admonished, gently, holding his own smoking coffee cup in both hands, eyeing the two men warily.

Davis turned to him. "Who's he riding with tomorrow?"

"Both of us, I reckon."

"He should ride with the boy," Davis insisted. "The boy's light."

Angus said, "He's not riding with the boy. He's yours. He'll ride with you, takin' turns, 'till we can find him another horse."

Davis turned his angry eyes on him. "I'm gettin' tired of you playin' cock o' the walk, you one-armed old scudder!"

Angus slid his Spencer across his lap, the barrel aimed generally but not overtly threateningly at Leech Davis. "Get your hand off your pistol." His tone was low, quiet, grave. All his previous humor was gone from it.

Davis looked at the Spencer resting across Angus's lap.

He lifted his gaze to Angus's eyes. His own eyes were dark and flat save for the firelight dancing in them. The light did not reach back very far. He was filled with darkness and anger. He hardened his jaws, flared a nostril.

"Leech," Jackson said. "Take your hand off your pistol!"

Keeping his eyes on Angus, Davis said, "I'm tired of this one-armed old grayback runnin' things."

There was a ratcheting click and Angus shuttled his gaze over to where Jackson aimed his Smith & Wesson at Davis, his arm fully extended, all business in his eyes. "Get your hand off your pistol, Leech!"

Davis looked at him. He looked at the big Smithy in

Jackson's hand. He nodded slowly, grimly, fatefully. "All right, all right." He held up a hand to Jackson, palm out. "There it is. You happy?"

"No more of this crap—you understand?"

Again, Davis nodded slowly. "Sure, sure." He picked up his cup and sipped his coffee, planting his own brooding gaze on the fire.

Meanwhile, the whiskey had finally put Dutch to sleep. He sat against his saddle, head sagging toward his chest, snoring quietly and muttering restively.

Angus turned to Nathan. He'd kept his gaze on the fire even during the verbal foofaraw. Angus nudged him with his elbow and said, "You all right, son?"

Nathan looked up at him. He pulled his mouth corners down and nodded.

"Scary thing, havin' a bruin like that run toward you."

Nathan returned his gaze to the fire and nodded again.

He jerked his head up with a gasp when a bugling cry of raw, savage fury rocketed down from a ridge to echo around the night-dark valley.

CHAPTER 19

Big Nick kept his hand clamped tightly over Annabelle's mouth as he finished cutting the rope tying her to the tree.

He slid his long, craggy face up to hers again, his eyes two burning, black coals of raw threat. He held the knife up to show her again, then jerked his chin up, silently ordering her to rise.

Meanwhile, the other outlaws snored in their soogans, some curled on their sides. Machado was the only one who lay flat on his back in an almost casual slumbering pose, ankles crossed, his pistol on his chest, hand around the grips even in sleep. Anna wished the outlaw leader would wake up. She suddenly found herself in the improbable position of seeing him for once as her possible knight in shining armor.

Or at least he'd save her from whatever Big Nick had in store for her.

She had a pretty good idea she knew what that was.

She pushed back against the tree to help lever her to her feet. Big Nick kept his hand clamped tightly over her mouth. The skin of that hand was hard and crusty as a clam shell; it reeked of sweat, the leather of his gloves, whiskey, and camp smoke. When she'd gained her feet, Big Nick looked cautiously around the near-dark camp—the fire had burned down to a few orange coals—then stepped around Anna and, keeping his hand on her mouth, shoved her forward and straight out into the brush, away from the camp.

Hand held fast against her mouth, Big Nick shoved her a good ways down a deer path until she could just barely see the glowing coals behind her. He gave her a shove into deep grass. He shoved her again, harder, and she stumbled forward and fell.

"One sound and I cut your throat!" His voice was raspy with menace. More animal than man.

Anna shoved up to a half-sitting position, propped on her hands. "You go to hell!" she raked out through gritted teeth. "If you think you're gonna savage me, Big Nick, you got another think coming! You'll have to kill me and ravage a corpse!"

Big Nick gave a mirthless laugh. She saw the off-white line of his teeth in the darkness. He removed his hat, tossed it away, and threw himself down on top of her.

She groaned with the force of his big body on hers.

He nuzzled her neck and pawed her, grunting, pressing himself down hard against her. Anna struggled against him, but he was so much stronger. Her fear and exasperation made her feel small . . . tiny. Insignificant. This man would do to her what he would and there was nothing she could do about it . . . until her right hand strayed to the handle of the big Bowie knife poking up from his shell belt.

As Big Nick pawed her and ground against her, Annabelle unsnapped the keeper thong from over the knife's hilt, slid it from its scabbard, wrapped her hand tightly around the ridged, horn handle, and raised it until starlight glinted off the long, wide, razor-edged blade.

"Hope you had your fun," Anna grunted. "Because it cost you big-time . . . Big Nick."

Big Nick lifted his head and stared down at her, brows ridged. His lips were wet. "Huh?"

Anna smiled at him, then gritted her teeth as she rammed the upturned end of the Bowie into the side of Big Nick's neck. His eyes widened in sudden shock. His mouth opened as though to scream and, still smiling through gritted teeth, Anna closed her left hand over his wet mouth and ground the knife deeper into his neck. He stared at her, imploringly. That made her grind the knife all the deeper into the pig's neck.

Blood geysered out around the Bowie's blade, flowed hotly over Annabelle's hand and wrist.

Big Nick lay stiff as a board on top of her, quivering, groaning into her hand. He clawed at the ground to each side of him with his hands. She knew he was trying to gain the purchase to pull away from her, but that made the moment all the more delightful. He wasn't going anywhere and deep down inside him, he knew it.

He knew he was already dead.

His expression changed from one of beseeching . . . a silent plea for mercy . . . to one of astonishment and fury.

"Told you, Nick," Anna said, holding the knife fast in his neck. "It was gonna cost you. Did you have fun? Huh? Was it worth it?"

He coughed into Annabelle's hand. His head bobbed, shook, his lids closed down over his eyes several times, haltingly, before they stayed shut. His death spasms died with the rest of him and then Anna pulled the knife out of his neck and kicked him off her, struggling out from under the big man's dead carcass as she did. She tossed the knife into the brush.

The stream they'd camped along was close by. She strode over, stumbling with exhaustion. She dropped to her knees and washed the blood from her hand and wrist. She bathed her face, drank, rose, and returned to Big Nick's dead body. He lay on his back, his death grimace in place as he stared up at her through half-open eyes.

She glanced toward the camp. No movement there.

Machado had sent two men out on guard duty. Big Nick and one of the others. The other man must be holding his position on the other side of the camp.

Good.

Anna crouched to pull Big Nick's six-shooter from its holster. She'd lost the drover's gun in the river. Well, she had another one now. She shoved it down snug inside her belt, glanced once more at the camp, then began walking downstream. She had no idea where she was or where she was going, but something might come to her as she walked. All she wanted was to put as much distance between her and Machado's camp as she could.

She'd walked maybe a couple of hundred yards before she realized her feet were getting heavy. Very heavy. Stonelike heavy. She was exhausted. She pushed on, weaving through the willows and aspens lining the creek. A thumbnail moon had risen without her realizing it until she found herself staring at what appeared to be small buildings on a rise on the other side of the creek. The sliver of moon didn't give much light, but it gave enough to tell her that what she was looking at was no collection of widely scattered boulders but man-made structures of some kind. They were too perfectly formed of square angles to be natural rock.

Annabelle crossed the stream, which was only about a foot deep at its deepest.

She was so exhausted she didn't even feel the water soaking her boots and the cuffs of her denims. There was no bank to speak of, so she merely stepped out of the water and onto the opposite shore. She moved toward the unnaturally shaped objects, limned slightly by milky moonlight, and soon found herself at a low, adobe brick wall against which tumbleweeds had piled themselves high. There were several breaks in the wall including, a few feet away on her right, a large one where a bottom corner of a wooden gate angled into the dirt.

A rusted steel hinge had broken away from the gatepost. The gate was splintery, moldering, as was the rest of this place, she could tell, even without being able to scrutinize it very carefully in the darkness relieved by only the thumbnail moon and the stars. Some sort of old military outpost, she assumed, that had fallen on bad times. She saw several splintering arrows in the sand and gravel around her boots. A spear was lodged in a wooden casing of a glassless window of the first, square, adobe brick building she came to.

The dwellings—some long and L-shaped and that had likely been barracks—were spaced at regular intervals. As she moved to the far end of the old outpost, she spied a large flat area that likely served as a parade ground. A tall cedar post was all that remained of a flagpole. Beyond, the country looked pale and lumpy even in the darkness, like a city of domed buildings. She walked across the parade ground and across a small cemetery with maybe twenty or so graves in it, all marked by tilted wooden crosses, to find herself standing at what could only be the Dakota Badlands.

That devil's maze of upturned, eroded, chalky, red earth spread out before her, a vast, forbidding, wild country of sandstone cathedrals and ancient riverbeds she'd only seen photos of until now. She took a deep breath of the breeze blowing up out of it. It smelled like sand and stone, possibly touched by the late-summer gaminess of a distant spring. It smelled like the wildest country she'd ever known. The vastness of it frightened her the way the vastness of the night sky once frightened her as a child.

She stood on the lip of it, overlooking that deep, dinosaur's mouth of a canyon, and felt as though a firm hand were pushing her forward, threatening to send her plunging into all that wildness, never to be seen or heard from again.

She spread her arms and sent herself stumbling backward.

She dropped to her knees and suddenly found herself bawling. She lowered her head to the sandy ground and let the emotion pour out of her, crossing her arms on her belly and just letting it flow, purging herself of all the raw emotion that had been for a long time licking up and threatening to spill over the top and down the sides of her being.

You can't give up, she told herself. *You owe it to yourself, to Hunter, to Angus, and to Nate.*

Don't give up.

It's not only you in trouble here. It's your whole family.

She was so exhausted, however, she didn't think she could go on. She wasn't even sure, after she'd vented the last of her sorrow and terror, that she could even stand. She gritted her teeth and pushed off the ground with her hands, heaved herself to her feet. When he found her this time, he'd kill her. Of course, he'd find her again. She didn't have the strength to run. She stumbled back across the cemetery and the parade ground, entered the first hollow shell of a hovel she came to, sat down against the wall opposite the doorless doorway, and fell asleep.

Fast asleep, she didn't hear the angry shouts coming from a couple of hundred yards upstream from her.

A beam of sunshine angling through a near window felt like a brand laid against Annabelle's right cheek. It was in sharp contrast to the morning chill that made her shiver.

She felt that hot beam for a long time before it finally woke her.

She lifted her head from her knees around which she'd wrapped her arms.

She glanced to her left and a shrill scream erupted from deep in her lungs. She'd spent the night with a skeleton half-clad in tattered cavalry gear including a saber around whose gold handle the skeleton's skeletal hand was wrapped. Enough of the man's uniform and dark red longhandles remained that she could see the yellow stripe running down a tattered patch of dark-blue uniform pants clinging to a short stretch of bony thigh. A leather-billed cavalry kepi remained on the bony head, most of the flesh and the eyes weathered away or likely pecked away by birds. The man's stovepipe black boots remained on the skeleton's feet.

A wooden saber with faded ochre and yellow designs painted on it protruded from the man's skeletal belly, the stone tip lodged deep inside the sun-bleached rib cage.

The soldier was dusty and sooty, and cobwebs filled his mouth and nose, as though the entire head had become the home of web-spinning spiders. Just then a black widow emerged from the man's mouth, picking its way through the long, crooked, yellow teeth. Annabelle slapped a hand to her mouth to quash another scream.

But the damage had been done.

When she turned her head forward, she gasped yet again. She stared out the glassless window right of the doorless doorway . . . and into the eyes of none other than Saguaro Machado himself, sitting his horse about ten feet from what had probably been a small office building, staring through the window at her with his one, flat, dung-brown eye, his single, gray-brown braid hanging down his back. The morning breeze played with the strings running down the sleeves of his buckskin tunic.

Another sob exploded from between Annabelle's lips.

Fear and anger were awash inside her.

Heart quickening, she pulled Big Nick's revolver from behind her belt, extended it straight out before her in both hands, and ratcheted back the hammer. She aimed down the barrel, her vision made watery and uncertain because of the tears filling them. Her hands shook, making the revolver shake violently. She wanted desperately to pull the trigger, but something kept her from doing so. She couldn't pull her finger back against the trigger.

Machado gave a disgusted chuff. He swung down from the saddle and walked through the empty doorway. He glanced at the skeleton and then strode over to Annabelle. Annabelle kept the cocked pistol aimed at him, sobbing, shaking, unable to squeeze the trigger.

Machado held out his gloved hand, palm out.

His lone eye blazed at Annabelle. He said nothing, just held out his hand for the gun.

Sobbing against her weakness, Annabelle depressed the hammer and, her hands still shaking, set the pistol in the man's hand. He shoved it down behind his cartridge belt, then held out his hand again. Annabelle stared up at him, terrified, befuddled.

She placed her shaking hand in his. He pulled her to her feet . . . almost gently, which astonished her.

He led her out of the little shell of a building and over to his horse.

He helped her up onto the horse's back, then swung up in front of her, gave the mount the spurs, and galloped off in search of the rest of his gang that must have separated to look for her.

CHAPTER 20

"Well, I'll be hanged," said Powwow Billy. "That's part of a boat, ain't it?"

The day after Hunter had learned from Henrietta about Annabelle's fate at the River Bend Station, Hunter had stared down in horror at the prow of a wooden boat and one wood bench seat that had snagged against a cottonwood whose roots some wind had pulled up out of the ground, knocking the tree out over the river, its still-green leaves glinting in the midmorning breeze.

The rest of the boat lay in pieces scattered across sandy shallows on the other side of the Cheyenne River, which ran slowly here, a couple of hundred yards beyond the falls.

Bobby Lee was sniffing the wreckage on this side of the river and mewling.

"That is a boat," Hunter said, tonelessly. He poked his hat up to scratch the back of his head, darkly pensive. "Don't look good. Not good at all."

Bobby Lee stopped sniffing and looked up at him, tail curled up over his back.

"We'll find her, boy. Don't worry." Hunter did not add aloud what he added silently to himself. *If she's alive, we'll find her.*

"I got some tracks over here."

Powwow was riding his horse slowly beyond the fringe of willows lining the stream. As he rode, he leaned far out from his saddle, scrutinizing the ground. "Some apples, too." Powwow stopped and stepped down from his saddle.

Hunter rode Nasty Pete through the willows and stopped where Powwow was crumbling a horse apple between his fingers and sniffing. He dropped the crushed manure and looked up at Hunter. "Two-, three-days old, I'd say. Hard to tell for sure because of the humidity along the river."

Hunter winced. If the manure was two- or three-day's old, he and Powwow still had some riding to do before they'd catch up to Machado. Frustration was a hot tidal wave rolling through him. His damnable ribs had slowed him down, that extra night they'd taken at Cynthia McGovern's ranch. A needless dalliance. He should have pushed on, pushed through the pain, just kept abating it with hooch.

Bobby Lee sniffed the tracks, tipped his head back with a mournful howl, looked at Hunter, and wagged his tail, giving his entire gray-brown body a quick shake.

"She with 'em, Bob?" Hunter said, hope rising in him. "Is she ridin' with 'em, Bob?"

Bobby Lee gave a yip in the affirmative and, nose to the ground, began running downstream along the tree- and shrub-lined river.

"Let's go," Hunter said, and booted Pete along the game path Bobby Lee was following, stopping often to sniff the ground.

They followed the trail for several hours. Machado's bunch had ridden along the river for several miles. Then, when thick woods and high bluffs closed down along the river, Hunter had picked out the tracks of seven shod horses angled out away from the river and into open prairie— Machado and his men and, hopefully, Annabelle. They camped that night well after dark, Hunter reluctant to give up the trail despite the danger of night travel to the horses, then headed out early again the next morning.

They pushed hard, Bobby Lee leading the way.

In the early afternoon, Hunter checked Pete down to a stop and curveted the mount, gazing straight ahead toward a fringe of cottonwoods lining what appeared to be a wide, narrow stream cutting through the vast prairie in this southwestern corner of Dakota Territory.

"You see somethin'?" Powwow said, reining up beside Hunter.

Hunter gestured with his chin.

Bobby Lee had seen it, too. Or *them*. He sat down roughly twenty feet beyond Hunter and Powwow, staring straight ahead toward the fringe of cottonwoods. Or rather at the turkey buzzards swarming in the brush beyond them, some turning slow circles twenty feet in the air, others skirmishing along the ground, squawking and barking like dogs fighting over a particularly tasty cache of meat.

Terror was a hot saber rammed through Hunter's heart.

Buzzards meant death.

"Let's take a look," he said, trying to keep his tone even, himself calm while at the same time stealing himself against what he'd find in the brush on the other side of the cottonwoods.

She'd escaped once. Had she tried to escape again and pushed Machado too far?

According to Henrietta, the harlot at River Bend, the vermin outlaw leader intended to sell Anna to a Missouri River slaver named Corazon. A beautiful redhead, Annabelle was a special catch for Machado, who supplied slaves to an even bigger slaver in Corazon. Redheads were rare and big money-makers. From what Henrietta had overheard in River Bend's main drinking hall, Annabelle was all the more desirable because she was married to the famous—

Yankees would say *in*famous—ex-rebel freedom fighter, Hunter Buchanon.

A beguilingly dangerous prize, indeed.

Thinking of Annabelle being in the hands of slavers was as raw as the prospect of what Hunter would find in the brush beyond the cottonwoods.

He and Powwow galloped after Bobby Lee down the sight rise and, passing a fire ring in which several bottles and airtight tins lay in a small pile of gray ashes, through the cottonwoods and willows. They swung right, downstream, and followed Bobby Lee over to where a good dozen buzzards were squawking and barking as they skirmished over whatever lay in the tall brown brome grass.

Bobby Lee rushed the birds, barking furiously, until they'd all taken flight and, still barking and squawking defiantly, flew up into the trees and lit on branches to glare down at the interlopers, squawking and mewling and barking their disdain for the intrusion on their meal.

Hunter and Powwow swung down from their saddles, dropped the reins of the uneasily whickering horses. They didn't like the sickly sweet smell of death any better than Hunter did. He raised his neckerchief to his nose and mouth. Still, his eyes watered as he stood gazing down at the hideous remains of a dead man—a man in buckskins and with a thick tumbleweed of coarse, gray-brown hair. His eyes were gone and his face had nearly been pecked away by the buzzards. He was bloating up and turning purple, splitting his buckskins at the seams, which meant he'd been dead at least a couple of days.

Hunter leaned down, pressing the neckerchief tighter to his mouth and nose, and canted his head to scrutinize the deep, wide gash in the side of the man's neck.

"Anna." Hunter gave a dry chuckle. "She's still alive. Hah! At least two days ago. Givin' 'em their just desserts!" His heart feeling lighter and more buoyant than it had been only a few minutes ago, he turned and grabbed Nasty Pete's reins. "Come on, boy. Let's get after 'em. Anna's doin' her part in gettin' shed of those snakes. It's high time I do my part!"

He and Powwow mounted up and galloped along behind Bobby Lee, who was hot on the kidnappers' trail. They rode hard for the next hour, crossing an old military outpost showing the tracks of one horse, which soon joined the rest of the gang and continued to the northeast, around the deep canyons of the Dakota Badlands.

Later that afternoon, Hunter, Powwow, and Bobby Lee topped a low rise, and Bobby Lee stopped dead in his tracks and turned to peer off to the right, the southeast. He lifted his long, pointed snout and sniffed the air with leathery black nostrils, half-closing his eyes, concentrating his energy into his sniffer.

Hunter checked Nasty Pete down, and Powwow reined up just behind him.

"What is it, Bobby?"

The coyote gave a soft yip and a mewl and then Hunter saw what the coyote had detected with his nose.

Five riders were just then riding to the top of a low rise roughly a hundred yards away. They were climbing the rise's opposite side, their hatted heads showing first and then the heads of their horses and then, finally, the rest of both the men and the horses as the five riders drew rein at the top of the rise. They sat their mounts spaced about seven feet apart; they just sat there, all five staring toward Hunter, Powwow, and Bobby Lee.

It was hard to tell much about them from this distance.

They were all dressed dissimilarly though they were all similarly armed. Even from this distance, Hunter could see holstered pistols bristling on their hips or thighs, rifles jutting from saddle scabbards. Two had cartridge bandoliers crisscrossed on their chests. One wore a steeple-crowned sombrero and a what appeared to be a white cotton tunic, marking him a Mex. One wore a bowler hat. The others, including one Indian wearing a calico shirt and buckskin breeches, wore weathered Stetsons.

"Who do you suppose they are?" Powwow said, thumbing his battered Stetson up on his forehead.

"Parasites," Hunter said, knowing instinctively it was true. "Common road agents, outlaws. Rustlers, maybe. Train or stagecoach robbers on the run."

"Don't like the way they're givin' us the woolly eyeball."

"You can't see their eyeballs."

"No? Well, I got a good imagination. They're trouble or I've missed my guess."

"Got me a feelin' you're right on both counts. They're givin' us the woolly eyeball, all right. Might think we're law."

"Well, then they just got guilty consciences an' oughta see the error of their ways an' change 'em!"

Hunter chuckled without mirth. "Why don't you ride over an' explain it to 'em, preacher?"

Powwow gazed up the rise at the five renegade riders. "Yeah . . . maybe not."

Bobby, sitting ten feet ahead of Hunter, lifted his snout to give a brief howl. He didn't like how those strangers looked any more than Hunter did. Even the coyote recognized the "lead swap" look.

Hunter booted Nasty Pete ahead. "Let's just keep ridin', see what they do."

As he and Powwow continued following Bobby Lee to the northeast, Hunter glanced back. The five riders held their positions atop the rise.

Good. Maybe the five renegades—he had little doubt they were renegades, all right—were just curious and wanted a look-see at the two pilgrims and the coyote they were following. Bobby Lee always drew interest. And if he and Hunter weren't careful, he'd also draw lead.

Hunter, Powwow, and Bobby Lee rode another few yards,

and Hunter cast a glance over his right shoulder. His heart sank. The five riders were just then starting down from the crest of the rise, spurring their mounts into hard gallops, angling toward Hunter and his two unlikely trail pards.

"Ah, hell!"

"What is it?"

"Those sharks smell blood. Let's ride, look for cover! Hightail it, Bobby, or we're gonna be dancin' to those fellas six-gun serenades!"

The words had no sooner left Hunter's lips and he'd booted Pete into a gallop than the guns began barking behind him. He could tell they were not six-guns, however, but rifles—likely various calibers of Winchesters and at least one Henry rimfire .44. Whooping and hollering followed. The renegades sounded like Indians on the warpath who'd just spied a succulent stagecoach sporting a strongbox filled with white eyes gold.

Which is exactly what they wanted to sound like to inflict fear on their intended victims. Hunter had little doubt that they assumed he and Powwow were either lawmen or bounty hunters, and they intended to scour the range of them and steal their horses. Renegades like the one galloping and shooting behind him now enjoyed the sport of hunting and killing. They were human buzzards, combing the Dakota prairie for something to eat . . . or steal. Or just for the mere satisfaction of killing and stealing and then heading for the nearest town and inflicting fear there on the citizens and law, as well.

As bullets plumed dirt and tore up sage branches just behind him, Powwow, and the full-out running Bobby Lee, Hunter glanced behind him again. The renegades were on fast horses, likely fresher than Hunter's and Powwow's. They were steadily closing the gap between them and their prey.

Ahead and left lay a steep, chalky ridge. Another one rose on the right, forming two long bastions of chalky, eroded soil on which pockets of buckbrush and cedars grew. As Hunter and his cohorts rode between these two escarpments, Hunter spied what appeared a notch cave atop the steep apron slope rising to the base of the greater formation on the left.

"Up there—a cave!" he shouted, pointing. "We'll cover there!"

"The high ground—right behind ya, Hunter!" returned Powwow.

"This way, Bobby!" Hunter yelled as he angled Nasty Pete to the left.

The part of the ridge the cave was in was deeply recessed from the rest of it. The slope leading up to the cave was steep but not so steep that two good horses couldn't take it at a fast clip and at an angle, weaving around several small boulders that had likely tumbled from the ridgecrest. The boulders offered cover, and several bullets plowed into them as Hunter, Powwow, and Bobby Lee traced a meandering course through them toward the notch cave in the ridge wall.

Bobby made the cave first and stopped and turned back to watch Hunter and Powwow approach on their blowing, sweat-lathered horses. Both men leaped from the horses while they were still moving, sliding their rifles from their saddle boots, then slapping both mounts off into the boulders at the far shoulder of the slope and out of the line of fire.

Hunter scrambled into the cave, whose ceiling was only about six-feet high. He doffed his hat, dropped to his hands and knees and, jacking a live cartridge into the Henry's action, lay belly down, and aimed down the slope, toward where two riders were pulling away from the others as they galloped up the slope, triggering rifles, some with their reins in their teeth.

One of the two riders breaking ahead of the pack was a black man in buckskins and tan Stetson; the other appeared a half-breed with wildly flying hair behind a red bandanna tied around his forehead. The black man got a shot off before Hunter did. Hunter's aim was better. His bullet took the black man high in the chest, knocking him ass over teakettle over his mount's arched tail. The black man's bullet hadn't entirely missed, however; it had carved a nasty burn across Hunter's left cheek before plunking into the cave wall behind him and evoking a frightened mewl from Bobby Lee, who'd taken refuge against the cave's rear wall.

Powwow fired at the half-breed once, twice, three times. His first two shots missed because the breed was crafty enough to run his paint horse in a weaving fashion. He got so close that Hunter could see the white line of his gritted teeth between his thin lips, could see the pitted, copper skin of his face and his dark-brown eyes slitted angrily.

Powwow's third shot took the breed high in his right arm just as he was about to fire the carbine in his hands from thirty feet down the slope. That made the breed reconsider. He reined his pony around sharply and hightailed it back down the slope, weaving around boulders and avoiding both Powwow's and Hunter's flying lead. The other three had gone to ground behind boulders but now as the breed galloped past them, they mounted up and hightailed it after him, bottoming out on the prairie below and galloping back in the direction from which they'd come as though their horses had tin cans tied to their tails.

The black man was on his belly, crawling toward the Spencer repeater he'd dropped when Hunter had shot him off his horse.

"Don't do it!" Hunter yelled.

To no avail.

The black man grabbed the carbine, fumbled the cocking mechanism open and closed and, gritting his teeth, frothing blood oozing from the wound in his upper chest, swung the Spencer's barrel toward Hunter and Powwow. Powwow tried to shoot him, but his rifle hammer dropped on an empty chamber. Hunter shot the man through the forehead a half-second later, the black man rolling onto his back and triggering the Spencer skyward before arching his back in a death spasm and then relaxing as his Maker came calling.

Hunter sighed, mopped sweat from his brow with his shirtsleeve. He glanced at Powwow lying belly down beside him. "You all right?"

Powwow's face acquired a troubled expression. "I, uh . . . I think so . . ."

He lowered his right hand to his right leg. When he brought it back up to look at it, there was blood on it.

"Oh, hell," Hunter said. "You're hit, kid!"

CHAPTER 21

Dutch McCrae jerked his head up from his drunken doze, his broad, bearded, sweaty face bronzed by the dancing firelight. "What was *that*?"

"Holy moly—that was loud!" said Pinkerton Leech Davis, looking around warily.

Again, came the bugling cry, echoing across the night, the echoes dwindling as they chased one another toward the star-filled sky.

"It's back," Nathan whispered dreadfully beside Angus.

Slowly, Angus reached back for his Spencer .56, pumped a cartridge into the chamber, and rested the long gun across his thighs.

Dutch turned to him. "That's him, ain't it? He's back."

"Easy," Angus said. "He won't come near the fire."

The horses whickered edgily, pulling at their picket line.

While the others stared, frozen with terror, into the murky darkness beyond the fire, a darkness alive now with an even darker specter, Angus reached forward and chunked more wood on the fire, building up the flames, glowing cinders spiraling as they rose toward the pine boughs.

Another bugling cry, even louder than before, vaulted across the night.

Beside Angus, Nathan gasped, stiffened.

"He's huntin' us," Dutch said, his dark eyes wide as 'dobe dollars, his broad, lumpy chest rising and falling sharply. "Sure as donuts an' coffee—he's huntin' us." He turned to Angus. "Ain't he?"

Angus didn't say anything. There was no point in pouring more proverbial fuel on the fire of the man's fears. Fear had brought Dutch near the edge of desperation, and you just never knew what such a man might do. Like people lost in the wilderness—sometimes they shed rationality and did the opposite of what they *should* do. Angus didn't like having to contend with the bear . . . another damn bear! . . . and Dutch, too.

"Ain't he, Jackson?" Dutch said, turning to the head Pinkerton sitting to his left. "He's huntin' us."

Jackson turned to him. "Shut up, Dutch. Keep it together."

Another screeching wail of ancient, savage fury rolled across the night, sucked straight up out of the sky as though by some unseen god. Another followed, louder than the previous one. Now Angus could hear thrashing, snapping sounds off in the darkness, straight out ahead of him, beyond the horses.

"Oh, hell," Dutch said, rolling his head around as though to loosen the muscles in his neck. "He's comin' closer. He's huntin' us, sure enough, an' don't you go tryin' to tell me this fire is gonna keep him away, Buchanon!"

One of the horses whinnied and reared, craning his neck to peer into the darkness behind him.

"Easy, easy," Angus told them, raising his voice, pushing off the ground with his hand, rising with a grunt, old knees creaking. "Nate, you stay here. I'm gonna try to settle the horses."

"Don't go far, Gramp . . . I mean, Angus."

Angus glanced at him in vague surprise at the moniker he'd clipped, obviously embarrassed by it. Nate had never called him anything but Angus before. Holding the Spencer in his lone hand, the rear stock clamped under his arm, he strode around the fire and out to where the horses were whickering and skitter-stepping, pulling at their halter ropes tied to the taut picket line strung between two large aspens. The aspen leaves made faint scratching sounds as a slight, vagrant breeze toyed with them.

Save the blows and whickers of the nervous horses and the leaves, the wheezing, crackling of the fire behind Angus, the night was eerily silent.

"Easy, fellas," he said, running his hand down the snout of Nate's steeldust. "All is well. He won't come near the fire." At least, I don't *think* he will, he silently, begrudgingly added to himself.

He could hear the bear thrashing around in the brush up a rise maybe seventy yards away, if he remembered correctly from his survey of the area before dark. The thrashing was growing gradually louder.

Another bugling wail.

The horses leaped together like puppets joined by the same string.

Behind Angus, Dutch said, *"Damn!"*

The big man gained his feet unsteadily, drunkenly, and glared at Angus, pointing angrily. "Don't you tell me this little bitty fire is gonna keep that bruin away, old man!"

Nate cast his wide-eyed, frightened gaze from Dutch to Angus, as though he wanted reassurance, too.

Angus turned to Jackson. "Keep him quiet."

Jackson turned to Dutch. "Sit down, Dutch. Sit down and keep your damn trap shut!" He reached into his saddlebags for a bottle, tossed it to the big, bearded man standing to his right. Dutch caught the bottle against his chest, looked down at it in hushed surprise. Slowly, he sank back down against his saddle.

Angus stepped out away from the horses. Judging by the continuing thrashing, snapping, and crackling sounds, the bear had moved to Angus's right. It seemed to keep moving in that direction. Angus could hear it grunting and blowing, growling deep in its chest, stopping occasionally to loose another of those bone-splintering menacing bugling cries of ancestral fury. Angus wondered what had spawned such hatred.

Had he and his trail partners intruded on territory the bruin had claimed as his own? If so, he'd claimed a broad territory. Angus and the others had ridden a good way since the first time they'd seen the beast in the brush near the top of the ridge.

Maybe it was after the horses.

Or . . . and this was even more troubling:

Had the bruin acquired a taste for human flesh?

Angus knew that some bears did. Human flesh was a delicacy that, once acquired, they could not resist.

The thought tied a knot in his guts and made his mouth go dry.

"Ah, hell, I think he's over there now!" Dutch yelled as he twisted around to peer into the darkness behind him.

Again, the horses stirred. They all stared in the same direction, the same direction in which Angus found himself staring now, as were the others around the fire. The thrashing sounds told him that the beast had circled the camp and was now to the west of it. Also, judging by the sounds, he was moving closer.

Gradually, but surely . . .

Angus moved out away from the horses, walking around the camp to the west side of it. He strode out into the darkness. He took two more steps, feeling as though he were swimming out in a dark ocean away from the safety of an anchored boat. He stopped, shouldered the Spencer, and fired into the darkness from where the thrashing was now coming.

He dropped to a knee, racked another cartridge into the Spencer's action, and fired another round, then another.

That evoked another screeching, bugling, grating roar that seemed to infect the entire night, the entire world with the sheer, spine-splintering menace of it.

Angus fired again and again until he'd fired all seven shots, the big-calibers gun's roar replacing the horrific cries of the grizzly.

Another bugling cry, more thrashing.

Only, now the thrashing sounds were dwindling. The bear was moving away, likely up the western ridge. Angus held the Spencer under his arm, listening to the fading sounds of the bruin's retreat.

They faded to silence.

The silence was heavy. Complete. All Angus could hear was the ringing in his ears from the shots he'd fired.

He used the rifle to lever himself to his feet. His legs were stiff from fear. Beneath the ringing in his ears, he could hear his knees popping. His ankles ached. He ambled back to camp. All three men and Nate stood with their rifles in their hands, gazing expectantly at Angus.

"The damn thing gone?" Jackson said.

Angus nodded. "I may have hit him—I don't know. Normally, a fifty-six would take down a bear . . . even a grizzly. But this one—" He shook his head as he entered the camp and walked over to a log against which he'd propped his saddle. "Not sure about this fella. Reminds me too much . . . too damn much . . ."

With a sigh, he sat down on the log, rested the Spencer across his thighs, withdrew the spring assembly from the butt plate, and began refilling the tube with fresh shells from his cartridge belt.

"Of last year's bear . . . Grandpa?" Nate said, haltingly, looking at Angus as though wondering how the moniker would register.

Angus smiled at him, tenderly, nodding slowly. "Yeah . . . like last year's bear."

"Well, if we can't kill it," Dutch said while the other two Pinkertons retook their own places around the fire, "what the hell we gonna do if it comes again?"

"Time we became good God-fearin' men, I reckon," said Leech Davis with a dry chuckle, sipping from his coffee cup.

"Oh, we can kill it," Angus said. "The fifty-six will kill it. I just need a heart shot. I wounded him before, an' that's likely why he's so mad. Given time, he'd bleed to death . . ."

"If he doesn't kill us first," Jackson said, staring into his own coffee cup as though looking for the answer to their travails and finding none.

"Let's just hope he wanders away an' dies," Angus said, shoving the loaded tube back into the Spencer's stock and flicking the steel locking latch home. "That's most likely what he'll do now. You fellas get some sleep. I'll keep watch." He glanced at Nate. "You, too, boy. Try to get some shut-eye."

Nate gave a stiff nod, casting his wary gaze off into the darkness where they'd last heard the bear. He sank low against his saddle and drew his blankets up to his chin, gazing skyward.

He was still uneasy, of course. As was Angus. None of them were likely to get much sleep, but he wanted the others to try. They needed to be rested for the next day's trek higher into the hills. He was as wide-awake as he'd ever been. No way he was going to get any snooze time in. He hadn't felt this uneasy since the war, when he and the other men in his platoon had sat up late without a fire, listening for Union snipers who had tried to pick them off one at a time.

It was to one such sniper Angus had lost his arm.

Before he'd passed out, he'd shot the bluebelly out of the tree where he'd hunkered like a damn, Springfield-wielding monkey and done a wicked, little rebel dance over him.

Next thing he knew, he was on a surgeon's table having his arm sawed off without benefit of anything but whiskey—raw, Smoky Mountain distilled white lightning. He couldn't drink the stuff anymore. He preferred his own malty, dark ale to which no bad memories clung.

He refilled his coffee cup from the pot sitting on a flat rock in the fire ring. He looked up at Dutch, who remained standing where he'd been standing when Angus had returned to camp—at the edge of the firelight, gazing out into the darkness, holding his Winchester in both hands across his belly.

"Dutch," Angus said. "Lay down, get some sleep. I'll keep watch."

Dutch turned to him, gave an angry chuff. "Yeah . . . right."

He tossed down his hat, leaned his rifle against a rock to the right of his saddle, then sank down into his bedroll. He picked up the bottle Jackson had tossed him, popped the cork, and took two deep swallows. Angus heard the bubble rising and falling as the man's throat moved as he drank.

Dutch sighed, returned the cork to the bottle, and turned over on his side, giving his back to Angus.

Angus turned to Nate, who lay gazing up at the stars. Angus knew he wasn't seeing the stars. He was seeing that big bruin running up the slope toward him, getting bigger and bigger before him, muscles rippling, long fur jostling in the wind. Eyes large and flat with all the savage indifference of the vast, cold universe, which cared nothing about men or beasts or anything else except feeding itself. When a beast like that comes running at you, the world quickly becomes Godless.

"Angus?"

Angus sipped his coffee and looked down at Nate lying in his blankets to his right. "What happened to Grandpa?" He smiled.

Nate blushed. "I was just trying it out."

"I thought it came out all right."

"Did you?"

Angus shrugged a bony shoulder.

"All right, then—Grandpa?"

"Yes, son?"

"When that bear was running after Dutch an' me . . . on that slope . . . I could have shot him, but I froze." Nate looked at Angus, eyes deeply troubled. "It was like my finger turned to stone. I couldn't pull the trigger."

Angus ruffled the boy's hair. "It happens. Don't worry about it. You're young. You'll outgrow your fears. Some of them, anyway, though just between you an' me, I'll never outlive the fear of a bruin like that one!"

"You afraid, Angus?"

"Only a fool wouldn't be afraid, boy. The trick is not to let your fear get in the way of what needs to be done. Believe me, that's some trick. It takes experience, practice. Try to get some sleep now. I'll keep watch. You're safe."

"All right. Good night."

"Good night, boy."

Angus sat on the log, sipping his coffee, occasionally adding wood to the fire, keeping it built up.

Only one of the other men was snoring. That was Leech.

Neither Jackson nor Dutch McCrae were asleep. Or, if they were, it was not a restful sleep, both men moving around as though to get comfortable. Finally, the whiskey must have done its work, for about an hour after he'd turned in, Dutch started to snore albeit intermittently between mutterings. Nate lay on his side, facing Angus. Angus thought he was asleep. At least, he didn't move around much. He was giving it a good try, anyway.

Angus smiled.

Grandpa . . .

That made him think of Hunter and Annabelle. He wanted nothing more than for his son and daughter-in-law to start dropping little Buchanon urchins all over the Box Bar B while Angus still had enough wits about him to enjoy the rascals, to bounce them on his knee, lift them onto ponies, and lead them around the corral. If he was lucky enough, maybe he'd even live long enough to give the oldest one his first rifle and to teach him how to shoot it.

He wouldn't be able to take him up here, however, into his beloved mountains.

He had little doubt this would be his last trek into these vast, mysterious, majestic reaches.

Yes, still vast and majestic despite their bear problem. It didn't ruin the trip for Angus though he wouldn't doubt if the Pinkertons decided they didn't really need to hunt down their quarry as badly as they'd thought, and elect to head back to lower, safer ground.

Angus wouldn't hold it against them.

They weren't used to this sort of thing. Hell, Angus had gotten used to it last summer—far *too* used to it—and his blood was still frozen in his veins, his marrow turned to lead in his bones. Still, the wild was a mystery. A beguiling one at that. One he lived in dread of finally having to turn his back on for good, of having to restrict his adventures to his upstairs bedroom back at the Box Bar B headquarters . . . to his memories.

A bugling cry caromed across the night. It was like a clenched fist that nearly knocked Angus off his log. He dropped his coffee cup and, old heart racing, reached for the Spencer.

CHAPTER 22

"Let me take a look at that, kid," Hunter said.

"Ah, hell, it's nothin'."

"I'll be the judge of what's nothin' an' what's not nothin'."

Hunter set the Henry down and rose onto his knees, turning to Powwow. "Sit up," he said, motioning with his hand.

Powwow sat up, his back to the cave entrance and the long, boulder-strewn slope where the dead black man lay in a bloody heap.

Hunter winced when he saw the blood oozing from a hole in Powwow's denims, on the outside of his left thigh. He canted his head to see the backside of the kid's thigh, where another hole in the denims oozed more blood.

"You must've got hit when you were still in the saddle. Didn't you feel it?"

"Just a pinch."

"Well, it went all the way through, anyway."

"Oh, Lordy."

Angus looked at Powwow. The kid's face had gone nearly as white as a sheet. He listed a little this way and that, as though he were about to pass out.

"Hold on, kid. Hold on. I think it's just a flesh wound. Does it feel like it hit the bone?"

"Oh . . . bone. Oh . . . blood. Oh, man . . ."

"Stay with me, kid. You're gonna make it." Hunter removed his neckerchief and pressed it over the wound in the back of the kid's thigh, which was the entrance wound. The bullet had exited the kid's leg through the front. "Hold that down over the wound. Hold the other end over the—hey, you with me?"

"I, uh . . . I gotta confession to make."

"What's that?"

"I, uh . . ." Powwow shook his head as though to clear the cobwebs. "I, uh . . . can't stand the sight of blood. 'Specially . . . 'specially . . . my *own*!"

He gave a ragged sigh and fell onto his right hip and shoulder and lay there motionless on the cave floor, dead out. He began snoring raspily.

"Oh, hell!" Hunter said.

Bobby came over, sniffed Powwow's bloody leg, gave a little mewl, and turned to Hunter, nervously wagging his shaggy tail.

"Yep, it's one thing after another, Bobby," Hunter said, rising to a crouch and dragging Powwow deeper into the cavern in case their assailants returned. "I'm gonna have to clean that wound, get the bleeding stopped. You stay here with him. I'm gonna fetch my saddlebags."

Hunter moved to the cave entrance, gazed down the slope beyond the dead man. No movement. Their assailants must have realized the error of their ways and were staying gone. At least, Hunter hoped they'd stay gone. He needed no more complications.

He hated the added delay, but he had no choice but to get the kid's wound cleaned, the bleeding stopped. To that end he moved down into the boulders on the side of the slope and found Nasty Pete and the kid's dun grazing wiry brown grass around one of the boulders and from beneath which clear water bubbled, making a miniature geyser and forming a freshet that trailed off down the slope.

A spring.

Good. He'd need water.

He quickly unsaddled both horses and tied them to a wind-gnarled cedar in the shelter between boulders, within reach of the spring, then hauled his saddlebags and both his own and the kid's bedrolls back to the cave, where Bobby Lee was sitting in worried vigil over the still slumbering Powwow. He dropped it all down near the kid and Bobby Lee, then took his canteen down to the spring to fill it.

When he'd returned the canteen to the cave, he quickly gathered rocks to form a fire ring in the middle of the cavern. There were pines and cedars growing along both sides of the slope, and after two trips and two armfuls of dead wood and branches and pinecones and twigs for kindling, he built a fire, taking his time, coaxing it to life though feeling the nettling impatience, knowing the kid was likely losing a lot of blood while he tended his chores.

They were necessary chores, however.

He set water to boil in the coffeepot, which he hung from his iron tripod, then pulled the kid's boots off. "Oh," Powwow said, as each boot was removed. "Oh . . ."

Hunter pulled the kids denims off, tossed them aside, then with his bowie knife he cut a neat round hole in the kid's longhandles, around the wound. That task accomplished, he rolled the still slumbering Powwow onto his side so he had better access to both wounds. He cleaned each thoroughly with warm water.

Cynthia McGovern had slipped a bottle of whiskey into the possibles bag she'd packed for Hunter and Powwow. He hadn't needed much of it due to the poultice she'd made for his ribs, but he was glad to have the bottle now.

He popped the cork and poured whiskey over the kid's leg, letting it dribble over each wound, cleaning them more thoroughly than water could. The kid's body stiffened, and he awakened with a screech, saying, "Oh, God! Oh, God—that burns like the smokin' gates of the devil's own *hell*!"

"That's just for starters," Hunter said. "I'm gonna suture those wounds closed. Now, I'm no sawbones, so it ain't gonna be a very neat job, an' it might be a tad on the painful side, so you'd best have you a swig." He extended the bottle to Powwow. "Take a big one."

"Don't normally imbibe in the daylight hours—ain't the way I was raised—but since you insist."

Powwow took the bottle and took a drink.

Then another.

He winced as the busthead raked its way down his throat.

"Have another one," Hunter said, threading the needle he'd produced from his small, leather sewing kit.

Powwow took another drink, then thrust the bottle over his hip toward Hunter. "Lordy . . . that's enough." He sighed and rested his head on the cave floor, one hand wedged beneath it.

When Hunter began sewing him up, again the kid stiffened and gasped. He glanced back at Hunter's handiwork, saw the blood, and promptly passed out again. Hunter chuckled. "Well, that's one way to skin a cat," he told Bobby Lee, who was sitting and watching him intently from only a few feet away.

Bobby mewled and shifted his weight from one front paw to the other.

As he continued sewing the exit wound closed, Hunter glanced at the coyote. "You worried about Annabelle?"

As soon as Hunter said her name, Bobby lifted his long, clean snout and cast a low, mournful howl at the cave ceiling.

"Yeah," Hunter said, pinching up the flesh along the wound and poking the needle and catgut through. "Me, too. Don't reckon I've ever been so worried about anyone in my life. Maybe ol' Pap during the war, wondering how he was gettin' along. They separated us as soon as we signed up together."

He stretched his lips back from his teeth and shook his head. "Never been as worried since . . . till now."

Bobby Lee gave a clipped cry, then lay belly down, resting his snout on his front paws. He gave his tail a sympathetic wag, then just lay there, watching Hunter finish closing the exit wound before once more cleaning the entrance wound with water and whiskey, evoking a groan from his patient, then suturing the entrance wound closed, as well.

He wrapped a tight bandage around the kid's leg, rolled him onto his back, and covered him with his soogan. Powwow didn't stir. He lay with his eyes tightly closed, moving his lips a little and whimpering softly against the pain. Hunter cleaned up, returned his sewing kit to his saddlebags, then retrieved his and the kid's saddles, setting the kid's down and leaning his head up against it so he was not lying on the cave's bare, gravelly floor.

Hunter filled the coffeepot at the spring, brought it back to the cave, hung it over the fire, and was soon resting back against his own saddle, sipping the mud and nibbling bits of jerky he shared with Bobby Lee who sat beside him, twitching his ears and tilting his head expectantly this way and that, awaiting the next treat.

Hunter was about to freshen his coffee when the kid sat abruptly up and yelled, "Laurel!"

Bobby Lee leaped to his feet and barked at the kid, frightened.

One of the horses whinnied.

Placing a calming hand on Bobby Lee's head, Hunter turned to the kid still sitting up and staring wide-eyed out the cave entrance where the light was fading toward dusk.

"Easy, kid. Powwow . . . easy." Hunter placed an arm on the young man's shoulder. "Just us here . . . you, me, an' Bobby Lee."

The kid seemed to come out of it, rationality returning to his gaze. As it did, the pain of Hunter's makeshift sutures must have returned to him, as well. Stretching his lips back from his teeth, he placed both hands on his upper thigh and squeezed.

"Oh, man . . . burns."

Hunter pulled another cup out of his saddlebags, filled it three-quarters full with coffee, then filled it the rest of the way with whiskey from Cynthia McGovern's bottle. "Here. Drink that. Take out some of the sting."

Powwow accepted the cup in both hands, his hands shaking a little. He brought the cup to his lips, swallowed, sighed, then rested back against his saddle. "Does file the edge off it some."

"Coffee and whiskey, a couple handfuls of jerky, is all a man needs when you get right down to it."

Powwow chuckled, then winced again at the pain.

"Sorry, kid. I did as well as I could. I learned from watching the surgeons back during the war. I can set a bone if it ain't too badly broke, and I can sew a wound closed if it ain't too big, but I'm not sayin' I do a nice, neat, pain-free job."

Powwow looked at him, the kid's eyes serious, maybe a little incredulous. "You saved my life."

"Ah, hell."

Powwow laughed as he stared out the cave entrance. The light bathing the slope had turned a soft blue. "I can go around for the rest of my life now, crowin' to folks about how my life was saved by Mister Hunter Buchanon his ownself."

"Careful, kid. Might get yourself shot. We're above the Mason-Dixie line."

"Hell, down South you're a legend. I'm from Texas, an' I grew up hearin' your name spouted this way an' that by the veterans from every loafer's bench in the town square!"

Hunter was ready to change the subject. He couldn't do much about his troubled memories of the war, but he could put an end to talking about that bloody time.

"Where you from in Texas, Powwow?"

"Little ranch outside San Antonio."

"Brothers? Sisters?"

Powwow sipped his whiskey-laced coffee, grimaced, and sighed as he set the cup down on his right thigh, atop one of the blankets comprising his bedroll. "Two brothers, two sisters."

Powwow turned to him. "I had two brothers. They died . . . in a bad way." But honorably, he did not add. Shep and Tyrell died helping him fight for the girl he'd been in love with. Whom he'd always be in love with no matter how far apart the fates might take them.

Powwow nodded grimly.

Hunter sipped his own whiskey-laced brew and said, "Who's Laurel?"

Powwow turned to him sharply. "Who?"

"The girl whose name you called out in your sleep."

"Oh." Powwow ran his hand down his face. "Didn't realize I said it out loud."

"Who is she? I mean, if it's none of my business just—"

"Laurel McKinney. Girl from a neighboring ranch I once knew."

"Uh-oh. One of those girls-from-a-neighboring-ranch stories, eh?" Hunter chuckled. "Got one o' them myself."

"Laurel," Powwow said, and took another sip of his coffee. "She was right special. I can still hear her laugh. We used to pick wild berries together on the way home from school. We sorta grew up together . . . as friends. Then, well, we started goin' to barn dances together. I reckon we were gettin' kinda serious, not just friends anymore, and her pa stepped in, wanted us to stop seein' each other.

Laurel's folks wanted her to marry the son of a wealthy man in town."

"Yeah," Hunter said with a fateful sigh, able to sympathize with that aspect of the story, as well. "So what happened?"

"We didn't stop. Couldn't seem to. We grew up together. We knew each other better than we knew anyone else. We kept meeting, sending secret notes about places to rendezvous. And then . . ."

Powwow picked up his cup. Hunter noticed his hand shaking as he sipped, then set the cup back down on his lap. Powwow swallowed the coffee, turned to Hunter with a sorrow in his eyes. "Laurel became in the family way. Her parents kept her home when she started showing. We couldn't see each other. Her parents forbid her to ever see me again. They were going to send her off to have the baby, to some relative back east, but she gave birth early and they both died, Laurel an' the baby."

Hunter just stared at him. He'd had a feeling the story was going to take a dark swing. He hadn't been prepared for how dark it had swung.

"Gee," he said. "I'm sorry, Powwow."

Mouth corners drawn down, Powwow stared out at the darkening night from which the only sound was the distant, grating cry of a hunting owl. "Everyone blamed me. Even my own folks. I couldn't go anywhere, do anything, without people givin' me the stink eye.

"Finally, one mornin', I packed my bags, saddled up, rode up to the cemetery where they buried Laurel and the baby, told them both goodbye and . . ." The kid's voice quavered. "Th-that I loved 'em both." He brushed a tear from his cheek with the back of his hand. "And then I rode on out of there . . . just started wanderin' . . . workin' where I could find it. Livery barns an' ranches, mostly. Swamped out a few saloons."

Powwow glanced at Hunter with a dry chuckle, his eyes still bright with emotion. "An' here I am . . . with the great Hunter Buchanon . . . helpin' him rescue his wife back from slavers."

"That's some life story."

"I oughta write it down some day."

"I'm sorry, kid. About Laurel an' the baby. I know that feeling of loss."

"It don't hurt as bad as it once did but I reckon it'll never stop hurting completely."

"No, it doesn't."

"I hope at least this part of it has a happy ending." Powwow glanced at Hunter again. "That we get your Annabelle back from Machado. I'm ready for a success like that."

"Yeah," Hunter said, finishing his coffee and tossing the dregs into the fire. "Me, too."

One of the horses gave a shrill, warning whinny.

Instantly, Hunter kicked out the fire and grabbed his Henry.

CHAPTER 23

The town of Lone Pine was aptly named.

The sod huts and tar-paper shanties and log cabins with a few wood frame buildings lining the main trail through town sat in a crease between large, low, fawn-colored bluffs. Atop the bluff south of town stood one lone pine tree. That was the only tree anywhere in sight, though scraggly shrubs lined the wash that cut around the south edge of the town, between the town and the bluff with the lone pine on it.

Age-silvered log shacks and sod huts lined the wash that appeared to be a trash dump for those living along it. Sickly looking men and wizened women milled around the huts, with sickly looking animals in stock pens and rudimentary stables hammered together with mismatched boards and stone. It was midday, but in a chicken coop down there along the wash a mixed up rooster was crowing. A dog sat atop the brush roof of one of the sod shanties—a black and white collie dog—barking at the newcomers riding into town.

Machado's bunch had been avoiding towns on their eastward trek toward the Missouri River, which Annabelle had heard one of the gang members mention was only an-other day or so away. She wondered why they were heading into Lone Pine but, as they did, Annabelle couldn't help entertaining the possibility that she might find help here.

The town wasn't much but surely it had a lawman.

The buoyant thought had no sooner swept through her brain than she saw a sign tacked to two unpeeled pine poles extending out into the main street.

It read simply CONSTABLE in unsteady black lettering.

That's all it needed to say to cause Annabelle's heart to pick up its beat.

The gang had pushed hard that day, but now they walked their tired, sweaty horses into the town. The constable's office was coming up on Anna's right—a weathered log shack with a tin roof, deeper than it was wide, loose chinking between the gray logs. There was a small, roofed stoop fronting the place. An old man sat in a chair to the left of the cabin's front door, which was half-open, exposing deep shadows within.

He was a little man, but he sported a bulbous paunch, and a bulbous red nose occupied a good portion of his badly weathered face with a thin gray mustache mantling his upper lip and a spade beard of the same color adorning his chin. His skin was ruddy and sun blotched, freckled. He sat in the chair, smoking a pipe with an almost dreamy air. A tin cup sat on a small, halved-log table beside him.

When he saw Machado, he smiled around the pipe stem, smoke wreathing his head topped with a battered tan Stetson. Annabelle eyed the man hopefully as she rode the horse Machado had stolen for her, killing its rider in cold blood. Surely the lawman would see that her wrists were tied to her saddle horn, that she was a captive in need of rescuing. She doubted the old man could do it himself but surely he'd gather other citizens, form a posse of sorts.

She felt that hope, that certainty only briefly.

It became clear to her that she was likely not the only captive Machado had paraded through Lone Pine.

It became even clearer to her when the old lawman started laughing.

He stared at her, and his little eyes were pinched up as he laughed, throwing his head back as though at the funniest joke he'd ever heard. He kept laughing as the gang and Annabelle rode on past him. She could hear him laughing even a block away, as they headed for a large, barrack-like, unpainted, wood frame, clapboard-sided building another block farther on, sitting perpendicular to the street that followed a bend around the large place, easily the largest building Annabelle had so far seen in Lone Pine. Girls in skimpy, brightly colored clothing—there were a lot of reds and blacks—lounged around on the wooden, second-floor balcony.

THE LONE WOLF HOTEL was painted in large, black, ornate letters across the top of the building's second story, just below the mansard roof.

Judging by the skimpy attire worn by the girls on the balcony—some of whom were leaning against the rail smoking cigarettes in long, wooden holders—the Lone Wolf was more than just a hotel.

Don't tell me, Annabelle thought, *that he's going to put me up in another hotel again?* After her attempt to escape from River Bend Station, she'd thought she was a goner. But he'd let her live. Even after killing Big Nick by ramming his own bowie knife into his neck, she was still alive!

She couldn't quite wrap her mind around it.

Ahead, Machado reined his horse to a stop in front of the building and smiled up at the *doves du pave* fluttering like colorful birds on the balcony. One of the girls, a pretty, green-eyed mulatto with shoulder-length, frizzy black hair, called through the open French door behind her, "Miss Delphine, Mister Machado is here!"

Silence.

Then Annabelle could hear footsteps growing in volume

until the front door atop the porch opened and a pretty, brown-eyed blond woman in a flowing, cream gown appeared. She threw a hand up against the doorframe to her left and took a drag off the long, thin, brown cheroot protruding from a long white porcelain holder.

"Well, Mister Machado," she said coquettishly, in a heavy, Southern, slow, beguiling accent from somewhere far below the Mason-Dixon Line, "what an honor to have you grace us here at the Lone Wolf with your presence again, sir!"

Even sitting her mount at the tail end of the back, Annabelle could hear Machado's seedy chuckles. He leaned out to the right of his saddle, placed an elbow on his knee, raised that hand, and beckoned the woman with his right index finger. At first, she frowned, befuddled, then, gown flowing around her in the breeze of her graceful passage, crossed the porch, drifted down the steps, and moved over to have Machado whisper into her ear at some length.

While he spoke into the pretty woman's ear, she cast her gaze around the uncouth ruffians to Annabelle and arched both brows as though in surprise.

"Oh . . . she pretty," Annabelle heard her say to the slaver leader.

Oh, no, Annabelle thought. *Another whorehouse madam in cahoots with the goatish ol' Saguaro.*

He pinched his hat brim to the woman, then reined his horse back down the street in the direction from which they'd come. The man who'd been leading Annabelle's horse dropped the reins and, along with the two others, followed Machado—likely to one of the several saloons Annabelle had spied on her way into town.

"Maggie, Patricia," the pretty Southern blonde yelled up to the balcony. "Your assistance, ladies, please!" she added, puffing on the long cigarette holder and eyeing Annabelle sitting her horse alone, a good thirty feet away from whom she figured was the Lone Wolf's madame. She was probably in her mid-thirties, and it was a hard-won thirties, but she was still pretty.

When two girls strode out of the Lone Wolf, Miss Delphine began strolling toward Annabelle, still puffing on the cigarette. A mousy redhaired girl and a pretty, lithe girl with long, black hair fell into step beside her, all three eyeing Annabelle as though she were a cut of meat they were thinking of purchasing in their local grocery.

"Well, hello, there," said Miss Delphine, stopping near Annabelle and crossing one arm on her chest while puffing the cigarette with her other hand, slowly blinking, her light brown eyes raking Annabelle up and down. "Pretty," she said, while the girl with long, black hair produced a stiletto from a sheath strapped to her right thigh and began sawing away on the ropes binding Annabelle's wrists to her saddle horn.

"What's happening?" Annabelle said, wondering if she had just been given another opportunity to flee. If so, she would not. He knew she would not. She was too broken, and she knew she would only be caught again.

She was so exhausted, she wanted to die. She thought if a gun were available, she might very well shoot herself. She wouldn't, of course, when it got right down to it. Because she would think about her beloved Hunter, Angus, and Nate.

The Box Bar B and all her beloved horses.

But was it all possible she would ever see them and the ranch again?

"What's happening, dear heart," said Miss Delphine, pulling the cigarette holder away from her mouth and blowing a long plume of smoke, "is that I might just be able to save your life if you cooperate."

Annabelle frowned curiously. "How?"

Miss Delphine tossed her head toward the sprawling building behind her. "Come."

"Where am I going?"

"Inside. We're going to make you presentable."

"Presentable?"

Miss Delphine gave a shrewd smile. "He's sweet on you, dear heart. Otherwise, I have no doubt you wouldn't have gotten this far. Come! Girls, help her!"

Maggie and Patricia helped the shaky Annabelle down from the saddle. She was so weak from exhaustion and hunger she could barely walk. Each girl wrapped a hand around her waist and led her up the porch steps, across the porch, and into the rambling building that smelled of wood smoke and cooking food. She found herself in a large, well-appointed parlor with a sprawling kitchen through a doorway on her left. She was led across the parlor and then up a narrow, winding, enclosed stairway, past one landing to a third and then down a hallway lit by windows on both ends.

Miss Delphine stood in an open doorway halfway down the hall, on the left side. "We'll put her in here. Leave her to me for now; fetch bathwater."

Miss Delphine led Annabelle into what appeared a suite of rooms. She eased Anna down into a soft, brocade sofa, then went to a cabinet, produced a cut-glass decanter, and half filled two cut-glass goblets. She gave one to Annabelle.

"Here. It'll cut the trail dust."

Annabelle accepted the glass but looked up sharply at the pretty blond woman as she stared down at Annabelle, the smoldering cigarette holder in one hand, the glass in her other hand. "You work with Machado?"

"Yes."

Annabelle drew her mouth corners down in defeat, nodded slowly.

"But not how you think," said Miss Delphine, her slow, dogwood blossom–soft accent strangely comforting. Maybe because it sounded like Hunter's when he was tired, weary after a long day gentling a horse in the round corral that

Annabelle hoped against hope she would live to see again. "I keep the girls alive. Those he sells to me, I make sure get returned to where they come from. If he sells you to me at a price I can afford, I will see you get back to where you came from. However, I think he'll want to save a pretty redhead like yourself for Corazon. He can afford you. I probably can't if he asks for what I think he's going to ask. I can save two girls for the price he'll likely ask for you. I can keep you alive, however. For now. How you fare when you leave here will be up to you."

Footsteps sounded in the hall, and then Patricia and Maggie came in with two steaming buckets of water apiece. They disappeared through a doorway Annabelle assumed led into a washroom, and she promptly heard the water being poured into a tub.

"First," Miss Delphine continued, "we have to make you clean and pretty. You're going out on the town tonight, don't you know?" She threw her head back and gave a tittering laugh. "I didn't think I'd ever live to see it, but he's tumbled for one. He's tumbled for you, Miss Annabelle Buchanon."

Suddenly, she frowned, deeply curious.

"Buchanon. That's a name from my Southern past. The war . . ."

"My husband is Hunter Buchanon," Annabelle said and took a sip of the brandy.

It went down well, almost immediately filing off some of the sharpest edges.

"Ahh," said Miss Delphine, removing the cigarette stub from the holder and mashing it out in an ashtray on the table before her. "That, too, will up the price."

Annabelle leaned forward, holding the glass in both hands on her knee, giving the madam of the Lone Wolf Hotel a pointed look. "Do you seriously believe I will go out 'on the town' with that man. The savage who beat my husband, possibly to death, and kidnapped me, intending to sell me to Missouri River *slave traders*?"

"Yes." Miss Delphine nodded. "Because you want to live. If you want to live, you must do what he wants you to do. For now, he wants you to be his woman. So be his woman. Go out and eat a nice meal, drink some French wine, and pretend to enjoy yourself. That way you might live to see another day. Aggravate him, and he will forget about Corazon and the tidy sum your pretty red head will fetch and stick a knife in your heart." The madam shook her head. "You'll never be seen or heard from by those you love again."

She poked another cigarette into the end of the holder and lit a match.

CHAPTER 24

"Get low, kid!" Hunter said, grabbing his Henry, then rolling to his left.

He gained his hands and knees and crabbed over to the cave entrance, doffing his hat and tossing it away, wanting to make as small a target as possible. He hunkered low on his chest and belly, keeping the rifle tight against him so no starlight would reflect off the barrel and give him away.

"Our friends from earlier, you think?" Powwow asked, tightly, quietly.

"Most likely. On the other hands, the whole damn Dakota Territory is crawling with owlhoots on the run. Good place to get lost, Dakota. They may want our horses."

"Without our horses . . ."

"Don't worry, they won't get 'em." Hunter studied the slope dropping away before him. There was enough starlight that he could see a pretty good ways, make out rocks, gnarled cedars, and boulders, which meant he should be able to see a man or men, as well.

However, he spied no movement.

He stayed there for a time, studying the slope, watching, waiting. He began to wonder if Nasty Pete—he'd recognized Pete's whinny—had gotten jumpy over nothing. A coyote or a rabbit, say. Maybe a hunting nighthawk.

But then it came again—another shrill whinny.

Hunter could hear the grullo shake its head and paw the ground.

Still no movement.

He glanced over his shoulder where he could see Powwow's silhouette lying belly down against the cave's rear wall.

"You got your rifle?" Hunter said just above a whisper.

"Yep."

"Keep it close and keep your eyes and ears skinned. I'm gonna check the horses, then take a little walk around, have a look-see."

"All right."

Hunter gained his feet and stepped quickly out of the cave and to the left side of it, crouching, looking around, listening.

Farther off to his left, down a short, steep slope, he could hear the horses moving around nervously, whickering, blowing. They'd detected something they feared. Could be a man or men, could be a wolf or a wildcat. Hunter was exhausted from the long ride with the battered ribs and wanted nothing so much as to get some rejuvenating sleep, but he admonished himself to stay alert. He didn't know what he might be walking into.

Slowly, he moved down the slope through large rocks and boulders. When he came to the relatively flat area where both horses were tied, he placed a soothing hand on Pete's rump. He could feel the muscles just under the hide twitch automatically, apprehensively.

Slowly, he moved up between the horses, running his gloved left hand along Nasty Pete's back and then placing a soothing hand on Powwow's dun.

"Easy, fellas. Easy. Just me." Hunter paused, stared into the darkness beyond the boulders. "What'd you wind, Pete?" he asked in a soft, slow whisper. "You see somethin' down there, did you?"

Pete jerked his head up, switched his tail, and stood staring into the darkness.

Hunter sniffed the still night air. If a mountain lion was close, he'd likely be able to smell it. They had a strong, distinctive odor. He'd smelled it before and had known he was close to a den. He smelled nothing now but the mushroom smell of the spring bubbling up before him and glinting in the starlight, and the clean tang of cool stone.

"All right," Hunter said. "I'm gonna check it out."

He gave Pete a pat on the snout then, holding the Henry up high across his chest, his gloved hand over the brass receiver, started walking slowly down the slope, weaving through boulders. He took one step at a time, treading lightly, wanting to make as little sound as possible. He stopped suddenly beside a wagon-sized boulder on his left, squeezed the Henry tensely in his hands.

An unfelt current in the otherwise still night air had brought to his nose the rancid, sweaty smell of a man. It was laced with the smell of wool, leather, and camp smoke.

He'd learned to trust his sniffer. Several times during the war, it had saved his life.

He waited, listening.

The smell grew in intensity. Then he heard the faint crackle of a stealthy footstep on sand and gravel.

Slowly, almost soundlessly, he backed up. He stepped around the boulder and stopped at its far end, cast his gaze up alongside it. Nothing. The man he'd smelled and heard was likely working his way around the far end, heading toward where Hunter had been standing.

Hunter moved forward, stopped at the corner of the far end, and peered along the backside of the boulder, on his right. A silhouette figure stood crouched before him, at the boulder's far corner. Hunter could make out the steeple-crowned sombrero of the Mexican who was part of the five-man pack that had stalked him and Powwow earlier.

Four-man pack, that was.

About to be three-man . . .

The Mexican moved suddenly around the corner of the boulder, lowered his rifle, and fired three quick rounds toward where Hunter had been standing a minute before. Vaguely, Hunter wondered if the Mex had detected him by his own smell. It had been a long time since he'd had a bath.

The Mexican stood crouched over his smoking rifle, moving his head, looking around, likely wondering where his target had gone.

"Here, *pendejo*."

The man gasped with a start and swung around sharply, bringing the smoking rifle around, as well. Hunter's Henry barked twice, both slugs taking the Mexican in the chest, lifting him a foot up off the ground, and then throwing him back into the rocks behind him. His rifle clattered as it, too, struck on the rocks.

A bullet slammed into the boulder less than a foot in front of Hunter. A rifle flashed and barked in the darkness maybe thirty feet away, on his left. Hunter whipped around and fired three more shots, triggering and pumping the cocking lever, the spent shells arcing up over his right shoulder and clinking onto the sand and gravel around him. The man screamed and dropped with a crunching thud, the rifle clattering onto the rocks around him.

The man lay groaning.

Hunter strode toward him slowly, keeping the smoking Henry aimed out from his right hip, tracking for any sign of more movement. There should be two more of these prairie parasites out here somewhere.

Ahead, he saw the man he'd shot trying to crawl away, a long lump of a man in the darkness. He was grunting and groaning. In the starlight, Hunter could see the dark blood staining the ground behind him. Likely a belly wound.

Hunter set his right foot down on the man's back, drove

him to the ground, and held him there. It was the Indian he'd seen earlier, long hair hanging in tangles down the back of his calico shirt. His tan Stetson lay in the sand beside him. He wore buckskin breeches and high-topped moccasins decorated with beads and porcupine quills. "What're you after?"

The Indian groaned, glanced over his shoulder, and spat, showing his teeth briefly in the darkness. Then he smiled. "Your friend . . . he's wounded, eh? That's why you holed up in the cave."

Hunter just stared down at the flat-faced Indian smiling up at him, dark eyes narrowed in self-satisfaction.

"My two amigos," he added in a lilting, flat-voweled Indian accent, "are probably carving him up right now. Those two like knife work. Consider themselves *artists!*"

Hunter shot him in the head, then ran through the boulders and up the slope toward the cave, which he could barely make out in the darkness. Ahead, a shadow moved—a man stepping around the side of a large boulder about twenty feet downslope from the cave. Ahead of that man and to his left, another man moved across the shoulder of the slope, heading toward the cave.

Hunter ran ahead, shouting, "Powwow—on the slope beneath you!"

The man nearest Hunter swung around, his rifle lapping red-orange flames. The bullet spanged loudly off a rock to Hunter's left. Hunter dropped to a knee, racked a fresh round in the fourteen-shot Henry's action, and fired twice. The first bullet slammed into the rock to the right of his target. The second bullet felled the man—likely a leg shot—as he tried to run behind a rock downslope ten feet and to his right, Hunter's left.

He squeezed off another shot at Hunter. That round whistled far over Hunter's head. Hunter dropped to his knee again, fired three more rounds, and watched in satisfaction as the vermin—an oblong shadow—rolled over on his back with a shrill curse.

A rifle flashed from farther up the slope. The bullet curled the air off Hunter's left ear. Hunter racked another round into the Henry's action but held fire when yet another rifle roared and stabbed flames from even farther up the slope and to the right of the man who'd just fired. The kid's rifle barked from the cave mouth two more times, flashing brightly.

There was a groan and a thud, the clatter of another rifle hitting the ground.

A long, ragged sigh, then silence save for the low rumble of distant thunder and a distant lightning flash.

"Kid?"

"Here," Powwow said. Another brief silence, then: "Dang."

His voice was clear in the heavy silence that had fallen over the slope in the wake of the lead swap. Absently, Hunter wondered why he couldn't hear the horses, both of whom should have been kicking up a fuss at the shooting.

He walked up the slope toward the cave. "What is it?" he asked Powwow.

No response.

Hunter moved through the rocks and stood crouched at the cave entrance, peering inside. Powwow was sitting down against his saddle, resting his head against the cave's rear wall. "You all right?"

He sat with his right knee drawn up, right arm resting over the top of it. The left, wounded leg lay straight out before him, the barrel of his Winchester resting against his knee.

"I ain't never shot anybody before." He gave an ironic laugh.

Now, you tell me, Hunter thought.

He was going after a gang of cutthroats who'd kidnapped

his wife to sell her into slavery with a kid who'd never shot anyone before tonight.

"Well," Hunter said, worrying his thumb over the top of the Henry's receiver, "you did real well. If you hadn't shot him, he might've shot me an' then shot you."

"Oh, I know, I know," Powwow said. "I'll build up the fire, make some more coffee."

"I'm gonna check on the horses."

Hunter cursed when he found that the reason the horses hadn't been kicking up a fuss was because they'd managed to rip their halter ropes from the cedar Hunter had tied them to. They hadn't strayed far, however, and Nasty Pete came when he whistled, so within a half hour he had both horses back tied near the spring.

When he returned to the cave, Powwow had rebuilt the fire and Hunter's coffeepot was hanging from the tripod, hissing softly as the water heated. Hunter had been hearing more thunder as he'd run down the horses. It had gradually grown louder, the lightning brighter. He hoped it wouldn't rain, which would likely wipe out Machado's trail.

Hunter leaned his rifle against the cave's rear wall. He removed his hat, tossed it down, then sat down against his saddle, knees raised, arms wrapped around them. He was beat, but he doubted he'd be able to sleep. Too tired, too enervated.

He sure hadn't figured on trouble like this when he and Anna had left the Box Bar B, herding those ten broncs to Arapaho Creek.

He turned to see Powwow absently poking a stick into the flames, letting it catch fire, blowing it out, then sticking it into the flames again.

"When we come to a settlement, and we should be comin' to one soon—I saw one on a map in my saddlebags, a little south and east of where we are now—I'm gonna get that leg of yours checked out by a sawbones. I'm gonna leave you there an' ride on alone, try to get back on Machado's trail."

Powwow whipped a sharp, surprised look at him. "Why? I can ride." He brushed his thumb across his bandaged left thigh. "Hell, it's just a flesh wound. You said so yourself."

Hunter shook his head. "I'm not gonna get you killed, kid. You're green. You're gonna stay back. Lounge around in a hotel room for a few days, eat some good food. Get you a girl."

"Oh, it's on account o' I told you I never shot nobody before."

Hunter didn't say anything. The water was boiling.

He got up, removed the pot with the leather swatch he used for removing hot pots and skillets from the fire, and removed the pot from the tripod.

"You said yourself I did well," Powwow insisted.

Thunder rumbled again, louder. Lightning flashed in the cave's entrance.

Damn.

Hunter reached into his Arbuckles pouch for a handful of the coffee Annabelle had ground before they'd left the Box Bar B and tossed it and one more into the pot. If he wasn't going to sleep, he might as well be good and awake. He returned the pot to the fire. It took only a minute for the water to return to a boil. He let it boil a minute, then removed the pot, set it on a rock near the flames, and added some cold water to settle the grounds.

He dropped to a knee to refill Powwow's empty cup. He added a little whiskey to it, then gave his own cup the same treatment.

"Hunter," Powwow said, poking the stick into the fire with a frustrated air, "I have to go with you." He gave Hunter another pointed look. "I have to help."

Hunter sipped his coffee and returned the kid's look

with a pointed one of his own. "It would be suicide. I'm not gonna let you commit it."

"It's suicide for you to go alone."

"Maybe, but we both know I have to. I have no choice."

"I have no choice but to ride with you, Hunter. All right, we'll get the leg checked out. If the sawbones says it's good, I'm ridin' along. You can't stop me."

Hunter scowled at him in exasperation. "Why are you so galldang intent on getting' yourself killed, boy?"

Powwow shrugged a shoulder and resumed poking the stick into the fire. "I've never been good at anything in my life. I grew up on a ranch, but I'm only half a rancher. You know why I'm out of work? Because I'm no good at it. I'm lazy. My heart ain't in ranch work, but it's all I know, and I hardly know even that. I can't read or write though my folks sent me to school, and . . . and . . ."

His voice broke a little as he added, "And I couldn't even save the girl I loved. Didn't have spine enough to stand up to her family though I knew she was waitin' for me to do just that. She loved me. Why, I got no idea. Guess she thought she saw somethin' in me. Some little bit of promise, maybe. Well, I reckon I fooled her. When she saw I didn't have it in me to defy her family . . . that I had no courage . . . she turned her back on me, gave into her folks' wishes. That's why she died. Why our baby died with her. Shame and heartbreak."

Powwow turned again sharply to Hunter. His eyes were bright with tears. "You know how it feels to have caused somethin' like that?

Hunter just stared at him. He had no response.

"That's why I have to ride," the kid said, breaking the stick over his knee and tossing it into the flames. Staring into the fire, he nodded. "I need a shot to do somethin' good.

To try, anyway." Again, he glanced at Hunter. "Know what I mean?"

Hunter sighed.

He nodded.

He cursed under his breath. He heard the ticks of the first raindrops.

CHAPTER 25

"Ah, hell, it's back!" Dutch McCrae said, sitting bolt upright against his saddle, his soogan slipping down his chest.

"Damn!" said Jackson.

"That beast is right angry or he's right hungry," said Leech Davis, sitting up in his own soogan and reaching for his rifle.

"Or both," Angus opined, wishing he hadn't said it when he saw Nate, also sitting up, looking up at him, wide-eyed. Angus tossed a crooked, sun-bleached chunk of solid drift-wood onto the fire. "He'll stay away as long as we keep the fire built up."

Dutch turned to look at the dwindling supply of wood beside the fire ring. "Yeah, well, it ain't gonna last long. An' whose gonna go out an' fetch more . . . with that demon on four legs stompin' around, hungry for more than a few morsels of human flesh!"

"Easy, now, easy," Angus said.

But he himself jerked with a start when another bugling cry rocketed out of the darkness.

"Whoah!" Nate said, stiffening and staring off to his right, the direction from which the second cry had come.

The first had come from straight off in the darkness beyond Angus.

Angus rose, his Spencer under his arm.

Jackson rose, too, his Winchester in both hands. He looked at Angus. "He's coming closer. Are you sure . . . I mean good an' sure . . . he won't come near the fire?"

No, Angus said silently to himself. He was no longer sure. He just knew that most bears would stay away from a fire. He had no idea what this one was capable of.

"Yes," he said aloud.

Jackson arched a knowing brow at him. "You're not sure."

Another bugling cry, and everyone in the camp jumped. Even Angus, though he thought he'd been prepared for it.

"Just keep your wits about yourselves," he said, quietly. "An' keep your long guns handy. If he comes into the firelight, aim for the heart. Shoot an' keep shootin'. One of our bullets is bound to penetrate that thick hide of his."

Again, came another bugling cry of the most intense anger Angus had ever heard given voice to by man or beast. He felt his own hand shaking as he clamped it around the Spencer, standing at the outside edge of the firelight. He whipped around, for that wail had come from behind him now as he gazed off to the east.

It had come from the west, and it had been closer than the last one.

Dutch gained his own feet now, looking around warily. "He's movin' around us. Tryin' to trick us. An' he's comin' in." He pumped a cartridge into his rifle's action. "Oh, he's comin' in for the kill, all right, an' let there be no mistake!"

"Dutch!" Jackson scolded.

"Easy, Dutch," said Leech Davis, staring westward, cradling his rifle in his arms.

Nate walked up beside Angus. "Grandpa, I got a confession to make. I'm—"

"Scared. Don't blame you a bit, boy. But it's going to be all right. If he charges the camp, I'm ready for him."

Of course, he'd been ready . . . or thought he'd been ready before . . . but he'd been too nervous to place any of his shots where they'd needed to be placed to kill the beast. Next time—and he hoped there wouldn't be a next time—he'd place his shots better.

The roars that turned the men's and the boy's guts to jelly continued along with the big beasts' heavy crackling footsteps and growling, thrashing sounds as it moved around the camp, pushing through shrubs and snapping fallen branches. At one point there came grating, sawing sounds accompanied by more angry wails that caromed from one near ridge to another, echoing madly.

The men and Nate, standing around the fire, turned to track the beast with their gazes. A couple of times, Angus got a brief glimpse of the bruin's silhouette as it moved around the camp, from one side to the other, circling, then stopping abruptly and switching course. At one point, Angus saw the two red, glowing eyes roughly fifty yards out beyond the circle of wavering, guttering firelight.

That made his heart hiccup, caused more cold sweat to pop out on his forehead and dribble down his bearded cheeks.

The horses were frightened, too. They also tracked the bruin's movements with their gazes, swinging their heads this way and that, whickering, stomping, pulling at the halter ropes tied to the picket line strung between pines.

Angus kept one eye skinned at Dutch McCrae. The big, bearded Pinkerton was also sweating profusely and flinching and starting with each new noise the bear made. The man was terrified. Angus was himself; only a fool would not be. But Angus found himself feeling almost as anxious about what Dutch would do in his irrationality as he was about what the terrorizing bruin might do.

Finally, wound up as tight as a Swiss watch, Dutch did it. The springs inside him finally sprung.

Angus couldn't have stopped him even if he'd been closer.

The man jacked a live round into his Winchester's action, and yelled, "That tears it! I ain't gonna stand around an' listen to this no more. I'm gonna put a *stop* to it!"

Jackson swung toward him, but McCrae had already stomped past him before he could grab him. Suddenly, Dutch was swallowed by the heavy darkness beyond the camp, shouting and cursing and bellowing: "You want some o' this, you big stupid beast, then come an' get it!"

Now there were two separate sets of thrashing sounds—those of the bear and those of McCrae, for whom the beast's rampage had driven him over the edge and into madness. His rifle was a .44. It would have to take a damn well-placed shot for a .44 round to penetrate the beast's thick hide. He'd either have to make a head shot or a heart or lung shot. Preferably, one of the former because the beast could live to do a lot of damage with a round lodged in only its lungs. Hell, Angus had heard of grizzlies running a mile, roaring, with bullets lodged even in the heart.

"Dutch!" Davis shouted.

"Don't do it, Dutch!" Jackson bellowed, cupping his hands around his mouth.

Angus strode quickly over to the side of the camp from which McCrae had made his exit and squeezed his old, trusty Spencer in his hand, which was soggy with sweat inside his glove. Another bugling cry exploded out of the dark woods. Two quick rifle shots nearly drowned by the beast's enraged wails, and then a man's bone-splintering wail of rarified terror.

Running footsteps growing louder, a man's shrill wail.

The bruin's bugling cry.

The horses screamed.

"Get ready!" Angus said, dropping to a knee and raising the Spencer .56 in his lone hand and arm, which, having to make up for the loss of the other one, was corded and sinewy, as strong as that of a much younger man. "Remember—aim for the heart!"

Two glowing eyes swam up out of the darkness.

Dutch was running toward them. He'd lost his hat and his rifle, and he was scissoring his arms and legs.

"Help!" he cried. "Help meee!"

The bruin was closing on him quickly, close-set eyes glowing as red as a fire burned down to embers.

Dutch burst into the camp, tripped over his own feet, fell, and rolled almost into the fire.

When the bear entered the outside edge of the firelight, it stopped and rose onto its back feet, glaring at the campers, throwing its head back, and loosing more enraged cries at the stars.

"Shoot!" Angus bellowed.

He fired the heavy Spencer. The other men fired, as well, save Dutch, who lay near Angus and was staring back at the mountain of a bear before him in mute shock. Nate fired from his own knee beside Angus, firing and cocking, firing and cocking, the empty cartridge casings glinting in the firelight as they arced back over his shoulder.

The bullets made the beast's long fur part. Dust billowed. It clawed at its wounds, oozing crimson blood in the fire-light, before dropping back down to all fours, turning, and lumbering off into the darkness.

A specter birthed by the darkest night on earth.

A demon not unlike the one that had haunted and terrorized the Box Bar B the summer before.

Gradually, the enraged wails and the heavy thrashing sounds dwindled to silence. They were replaced by the distant yammering of a lone coyote as if sending out queries across the night, wondering what all the fuss had been about.

Angus gazed through the pale, wafting powder smoke toward where the bear had disappeared.

Dutch was the first to speak. In a hushed, quavering tone, he said, brushing sweat from his forehead with a sleeve of his frock coat, "There ain't no killin' it, is there? The beast won't die. I seen blood, but . . ." He turned his terrified eyes to Angus. "He won't die."

Angus leaned against his rifle, the terror slow to die in him, his heart slow to ease its raucous drumming against his breastbone.

"Don't make him more than he is," he told Dutch, though he was speaking as much to himself as to anyone else. "He's a bear. That's all. With that much lead in him, he'll die. Likely just wants to choose his own place."

Yeah, like the one from last summer . . .

That one had likely been just a bear, as well, despite its uncanny ability to seemingly read the minds of the men, including Hunter's, who'd hunted it.

Angus had seen enough in his lifetime plus having been born and raised in the Smoky Mountains, the superstition capital of the South, to know there were some things that could not be explained.

Aside from Dutch, who lay on his side by the fire, they all stood staring into the darkness in which the bear had disappeared. No one said anything. The fire cracked, snapped, popped. Angus knew the others were as tense as he was, waiting for another bugling cry.

None came.

He looked east. There was a faint lightening in the sky over that way. It would be morning soon.

He said as much to the others.

"Let's try to get a little sleep. Even an hour would help. If that beast comes back, and I don't think he will, the horses will warn us."

Only now were the frightened mounts starting to settle down.

Angus knew none of his trail pards was likely to get any sleep. Not tonight. Probably not tomorrow night. Probably not for a long time.

But trying might help settle them all down. He could sense their nerves dancing around just beneath their skins, as were his.

Gradually, they got settled back down, as did Angus and Nate.

Angus was surprised to hear Leech Davis snoring not long after Angus himself had closed his eyes.

He was so exhausted, he found himself starting to doze.

Then he must have slept. When he opened his eyes, lemon sunlight was angling down through the forest canopy. Jackson, Davis, Nate, and even Dutch McCrae appeared to be asleep, rolled up in their soogans. Angus wasn't sure how he'd managed to fall asleep, but that was how tired he was, he reckoned. Not even the prospect of the specter's return had kept him awake.

He got up quietly. Might as well let the others rest for as long as they could.

Even Nate, lying belly down, head turned to one side, a little drool leaking down from a corner of his slightly open mouth, was snoring, albeit more quietly than the others.

He grabbed his hat, then moved off into the trees to tend nature and check the horses. They all seemed settled, so he picked up a few dead branches, then returned to the camp and set them down quietly beside the fire ring and its pile of cold ashes and a half-burned pine knot that had been too green to burn all the way.

As he did, Jackson stirred, rolled onto his back, yawned, ran a hand down his face.

Angus glanced at Dutch lying on the other side of the fire ring from him, then started crunching up a dry pinecone in his hand for tinder. Something made him look back at Dutch, quickly.

"Dutch?" he said, his heart quickening.

The man gave no reply.

Angus rose on creaky knees, went over, and dropped to a knee beside McCrae.

The man's eyes were open wide, but he wasn't looking at Angus. He was looking right through him, the man's eyes still owning the lunatic fear they'd shone a few hours before, when the bruin had been closing on Dutch, intending to rip, rend, and devour. His mouth was half open, twisted as though mid-scream.

Angus placed his hand on the big man's chest, over his bedroll.

Stillness.

Jackson yawned and looked at Angus. He frowned. Davis was starting to stir now, as well.

"What is it?"

Angus removed his hand from the big man's chest.

"Dutch is no more."

Scared to death.

CHAPTER 26

A nnabelle felt ridiculous.

She looked down at the gown—from Miss Delphine's own large closet—and at the pearls looped around her neck, the long, white gloves on her hands that matched the white silk of the gown that hugged every curve of her body as though it had been tailored for her. The two girls still doting over her, nipping and tucking and adjusting her garish face paint, looked from her to her image in the standing mirror.

Miss Delphine sat in a brocade armchair fronting one of the suite's two large windows, drawing on her cigarette holder and regarding Annabelle critically, nodding her approval.

"Fine, fine," she said in her heavy Southern accent. "You look just fine. Better than fine. When Machado gets a look at you, he's gonna swallow his tongue."

"Does the neckline need to be this low?" Anna asked, brushing a gloved thumb across her deep, freckled cleavage.

The girls were messing with her hair now, making sure it was adequately coifed after being washed and dried, then brushed out until it shone, then piled neatly and pinned with delicate silver clips atop her head. A few red sausage curls hung strategically down against her rouged cheeks.

"It does."

Annabelle drew her mouth corners down as she looked at the young woman in the mirror. She couldn't help wondering what Hunter would think if he saw her now, being outfitted for another man. Being decked out in something as revealing as the dress she was wearing, the matching elastic, side-button shoes pinching her feet. She hadn't worn anything so feminine since she'd worked in a saloon a couple of years earlier, when Hunter had refused to marry her until he'd gotten his gold stake—the stake for their marriage—back from who had stolen it.

That person had turned out to be Annabelle's own brother, Cass.

Guilt had compelled Cass to return the gold dust to Hunter, so he and Annabelle could be married at last and could start rebuilding the Box Bar B after Annabelle's father, Graham Ludlow, and his marauding men had burned most of it to the ground, killing Hunter's oldest and youngest brothers, Shep and Tyrell, respectively.

Life had not been easy for her and Hunter.

Now, looking at the stranger peering back at her through her own eyes in the mirror, she was reminded that it wasn't getting any easier.

"Drink." Miss Delphine had poured them each a brandy. She thrust the snifter at Annabelle now and sat back down in the chair, crossing her legs. "That will loosen you up. My God, something must!"

"How am I supposed to feel loose?" Annabelle snapped at the woman. "I feel like I'm being thrown to the wolves. Or at least to the leader of the pack. The man's a savage and you want me to step out with him . . . like he's sparking me or something?"

"Oh, he is sparking you, dear heart." Again, Miss Delphine sipped her brandy. "Make no mistake."

"Does he really think I could feel any *tenderness* toward

him . . . any desire to go out *dining* with him. What about after that—*dancing*?"

Miss Delphine pursed her lips, shook her head, and looked up at Annabelle from beneath her thin, perfectly sculpted brows. "Dear heart, you're going to have to change your attitude. Keep in mind." She placed a finger to her temple. "That man's crazy. Crazier'n a treeful of owls. For whatever reason, he's tumbled for you. I've never seen him like this. Never. Somewhere along the trail, he got to fantasizing about you . . . about how it might feel to be your man."

"My God . . ." Annabelle said, slowly wagging her head in exasperation. "He's an animal."

"Yes, but that animal has feelings for you. Those feelings might very well guarantee your safety for at least as long as the rest of the trip. If you play your cards right, he might even decide to keep you for himself."

"Oh, do you really think . . . ?"

"Shhh!" Miss Delphine pressed two fingers to her lips. "Keep your voice down. And, no, I don't think you'll go along with it but you'd better do a good job of pretending to or." She swept her index finger across her throat, giving Annabelle a grave expression. "One minute . . . one hour . . . one day at a time . . . until you can find a way to free yourself from the man's insane clutches."

Again, she tapped her finger against her temple. "Remember. Attitude. The crazy devil is sweet on you. Go with it. Use it to your advantage. Take *advantage* of him . . . and you might find yourself in a position to get away from him."

Soft footsteps in the hall.

Three light taps on the door.

Both Patricia and Mattie gasped with starts and stopped messing with Annabelle's hair.

Miss Delphine rose from the chair and, trailing cigarette

smoke from her holder, opened the door. Annabelle didn't turn but stared toward the chair Miss Delphine had just left.

"He's here," came a quiet, grave, female voice behind her.

The door clicked shut.

In the mirror, Annabelle saw Miss Delphine turn to her. "Ready?"

"God, no." Annabelle tried to suppress a shudder without success.

Ten minutes later, after a little last-minute primping by the Lone Wolf's madam and Patricia and Mattie, Annabelle was led downstairs, a light silk wrap draped across her shoulders against the possible chill of the coming evening. A lamb to the slaughter albeit a well-groomed, coifed, and dressed one.

Miss Delphine stepped outside ahead of Annabelle, with both Mattie and Patricia following, like bridesmaids at a wedding, Annabelle couldn't help thinking while trying in vain to suppress another shudder. He was standing at the base of the Lone Wolf's porch steps, near the high, red wheel of a leather carriage. A small, slovenly, elderly man in a black immigrant's hat and soiled coat over a soiled wool shirt sat in the carriage's front seat, holding the ribbons of a charcoal gray gelding and staring straight ahead.

Miss Delphine glanced at Annabelle. Annabelle knew the madam was thinking the same thing she was: *My God—he even hired a carriage and a driver!* The driver was likely a swamper from the livery barn from which Machado had hired the carriage. He had that air about him; Annabelle thought she could smell the stench of manure emanating from his clothes.

Just how ill was Saguaro Machado, anyway? Annabelle inquired of the madam silently with a look.

The outlaw leader was dressed in his usual crude and mismatched trail clothes, but he must have had a bath because he looked cleaner, and his long hair appeared still damp and freshly braided. He'd brushed the dust from his black top hat as well as from the hawk feather jutting from the band. The jagged scar cutting through the eye patch looked just as grisly as ever. He flushed—bashful??—as he pinched his hat brim to Annabelle, then turned to open the carriage's rear door.

Annabelle gave one last, frightened look at Miss Delphine, who merely drew deeply on her ubiquitous cigarette holder, lifted her fine chin, and blew the smoke into the cooling, early evening air. Behind her, Mattie and Patricia, remaining on the porch, wore wide-eyed, apprehensive expressions.

Stiffly, with a reluctance bordering on panic, Annabelle climbed into the carriage.

Machado climbed in beside her. He closed the door, gave a grunt, and the driver whipped the reins against the gray's back and turned the gelding out into the street, then down a meandering side street.

Annabelle clenched her hands together in her lap, wondering what else besides dinner the scoundrel sitting beside her, arm stretched across the top of the seat behind her, might expect of her this night.

Lamb to the slaughter . . .

Ten minutes later, Annabelle found herself sitting across from Machado in a tony dining room—at least, tony by Lone Pine's and probably all of eastern Dakota's standards—in a hotel named THE DAKOTA BADLANDS INN.

It had a façade of wood and stone and had likely been much more impressive in its and Lone Pine's heyday, for the wood portion was in badly need of paint and several windows were cracked. Annabelle knew nothing about the town, but she'd seen enough similar settlements to figure Lone Pine had once been large, prouder, possibly a little more civilized back when cattle had been herded through the area on the way to the gold camps in the Black Hills farther north and west.

Nowadays, more cattle were shipped by rail from Sioux City and Council Bluffs, and the obvious outlaws outnumbered the honest businessmen a good five to one, she had observed on her ride through town to the Lone Wolf Hotel, which, she'd learned, was no longer a hotel at all but a hurdy-gurdy house.

Still, the clientele in the Badlands Inn seemed a cut above the crowd of men Anna had seen in the street. To be sure, there were a few cow punchers in the place, as well as gamblers and obvious mule skinners, but the bulk of the crowd appeared ranchers or cattle buyers—ruddy-skinned, mustached westerners conversing in businesslike tones and clad in clean, stylish western attire including bolo ties and crisp Stetsons. Such men, likely knowing Machado's reputation, cast frequent, incredulous glances toward the cloth-covered table at which Annabelle sat across from the big, savage-looking, one-eyed outlaw, who so far had not spoken a single word to her but had communicated with hand gestures and grunts.

Annabelle kept glancing around, as though she could expect to find help here among these more civilized men than those stumbling from saloon to saloon out on Lone Pine's dusty street. No help, however, appeared imminent. Just as she realized she could expect no help from the Lone Pine lawman, she was realizing now that she could expect no help from any of its citizens or wealthy, law-abiding visitors, either.

Machado ordered red wine, which a liveried and obviously nervous waiter who wore a towel over one arm served with cultured aplomb, which was lost on Machado who kept his dark, flat, one-eyed gaze on his dinner companion. The waiter filled their glasses, told them he would return later for their order cards, and strode quickly away, chuckling nervously.

Finally, Machado said something. He looked at her Anna's untouched wine and said, "Drink. Bought for you."

She gave a start at the unexpected outpouring of words from the savage man. At least, an outpouring for Machado. He waved a big, brown, scarred hand at her glass.

Annabelle slid her hand to the glass. It was shaking. She couldn't hide it. She took a quick sip of the wine, then one more, hoping it would settle her down a little. It did not. She didn't think she'd be able to eat anything, either, and silently hoped her lack of appetite wouldn't rile the man paying for her meal and wanting—what?

Herself?

Did he really think that after all he'd done to her that he could win her with some wine and a meal?

If so, he really was insane and even more dangerous than she'd thought.

He threw back half his glass in three swallows, then re-filled it with the bottle the waiter had left on the table. Then he slid one of the menu cards and a pencil stub toward Anna.

"What's it say?" he asked.

She looked at the cards. She drew a breath, steeling her-self against her fear, and read the options on the menu card.

"Oyster stew with brook trout, fried chicken and mashed potatoes, pork roast with potatoes. All options come with pie and coffee for dessert."

"Mark down the chicken for me."

Annabelle scratched a check mark in the box next to the chicken on the card.

She wasn't sure what she would choose. None of it sounded good to her. In fact, all three choices made her feel sick to her stomach. While she was reviewing the choices, she spied movement in the big window to the right of the restaurant's big, oak door. Two horseback riders had just ridden up to the Badlands Inn.

Anna's heart quickened.

Both men wore moon-and-star badges of deputy U.S. marshals pinned to their coat lapels.

Her heart banged.

Lawmen. Federal lawmen.

Surely, she could at last find help from this promising new quarter!

To cover her interest in the newcomers just then climbing the porch steps and heading for the front door, she quickly scratched a mark next to the oyster stew with trout, dropped the pencil, and slid the card to the edge of the table.

When she looked up at Machado again, he was giving a crooked smile, staring at her as though he knew her every little secret.

CHAPTER 27

Annabelle's heart quickened when she heard the front door open twenty feet away on her left, as she faced her captor.

She cast the two federal lawmen a quick glance—seeing one tall man with an upswept, gray mustache and a shorter man who appeared younger and who also wore an upswept mustache, brown, as though he were trying to pattern himself, or at least his mustache, after the older lawman. They were both in three-piece suits, the older man with a blue shirt, black vest, and black ribbon tie, the younger man in a white shirt, burgundy vest, and a black foulard tie. Both wore tan Stetsons. As they glanced around the room, removing their hats, the older lawman smoothing his straight, gray hair into place, Annabelle dared another quick glance.

The older man appeared somewhere in his fifties.

The younger man was a good thirty years younger. He wore a congenial smile while the older, more experienced lawman's eyes showed little emotion as they darted quickly around the room, getting the layout and likely trying to identify any possible threats. He was likely well aware that, like so many towns on this remote prairie, Lone Pine was another wide-open settlement populated with outlaws fresh off the owlhoot trail. The businesslike expression on his long,

angular face told Annabelle he was one federal lawman who
would not avoid such a town but take any trouble he found
there head-on.

Or so she hoped as she reached for her wineglass, noticing
with a wince that her hand was shaking. She suppressed the
shaking as she sipped the wine, which she couldn't taste, suppressed it again as she set the glass back down on the table.

The two lawmen made their way to a table halfway between Machado's and Annabelle's table and the dining
room's long, mahogany bar running along the wall straight
out away from Anna. She wasn't sure if her captor had seen
the two lawmen. He'd cast a quick glance toward the front
of the room when the door had opened, but if he'd noted
the badges pinned to the lawmen's vests he hadn't let on.
Annabelle chose to believe he had. A man like Machado, for
all his seeming ease and menacing lack of expression, took
note of things like badges.

However, he'd made no attempt to sit with his back to a
wall, which he could have done because several tables near
walls were available. That told Annabelle the man was confident no one would try to shoot him in the back. That was
the intensity of the air of danger that the man moved through
the world firmly ensconced in. He was a confident brute, a
killer without even the good manners to remove his ridiculous top hat with its hawk feather jutting from the band.

Why the charade? she couldn't help wondering as the
waiter, humming pleasantly, disappeared into the kitchen
through a swinging door to the right of the long bar at which
a half-dozen men in trail garb stood, a few conversing, one
reading a newspaper, the others enjoying their drinks in
silence.

Did Machado have feelings for her?

The thought was almost laughable.

On the other hand, that was probably the reason she was
still alive after several escape attempts.

She found him regarding her with a dubious expression on his hideously scarred, one-eyed face. He turned his wineglass by its stem with his enormous right index finger and thumb. She was surprised he didn't break the stem off the glass.

She had trouble meeting his gaze.

She also had trouble keeping her eyes off the two lawmen sitting ten feet away from her. They'd set their hats on their table, ordered beers from a slender, middle-aged woman with an apron and no-nonsense air, and were conversing in low but pleasant tones, the younger one smiling and occasionally looking around with his affable, blue-eyed gaze.

Annabelle's first thought when she'd seen the lawmen ride up to the restaurant—her first hope—was that they were here looking for her. That hoped died in her, however, for neither man had the air of hunters. Neither one had so much as given her and Machado a passing glance, and Anna didn't think either one was feigning nonchalance. Something told her they were just passing through Lone Pine, maybe hunting other outlaws. Their only interest in the restaurant was likely drink and food.

No different from the other customers.

She looked at the menu cards on the table, wedged between a green cut-glass vase with blue paper flowers in it and a black, stone horse standing on its back feet, clawing at the sky with its front hooves. The horse seemed to be looking at Anna a little askance, as though it was somehow aware of her dangerous situation.

Anna glanced at the menu cards again, heart fluttering.

The backs of the cards were blank. The stub of a pencil rested on the table before them.

She had to get a note to the lawmen.

But how . . . ?

She turned to Machado again. He sipped his wine, set it back down on the table, and returned his gaze to her, one brow slightly arched, as if he were waiting for her to say something.

"Well," she said, deciding to oblige him. He was certainly no conversationalist, and if his mind was anywhere on the two deputy U.S. marshals, she wanted to try to get it off them. "Shall we try to have a conversation?"

"About what?" he said in his deep, throaty voice. His tone sounded a little defensive as though he were silently weighing her motives.

Well, she was weighing his, as well . . .

"Why?" she said, taking her glass in both hands, slowly turning it between her palms, trying to keep them from shaking. They were moist with nerve sweat.

"Why what?"

"Why . . . this?"

Machado shrugged a heavy shoulder. "You're tough." His eyes bored into hers. "And beautiful. I wasn't expecting such a beautiful woman to be so tough." He shrugged again. "I admire courage. Even most men don't have that much courage . . . to stand up to Saguaro Machado."

He gave a crooked smile. His lone, dark eye glinted with self-satisfaction.

Again, he shrugged his shoulder. "You might even come to like me . . . someday."

She couldn't help betraying a little of the exasperation with her voice. "You kidnapped me. Intend to sell me to slave traders."

"We'll see."

"We'll see what?"

"If Corazon appreciates you as much as I do."

"I don't understand."

Machado topped off her wineglass then topped off his own. "You will." He set the bottle back down on the table. "I might get more money for you in Mexico. Unless . . ."

He sipped his wine deeply, taking several swallows, the

way most men drink beer. His lone-eyed gaze was getting glassy. Anna wasn't sure if his getting drunk was good or bad. Likely, bad. On the trail when he'd been drunk, he'd gotten quiet. Dark. Brooding.

He pursed his lips, canted his head to one side, and made an offhand gesture with his hand. "Unless you decide to be my woman."

Annabelle wanted to laugh. She wanted to laugh and slap the table.

But she kept her face stony, impassive. She wasn't sure what to say to that, so she said nothing. Her honesty might only hasten her demise. On the other hand, was this man really stupid enough to believe that she would ever willingly become his woman? If so, then she would take advantage of his stupidity for as long as she could. At the very least, it might keep her alive. For how long, was anyone's guess. If she was turned over to the slave trader named Corazon, she had little doubt she'd want to be dead.

So far, Machado and his men—aside from Big Nick, that was—had resisted ravaging her. Machado had warned them off. She hadn't seen it or heard it, but she sensed it by the obviously frustrated way the other men eyed her sometimes.

"You miss your husband," Machado said. It wasn't a question.

"Of course," she couldn't help snapping, wrinkling her nose at the big man with brash disdain.

He smiled, showing tobacco-stained teeth. "He is weak. He couldn't protect you."

"You jumped us. Hunter was outnumbered."

"You think about it," Machado said. "I might not be so bad."

She didn't respond. She knew what he meant. He wanted her to think about becoming his woman, though now the thought wasn't laughable but very grave, very frightening, indeed.

When their meals came, Annabelle almost felt sick looking at it. She was hungry, but she was also nauseated. She wasn't sure she could hold any of it down. Machado ordered another bottle of wine, and as she poked at her food, trying to eat small bites, and the waiter returned with another bottle of the French wine, her thoughts returned to the marshals.

Somehow, she had to let them know she was in trouble. She knew they'd both seen Machado, for she'd seen their gazes slide across him, hold briefly, then continue to sweep the room. Obviously, the big, one-eyed man was attention-grabbing, but neither lawman had seemed to recognize him. They'd probably seen that he was trouble—obviously so!—but their interest, Anna could tell, was on other quarry.

Picking at her fish, she glanced again at the small menu cards and at the pencil stub. Deciding there was no way to get a note to the two marshals without Machado noticing, she decided to try another tactic. There was no way she could leave the restaurant without at least trying to get word to the lawmen that she needed help.

Her heart quickened again when a thought occurred to her. She looked around as though for the waiter, frowning.

"Excuse me," she said, setting her napkin on the table and starting to slide back her chair. "I need some milk. The wine isn't going down very—"

"I'll tell the waiter." Machado looked around for the man.

"I haven't seen him in a while," Anna said. "I think he must be occupied with something in the kitchen." She could hear him talking back there with two other men beneath the sounds of cooking food and pots and pans clattering together, the squawk of an opening and closing stove door.

She slid her chair back a little farther. "I'll fetch him."

"No!" Machado gave her a hard, commanding look. "I will."

He slid his chair back, rose, and walked toward the door to the right of the bar.

Immediately, Annabelle grabbed one of the menu cards and the pencil, and scribbled HELP ME in large, dark letters on its back. Hearing Machado's gruff voice, she returned the pencil to its place beside the vase, then folded the card quickly and slipped it into her low-cut bodice, shoving it down out of sight in her cleavage and smoothing it down so it wasn't noticeable.

She looked up quickly to see Machado moving back to the table in his slow, heavy-footed way, his big, broad face a little red with pique.

Had he seen her stuff the card in her bodice?

Her heart raced. She felt a bead of sweat pop out on her brow.

But he merely grunted, returned to his chair, and dug back into his meal, which he'd nearly finished eating with animalistic fervor while Annabelle had hardly touched her own.

Annabelle stuffed a few more forkfuls of fish and oyster stew into her mouth, drank some of her milk, and said, "I have to use the privy."

Machado lifted his head, reached across the table, and placed his big left hand on her right one. He gave another, louder grunt and cast her a threatening look.

"I'm too exhausted to try to flee again," Anna said with a sigh. "Besides, how could I possibly try to run in this get-up?" She kicked her left foot out from under the table, held it high. "And in these shoes."

Machado looked at the shoe, grunted again, smiled, then released her hand and went back to work on his nearly empty plate.

Anna rose, moved around the table, and headed toward the back door in the room's rear wall, adjacent to the door to the kitchen. Her route would take her past the lawmen's table. She was so weak from anxiousness she thought she would pass out. Her feet felt heavy and the room sort of swirled around her.

She was six feet from the lawmen's table when she glanced into the back bar mirror. Machado was still hunkered over his plate, his back to her and the lawmen, giving his full attention to polishing off his meal. Anna quickly slipped the folded menu card out from her bodice and, as she passed the lawman's table, dropped it on the table between them, giving it a little toss so they'd be sure to see it right away.

Both men frowned down at the folded card. They frowned up at the pretty redhead, deep lines of incredulity cutting across their foreheads. Anna gave them each a dark look of silent beseeching, then continued across the room and out the back door. She went into the two-hole privy and endured the stench issuing from another customer in the compartment beside her for a couple of minutes, wondering what was happening inside the restaurant.

The silence was frustrating.

Would the lawmen help her, or had they recognized Machado and, as afraid of the outlaw as most other men, decided they'd leave well enough alone and live to arrest less dangerous criminals another day?

Curiosity added to Annabelle's anxiety.

Finally, hearing her neighbor grunting and cursing under his breath in the other stall, Anna tripped the latch, opened the door, followed the deeply worn path to the restaurant's back door, and went inside.

The lawmen had been served and were eating.

They spoke as they cut their food and chewed, both men

not looking at Anna, though she knew they'd seen her enter the restaurant. The note was no longer on their table. Anna walked past them, her feet feeling even heavier than before. Still, the two lawmen did not look up at her.

She walked past them, and their seeming indifference to her made her want to cry.

Shakily, she moved past Machado and retook her place across from him.

His plate and hers were gone.

He looked up at her with reproval. He'd bought her a meal, most of which she hadn't eaten. The second bottle of wine was nearly gone. Machado's glass was half-full. But not for long. As soon as Anna had retaken her seat, he threw back the rest of the glass in three deep swallows. He scrubbed his shirt sleeve across his mouth with a snort and a grunt, adjusted his hat, and, holding his holstered revolver in place against his right thigh, rose from his chair.

He fished some coins out of a pocket of his black, sun-coppered trousers, tossed them onto the table. Without even looking at Anna, he turned and headed toward the restaurant's front door. Anna followed, glancing quickly at the two lawmen who were still talking and eating, wiping their mouths with their cloth napkins, the old man raising his left forearm and sneezing into it, loudly.

"Bless you!" said the other man over a fork load of fried chicken and potatoes.

Crestfallen, deeply frustrated, even exasperated at the lawman's inaction, Anna followed her tormentor out onto the porch fronting the building, then down the porch steps toward where the old, scrawny man whom Anna assumed was a liveryman still sat in the smart-looking carriage's driver's seat. The ribbons were wrapped around the brake handle. He didn't look at either her or Machado, who opened the carriage door for her. She was on the verge of tears.

She'd just started to climb up into the rear seat when the Inn's front door opened.

The two lawmen stepped out, the older one first, followed by the younger one, both men smoothing their hair and thick mustaches down and setting their hats on their heads. Machado froze in place beside the carriage's rear, open door, regarding the two men blandly. He cut a quick look at Anna, then returned his attention to the lawmen.

"Excuse us, there," said the older lawman, moving down the steps a little stiffly, as though his knees bothered him.

When he reached the bottom of the steps, he turned to face Machado who stood roughly eight feet away from him, on the street fronting the boardwalk. The younger lawmen stopped beside the older one and turned to face Machado, as well. His earlier good nature seemed to have soured. Now it was the older man who was smiling, his gray eyes lit with ironic humor, though Annabelle could see he was merely trying to disarm Machado. The outlaw stood hulking before the two lawmen, the older, taller one standing a good four inches shorter, the young one a whole head and a half shorter than that. Both lawmen let their right hands hang down over the walnut grips of their revolvers.

"What do you want?" Machado growled.

"Just wondering if everything's all right," asked the young lawman, who made the somewhat cocky mistake of hooking his thumbs behind his cartridge belt. Right away, Annabelle saw it was a mistake. Machado was fast. She'd seen him shoot. And the younger lawman had far too much brass for his own good.

He was trying to show off for Annabelle, she knew, a dark wave of dread washing through her. He drew a deep breath, canted his head slightly to one side, and spread his feet a little wider apart.

"Is it?" he asked the silent Machado. He glanced at Annabelle, then returned his all-business gaze to the outlaw.

Machado said nothing. He just stood staring down at the two men, a slight grin twisting his lips.

Seconds passed. Long, stretched seconds.

A minute.

The two lawmen glanced at each other uneasily.

The older lawmen said, "Just want to make sure the young lady's all right is all."

Machado glanced at Annabelle. "You all right?"

Anna sobbed. She couldn't help it. The emotion exploded out of her.

Then another sob exploded out of her, and her vision became blurry from the tears rushing to her eyes.

The lawmen shared another uneasy glance.

Stiffly, they looked at Anna and then returned their gazes to Machado, who stood as before, that odd frown twisting his thick, chapped lips, bits of his meal clinging to his bushy, tangled beard.

Oh, God, Anna thought, sucking back a scream that wanted very much to bound up out of her lungs. *Oh, God!*

The younger lawman drew first.

He was the first to get a bullet drilled into his guts.

Before the older one had even started to pull his own gun from its holster, he, too, went twisting around on the board-walk, yelling and clutching his hands to his belly from which blood and bowels were erupting. The two men, losing their hats, piled up beside each other, writhing and yelling, dying hard.

Machado laughed.

The liveryman drew back hard on the reins of the horse hitched to the carriage; it leaped in place and regarded the two loudly dying, writhing lawmen with terror in its eyes. A terror akin to that nearly making Annabelle's heart explode.

Laughing, leaving the lawmen dying on the boardwalk from the agonizing belly wounds, Machado climbed into the carriage, closed the door, and slapped the seat back ahead of him.

The liveryman, trying desperately to keep the frightened horse from bolting, swung the carriage out into the street and turned the skitter-hopping horse back in the direction from which they'd come.

Machado lolled back in his seat, holding his own belly against the mirth making his ribs ache, roaring.

CHAPTER 28

The rain came down hard for a good hour, effectively wiping out Machado's spoor, which Hunter found the next morning when he tried to get back on their trail.

He was bereft, hopeless, feeling as though a rusty pig-sticker had been poked through his heart.

The one true love of his life had been taken from him. He doubted he'd ever get back on their trail again though he likely would have lost it, anyway, for he was heading for a settlement and a sawbones for Powwow, who rode beside him, looking pale and drawn from the wound in his leg. Hunter was afraid infection was setting in. That's why he knew he had no choice but to head for one of the few towns marked on the old government survey map in his saddlebags.

The town was called Bull Hook Bottoms. Though he'd never been there, Hunter had heard of it—a somewhat notorious hide hunter's camp back when there were still a few buffalo left roaming this short grass prairie spiked with sage and prickly pear and bunches of late-summer, fawn-colored bunch grass. Hunter had heard the usual riffraff had frequented the shaggy-headed place back in the day, including Buffalo Bill and his sometime sidekick, Calamity Jane, whose salty language equaled and sometimes beat all to hell that spewed by the roughest, most Irish of railroad track layers and gandy dancers.

Remembering dear old Calamity as he rode, following an old stagecoach and likely buffalo hunter's trail, Hunter almost cracked a smile. Almost. Then he remembered seeing Anna wrestled away from him, heard her screams in the Yellow Hotel in Lusk. His heart returned to ashes.

"Hunter," Powwow said, riding beside him, a constipated look on his pale, sickly features. "Please go after your wife . . . Machado. I can find my own way to Bull Hook Bottoms."

"You're liable to faint and tumble from your saddle."

"I won't. I promise."

"Besides," Hunter added, "I have no trail to follow. The rain wiped it out. Was bound to eventually, anyway. I'll get back after Machado soon enough. If Anna's still alive, I'll find her. Sooner or later."

He hated the doubt he heard in his own voice.

Following behind him and his trail mate, Bobby Lee stopped to give a low, mournful howl, then continued dogging his master's trail. That almost bought a tear of raw emotion to Hunter's eye. The coyote knew the stakes. Was likely missing Annabelle as badly as Hunter was.

It was late in the afternoon when they crossed a long, broad curve in the trail still muddy from the previous night's rain, though the hot Dakota sun was drying it out quickly now. Staring straight ahead, Hunter saw the motley-looking settlement spread out at the base of a rise on which one lone pine grew, listing a little to the southeast and looking like the loneliest tree in the world.

A sign slid up in the brush off the trail's right side.

LONE PINE it read in faded lettering.

Hmm, Hunter thought. The town fathers must have changed the name to something sounding a little more respectable, a little more civilized. A modicum of hope rose in Hunter. The town looked larger than the hide hunter's camp it had started out as. Surely, at least he and Powwow would find a sawbones there so they wouldn't have made the trip for nothing.

They rode on into the town.

Hunter had to inquire several times before any of the rough characters populating Lone Pine would answer his request for the location of a pill roller. One man only threw out an arm to indicate a straight ahead on the main drag's left side, grunted, and strolled on, belching his sour beer and whiskey breath.

Dr. Wesley Mordecai Robertson's office occupied the second story of a furniture shop. Access was gained to the humble, unpainted, clapboard building's second story via stairs running along the outside. Hunter helped Powwow negotiate the narrow steps, moving slowly, Powwow grunting with each step he took with his left foot, clamping his left hand over the bandage Hunter had wrapped around his thigh and that he could see through the hole Hunter had cut in the denims.

The bandage was liberally spotted with blood.

Which meant that the previous night and today, Powwow had lost a good bit of the precious stuff. That's why he was so blamed weak that Hunter found himself almost carrying the younger man up the steps.

Wisely, Bobby Lee had found a rabbit to chase out in the country just before they'd reached town, so at least Hunter didn't have his loyal coyote to worry about. Many a westerner—and not just stockmen—would shoot a coyote on sight.

Just as Hunter and his charge gained the top of the stairs, the door to the doctor's office opened and a man in his fifties stumbled out, groaning and holding his right arm, which was secured by a white cotton sling, close against his chest. He wore a denim jacket over a wool shirt, faded dungarees, and hobnailed boots; his face was deeply tanned above the salt-and-pepper beard he wore. Likely a mule skinner who hauled freight from the Union Pacific Depot in Cheyenne. Hunter had seen plenty of those rigs, pulled by braying mules under the whip crack of the skinners' blacksnake, along the trail.

"Riley, go easy on that laudanum now," said a man in a shabby wool vest coming up behind him, a stethoscope hanging around his neck, steel-framed spectacles hanging low on his nose. "It's highly addictive. Just a conservative sip every now and then when the pain is particularly bad." He was stoop-shouldered, potbellied, and bald on the top of his head, with long, gray, unkempt hair hanging down from the sides.

"Yeah, yeah, all right, Doc—I hear ya!" said the man called Riley, groaning as he negotiated his way down the steps. The neck of a flat, blue bottle jutted from a corner of his jacket.

The doctor turned to Hunter. "Damn fool is gonna go over to his flophouse and drink the whole bottle. I just know it. He'll be in the bag for the next three days!"

"You're the sawbones, I take it."

"You take it right. Wesley M. Robertson, M.D." The sawbones looked at Powwow, who had one arm wrapped around Hunter's neck and was stretching his lips back from his pain against the torment in his leg. "What's ailing him?"

"Flesh wound in his leg. I cleaned and stitched it closed but it opened up during the ride here."

"All right, all right." The doctor turned and began walking into his office, beckoning. "Bring him on in here and let me take a look." More groans came from the dark hall down which he led his Hunter and his new patient. "Been a busy day. Been a busy week. Hell, it's been a busy year.

What these men won't do to each other after a few tipples of the ol' who-hit-John. Savages!"

He opened the third and last door at the end of the hall, on the right, and went in. Hunter helped Powwow through the door in which dimming, late-day sunlight pushed through a single window in the wall over a leather examination table.

"Lay him out on that," said the sawbones.

When Hunter had eased Powwow onto the table after first removing his hat and pegging it by the door, the doctor said, "Let's get that hogleg off him and pull his pants off."

Hunter removed Powwow's pistol and hung the shell belt by his hat. Then he wrestled Powwow's pants off, Powwow groaning and apologizing for taking the bullet.

"You didn't have too much say in it, Powwow," Hunter said. "It was the luck of the draw."

"Who shot him?"

"Owlhoots."

"His name's . . . ?"

"William Tecumseh Lancaster," Powwow said through another groan. "Powwow for short." He tried a smile and held up his right hand, the index finger and thumb a half inch apart. "I have about that much Comanch blood. Hale from the Red River country, don't ya know."

The doctor was cutting off the bandage from Powwow's leg with a small scissors he'd produced from a steel wall cabinet above a steel table adorned with many small, colorful bottles and grisly looking surgical instruments including a bone saw. After the bloody war he'd endured four long years of, Hunter had hoped he'd never see such an instrument again. He'd seen plenty of arms and legs stacked outside surgical tents on bloody Southern meadows. He saw those in his sleep.

"I see, I see," the doctor said, removing the bandage. He held it up to inspect it. It was soaked with blood.

Powwow looked up at it through one narrowed eye and passed out with a ragged sigh.

Dr. Robertson turned to Hunter with a curious frown.

"Can't stand the sight of blood," Hunter said with an ironic smile. "Least of all his own."

"Ah."

While the doctor fetched a basin of water and cloths and began working on Powwow's bloody left thigh, Hunter went to the window and stared absently into the street below that was still busy now at nearly six o'clock, suppertime. More horses had been tied to hitchracks fronting saloons and hurdy-gurdy houses than when he'd first ridden into town. He could hear the tinny patter of a piano emanating from one such establishment up the street on his right.

A man shouted angrily. Another shouted back at him.

"Ah, the wolves are starting to howl," said Dr. Wesley M. Robertson, M.D., as he gently snipped Hunter's sutures and cleaned the wound with a damp, bloody cloth. "There'll be a few in here before midnight, a few after with others becoming the delight of our local undertaker, who keeps a welcoming beacon in his office window all night long."

The middle-aged sawbones clucked disgustedly and shook his head.

"Sounds like Lusk," Hunter said, anger rising in him, remembering.

"Hell, it is Lusk . . . just by another name. These remote, prairie towns always attract the worst of men."

The doctor had no sooner made the statement than Hunter saw a buckboard wagon pull up in front of the undertaker's shop on the other side of the street, strategically positioned, he silently opined, across from the doctor's office. Hunter wouldn't doubt it if the old pill roller and the undertaker were in business cahoots. He'd heard of it before, though it seemed to him to be rife with conflict of interest, at least on the sawbones' part. But a man had to make a living, and in a place like Lone Pine, the doctor likely had to find other sources of cash.

Hunter frowned down at the wagon. Two bodies lay in the box, belly up. They were covered with wool blankets, but they were dead bodies, all right. Bloody shirts and vests were piled in a corner of the wagon by the tailgate, which the scrawny, elderly man who'd driven the wagon opened. As he did, he was joined by a tall, sharp-featured, bald man, who surfaced from the undertaking parlor, clad in a bloody apron.

Hunter's frown grew more severe when he saw clothes—bloody shirts and vests, it appeared—piled in a corner at the rear of the wagon. To one vest was pinned a badge.

Hunter scrutinized the badge more closely, squinting through the window, until he recognized the moon-and-star badge of a deputy U.S. marshal.

"I see the undertaker has him some fresh business," Hunter said, still staring through the window as one of the bodies was pulled out by the undertaker and the man who'd driven the wagon.

"Ahh, Glenn Steinmark," the doctor said as he threaded a needle with catgut, his tone absent, distracted. "He owns the furniture store below as well as the undertaking parlor. Business got so good in recent years that he had to branch out, bought the old grocery store across the street. Really been packing them in over the past year or two. He an' the missus journey to Denver frequently to wine and dine, enjoying a little rest and relaxation. Steinmark's damn near the richest man in town!" the sawbones added with an ironic laugh.

"Looks like one of his new clients is a federal badge toter."

"They both are." The doctor sighed as he went to work sewing up Powwow's leg, the young patient grunting and groaning as the needle poked through the skin the sawbones was pinching up between thumb and index finger. "Both

were shot yesterday afternoon. I had them hauled into the
Badlands Inn, worked on them both for hours, trying to dig
the bullets out of their guts while a couple of bouncers held
them down. Never heard such yelling. A bloody mess. They
were shot in just the right place to inflict the maximum,
longest lasting pain. Mercifully they both died around three
this morning and I was able to pack up and come home for
an hour's worth of sleep and a few eggs."

Again, the doctor sighed as, sitting in a chair beside the
examination table, he pulled the catgut through once more.
"I'm getting too old for this. A fella needs his sleep."

Hunter had barely heard that last statement. Something
else of significant interest had just caught his eye on the
street below the doctor's office. Or *someone* else, rather—a
horseback rider in a brown vest and battered tan Stetson was
just then riding past the doctor's office, riding from Hunter's
left to his right, opening his vest to adjust something—an
envelope?—poking up from the vest pocket of his shirt.
Hunter couldn't see the man's face from this angle. But the
rest of him looked familiar. Hunter looked more closely at
the horse the man rode and recognized a coal black with one
white stocking.

It was one of the broncs Hunter and Annabelle had sold
to Rufus and Lucinda Scanlon at their Arapaho Creek Ranch
in Colorado. The Arapaho Creek "A/C" brand had been
freshly burned into the black's left wither.

Deep curiosity laced with a rising apprehension rose in
Hunter.

He hadn't seen the face of the man riding the black well
past the doctor's office now. But he knew who he was—
Jack Tatum, foreman at Arapaho Creek and former deputy
sheriff in Deadwood with whom Hunter had once scrapped,
drunkenly, in a Deadwood Saloon.

What in holy blazes was Tatum doing here, in Lone Pine?

As he watched, Tatum angled his horse toward a saloon

on the opposite side of the street from the doctor's office, one block beyond.

Scowling deeply as the blood quickened its course through his veins, Hunter turned to the sawbones, who was just then finishing the stitching of Powwow's wound.

"Doc," Hunter said, "who was it who shot the federals?"

The medico snipped the catgut down near the wound he'd sewn shut and said with another wag of his head and a fateful sigh. "Truly, a demon from hell who walks this earth as—"

"Saguaro Machado."

The doctor cast Hunter an incredulous look. "How'd you know?"

Hunter didn't take time to respond.

In seconds, he left the exam room, crossed the office, opened the door, and ran down the stairs three steps at a time.

CHAPTER 29

Hunter ripped the grullo's reins off the hitchrack fronting the doctor's office, fairly leaped into the saddle, and galloped along the street for one block before swinging toward the two hitchracks fronting the Angry Dog Saloon and Brewery.

He put the grullo up next to Jack Tatum's black, who, recognizing Hunter, gave a friendly whinny and one friendly switch of his tail. Hunter ran his hand down the black's snout, mounted the boardwalk, and pushed through the batwings, finding himself in the twilight world of a smoky bar with only a few of its lamps lit against the coming dusk.

Three men stood at the bar at the room's rear. They were spaced roughly ten feet apart, one foot planted on the brass rail running along the base of the bar where several brass spittoons were strategically positioned. The man on the far right was Tatum, who stood over a frothy beer mug. A door to his right, flanking the bar, was marked BREWERY.

The barkeep was just then filling the shot glass on the bar before Tatum's beer schooner. He held out his hand and Tatum tossed a coin at the man too hard for the man to catch it. The coin bounced off the apron's broad chest and clattered to the floor behind the bar.

The barman scowled, then scowled to retrieve the coin.

Tatum chuckled. He glanced to his left to see if the man standing over there had found the high jinks as amusing as Tatum had. Hunter could see in the back bar mirror that the man hadn't. Leaning forward with his elbows on the bar, wearing a bland expression and pointedly ignoring Tatum, he took a sip of his own, black, frothy ale. Tatum must have glimpsed Hunter standing to one side of the batwings out the corner of his left eye. He turned his head farther around to get a better look at the newcomer.

He turned his head forward and then, his brain registering who the man had seen, swung it back around so quickly he was liable to snap his neck.

His eyes widened when he saw the big blond man in the buckskin tunic and holstered LeMat, and he turned his head quickly forward once more, shoulders tightening in his pin-striped, collarless shirt and brown leather vest. He raised his shot glass, tossed back half the whiskey and, glancing quickly, furtively into the back bar mirror at Hunter, flinched. Needing a bracer, he threw back the rest of the shot.

Smelling the beer wort emanating from the brewery flanking the saloon, which reminded Hunter of old Angus's own malty ale, Hunter made his way toward Tatum, whose right hand, Hunter saw, had dropped to the walnut grips of the Schofield .44 holstered for the cross draw on his left hip. Hunter increased his pace, shouldered up hard against Tatum, and said in a raking, angry rasp through gritted teeth, "Go ahead an' pull that hogleg, and I'll blow your brains all over that mirror!"

Tatum's face blanched behind three- or four-days' worth of salt-and-pepper beard stubble. His chest rose and fell sharply. When Hunter saw him remove his hand from the Schofield's grips, Hunter looked at the jowly bartender, who was regarding him dubiously. "Not thirsty," he said. "Go about your business."

The big man shrugged, drew a breath, and walked over

to where one of the customers sitting at a table had walked up to the bar with his empty beer mug.

Hunter opened Tatum's vest and pulled the manilla envelope out of his shirt pocket. He recognized the envelope Rufus Scanlon had given him. Peering inside, he recognized the crisp bills amounting to the full two thousand dollars Saguaro Machado had stolen from him when he'd taken Annabelle.

Tatum opened his mouth to object but before he could say a word, Hunter spun him around and gave him a hard shove toward the door marked BREWERY.

"Hey, hey, hey!" Tatum said, stumbling forward. "Someone help me. I'm bein' robbed in broad day—"

Hunter gave him another hard shove through the door and out into the Angry Dog's backyard where a cabin sat to the left of a two-hole privy. The cabin door was open. A tall man in overalls stood to the right of the cabin's open front door. In the same patch of shade, a medium-sized, shorthair, brown dog lay. Between the cabin and the saloon, another man, also clad in overalls, stood stirring a large steel tub with a long-handled wooden paddle. The tub sat on a stone fireplace. Steam rose from it, smelling like brew day out at the Box Bar B.

The two men, the man by the cabin smoking a brown paper quirley, stared at Hunter and his quarry. Growling and showing his teeth, the dog leaped up and ran over to bark and run a single circle around the two combatants before running back to the cabin and taking up his position beside the man smoking the quirley.

Both men wore immigrant hats and wore beards but no mustaches.

Hunter gave the back of Tatum's right knee a savage kick. The man went down, yelling, "You got no right. You got no damn right, Buchanon!"

Hunter kicked the man onto his back, drew his LeMat,

clicked the hammer back, and pressed the barrel against Tatum's forehead. "Where'd you get the money? Was it Machado?"

Tatum stared up at him, eyes wide. He didn't say anything.

"You have three seconds to tell me where you got his money. One . . . two . . . th—"

"Yes, Machado!"

"Is he in town?"

"No! He rode out."

"When."

"Fifteen, twenty minutes ago." A faint smile quirked one corner of the Arapaho Creek foreman's mouth briefly.

"Where'd he leave from and which way did he head?"

"Lone Wolf Hotel. East."

"Was Machado working for Scanlon?"

That appeared a harder question for Tatum to answer. He flinched slightly, hesitated.

"Why?" Hunter asked, pressing the LeMat even harder against the man's forehead.

"You, uh . . . you killed Scanlon's son . . . the girl's brother . . . in the war. He was a picket guarding a bridge you and several of your grayback friends blew. One of the other soldiers saw it all . . . heard the way Billy Scanlon pleaded for his life even while he lay dyin'. The Union soldier recognized you. Told Scanlon after the war. Stealin' that money back . . . usin' Machado to do it . . . and sellin' your wife into slavery was his way of gettin' back at you. He wanted you to live in the same agony he lived with every day."

"Lucinda was in on it too?"

"Yes," Tatum said. "She was just a baby when Billy died, but she had to live with her father's heartbreak. She believes it's that heartbreak that's finally killin' the old man."

Hunter's mind was whirling.

He remembered the young Union picket lamenting his

own death, sobbing for his family and his girl while the blood and viscera spilled out of his belly. Hunter had felt wretched. But it had been his job to blow the bridge to keep trains hauling munitions from crossing it at the cost of more Confederate lives.

Still, it was that poor kid's death that still haunted his sleep more than any of the countless others he'd killed.

Hunter pulled the LeMat away from Tatum's forehead.

A little color returned to the frightened man's cheeks.

"Get out of here. Go back to Arapaho Creek. Tell them they failed. They both failed. What I did was in war time. It was the natural cost of war. What they did is not. They'll pay. Both of them. Maybe not soon. But someday they'll both pay big. Tell them to live with *that*!"

Hunter holstered the LeMat, snapped the keeper thong closed over the hammer, then went back into the saloon, crossed it quickly, went outside, stuffed the envelope into his saddlebags, and climbed up on Nasty Pete's back. Pete was tired. He needed a long rest. But there was no time.

Machado and Annabelle were close. Hunter might not ever get this close again.

Machado's trail was fresh.

Hunter picked it up even in the failing light out front of the Lone Wolf Hotel and followed the tracks of the six horseback riders east of town on a secondary freight trail, probably one that hadn't been used in a good ten years, replaced by easier routes. It was rocky and sage pocked and washed out in areas, so Hunter had to hold Pete to a fast walk. In clearer areas he trotted the mount, impatience nearly exploding inside him.

Why Machado had left so late in the day was anybody's guess, but it was Hunter's guess the man wanted to stay ahead of any possible bounty hunters intending to backshoot the big killer and collect the reward money that would likely be offered for his head for killing the federals. Hunter himself should have known better. He wasn't going to catch up to the gang, all likely riding fresh horses when his own was weary. He should have stayed in town, given both himself and Nasty Pete a good rest, but he just hadn't been able to do it.

However, just after good dark, when he was a little over an hour out of Lone Pine, he checked Pete down atop a ridge. He curveted the mount and gazed out into a flat beyond, one that was scored by a shallow ravine that Hunter had taken a better look at when there still had been light. A thin, meandering thread of water ran through the bottom of the arroyo. A fire flickered in a cottonwood copse a hundred feet to the left of the ravine, roughly a half a mile from Hunter's position.

His blood washed through his veins, tingling with expectation.

Machado?

Hunter booted Pete down off the ridge and into some rocks and cedars off the side of the trail.

He was breathing hard, heart drumming at the prospect of having finally closed the gap between himself and Machado and the outlaw's four remaining riders after Annabelle had given the man Hunter had seen in the brush a deadly shave with the man's own pig sticker.

Annabelle.

Hunter couldn't wait to set eyes on her again.

To hold her again, tightly, and never let her go again . . .

He tied the blowing, sweating Pete to a tree and released the grullo's saddle cinch so he could breathe freely. He slipped the bit from Pete's mouth, set his hat on the ground, and poured into it what little water he had left in his canteen. The horse needed it worse than Hunter did if the mount was going to get him and Anna back to town.

Unless Hunter could secure a couple of the outlaws' mounts.

That meant he'd have to kill them all, and that might be a little more of a bite than he could chew. He was hungry, exhausted, and his ribs still ached. Also, he knew that because of all those factors, and how madly, desperately he wanted to rescue Anna, he wasn't thinking clearly.

"You stay, Pete," he told the grullo, giving its rump an affectionate pat. "Hopefully, I'll be back soon with the lady of the Box Bar B."

He trotted off into the night, toward the orange flames of the fire flickering before him.

Crouching, he strode up and down natural prairie swells and low hills, meandered around thick stands of cedar and cottonwood. As he closed the gap between himself and the fire, he could see the outlaws sitting around the fire, eating. He thought the horses must be picketed in the trees ahead and to Hunter's left.

He couldn't see Anna. But then as he moved slowly to his right, opposite the fire from the horses, partially circling the fire around which the men had tossed down their gear, he saw the red of her hair on the fire's near side, sitting with her back to a cottonwood.

He stopped, dropped to a knee, heart hammering expectantly.

All he could see was her hair from this view. Her head seemed to be dipped forward, her red tresses hanging down over her face so that all he could see was a patch of the paleness of her chin and part of her cheek. But mostly her hair, the firelight dancing in it.

That was enough.

She, too, was likely exhausted, sleeping.

She was alive.

For now, that was enough for Hunter. Now he had to

figure a way of getting her out of there without the horses giving him away.

Anna had trimmed the odds against him. Still, in his condition, they were long odds.

He counted the men milling around the camp. He couldn't see any in detail but he counted four.

Where was the fifth?

Likely on picket duty, which would complicate Hunter's job.

That's all right, he silently told himself. *You've faced these odds before. Many times during the war, albeit you'd been younger and in better condition. You knew the key. Patience and silence. The ability to move with the slow, plodding determination of a tortoise and then, when the time was right, kill with the ferocity of an Apache on the warpath.*

Slowly, he got belly down against the ground and began crawling slowly, angling around sage shrubs and patches of prickly pear. As slowly as that tortoise, he crawled. He'd crawled maybe thirty yards, bringing the camp into closer view so that he could make out some of the men's firelit faces, including that of the savage, one-eyed Machado. The outlaw leader sat on the far side of the fire, against his saddle, one knee raised. He was hungrily eating what appeared to be a rabbit haunch or a chicken leg, wiping his hands on his pants.

Cigarette smoke touched Hunter's nostrils.

He'd gotten only a slight scent, and then it was gone.

He lay flat against the ground, between a large sage shrub and a rock. He kept his gloved right hand wrapped around the Henry's brass breech.

Slow footsteps sounded to Hunter's right.

He slowly turned his head that way. Presently, a man-shaped shadow gained definition roughly forty yards away. The man moved toward Hunter, at the edge of the firelight so that the dancing flames shone the man's bearded face beneath a low-crowned, flat-brimmed black hat, holding a rifle on his shoulder. Two pistols and a knife bristled on the man's hips clad in baggy canvas trousers. He wore a long, black duster and the brass buckle of his cartridge belt glinted in the firelight, between the duster's two open flaps.

The cigarette in his mouth glowed orange as he drew on it. The orange glow faded as the man blew out the cigarette smoke through his nose.

Moving slowly around the camp, at the edge of the firelight, the man walked slowly toward Hunter. He was around thirty feet from the fire. Hunter was around fifty feet from it. If the man's course stayed the same, the lookout should pass within twenty feet of Hunter's position.

He did.

He continued past Hunter, smoking, and headed toward the horses picketed on the fire's far side.

Hunter heaved a sigh of relief, then backed slowly away from the camp.

He couldn't give in to impatience. He had to bide his time, wait for the other men to roll up in their soogans. They were passing a bottle, so it shouldn't be too long before they slept.

He continued crawling back the way he'd come when a man's sharp voice said, "Hey, Mrs. Hunter Buchanon. Wake up. Time to clean dishes!"

Hunter stopped and looked toward the camp.

Machado himself stood before Anna, a hulking, one-eyed figure in the flickering firelight.

He took a pull from the bottle in his hand, then kicked Anna and repeated, "Take the dishes to the creek."

Anna groaned and lifted her head.

Machado glanced behind him and said, "Fat Charlie— follow her." Turning back to Anna, he said, "Any more tricks and I *will* blow your purty head off!"

CHAPTER 30

"He's dead?" Nathan had crawled out of his bedroll to stand beside Angus, looking down at Dutch, the big man's bearded face still twisted in horror at the raging bruin that had indirectly killed him.

Killed him in his sleep. In his dreams. Nightmares . . .

"He's dead, boy," Angus said, pulling the man's top soogan blanket up over his face.

Jackson and Davis stood gazing down at the dead man. Jackson was stepping into his boots.

He said, "Well, I say we skip coffee an' breakfast. Eat some jerky on the trail. The sun's already up. We gotta get a move on."

He grabbed his frock coat from where it lay over a log and shrugged into it.

"What're you talkin' about?" Angus said. "You gotta bury your dead."

Leech scowled down at him. "No time, old man. We've wasted enough damn time. Jackson is right. Let's saddle up an' get movin'."

Angus couldn't believe what he was hearing. A man always buried his dead. Always.

"Don't tell me you'd just leave him"—he threw his arm out to indicate the dead man—"like this!"

Jackson had built a cigarette and, smoking, quickly rolled his soogan inside his rain slicker. "We'll bury him on the way back."

Angus gave a deep sigh and stooped to retrieve his folding camp shovel, which he'd carried strapped to his saddle. He thrust it out at Leech, narrowed one eye angrily, and said, "Bury your dead. Don't leave it to me an' the boy. You both have two arms. You'll make faster work of it than I would."

Jackson rose angrily. "That'll take a good hour. We don't have a good hour!"

"Like I done told you," Angus said, "the only way down out of these mountains is the same way up. If those train robbers decide to make another run for it, they'll have to come down that trail right there!"

He pointed toward the two-track mining trail they'd been following, rising and twisting up one pine-clad ridge after another.

Angus added, "Even if we leave in an hour, we should make Ghost Mountain in good time. We're only a couple of hours away." Again, Angus thrust the shovel toward Leech Davis. "Best get diggin'. We're burnin' daylight!"

The two Pinkertons shared an exasperated glance.

Their eyes were flat and hard, deeply angry.

Jackson turned to Angus, and his right eye glinted furiously in the morning sunlight washing down through the pine boughs. "What if we just kept following the trail?"

"Good luck. There's plenty of unmarked forks leadin' to mines and prospector diggin's, each one a chance for a man to get forever lost." Angus dropped the shovel at Davis's feet, then knelt to begin building up the fire for coffee and beans. "It won't be as easy as you think." He glanced up at Jackson, narrowing one eye, shrewdly. "And do you remember your way back down?" He smiled, again shrewdly. "Many men have climbed into these reaches . . . never to be seen or heard from again."

He glanced at Nate, chuckled, then set some crushed pinecones on smoldering embers in the fire ring and slid his head low to blow on them.

Jackson and Davis shared another glance.

Davis sighed, stooped to pluck the shovel off the ground, swung around, and began tramping out into the forest. "I reckon I'll get started . . . buryin' poor old Dutch!" He gave an exasperated laugh and started digging.

Jackson gave a frustrated sigh of his own, then sat down on the log to smoke his cigarette. Nate had gone off to tend the horses' morning needs and to fetch more firewood. The raspy snicks of the shovel as Davis dug the grave mixed with the morning piping of the birds. When Angus had gotten a fire going, brewed coffee, and set a pot of beans and fatback to boil, he and Jackson sat on either side of the fire from each other, sipping their coffee.

Angus set his cup aside to roll a smoke of his own from his making's sack. Firing a match to life on his thumbnail, he narrowed an eye again as he peered across the fire's low, dancing flames at Jackson, who regarded him stonily. Nate had gone off to remove the feed sacks from the horses' snouts and to saddle his and Angus's mounts.

"Who are you?" Angus said, dropping the match and mashing it out with his boot.

"What?" Jackson said, incredulous.

"Who are you?" Angus repeated. "Really." He smiled and wagged his head slowly. "You ain't no Pinkerton. Neither is Davis. Neither was Dutch. A Pinkerton wouldn't balk at buryin' his dead. No *good man* would balk at such a thing."

Jackson continued staring at him, stone-faced. He brought his quirley to his lips, drew on it, blew the smoke out his nostrils. He jutted the index finger of the hand holding the quirley at Angus and said, "All you need to do is get me an' Leech to Ghost Mountain. That's all you need to worry your gray head about, old man."

Nate had just walked into the camp. He stopped suddenly and looked from Jackson to Angus, apprehension in his eyes.

"Come on, boy," Angus said, picking up his coffee cup. "Beans is ready. Eat your fill, then you an' me are gonna mount up an' track the bear."

"What?" Jackson said, scowling. "Why?"

"Because I don't want no more surprises outta that monster," Angus said and sipped his coffee.

It wasn't a monster after all, Angus was relieved to see a half hour later, when he and Nate, following the blood spoor, had tracked the bear to its destination.

The horses were jumpy at both the smell of bear and of death. Angus and Nate held them under tight rein as they stared down at the huge bruin sitting back against a rock, rear legs stretched out before it, front legs hanging down against its sides. The bruin's head to its chest made bloody by the several shots Angus and the others had drilled into it.

The old bruin looked nothing so much like it had just decided to sit down here for a bit and take a midmorning nap. Except for the blood. It's still-open eyes staring at nothing.

"By God, that bruin had some hate in him," Angus said, shaking his head in disbelief. "I must've put two rounds in his heart. Two fifty-sixes. Still, it ran a good mile!" He paused, staring down at the beast every bit as large as a bull buffalo. "Gotta admire him, in a way." In the way he'd admired and was terrified by last summer's bruin, the one who'd fed on both Bar Box B stock and the men who'd tended them, almost killing Hunter, as well.

Such wildness. Like the wild of the world at the beginning of time.

"Why do you think it hated us so much, Grandpa?" Nate asked.

"I don't know. I reckon we were trespassers on its territory. On what it had marked out as its territory. He had a right. He fought us for it the same way we fought the Indians for it. We fought back. We won. The bear lost." Angus drew a deep breath. "Maybe people should stay where they belong, leave the wild country to the wild creatures who call it home."

"What about the Box Bar B?"

Angus gave a droll chuckle and shook his head. "Yeah," he said. "What about it? I don't know, son. I don't know about our place there. Fought so hard for it. Two of my boys died for it. As they say in the army, that's above my pay grade. Sometimes I think it's *all* above my pay grade." He reined the dun around, booted him back in the direction of camp. "Come on, son. Them Pinkertons . . . or whoever they are . . . is likely chompin' at the bit."

"Whoever they are?" Nate asked, frowning curiously.

"Just stay close to me, boy. Stay close. I'm not sure who we're dealin' with, but if they're Pinkertons, I'm a monkey's uncle."

"Who do you think they are?"

"I don't know. Bounty hunters, maybe. I got a feelin' we'll find out soon." Angus glanced at Nate, warningly. "Just stay close to me, grandson."

Nate nodded. "All right, Grandpa."

"Well, look what the cat dragged in," grouched Leech Davis as Angus and Nate rode up to the camp twenty minutes later. "What've you two been doin'? Off enjoyin' the scenery, havin' you a nice little morning ride." He squinted at the sky. "Or is it afternoon by now?"

"Nope, still mornin'," Angus said in his customarily affable tone, devilishly, knowing how it graveled the Pinkertons . . . or whoever they were . . . and not caring.

Leech and Jackson were sitting on the log by the fire, each with a steaming cup in his hand. As they'd ridden in, Angus had noted the freshly mounded grave piled with rocks between a pine and a fir tree, a makeshift wooden cross angling up out of the ground ahead of it.

"Nice work," he added. "Dutch should have him a peaceful rest there."

Jackson tossed his remaining coffee into the fire, removed the iron tripod, and kicked dirt on the flames. "Let's go!"

He and Davis strode over to their horses, both saddled and ready to ride. They mounted up, and Angus gave another warning look at Nate, silently reminding the boy to stay close to him. Angus had no idea what they were in for at the end of the trail, but he had a feeling he'd be surprised. Probably not in a good way. He reined the dun down the grade to the rocky, two-track trail and swung northwest, toward where Ghost Mountain rose, its long, apron slope a furry blue green in the buttery, late-morning light.

Angus swung off the two-track trail and followed a narrow canyon up the ridge, a stream roiling down the grade, foaming over the ladderlike rungs of rock, on the riders' left side. As he and the others climbed, Nate keeping his steeldust close off the tail of Angus's dun, the craggy peak of Ghost Mountain grew before them, more and more of the mountain exposing itself, the lower fur forest sliding up until Angus could see where the forest stopped and the stone face of the mountain jutted straight up in the air for two hundred feet, cracked and fissured. Boulders balanced precariously on granite shelves, pines and firs stubbornly growing from narrow cracks in the bastion's face.

At the top of the ridge, the canyon dead-ended at a stone outcropping from the base of which the spring that formed the stream bubbled, so cold that when Angus stopped to let his horse drink and to slake his own thirst, he thought the last of his old teeth would crack. Nate let his own horse draw the cold water while he filled his canteen. Jackson and Davis, understanding that their own horses were weary from the steep climb, and tired themselves, stopped without argument.

In ten minutes, they were all back in the saddle.

Angus led them up out of the canyon via a game trail spotted with mule deer and elk beans. Ten minutes after that, the weary riders stopped their horses at the bottom of a broad stone escarpment maybe fifty feet high. Angus shucked his Spencer and climbed the rocks leading toward the stony ridge's flat crest. When he reached it, he thought his heart was going to explode, his knees splinter and cut through his skin. He hadn't made a climb like that in years.

He was surprised as well as impressed that he'd made it.

He wasn't breathing too much harder than the others, including the boy, when he gained the broad flat crest of the ridge, walked to the opposite side, and hunkered down in the rocks at the formation's edge. From here he could see the canyon opening on the other side of the scarp. On a shelf jutting out of the slope on the far side of the stream running along the canyon's bottom sat a humble, gray log cabin with a mossy, shake-shingled roof.

The shack sat at the very base of the stone wall that jutted straight skyward to the craggy crest of Ghost Mountain.

"Here we are," Angus said.

He'd hung his spyglass around his neck by a leather thong.

He raised the glass and adjusted the focus. After he'd taken a long gander at the cabin and the terrain around it, he lowered the glass and turned to Jackson. "Smoke rising from the chimney. Looks like someone's enjoyin' a nice fire, anyway."

"Let me have a look."

Jackson took the spyglass from Angus and inspected the cabin. He returned the glass to Angus and said, "All right. We'll take it from here, old man."

Jackson grabbed his rifle and flinched. "Oh!" he said, slapping a hand to his left ear.

As he did, a rifle barked from a near ridge.

When Jackson pulled his hand away from his ear, Angus blinked in shock.

The top of the man's ear had been blown off, leaving a ragged nub.

CHAPTER 31

"Whoa!" Nate said, staring wide-eyed at Jackson's ear. Another bullet came whistling in from somewhere above and to Angus's right, up higher on the escarpment. The slug spanged off a rock just behind where Davis knelt beside Jackson, gazing in disbelief at what was left of his partner's ear. Angus glanced up the escarpment just as the shooter, perched in a niche in the rocks roughly a hundred feet away, and owning the high ground, racked another cartridge into his rifle's breech.

"Down, boy!" Angus yelled and threw his wiry old body at Nate, grabbing the boy around the waist with his arm and rolling with him under a stone overhang, out of view from the shooter above.

As he did, Angus silently opined the shooter had likely been on guard duty, watching the canyon that was the only access to the remote cabin.

Jackson and Davis cursed loudly as they scrambled with their rifles under the stone overhang with Angus and Nate, Jackson to Angus's right as they sat with their backs to the stone wall behind them, and Davis to Angus's left, on the other side of Nate. Angus had left his Spencer leaning against a rock at the lip of the scarp, where he'd been when the first shot had pulverized half of Jackson's ear. Now as another bullet buzzed like an angry hornet from above, and blew up sand and gravel two feet in front of Angus's right foot, the old Confederate said, "Stay here an' stay down, Nate! Gotta fetch my long gun!"

"Grandpa!" Nate cried.

Too late.

Angus made a mad dash with far more fleetness than he thought he had left in his withered old body, grabbed the Spencer, and made another mad dash back under the overhang just as another bullet plumed gravel only inches from his right boot heel. He sat back down between Jackson and the boy and ran the sleeve of his wool-lined denim jacket—it was cool this high in the Hills—across his forehead to mop sweat from his brow.

He was breathing hard, raspily. He felt an ominous pull in his chest.

Don't sit here and have a heart attack, you damn fool, he chastised himself. *Not here. Not after you've come all this way. Not in front of the boy who loves you more than you deserve.*

Nate placed his hand on Angus's leg. "You all right, Grandpa?"

Angus nodded, again wiped more sweat from his forehead. His chest rose and fell sharply, achingly.

Meanwhile, Jackson held a handkerchief over his ruined ear and was cursing under his breath, showing his teeth beneath his thick dragoon mustache, like an angry cur. He glanced at Davis, who was leaning forward and twisting around, trying to get a look up the ridge behind them.

"That's Thayer," Jackson said. "It's Robbie Thayer. I know it is." He choked out a bitter laugh. "They knew we'd come. Eventually."

"Yeah, they were waitin' for us," Davis said, and cast Angus a hard glare. "Good scoutin', old-timer. Led us right into that rifle!"

"Go to hell," Angus said, trying to catch his breath. "My job was to get you to the cabin. What you do after that is up to you. Me an' the boy"—he shook his head—"we want no part of it." He returned Davis's hard look with one of his own. "You're one o' them." He jerked his chin in the direction of the cabin. "What'd they do—double-cross you? Run off with the loot after you robbed the train?"

"Shut up!" Jackson said.

He leaned forward like Davis had done, cupped his right hand around his mouth, and shouted hoarsely, furiously, "Robbie, I know it's you up there. You damn near shot my ear off, you rancid spawn of a dirty old whore. When I catch you, I'm gonna cut both of your ears *off,* an' I ain't sharpened my Bowie in a month of Sundays!"

Again, he laughed raucously, mirthlessly.

Another bullet came whistling in to pound into the small clearing just beyond where Jackson had poked his head out from under the overhang. The bullet was followed by another rocketing report. Jackson pulled his head back quickly, still cupping his bloody handkerchief against his bloody ear.

"Hah!" came an odd-sounding laugh from above. "It ain't Thayer that shredded your ear for you, Bryce. It was *me!*"

Another loud, odd-sounding laugh. At least, odd-sounding for a man.

But not for a woman.

"It's Frannie from San Francisco, you double-dealing card cheat, you double-crossin', back-shootin' worthless son of a—"

"Frannie!" Jackson shouted, sharing an incredulous glance with Davis. "You blew my damn ear off, sweetheart! An' in case you've already forgotten, you, Robbie, and Bull are the double-crossers!"

"Only 'cause you had it comin', *my love,*" said the young woman's sarcastic, jeering voice from above.

Another bullet slammed into the sand and gravel just

outside the overhang. It was followed by the rifle's angry whipcrack.

Nate flinched. He looked at Angus, a big question in his wide, brown eyes.

"Got no idea, boy," Angus said, his heart still pounding, sweat dribbling down his cheeks, soaking his beard. It was a cold sweat. "Got no idea. Just know"—he glanced from Jackson to Davis then back to Nate—"we got ourselves led into a whipsaw. Between *friends*," he added with his own sarcasm.

"Yep, you did," Davis agreed.

He looked across Nate and Angus at Jackson. "What do ya say we go get her?"

"She's pretty damn good with that rifle."

"You scared of the little lady? *Your* little lady, Bryce. Until you cheated on her with that showgirl from Tulsa! You're the one who got us into this mess."

"I don't know how she found out," Jackson said with a bewildered air.

"Oh, hell, they always find out!"

Nate glanced at Angus. "Find out what?"

"Never mind, boy. Grown-up stuff." Angus glanced at Jackson and wrinkled his nose distastefully. "So, you two-timed the girl, and she threw in with the other two owl-hoots." He smiled. "If the boy weren't involved, I'd admire the justice in that. Hope that ear don't hurt too bad!"

"Shut up, you old grayback!" Jackson looked back at Davis. "I saw a sheltered way up the rocks on this side." He canted his head to his right. "You try to find one from your side. We'll meet at the top of the scarp . . . at little Miss Frannie from San Francisco."

"If I get her in my sights . . ."

"Shoot her," Jackson said. "Just don't kill her." He thumbed himself in the chest. "I wanna do that!"

Davis racked a round into his Winchester's action and

said to Jackson, "I'll cover you. You go first, then cover me an' I'll go."

Jackson glanced at Angus and the boy. "What about them?"

"The old man isn't goin' anywhere. He's not lookin' so good."

"Right." Jackson set himself to make a run for it. "All right!"

Davis bounded out from under the overhang, twisted around, and fired the Winchester three quick times toward the top of the scarp. Jackson bounded out from the overhang, as well, disappearing around the corner to Angus's right. Davis fired two more rounds. When Jackson started firing from above, Davis disappeared up the scarp on Angus's left.

More shooting, then a lull.

Jackson and Davis were either dead or reloading.

Nate looked at Angus. He unknotted his red neckerchief, folded it into a pad, and swabbed Angus's forehead with it. "You ain't lookin' so good, Grandpa."

Angus winced. He felt as though a fish were nibbling his heart from behind. "I'll be all right. Just a little high here's all. Got a knot in my chest. It'll loosen soon."

Nate gave Angus's forehead another swab, then ran the cloth through the sweat dribbling down his cheeks. "So, they're all bad, ain't they?"

"Yep, they're all bad. I got sold a bill of goods." Angus looked at the boy, who looked sunburned, weary, and worried. "Sorry, boy. I was so enthused about another ride high in the Hills again, I wasn't thinkin' straight. The fact is, I'm old. An' stupid. Never shoulda hauled you up here, got you into this."

"I'm glad I came."

"You are?"

Nate nodded. "I belong with you. I mean, I love Hunter

an' Annabelle an' all. But I like bein' with you. You an' me are a lot alike, I think."

"Oh?" Angus laughed. "How's that?"

Nate smiled. "We like adventure."

Again, Angus laughed. He reached across his lap to tussle the boy's sandy hair with his hand. "We do, don't we?" He leaned back, drawing deep breaths, trying to fend off that toothy fish nibbling his old ticker. "Well, we've had that!"

He coughed, winced at the pain in his chest, which he pounded with the end of his clenched fist.

Suddenly, more shooting erupted on the scarp above and behind Angus and Nathan. Several loud, angry shots.

The men shouted.

The girl screamed.

A voice that Angus recognized as Davis's cursed several times, shrilly.

The girl laughed her raucous, unladylike laugh.

Silence.

After nearly ten minutes, Angus heard a rock rolling down more rock. The rock rolled down from above, to Angus's right, and rolled to a stop just beyond where he and Nate had remained under the overhang. He wished he could have gotten Nathan out of here, but he didn't think he had the strength. He needed to rest awhile.

Now it was too late, anyway. Shadows moved on his right and then a girl gave an indignant yell and suddenly appeared, stumbling down the rocks and falling in the clearing near the blood splatters from Jackson's ruined ear.

She sat halfway up and cursed at Jackson and Davis coming down out of the rocks, as well—Jackson leading, Davis following, limping badly and holding his left hand against the bloody wound in his left thigh. Davis shouldered Jackson aside, limped over to the girl, stooped slightly, and slapped her left cheek with his gloved, bloody right hand. Called her a name a gentleman should never call a woman—especially with an impressionable boy present.

She cried out as the blow jerked her head back and to one side, her hair covering her face.

"Hey!" Angus said. "That'll be enough of that!"

The girl, not much over twenty if that, Angus observed, raised a hand to her cheek and glared up at Davis. "You had it comin'. If I didn't shoot you, you woulda shot me!"

Dropping down against a rock, wincing and clutching his thigh with his hand, Davis shook his head. "No, I wasn't. I was gonna leave you to Jackson!"

He gave a humorless laugh, reached into a pocket of his wool coat, and pressed a handkerchief down hard against the wound.

Jackson turned, dropped to a knee, and gazed over the rocks at the cabin in the canyon below.

"Yeah, you'd best worry about Robbie an' Bull," the girl spat at him, her amber eyes aglow with rage. Her short, curly, dark-red hair caught the late-day sunshine and fluttered in the breeze. She had a pretty, heart-shaped face, lightly tanned, and with a wide, full, expressive mouth. Maybe a tad too expressive for Jackson and Davis. "They're on their way. I'm sure!"

Jackson glanced at her. It looked to Angus that he'd nearly gotten the blood from his ear stopped. "Which one'd you throw in with, Miss Frannie from San Francisco? Bull or Robbie?" He gritted his teeth and flared a nostril. "Or both?"

"Go to hell!"

"Please! Your language!" Angus admonished. "A child is present, dammit!"

The girl turned to him and the boy, both still sitting under the overhang. Angus's chest was still tight, and he was sweating. He was still having trouble getting his heart to slow down. It was as though the girl saw them both for the first time.

"What're they doin' here?" she asked Jackson.

"Shut up." He was on his knees, staring over the rocks toward the cabin, leaning on his rifle, which he held barrel up in his right hand. He glanced over his shoulder at her. "Where are they—Bull an' Robbie?"

"Prob'ly on the way up here to blow your lights out!"

"She might be right," Davis said, pressing down hard on his thigh, stretching his lips back from his teeth in misery. He held his rifle in his right hand, angled across that leg and aimed at Little Miss Frannie from San Francisco. "I'm gonna need a doctor, I do believe." He glared at the girl sitting between him and Jackson. "You, though—you ain't gonna need one. I'm gonna drill you one so deep—"

"Shut up!" Jackson said.

"Don't tell me to shut up!" Davis returned. "Look what she did to me!"

Jackson whipped another hard glare at his partner over his shoulder. "I said shut up!"

Davis looked astonished. "Why . . . you're still sweet on her, ain't you? Why . . . I can't believe it. She put us through this hell, you know—throwin' in with Bull an' Robbie after you—"

Jackson whipped full around to face the wounded outlaw. "Don't you understand English?"

"I understand it just fine," the girl said, saucily, lowering her head then tossing it back to throw her curly hair out of her face. "What're you gonna do, Bryce? Gonna be dark soon. Best make up your mind."

She was right. The light was fading fast, the forest to the west sliding long shadows across the escarpment. Birds piped in the trees behind the escarpment and in those fronting it, between the scarp and the canyon in which the cabin sat.

"Best make up your mind, Bryce," Davis said, his chest rising and falling sharply, the salmon light glistening in the sweat streaking his unshaven cheeks. "Meanwhile . . . I do believe I'm gonna need a sawbones."

Staring into the canyon, Jackson said, "Yeah, well, I'll just grow a pair of wings and fly down to Tigerville and fetch one up here pronto."

Davis seemed to find that amusing. He chuckled. The chuckle was broken off abruptly by a pain spasm. He gritted his teeth and threw his head back, sucking air through gritted teeth.

Angus turned to Nathan. "Boy, go down yonder, fetch my medical pouch out of my saddlebags. Haul it up here then go back down an' tend the horses while there's still light."

"All right, Grandpa."

Nate crawled out from under the overhang and gained his feet.

"Hold on, hold on," Jackson said, raising his rifle. "Where's he goin'?"

"To fetch my medical bag," Angus raked out at the man, his fury at this trio doing nothing to make his heart settle down. "In case you hadn't noticed, your partner's about ready to bleed dry. That wound needs to be cleaned and wrapped."

"That's not gonna save him," Jackson said. "Bullet prob'ly broke his damn leg."

"You go to hell!" Davis shot back, aiming his rifle at Jackson now. He glanced at Nate standing over him. "Do it, boy."

As Nathan turned to start clambering down the rocks toward where they'd left the horses, Angus said, "Bring my canteen, too, boy."

Nate threw up an arm in acknowledgement and continued down the rocks.

The girl turned to Angus. "Handsome young man. He need a girlfriend?"

"No," Angus said with a wan half smile. "But I do."

The girl laughed and turned to Jackson who'd returned to studying the cabin. "I like him. Where'd you find that one-armed rack of old bones, anyway?"

"This rack of old bones, honey, was the only one stupid enough to guide those two up here. Three before Dutch got taken down by a nightmare."

"Oh." Again, the girl turned to Jackson. "I thought he might've just taken a pill he couldn't digest. You know, to make the dividing up of the loot a little more lucrative. Fewer players . . ."

"That's right." Jackson fingered his ear gingerly. "And we're about to be less two more." He looked over his shoulder at the girl again. "Possibly three."

"What do you mean 'possibly'?" Davis said, sliding his rifle barrel toward Frannie once more. "I'll shoot her right now."

Frannie laughed. "What? You think he's gonna let you live? If that bullet in your leg doesn't kill you, he will." She tossed her pretty head toward Jackson.

Nate just then climbed up out of the rocks and dropped to his knees so he wouldn't be seen from below. "Here you go, Grandpa."

He held a large burlap pouch and a canteen.

"Set up down by him, boy," Angus said, nodding toward Davis. "Go down an' tend the horses. Looks like we'll be spending the night right here."

Angus crawled out from under the overhang, opened the pouch, and withdrew a flat, brown bottle. He popped the cork and handed the bottle to Davis.

"Have you a few swallows of that. Ease the pain a bit."

"Whiskey!" the girl intoned. "Now, we're talking. Let's build us a campfire and have us a party." She clapped her hands.

Jackson crawled over to the backside of the scarp and yelled, "Boy, fetch the rope off my horse!" He turned to Frannie. "Gonna tie you tight an' go down there an' kill your double-crossin' trail mates."

While Angus used a small scissors to cut away Davis's pants and underwear from around the bloody wound, Davis said, "I'll kill her right now. Get it out of the way!"

Jackson reached down and pulled the Winchester out of the wounded man's hand. He tossed it under the overhang. He pulled both the man's pistols and knife belt scabbards, and tossed them under the overhang, as well. "Not yet." He glared at Frannie. "Let her wait on it. If anyone kills her, it's gonna be me!"

"What?" Davis said through another grimace as Angus worked on his leg. "Double-crossin' us an' two-timin' with Robbie is worse than shootin' me in the leg?!"

Jackson kept his eyes on the girl, who stared up at him defiantly.

"Yes."

When Nate brought the rope, Jackson wrestled the girl down, tied her ankles together and her hands behind her back. He tossed the excess rope away and turned to Angus who was cleaning Davis's wound with a cloth soaked with whiskey and water.

"You leave her tied like that, old man, or there'll be hell to pay when I get back!"

"I got no dog in this fight," Angus said.

"Yeah, you do, an' you know it."

He was right. And Angus knew it.

"Should be back with those two nitwits' heads in a sack shortly," Jackson told Frannie.

She cursed him.

He laughed.

Then he was off, clambering down the rocks toward the fast-darkening canyon below.

CHAPTER 32

"Fat Charlie, shoot her if she tries to make a run for it," Machado said. "She's had all the chances she's gonna get!"

Hunter's gut tightened. He'd crawled back several feet farther from the fire and hunkered down behind a rock a little larger than a grave marker. Peering around the rock's right side, he gazed toward where the fire shimmered in the cottonwoods. He'd been hearing the clatter of pans and eating utensils, and now his gut tightened again when he saw Anna step out away from the camp and into the darkness, her red hair darkening as though a flame had been doused. She was a female-shaped shadow now, carrying behind her shoulder what appeared a heavy burlap sack bulging and clattering softly with cookware.

She slumped forward against the weight of the bag, whose mouth she held with both hands against her shoulder. A big, man-shaped shadow wearing a broad-brimmed, low-crowned sombrero and Mexican striped serape followed her out from the camp and into the darkness beyond. She and Fat Charlie were heading for the ravine and the stream bisecting it.

Hunter's heart thudded.

Cold sweat broke out across his back.

Now was his chance!

He watched the two shadows, the smaller one Anna's, walking twenty feet ahead of the stout-hipped and big-gutted Fat Charlie, who aimed a rifle at her back straight out from his left hip.

Anger burned in Hunter, made him grind his molars.

Don't you hold a gun on my wife, you fat slob.

When Fat Charlie had followed Anna down into the streambed, both figures disappearing from Hunter's view fifty yards ahead and to his right, he looked around carefully, making sure there was no sign of the picket. Not seeing the man, he got down on all fours and crawled through the buckbrush and sage, pulling the Henry along in his right hand. He moved more quickly, and made more noise than he wanted to, but urgency compelled him to risk it.

This might be his only chance to rescue his wife from these slave-trading curs, all of whom needed to die hard, howling.

The voices of the men conversing by the fire, and the faint snapping and crackling of the fire itself, dwindled as Hunter angled away from it, toward the dark cut that was the ravine. If he could get her away from Fat Charlie . . . away from the horses that might very well wind him and give him away . . . away from the smoking picket . . . they had a chance. They wouldn't be in the clear by any means, because they would both be on foot until they reached Nasty Pete. And even when they reached Nasty Pete, they'd have to ride double. Pete was already tired, and there was no way even the steadfast, stalwart grullo could outrun a half-dozen relatively fresh horses.

When he gained the lip of the ravine, he stopped, dropped to his chest, and peered down into the ravine. The stream was a gleaming, serpentine snake at the bottom of it, another fifty yards away from Hunter. He could see the broad, tall figure of Fat Charlie and the smaller, shorter figure of

Annabelle silhouetted against the dark, shining skin of the water.

There was a loud clattering as Annabelle upended the sack and spilled its contents out on the ground beside the water.

Fat Charlie didn't help her at all. The fat dog sat down on a rock nearby, his back to the bank on which Hunter lay, keeping his long gun aimed at Annabelle, whom he spoke to in low, harsh, jeering tones. Anna ignored him as she knelt to begin cleaning pots and pans in the stream with handfuls of sand.

Rage burned hotter in Hunter.

Slowly, quietly—he had to be very quiet now as well as patient—he slid down over the lip of the ravine and onto the side of the embankment. He pressed his chest to the ground again and crawled down the decline. When he reached the bottom, out of sight from the camp behind him now, he rose and moved slowly through the grass growing lushly at the arroyo's floor.

Again, cigarette smoke touched his nostrils.

Then he saw the pale smoke wafting back over Fat Charlie's right shoulder, buffeting in a vagrant breeze like a tattered cream guidon. The man's broad back with sloping shoulders clad in the striped serape grew larger and larger before Hunter, as he approached one slow, careful step at a time. He didn't want Anna seeing him, either. She would see only a big man's moving shadow and give a start. He didn't know his wife to scream, but that didn't mean she might not with her nerves likely drawn as taut as they were.

Eight feet from Fat Charlie, Hunter saw the glow of the cigarette as Fat Charlie drew on it. He turned his head to the right and blew the smoke plume into the darkness. As he did, he must have glimpsed Hunter behind him. He grunted and began to turn his head to see behind him.

Heart racing, Hunter dropped his Henry and leaped forward, drawing his Bowie knife with his right hand and wrapping his left hand around Fat Charlie's big head, closing it taut over the man's mouth, and sliding the savagely upturned tip of the Bowie deep into the man's back, just beneath his hat.

Hunter suppressed the image of the dead young Billy Scanlon whom Hunter had killed in the same way, as he drove the tip of the Bowie up hard and into the backside of the big man's heart. He pulled the man's head back as Fat Charlie dropped his rifle and his cigarette, which bounced and sparked. Charlie groaned deep in his throat, suddenly shocked and terrified, and flailed his arms, trying desperately to reach back for the man who was killing him.

As Annabelle suddenly stopped scrubbing the pot in her hand, and having heard Fat Charlie's muffled screams started to turn around, Hunter said quietly, "Anna, don't scream. It's your husband!"

Anna gasped and, leaping to her feet, swung around.

She stiffened and closed both hands over her mouth in mute astonishment as Hunter continued to drive the Bowie deep into Fat Charlie's heart.

Warm blood flowed out of the man's back and around the knife hilt, quickly bathing Hunter's gloved right hand.

The man spasmed violently, trying to reach behind him toward his assailant, waving his clenched fists. Gradually the spasms died. The man stopped swinging his fists, opened them, and his arms dropped down against his sides. He gave a last groan and then his big body went slack.

Hunter pulled the Bowie out of his back and, keeping his hand drawn taut over the man's wet mouth, eased his large, slack body down off the rock and into the grass growing up around it. Hunter had no sooner straightened than Annabelle threw herself into his arms. Arm, rather. Hunter held the bloody knife out away from her, held her with his left. Burying her face in his chest, she convulsed with a sob and squeezed him around the waist until he groaned.

She pulled away from him, looked up at him, eyes showing concern in the starlight.

She flicked his hat brim with her index finger. "About time you get here! And when's the last time you heard me scream?"

Hunter chuckled, remembering an incident involving a mouse she'd found in the stable early one morning. He didn't mention it. He kissed her then, knowing there was no time to waste, moved quickly around her, cleaned his knife and his hand in the stream, sheathed the knife, and took Anna's hand in his own.

"Let's go. Fast but quiet. Nasty Pete's tied up yonder."

He led her quickly along the narrow creek but slowed his pace when he realized, by her sluggishness, that she was exhausted. When they'd moved a hundred yards upstream, the ravine began to make a leftward curve. Nasty Pete was up on the tableland to their right. Hunter found a game path; he led Anna up the path and into the brush and sage of the flatland above.

They'd no sooner gained the top of the cut than a man's shrill voice cut through the night behind them. "Boss! Fat Charlie's dead an' the girl's gone!"

The picket had found Fat Charlie. His voice echoed menacingly across the starry night.

A silence just as menacing from the camp was the picket's only response. A glance back toward the fire told Hunter the other three men were scrambling for guns and possibly horses.

Hunter turned to Anna. "I know you're tired, honey, but we best make a run for it."

Annabelle nodded, squeezed his hand. "Let's go. I believe this cat has done run out of all nine of her lives!"

Hunter turned and, holding his wife's hand tightly in his

own, ran back in the direction he'd left Pete, hoping like hell he'd be able to find the horse in the darkness. It just now occurred to him that he'd been in such a hurry to get to Anna that he hadn't taken adequate note of where he'd tethered the grullo. Steering by instinct, he adjusted his course slightly. He and Anna had run a good fifty yards when he felt Anna slowing. Hunter had just started to turn back to her when he tripped over a rock and fell. Anna gave a clipped, involuntary cry and fell on top of him.

They rolled together several feet, and Hunter's heart hiccupped when he heard, "Over there!" shouted back in the direction of the fire.

Only, Machado and his men were no longer at the fire.

He could see three man-shaped shadows running out away from it, silhouetted against it, dusters or jackets winging out around them. Another man was running toward Hunter and Anna from the direction of where Hunter had blown out Fat Charlie's wick.

They were on foot.

Good.

Now, if Hunter and Anna could just reach Pete.

Hunter turned to Annabelle lying across his lap. A lock of her hair was in his mouth. Annabelle rose, slid her hair from his mouth, and said breathlessly, "That was a very rare scream, and it was no fault of my own, bucko!"

"Really glad to have you back again, honey." Grunting against the lingering ache in his ribs, Hunter set his hat back on his head, scrambled to his feet, took Anna's hand again, pulled her to her feet, and took off running once more.

"There they are!" came a deep, angry voice behind them. Machado's most likely.

Hunter glanced back to see the running shadows adjust their course and come straight toward Hunter and Anna, both of whom were so exhausted that Machado's remaining four men were closing in on them.

Pistols flashed and popped.

Bullets thudded into the ground just behind them and to either side.

"Oh, God, Hunter," Anna said behind him, slowing, even more breathless than before. "I'm not gonna make it. My feet are lead." She bent forward, hands on her knees, trying to catch her breath. "My heart's gonna explode!"

Guns continued to pop and flash.

Hunter grabbed her hand and pulled her along behind him once more. "You're comin' with me, lady! Whether you like or not!"

"You're gonna . . . you're gonna kill me!"

"No, I'm not. We're both makin' it back to the Box Bar B in one piece. Think of Angus. Think of Nate. Run!"

They'd just crested a low hill and ran several feet down the other side. Hunter released Anna's hand and yelled, "Pete should be up there around those rocks. Tighten his cinch, shove his bit in his mouth, and ride. I'm gonna stay here and feed those snakes so much lead they'll be rattling when they shake hands with ol' Scratch!"

Anna ran a few feet, slowed, bent forward again. "I can . . . I can't . . ."

"Go, Anna!"

To his surprise, she continued running, albeit slowly and as though her knees would buck at any second.

Hunter threw himself to the ground at the crest of the ridge. He tossed away his hat, racked a round into the Henry's action, and aimed straight out from his right shoulder.

He flinched when he heard Anna fall to the ground behind him.

"Hunter," she sobbed. "Oh, Hunter . . . oh, God, honey . . . I'm *sorry*!"

CHAPTER 33

"Thanks for tryin', old man," Leech Davis said when Angus had finished wrapping his leg, cut the cloth, and tied it off tightly enough to stem the bleeding.

To *stem* it. Angus knew it wouldn't stop it.

"Can't say as I'd do the same for you, in a losin' cause, but I do appreciate it." The drunk man chuckled drunkenly. "Now how 'bout you fetch my rifle so I can have my revenge before I die?"

He glared at Frannie from San Francisco, ankles and wrists bound where she sat back against a rock at the edge of the scarp, to Davis's left.

"No," Angus said. "That's as much as I'll do for you. Not quite sure why I even did that."

"Fair is fair," the girl said. "You wrapped his leg. Cut me loose."

Angus sat down beside Nate, who had finished tending the horses, unsaddling them all and feeding and watering them, and tying them all to a picket line at the base of the formation, in good grass.

"You know, young lady, cutting you free, a train robber who threw lead at me oh a little around an hour ago, is not at the top of my to-do list, either. All I want is to get this boy back down out of these mountains, safe an' sound. Along with my own withered carcass. I would do just that even in my less-than-spry condition if it weren't dark and we likely would never make it. So, I reckon I'll take my chances right here, an' we'll see what tomorrow brings."

He jerked with a start when loud rifle fire erupted from the valley in which the cabin sat. It was twilight, and Bryce Jackson must have tried taking advantage of the failing light to storm the shack. Men shouted, cursed, their voices nearly drowned by the fusillade—three rifles, it sounded like, being triggered quickly, angrily.

More shouting.

A man belted out a curse.

The shooting became sporadic, then ceased altogether.

"Well, well," Davis said. "Who do you suppose came up the winner?"

"Maybe they all shot each other," Frannie opined. She curled her nostrils. "None of 'em deserve any better."

"Well, then, Miss Frannie, all the loot's ours, I guess." Davis smiled. "You an' me can ride down to Mexico, lay back on the sand, kick our boots up, enjoy the high life for a change."

"Go to hell." Frannie turned to Nate who regarded her silently, knees drawn up to his chest, his arms around them. "Pardon my French, kid."

Nate said nothing.

She turned to Angus with a seductive smile. "How 'bout you, old man? Wanna go to Mexico?"

"Nah. I got nothin' against Mescins. It's just that their food"—Angus rubbed his belly pouching behind his buttoned jacket—"gives me gas."

"You're no fun. Neither are Robbie an' Bull. They didn't want to go to Mexico, either. They just wanted to hole up in that nasty, old cabin of theirs—smelled like a coyote den!— play cards, drink rotgut they brewed in a tub, and pinch my a—" She stopped abruptly and glanced at Nate. "Behind."

She smiled her saucy smile.

She stared at Angus, pensive, amusement growing in her eyes. "Wanna know where the loot is?"

"Where?" Davis said.

She whipped her head toward the wounded outlaw. "Never you mind! I wasn't talkin' to you!"

"Excuse me!"

"There's no excuse for you." Frannie turned to Angus with that smile again. "Wanna know?"

Nate said, "I'd like to know!"

"Oh, you would—would you? And what would you do with thirty thousand dollars in freshly minted gold coins? Enough payroll money for three separate mines around Salida an' Gunnison!"

"I'd buy Grandpa a new boiler for his brew barn and a new wagon for hauling it to town." Nate smiled at Angus, sitting beside him. "One with leather seats so it wasn't so hard on your behind, Grandpa." His smile broadened.

Angus smiled back at him. "I don't deserve you, boy."

"You deserve me," Frannie said.

"No, I don't deserve you, either."

"A young lady to keep your feet warm at night . . . ?"

Angus glanced at Nate and scowled. "Don't talk like that."

"Build a fire," Frannie said. "I'm cold. Don't worry about Jackson. I got Jackson wrapped around my little finger." She smiled again, broadly.

"She's right," Angus said to Nate. "We're gonna need a fire." He felt the cold down deep in his bones. He didn't think there would be any more danger here with a fire than there was in the darkness. Whatever would play out tonight would play out either in the light or the dark.

Nate rose and clambered down the rocks. He returned a few minutes later with an armload of dead branches and kindling. Angus laid out a ring of stones and coaxed a fledgling fire to life, which he gradually grew with the branches Nate had gathered.

When a sizable blaze spread its umber light around the sandy, semicircular area Angus, Nate, Davis, and Miss Frannie occupied, and Angus was about to add another pine branch to it, he stopped suddenly when a shrill scream rose from the darkness of the canyon in which the cabin lay.

The scream was followed by a shrill cry of pleading: "No! Oh, God—Jackson, no!"

"What's that?" Nate had just returned to the scarp once more and stood holding another armload of wood, staring off toward the canyon.

Davis chuckled.

"Poor Robbie," Frannie said.

Angus looked up at Nate. "Don't listen, boy."

Nate started and gave a slight gasp when another, agonized scream rocketed across the night. It was followed by loud sobbing, pleading.

"Boy," Davis said. "He's really goin' to town on Robbie. Musta killed ol' Bull." He laughed and glared at the girl. "That's what you get for double-crossin' ol' Bryce Jackson."

"He's tryin' to get him to tell him where the loot is," Frannie said. "He could have just asked me."

"Where is it?" Angus said.

"Take a lit branch," Frannie said, nodding to indicate the overhang.

Angus plucked a burning branch from the fire, then, drawing a deep breath against the tightness in his chest, crawled into the overhang, thrusting the burning end of the branch out ahead of him. Nate crawled in beside him. Angus studied the overhang's back wall.

"See it?" Frannie said. "A big rock, almost square. It comes out if you dig around it with a knife. I found it when I was on the scout up here and crawled into the overhang for a nap. Just foolin' around; then I noticed the rock looked loose."

Angus saw the rock she'd described. It protruded roughly a half inch from the otherwise solid stone wall.

Both Angus and Nate started as another scream of raw pain and terror vaulted across the night in which more and more stars were kindling.

Behind them, Davis chuckled.

Angus pulled his Bowie knife from the scabbard on his right hip, thrust it at Nate.

"Dig around it, boy. Try to wedge it out."

Chewing his bottom lip, Nate sawed around the side of the stone with the knife. He worked with the knife with one hand and pulled on the rock with the fingers of his other hand. He grunted softly as he worked. He grunted more loudly when a pistol blast caromed out of the dark canyon housing the cabin.

Just one blast, then silence.

Nate looked at Angus in the flickering firelight. Angus returned the look with a dark one of his own, then lifted his chin, silently prodding Nate to continue his work.

The boy did. Ten minutes later, he'd worked the rock free of the wall, set it aside, revealing a black hole in the same shape as the rock that had covered it. Nate slid to one side and let the firelight seep into the hole.

His eyes widened when he saw the contents of the hole.

Angus nodded at him.

Nate reached inside and pulled out a large burlap pouch, setting it on the ground between him and Angus. He reached into the hole again and pulled out a second burlap pouch that rattled with the coins inside it.

Davis must have been able to see into the overhang between Angus and Nate; suddenly, he laughed. It was a high, queer, jaded laugh. A deeply cynical laugh.

"It didn't need to be this hard," Davis said, looking at Frannie. "Didn't need to be so complicated, Frannie."

"Tell that to Bryce," Frannie said, coldly.

"Well, now you're just gonna die." Davis chuckled. "No way he's gonna let any of us get down off this mountain. Oh, sure, he'll keep the old man and the boy alive long enough to show him the way down, but after that . . ." He ran his index finger across his throat. "Me? I don't mind. I'd never get down, anyway . . . with this leg."

"Let's pull 'em out," Angus said to Nate.

Crawling out from under the overhang, the pair each pulled a money sack out into the firelight. Angus untied the twine holding one of the bags, reached in, and pulled out a handful of coins. He dropped them onto the sandy ground by the fire.

The gold coins glowed like miniature suns.

"Holy cow!" Nate said.

"Look at that," Davis said, the reflected light from the coins dancing in his eyes. "Look at . . ."

His voice trailed off.

He smiled. His head sagged to one side. His chest fell still after one, last, raking sigh.

"Gone," Frannie said, staring at the dead man. She turned to Angus sharply. "Cut me loose. Let's get out of here. Quick! Before he comes back!"

"He's back."

A large shadow emerged from the rocks behind her.

Jackson's shadow stepped into the firelight and revealed his mustached face beneath his Stetson's brim. He aimed his Winchester straight out from his right hip. A dark line of blood streaked down over his ear and neck to disappear under the collar of his jacket. His eyes glittered darkly as he stared down at the freshly minted payroll coins.

He squatted down beside the fire, rested the rifle across his knee.

Staring at the loot, his eyes black, his face stony, he shook his head slowly, fatefully. "Coulda all been ours, Fran. If you'd thrown in with the right fella. Now . . . hate to tell you this . . . but you come to the end of the road, my dear."

He turned to her, smiled grimly.

Frannie stared up at him, fear in her eyes.

Jackson rose, slowly slid the Winchester toward her.

Frannie closed her eyes.

A rifle blasted.

Frannie gasped and jerked her head up with a start.

She looked down at herself, searching for blood. Not seeing any, she looked up at Jackson once more. His hands opened, and the rifle dropped from his fingers. Blood spread a stain across his chest. He turned his head and looked down at the smoking Spencer angled up from Angus's lap.

Disbelief showing in his face, he staggered backward, nearly fell, then caught himself. He glared down at Angus, and said bitterly, "Damn fool. I . . . woulda . . . paid you well . . ."

"Yeah," Nathan said, on his knees beside Angus. "With a bullet."

Jackson convulsed, then fell in a pile, jerked out his life, and died.

Frannie stared at the dead man in disbelief. Slowly, a smile shaped itself on her full, wide mouth. She turned to Angus, grinning. "Cut me loose, old man. Once we're down out of these mountains, I'll give you an' the boy a cut!"

Angus regarded her sadly, shook his head slowly.

"You'll remain tied until we're out of these mountains, Miss Frannie . . . an' you're locked away in the Tigerville jail while this loot gets returned to its rightful owners. That's a lotta money, but I haven't lived all these years to turn outlaw now."

Frannie's face twisted into a mask of raw fury. She cursed him bitterly.

Angus chuckled and turned to Nate. "Close your ears, boy. Try to get some sleep. We'll get an early start tomorrow."

"You gonna be all right, Grandpa?"

"I'll be all right, Grandson." Angus chuckled. "At the moment, I'm too rich to die."

He rested back against a rock and pulled his hat brim down over his eyes. "Time to go home."

CHAPTER 34

Hunter caressed the Henry's hammer as he watched the shadows of the four slave traders running toward him, silhouetted by the distant fire in the camp behind them.

He glanced over his shoulder toward where Annabelle lay silently on the flat tableland forty yards away. She made no sound; she wasn't moving. Passed out from exhaustion, most likely. He hoped that's all it was. Worry racked him.

He turned his head forward and levered a fresh round into the Henry's breech, raking out, "We're almost done here," through gritted teeth.

The four men, running abreast roughly eight feet apart, came on quickly. The muffled pounding of their running feet grew louder until Hunter could hear the breaths raking in and out of their lungs. They held their rifles up high across their chests. He watched as they dropped down into a trough between rises. He waited. He could still hear them but he couldn't see them.

They reappeared, running up from the bottom of the rise he was on—first their hats and then the dark silhouettes of their faces . . . their chests, two of which were criss-crossed with cartridge bandoliers, the casings glinting in the starlight. Then their pumping arms and scissoring feet. Quickly, they closed the gap between Hunter and themselves. When they were fifteen feet away, one of them said, breathlessly, "Where the hell is he?"

Hunter gained his feet and snapped the Henry to his shoulder.

"Right here."

He shot the man on the far left first and kept shooting, jacking and shooting, jacking and shooting, until all three were screaming and twisting around, falling, dropping their rifles, and losing their hats.

Hunter stared through the wafting powder smoke, frowning, apprehension a cold finger tickling the back of his neck.

"Three?" he whispered.

Where was the fourth one?

Machado.

Hunter racked a fresh round into the Henry's breech and moved slowly forward. Cold sweat bathed his face and the insides of his gloves as he nervously squeezed the Henry's neck and forestock. He stepped over one of the dead men, a half-breed with long, greasy hair and a death snarl frozen on his lips, and continued down the rise into the rough in which the four slavers had briefly disappeared.

He stopped and looked around.

"Saguaro?" he said. "Come out, come out—"

He cut himself off. The sickly sweet smell of some animal touched his nostrils.

He was about to whip around when something cold, hard, and round was thrust against his back, between his shoulder blades.

An animal, all right. The human kind. The worst kind.

"Drop the rifle or take it in the back, Buchanon," came the outlaw's guttural snarl from behind him. As big as he was, he could move as quietly as an Apache.

Hunter's blood rushed like ocean waves in his ears.

"Drop it," Machado repeated with menacing quiet, "or I blow your grayback heart through your breastbone."

Hunter sighed, tossed the Henry into the sage.

"Think I'll take her to Mexico," Machado said quietly, jeeringly, in Hunter's left ear. "Kept my hands off her till now." Hunter heard the infuriating smile in the man's mocking voice: "But tonight, I'm gonna find out what I been missing."

The rage of a wild stallion inside him, Hunter started to whip around, intending to thrust the outlaw's rifle aside and deliver a hammering blow to his jaw. Machado was ready. Hunter wasn't halfway turned around before the butt plate of the man's Winchester smashed into the side of his head.

"Oh!" Hunter said, staggering backward and tripping over his own boots, striking the ground hard on his butt between sage shrubs.

He looked up, shaking the cobwebs from his vision.

The hulking, one-eyed bear of Saguaro Machado, wearing his customary opera hat, aimed the rifle at a downward angle. He spread his lips in a savage smile. "Two's company, Buchanon. Three's a crowd."

Hunter saw the man's right, gloved finger begin to draw back against the trigger.

He steeled himself, waiting for the bullet.

Rapid thuds sounded to Hunter's right, on the uphill side of the trough. Quick breaths and then a deep growl. Something long and gray leaped from Hunter's right to his left, three feet in front of him. Bobby Lee threw himself against Machado, closing his jaws around the man's right wrist just as the slaver squeezed the rifle's trigger.

Machado screamed as the Winchester stabbed orange flames, the bullet tearing into the ground only inches to the left of Hunter's head.

Machado dropped the rifle and staggered back and to one side, trying to fight off the enraged, snarling, and growling Bobby Lee biting into the man's left arm as though trying to rip it out of its socket. Machado bellowed like an enraged, wounded grizzly as he staggered backward, trying to fight off the coyote.

Finally, he gave an echoing cry of bald fury and, using both hands, grabbed the snarling beast around its neck and hurled the coyote away from him. Bobby was a gray blur in the darkness as he struck the ground ten feet away from the bear-like Machado, who turned to Hunter, his right hand dropping toward the revolver jutting from the holster on his right thigh.

Hunter's head was spinning, but his instincts kicked in, bypassing his brain.

Suddenly, as though of its own accord, the LeMat was in his hand and blasting and flashing once, twice, three times.

Machado wailed, triggering his own pistol skyward, as he staggered back and dropped with a grunt. He lay groaning, slowly kicking his legs, grinding his heels into the turf.

He cursed, lifted his head to stare toward Hunter. His chest rose and fell heavily as he raked breaths in and out of his lungs.

"Mierda," he said in his native Spanish. "Forgot about that . . . *whip hand*!"

His head flopped back against the ground. One foot shook, stopped shaking, and the man-beast was dead.

Hunter sat up, staring at the long, broad, lumpy form of the dead man from over the LeMat's smoking barrel.

A low yip sounded, and Bobby Lee hurried over to Hunter, whining and licking Hunter's face with his dry, rough tongue, wagging his shaggy tail.

Hunter chuckled. "There you are, you ol' devil! Where you been keepin' yourself? Out fraternizing with the opposite sex, I got me a feelin'."

Bobby Lee leaped up and placed his two font paws on Hunter's shoulders, continuing to run his tongue over Hunter's unshaven cheeks.

"Well, better late than never to the party," Hunter said,

shoving the coyote away and chuckling as he rose heavily, his head aching from Machado's blow. His ribs were on fire again, too. That was all right.

As long as he still had Annabelle.

He staggered up and over the rise and over to where Annabelle lay belly down. She wasn't moving.

"Oh, God," Hunter said. If he'd lost her now, after all he'd gone through to get her back.

He dropped to a knee, placed his hand on the back of her neck. Bobby sat beside Hunter, nuzzling Anna's neck.

"Honey . . . don't you die on me, Annabelle . . ."

She stirred, turned her head to look up at him through the screen of her tangled hair, grimacing against Bobby Lee's fervid ministrations. "Are they . . . ?"

"Yep."

"Even . . . ?"

"Yep."

Anna heaved a relieved sigh as she sat up. She hugged Bobby Lee tightly and then she threw herself into Hunter's arms and hugged him, too.

Hunter picked her up, rose, and began tramping off in the direction in which he'd left Nasty Pete, whom he could hear nickering in the darkness ahead of him. Annabelle looked up at him. "What about the money . . . for the horses?"

"Got it back . . . in Lone Pine. Intercepted a courier on his way to Arapaho Creek."

Anna frowned, deep lines cutting across her forehead in the starlight, which glinted in her bewildered eyes. "To the Scanlons?"

"It's a long story," Hunter said as he continued walking, Bobby Lee running ahead. "A long, sad story. Not sure what I'll do about it. Nothing, most like."

They'd been in agony ever since that dreaded Southern night during the war, just as Hunter had been. And would continue to be.

"Hunter, I don't understand."

"I'll tell you on the way home."

"Home," Annabelle said, resting her head back against her husband's muscular arm. "I like the sound of that."

"Mmm. Me, too."

"I like the sound of 'Angus' and 'Nate' even better."

Hunter chuckled. "Wonder what those two have been up to while we been gone."

"They've probably been sleeping in, waking at noon. Angus has probably been drinking his beer for breakfast. I bet they haven't gotten a thing done!"

"Nope," Hunter said. "Don't doubt it a bit. Just restin' and relaxin'. That's Angus."

"He's gonna infect that boy with his sloth!"

They laughed.

**TURN THE PAGE
FOR A RIP-ROARING PREVIEW!**

**JOHNSTONE COUNTRY. HOMESTYLE JUSTICE
WITH A SIDE OF SLAUGHTER.**

**In this explosive new series,
Western legend Luke Jensen teams up
with chuckwagon cook Dewey "Mac" McKenzie
to dish out a steaming plate of hot-blooded justice . . .**

A rotting corpse hanging from a noose is enough to stop
any man in his tracks—and Luke Jensen is no exception.
Sure, he could just keep riding through.
He's got a prisoner to deliver, after all.
But when a group of men show up with another prisoner
for another hanging, Luke can't turn his back—
especially when the condemned man keeps swearing
he's innocent. Right up to the moment he's hung
by the neck till he's dead . . .
Welcome to Hannigan's Hill, Wyoming.
Better known as Hangman's Hill.

Luke's pretty shaken up by what he's seen but decides
to stay the night, get some rest, and grab some grub.
The town marshal agrees to lock up Luke's prisoner while
Luke heads to a local saloon, Mac's Place.
According to the pub's owner—a former chuckwagon
cook named Dewey "Mac" McKenzie—the whole
stinking town is run by corrupt cattle baron Ezra Hannigan.
An excellent cook, Mac's also got a ferocious appetite
for justice—and a fearsome new friend in Luke Jensen.
Together, they could end Hannigan's reign of terror.
But when Hannigan calls in his hired guns,
they might be. . . dancing . . . from the end of a rope.

**National Bestselling Authors
William W. Johnstone
and J.A. Johnstone**

BEANS, BOURBON, AND BLOOD
A Luke Jensen–Dewey McKenzie Western

**Coming in August 2024,
wherever Pinnacle Books are sold.**

Live Free. Read Hard.
**www.williamjohnstone.net
Visit us at www.kensingtonbooks.com**

CHAPTER 1

L uke Jensen reined his horse to a halt and looked up at
the hanged man. The corpse swung back and forth in
the cold wind sweeping across the Wyoming plains.

From behind Luke, Ethan Stallings said, "I don't like the
looks of that. No, sir, I don't like it one bit."

"Shut up, Stallings," Luke said without taking his gaze
off the dead man dangling from a hangrope attached to the
crossbar of a sturdy-looking gallows. "In case you haven't
figured it out already, I don't care what you like."

Luke rested both hands on his saddle horn and leaned forward to ease muscles made weary by the long ride to the
town of Hannigan's Hill. He had never been here before, but
he'd heard that the place was sometimes called Hangman's
Hill. He could see why. Not every settlement had a gallows
on a hill overlooking it just outside of town.

And not every gallows had a corpse hanging from it that
looked to have been there for at least a week, based on the
amount of damage buzzards had done to it. This poor
varmint's eyes were gone, and not much remained of his
nose and lips and ears, either. Buzzards went for the easiest
bits first.

Luke was a middle-aged man who still had an air of
vitality about him despite his years and the rough life he

had led. His face was too craggy to be called handsome, but the features held a rugged appeal. The thick, dark hair under his black hat was threaded with gray, as was the mustache under his prominent nose. His boots, trousers, and shirt were black to match his hat. He wore a sheepskin jacket to ward off the chill of the gray autumn day.

He rode a rangy buckskin horse, as unlovely but as strong as its rider. A rope stretched back from the saddle to the bridle of the other horse, a chestnut gelding, so that it had to follow. The hands of the man riding that horse were tied to the saddle horn.

He sat with his narrow shoulders hunched against the cold. The brown tweed suit he wore wasn't heavy enough to keep him warm. His face under the brim of a bowler hat was thin, fox-like. Thick, reddish-brown side whiskers crept down to the angular line of his jaw.

"I'm not sure we should stay here," he said. "Doesn't appear to be a very welcoming place."

"It has a jail and a telegraph office," Luke said. "That'll serve our purposes."

"Your purposes," Ethan Stallings said. "Not mine."

"Yours don't matter anymore. Haven't since you became my prisoner."

Stallings sighed. A great deal of dejection was packed into the sound.

Luke frowned as he studied the hanged man more closely. The man wore town clothes: wool trousers, a white shirt, a simple vest. His hands were tied behind his back. As bad a shape as he was in, it was hard to make an accurate guess about his age, other than the fact that he hadn't been old. His hair was a little thin but still sandy brown with no sign of gray or white.

Luke had witnessed quite a few hangings. Most fellows who wound up dancing on air were sent to eternity with black hoods over their heads. Usually, the hoods were left in place until after the corpse had been cut down and carted off to the undertaker. Most people enjoyed the spectacle of a hanging, but they didn't necessarily want to see the end result.

The fact that this man no longer wore a hood—if, in fact, he ever had—and was still here on the gallows a week later could mean only one thing.

Whoever had strung him up wanted folks to be able to see him. Wanted to send a message with that grisly sight.

Stallings couldn't keep from talking for very long. He had been that way ever since Luke had captured him. He said, "This is sure making me nervous."

"No reason for it to. You're just a con artist, Stallings. You're not a killer or a rustler or a horse thief. The chances of you winding up on a gallows are pretty slim. You'll just spend the next few years behind bars, that's all."

Stallings muttered something Luke couldn't make out, then said in a louder, more excited voice, "Look! Somebody's coming."

The town of Hannigan's Hill was about half a mile away, a decent-sized settlement with a main street three blocks long lined by businesses and close to a hundred houses total on the side streets. The railroad hadn't come through here, but as Luke had mentioned, there was a telegraph line. East, south, and north—the direction he and Stallings had come from—lay rangeland. Some low but rugged mountains bulked to the west. The town owed its existence mostly to the ranches that surrounded it on three sides, but Luke knew there was some mining in the mountains, too.

A group of riders had just left the settlement and were heading toward the hill. Bunched up the way they were, Luke couldn't tell exactly how many. Six or eight, he estimated. They moved at a brisk pace as if they didn't want to waste any time.

On a raw, bleak day like today, nobody could blame them for feeling that way.

Something about one of them struck Luke as odd, and as they came closer, he figured out what it was. Two men rode slightly ahead of the others, and one of them had his arms pulled behind him. His hands had to be tied together behind his back. His head hung forward as he rode as if he lacked the strength or the spirit to lift it.

Stallings had seen the same thing. "Oh, hell," the confidence man said. His voice held a hollow note. "They're bringing somebody else up here to hang him."

That certainly appeared to be the case. Luke spotted a badge pinned to the shirt of the other man in the lead, under his open coat. More than likely, that was the local sheriff or marshal.

"Whatever they're doing, it's none of our business," Luke said.

"They shouldn't have left that other fella dangling there like that. It . . . it's inhumane!"

Luke couldn't argue with that sentiment, but again, it was none of his affair how they handled their lawbreakers here in Hannigan's Hill. Or Hangman's Hill, as some people called it, he reminded himself.

"You don't have to worry about that," he told Stallings again. "All I'm going to do is lock you up and send a wire to Senator Creed to find out what he wants me to do with you. I expect he'll tell me to take you on to Laramie or Cheyenne and turn you over to the law there. Eventually, you'll wind up on a train back to Ohio to stand trial for swindling the senator, and you'll go to jail. It's not the end of the world."

"For you it's not."

The riders were a couple of hundred yards away now. The lawman in the lead made a curt motion with his hand. Two of the other men spurred their horses ahead, swung around the lawman and the prisoner, and headed toward Luke and Stallings at a faster pace.

"They've seen us," Stallings said.

"Take it easy. We haven't done anything wrong. Well, I haven't, anyway. You're the one who decided it would be a good idea to swindle a United States Senator out of ten thousand dollars."

The two riders pounded up the slope and reined in about twenty feet away. They looked hard at Luke and Stallings, and one of them asked in a harsh voice, "What's your business here?"

Luke had been a bounty hunter for a lot of years. He recognized hardcases when he saw them. But these two men wore deputy badges. That wasn't all that unusual. This was the frontier. Plenty of lawmen had ridden the owlhoot trail at one time or another in their lives. The reverse was true, too.

Luke turned his head and gestured toward Stallings with his chin. "Got a prisoner back there, and I'm looking for a place to lock him up, probably for no more than a day or two. That's my only business here, friend."

"I don't see no badge. You a bounty hunter?"

"That's right. Name's Jensen."

The name didn't appear to mean anything to the men. If Luke had said that his brother was Smoke Jensen, the famous gunfighter who was now a successful rancher down in Colorado, that would have drawn more notice. Most folks west of the Mississippi had heard of Smoke. Plenty east of the big river had, too. But Luke never traded on family connections. In fact, for a lot of years, for a variety of reasons, he had called himself Luke Smith instead of using the Jensen name.

The two deputies still seemed suspicious. "You don't know that hombre Marshal Bowen is bringin' up here?"

"I don't even know Marshal Bowen," Luke answered honestly. "I never set eyes on any of you boys until today."

"The marshal told us to make sure you wasn't plannin' on interferin'. This here is a legal hangin' we're fixin' to carry out."

Luke gave a little wave of his left hand. "Go right ahead. I always cooperate with the law."

That wasn't strictly true—he'd been known to bend the law from time to time when he thought it was the right thing to do—but these deputies didn't need to know that.

The other deputy spoke up for the first time. "Who's your prisoner?"

"Name's Ethan Stallings. Strictly small-time. Nobody who'd interest you fellas."

"That's right," Stallings muttered. "I'm nobody."

The rest of the group was close now. The marshal raised his left hand in a signal for them to stop. As they reined in, Luke looked the men over and judged them to be cut from the same cloth as the first two deputies. They wore law badges, but they were no better than they had to be.

The prisoner was young, maybe twenty-five, a stocky redhead who wore range clothes. He didn't look like a forty-a-month-and-found puncher. Maybe a little better than that. He might own a small spread of his own, a greasy sack outfit he worked with little or no help.

When he finally raised his head, he looked absolutely terrified, too. He looked straight at Luke and said, "For God's sake, mister, you've got to help me. They're gonna hang me, and I didn't do anything wrong. I swear it!"

CHAPTER 2

The marshal turned in his saddle, leaned over, and swung a backhanded blow that cracked viciously across the prisoner's face. The man might have toppled off his horse if one of the other deputies hadn't ridden up beside him and grasped his arm to steady him.

"Shut up, Crawford," the lawman said. "Nobody wants to listen to your lies. Take what you've got coming and leave these strangers out of it."

The prisoner's face flamed red where the marshal had struck it. He started to cry, letting out wrenching sobs full of terror and desperation.

Even without knowing the facts of the case, Luke felt a pang of sympathy for the young man. He didn't particularly want to, but he felt it anyway.

"I'm Verne Bowen. Marshal of Hannigan's Hill. We're about to carry out a legally rendered sentence on this man. You have any objection?"

Luke shook his head. "Like I told your deputies, Marshal, this is none of my business, and I don't have the faintest idea what's going on here. So I'm not going to interfere."

Bowen jerked his head in a nod and said, "Good."

He was about the same age as Luke, a thick-bodied man with graying fair hair under a pushed-back brown hat. He had a drooping mustache and a close-cropped beard. He wore a brown suit over a fancy vest and a butternut shirt with no cravat. A pair of walnut-butted revolvers rode in holsters on his hips. He looked plenty tough and probably was.

Bowen waved a hand at the deputies and ordered, "Get on with it."

Two of them dismounted and moved in on either side of the prisoner, Crawford. He continued to sob as they pulled him off his horse and marched him toward the gallows steps, one on either side of him.

"Just out of curiosity," Luke asked, "what did this hombre do?"

Bowen glared at him. "You said that was none of your business."

"And it's not. Just curious, that's all."

"It doesn't pay to be too curious around here, mister . . . ?"

"Jensen. Luke Jensen."

Bowen nodded toward Stallings. "I see you have a prisoner, too. You a bounty hunter?"

"That's right. I was hoping you'd allow me to stash him in your jail for a day or two."

"Badman, is he?"

"A foolish man," Luke said, "who made some bad choices. But he didn't do anything around here." Luke allowed his voice to harden slightly. "Not in your jurisdiction."

Bowen looked levelly at him for a couple of seconds, then nodded. "Fair enough."

By now the deputies were forcing Crawford up the steps. He twisted and jerked and writhed, but their grips were too strong for him to pull free. It wouldn't have done him any good if he had. He would have just fallen down the steps and they would have picked him up again.

Bowen said, "I don't suppose it'll hurt anything to satisfy your curiosity, Jensen. Just don't get in the habit of poking your nose in where it's not wanted. Crawford there is a murderer. He got drunk and killed a soiled dove."

"That's not true!" Crawford cried. "I never hurt that girl. Somebody slipped me something that knocked me out. I never even laid eyes on the girl until I came to in her room and she was . . . was layin' there with her eyes bugged out and her tongue sticking out and those terrible bruises on her throat—"

"Choked her to death, the little weasel did," Bowen interrupted. "Claims he doesn't remember it, but he's a lying, no-account killer."

The deputies and the prisoner had reached the top of the steps. The deputies wrestled Crawford out onto the platform. Another star packer trotted up the steps after them, moving with a jaunty bounce, and pulled a knife from a sheath at his waist. He reached out, grasped the man's belt, and pulled him close enough that he could reach up and cut the rope. When he let go, the body fell through the open trap and landed with a soggy thud on the ground below. Even from where Luke was, he could smell the stench that rose from it. He didn't envy whoever got the job of burying the man.

"How about him? What did he do?"

"A thief," Bowen said. "Embezzled some money from the man he worked for, one of our leading citizens."

Luke frowned. "You hang a man for embezzlement around here?"

"When he was caught, he went loco and tried to shoot his way out of it," Bowen replied with a shrug. "He could have killed somebody. That's attempted murder. The judge decided to make an example of him. I don't hand down the sentences, Jensen. I just carry 'em out."

"I suppose leaving him up here to rot was part of making an example."

Bowen leaned forward, glared, and said, "For somebody who keeps claiming this is none of his business, you are taking an almighty keen interest in all of this, mister. You might want to take your prisoner and ride on down to town. Ask anybody, they can tell you where my office and the jail are. I'll be down directly, and we can lock that fella up." The marshal paused, then added, "Got a good bounty on him, does he?"

"Good enough," Luke said. He was beginning to get the impression that instead of waiting, he ought to ride on with Stallings and not stop over in Hannigan's Hill at all. Bowen and those hardcase deputies might have their eyes on the reward Senator Jonas Creed had offered for Stallings' capture.

But their horses were just about played out and really needed a night's rest. They were low on provisions, too. It would be difficult to push on to Laramie without replenishing their supplies here.

As soon as he had Stallings locked up, he would send a wire to Senator Creed. Once he'd established that he was the one who had captured the fugitive, Bowen wouldn't be able to claim the reward for himself. Luke figured he could stay alive long enough to do that.

He sure as blazes wasn't going to let his guard down while he was in these parts, though.

He reached back to tug on the lead rope attached to Stallings' horse. "Come on."

The deputies had closed the trapdoor on the gallows and positioned Crawford on it. One of them tossed a new hangrope over the crossbar. Another deputy caught it and closed in to fit the noose over the prisoner's head.

"Reckon we ought to tie his feet together?" one of the men asked.

"Naw," another answered with a grin. "If it so happens that his neck don't break right off, it'll be a heap more entertainin' if he can kick good while he's chokin' to death."

"Please, mister, please!" Crawford cried. "Don't just ride off and let them do this to me! I never killed that whore. They did it and framed me for it! They're only doing this because Ezra Hannigan wants my ranch!"

That claim made Luke pause. Bowen must have noticed Luke's reaction because he snapped at the deputies, "Shut him up. I'm not gonna stand by and let him spew those filthy lies about Mr. Hannigan."

"Please—" Crawford started to shriek, but then one of the deputies stepped behind him and slammed a gun butt against the back of his head. Crawford sagged forward, only half-conscious as the other deputies held him up by the arms.

Luke glanced at the four deputies who were still mounted nearby. Each rested a hand on the butt of a holstered revolver. Luke knew gun-wolves like that wouldn't hesitate to yank their hoglegs out and start blasting. He had faced long odds plenty of times in his life and wasn't afraid, but he didn't feel like getting shot to doll rags today, either, and likely that was what would happen if he tried to interfere.

With a sour taste in his mouth, he lifted his reins, nudged the buckskin into motion, and turned the horse to ride around the group of lawmen toward the settlement. He heard the prisoner groan from the gallows, but Crawford had been knocked too senseless to protest coherently anymore.

A moment later, with an unmistakable sound, the trapdoor dropped and so did the prisoner. In the thin, cold air, Luke distinctly heard the crack of Crawford's neck breaking.

He wasn't looking back, but Stallings must have been. The confidence man cursed and then said, "They didn't even put a hood over his head before they hung him! That's just indecent, Jensen."

"I'm not arguing with you."

"And you know good and well he was innocent. He was

telling the truth about them framing him for that dove's murder."

"You don't have any way of knowing that," Luke pointed out. "We don't know anything about these people."

"Who's Ezra Hannigan?"

Luke took a deep breath. "Well, considering that the town's called Hannigan's Hill, I expect he's an important man around here. Probably owns some of the businesses. Maybe most of them. Maybe a big ranch outside of town. I think I've heard the name before, but I can't recall for sure."

"The fella who was hanging there when we rode up, the one they cut down, that marshal said he stole money from one of the leading citizens. You want to bet it was Ezra Hannigan he stole from?"

"I don't want to bet with you about anything, Stallings. I just want to get you where you're going and collect my money. Whatever's going on in this town, I don't want any part of it."

Stallings was silent for a moment, then said, "I suppose there wouldn't be anything you could do, anyway. Not against a marshal and that many deputies, and all of them looking like they know how to handle a gun. Funny that a town this size would need that many deputies, though . . . unless their actual job isn't keeping the peace but doing whatever Ezra Hannigan wants done. Like hanging the owner of a spread Hannigan's got his eye on."

"You've flapped that jaw enough," Luke told him. "I don't want to hear any more out of you."

"Whether you hear it or not won't change the truth of the matter."

Stallings couldn't see it, but Luke grimaced. He knew that Stallings was likely right about what was happening around here. Luke had seen it more than once: some rich man ruling a town and the surrounding area with an iron fist, bringing in hired guns, running roughshod over anybody who dared to stand up to him. It was a common story on the frontier.

But it wasn't his job to set things right in Hannigan's Hill, even assuming that Stallings was right about Ezra Hannigan. Smoke might not stand for such things, but Smoke had a reckless streak in him sometimes. Luke's hard life had made him more practical. He would have wound up dead if he had tried to interfere with that hanging. Bowen would have been more than happy to seize the excuse to kill him and claim his prisoner and the reward.

Luke knew all that, knew it good and well, but as he and Stallings reached the edge of town, something made him turn his head and look back anyway. Some unwanted force drew his gaze like a magnet to the top of the nearby hill. Bowen and the deputies had started riding back toward the settlement, leaving the young man called Crawford dangling limp and lifeless from that hangrope. Leaving him there to rot . . .

"Well," a female voice broke sharply into Luke's thoughts, "I hope you're proud of yourself."

CHAPTER 3

Luke knew he should probably keep riding. Instead, he reined in and looked over at the woman who stood at the end of the boardwalk in front of the businesses to his right.

As he did that, a wagon rattled past on his left. From the corner of his eye, Luke saw that the man driving the rig wore a black suit and a black top hat.

The local undertaker, on his way up to the top of Hangman's Hill to retrieve the body that had been cut down. Had to be. That was going to be a mighty unpleasant task.

Luke turned his attention to the woman who had spoken to him. She was worth paying attention to. Blond, in her late twenties, pretty and well-shaped in a long brown skirt and a white long-sleeved blouse.

"You need a coat if you're going to be out in weather like this, ma'am," Luke said.

"I'm too hot under the collar to get chilled."

She looked angry, sure enough, as she gazed at Luke with intense blue eyes. He sensed that her anger wasn't directed solely at him, though. She seemed like the sort of woman who might be mad at the world most of the time.

Then she looked past him, up the hill, and sick dismay crept over her face.

"They hanged him," she said softly. "They really did."

"Friend of yours?" Luke glanced at her left hand and saw the ring on her finger. "Not your husband, I hope."

"What?" The woman looked confused for a second, then gave a curt shake of her head. "No, of course not. I barely knew Thad Crawford. Well enough, though, that I refuse to believe he was a murderer, no matter what the judge and jury said."

"Well, I didn't know the man at all, so I didn't feel like getting shot over something bound to happen anyway. If that's what's got you upset with me, you're off the mark, lady. There was nothing I could do"

She glared at him for a few seconds, then said, "I suppose you're right. Verne Bowen and his men would have killed you if you'd tried to interfere, and Thad Crawford would still be just as dead."

"Seems like the only logical way to look at it," Luke drawled.

"But I don't have to like any of it."

"No, ma'am, you don't. Neither do I."

She blew out an exasperated breath, shook her head, and turned to go back into the building behind her. Luke looked at the words lettered on the front window.

HANNIGAN'S HILL CHRONICLE.

So the blonde had something to do with the local newspaper. Maybe he would pick up a copy of the current issue while he was in town, Luke mused. He wondered if it would have something to say about the hangings.

He heeled the buckskin into motion again. He hadn't thought to ask the woman where the marshal's office was, but he didn't need to. He had already spotted the squarish stone building in the next block on the left with a sign over the door that had Marshal Verne Bowen's name on it.

"That was a pretty woman, even if she was mad as a hornet," Stallings said. "You should have introduced me."

Luke grunted. "Not likely. I don't reckon she would've had any interest in meeting a swindler. Anyway, I don't know her name, so I couldn't have introduced you, could I?"

"I suppose not. I wouldn't mind seeing her again, though."

"Give it up, Stallings. It's your weakness for women that got you caught in the first place, remember? If you hadn't bedded that ranch wife while her husband was away and then ran out on her, she wouldn't have been mad enough to put me on your trail."

"Well, she should have been smart enough not to believe me when I told her I'd take her to Cheyenne. I don't want to get tied down like that."

"So now you're tied anyway," Luke said. "At least, your hands are."

Stallings just sighed. Luke hoped that would shut him up for a few minutes.

On the way to the marshal's office, they passed a frame building that sat by itself on the corner of one of the side streets. The sign on the awning over its porch read MAC'S PLACE – GOOD EATS.

Luke's stomach responded instantly to the thought of a hot, well-cooked meal. Years of riding lonely trails had given him the ability to whip up biscuits, beans, and bacon, as well as boiling coffee, but after the long ride, an actual meal, maybe a steak, a heaping helping of potatoes, some greens, and a bowl of deep-dish apple pie, sounded mighty good. He would come back here after he got Stallings locked up, he told himself, and see if Mac's Place lived up to the sign's claim.

They stopped in front of the marshal's office. Luke swung down from the saddle and tied the reins of both horses to the hitchrack. He pulled his Bowie knife from the sheath on his left hip, behind the holster that held a Remington revolver rigged for a cross-draw, and cut the rope that bound Stallings' wrists to the saddle horn. He left the rope around the confidence man's wrists in place.

Something flickered in Stallings' eyes. Luke figured he was thinking about making a try for the knife. He was ready to grab Stallings' arm, jerk him out of the saddle, and dump him on the ground if he made any sort of suspicious move.

Then Stallings sighed, grasped the horn, and dismounted without trying anything as Luke stepped back. Whatever wild urge had gone through him for a second, he had thought better of it.

Luke took hold of his arm and steered him onto the boardwalk. The door to the office was unlocked. It was furnished like dozens of other small-town lawman's offices Luke had been in—a scarred desk with a leather chair behind it, racks on one of the walls holding rifles and shotguns, a map of Wyoming on another wall, some ladderback chairs, and a pot-bellied stove in the corner. To the right of the desk, an open door led into the cellblock in the rear of the building.

Marshal Bowen had said that he would be back soon, but Luke didn't see any point in waiting for the lawman to return. He marched Stallings through the cellblock door. The iron-barred cells were on the left. All four of them were empty, their doors standing open.

"One's as good as another," Luke said. He put Stallings in the first one and clanged the door closed behind the fugitive.

"What about these blasted ropes?" Stallings asked. "They've just about rubbed my wrists raw."

"Stick your hands through the bars."

Stallings did so. Luke drew his knife again and cut the bonds. Stallings sighed in relief as the pieces of rope fell away. His wrists did look a little sore, Luke noted, but that didn't generate any sympathy in him.

"When am I gonna get something to eat?" Stallings asked

as he rubbed his chafed wrists. "It's been a long time since breakfast this morning, and we were on pretty short rations, too."

"I'll talk to the marshal when he gets here. He may have some arrangements already made for meals to be delivered to prisoners. If not, I'll see about sending something in for you."

"Better not wait too long. I might just starve to death, and then how would you claim that reward?" A startled look appeared on Stallings' face as if he had just thought of something. "Wait a minute. That bounty the senator offered for me, it wasn't, uh, dead or alive, was it?"

Luke had to laugh. "No, they don't usually put dead-or-alive bounties on cheap swindlers like you, Stallings. All I had to do to earn it was apprehend you."

"Well, that's a relief anyway. Don't forget about the food."

"I won't," Luke said as he heard the front door of the office open and close again. Somebody had come in, and he figured it was Marshal Bowen.

He walked out of the office and stopped short as he realized the new arrival wasn't Bowen at all.

Instead, a woman stood there just inside the door, and she looked good enough to make Luke catch his breath.

Visit our website at
KensingtonBooks.com
to sign up for our newsletters, read
more from your favorite authors, see
books by series, view reading group
guides, and more!

Become a Part of Our
Between the Chapters Book Club
Community and Join the Conversation

Betweenthechapters.net